Obsession

ALSO BY KAREN ROBARDS

Obsession

KAREN ROBARDS

G. P. PUTNAM'S SONS
New York

║P

G. P. PUTNAM'S SONS
Publishers Since 1838
Published by the Penguin Group
Penguin Group (USA) Inc., 375 Hudson Street, New York, New York 10014, USA • Penguin
Group (Canada), 90 Eglinton Avenue East, Suite 700, Toronto, Ontario M4P 2Y3, Canada
(a division of Pearson Penguin Canada Inc.) • Penguin Books Ltd, 80 Strand, London
WC2R 0RL, England • Penguin Ireland, 25 St Stephen's Green, Dublin 2, Ireland (a division
of Penguin Books Ltd) • Penguin Group (Australia), 250 Camberwell Road, Camberwell,
Victoria 3124, Australia (a division of Pearson Australia Group Pty Ltd) • Penguin Books
India Pvt Ltd, 11 Community Centre, Panchsheel Park, New Delhi–110 017, India • Penguin
Group (NZ), 67 Apollo Drive, Mairangi Bay, Auckland 1311, New Zealand (a division of
Pearson New Zealand Ltd) • Penguin Books (South Africa) (Pty) Ltd, 24 Sturdee Avenue,
Rosebank, Johannesburg 2196, South Africa

Penguin Books Ltd, Registered Offices:
80 Strand, London WC2R 0RL, England

Library of Congress Cataloging-in-Publication Data

Robards, Karen.
Obsession / Karen Robards.
p.   cm.
ISBN 978-0-399-15416-4
1. Government investigators—Fiction.   2. Virginia, Northern—Fiction.
3. Drug addicts—Fiction.   4. Brothers and sisters—Fiction.   I. Title.
PS3568.O196O27   2007   2007003136
813'.54—dc22

Printed in the United States of America
1   3   5   7   9   10   8   6   4   2

BOOK DESIGN BY AMANDA DEWEY

This is a work of fiction. Names, characters, places, and incidents either are the product of the
author's imagination or are used fictitiously, and any resemblance to actual persons, living or dead,
businesses, companies, events, or locales is entirely coincidental.

While the author has made every effort to provide accurate telephone numbers and Internet
addresses at the time of publication, neither the publisher nor the author assumes any responsibility
for errors, or for changes that occur after publication. Further, the publisher does not have any
control over and does not assume any responsibility for author or third-party websites or
their content.

Peter, this book is for you, in honor of your graduation from Washington University in Saint Louis.

Christopher, this book is for you, in honor of your being named a National Merit Semifinalist.

Jack, this book is for you, for being, as always, an absolutely great kid.

Congratulations, gentlemen, and way to go.
You make your mother proud.

Acknowledgments

I want to thank everyone who made this book possible: my husband, Doug, who is always there and does mean carry-out in support of the creative process; my boys, who provide lots of comic (and sometimes not so comic) relief; my agent, Robert Gottlieb, for his indefatigable efforts on my behalf; my wonderful editor, Christine Pepe, who is the soul of patience and good advice; Leslie Gelbman and Kara Welsh and all my friends at Berkley; Stephanie Sorensen, who does great publicity; and Ivan Held and the rest of the Putnam family, with many thanks for your kind words and constant support.

Obsession

In the beginning . . .

June 8, 2005

"Nick. *Nick-ee.* Are you there? I'm in trouble. Real bad trouble."

Special Agent Nick Houston, FBI, stood in the kitchen of his small house in Alexandria, Virginia, head bowed, rubbing the back of his neck as he listened to the answering machine message. It was a little after eleven p.m. on a muggy Wednesday night, and he was dead beat. He'd already had the day from hell, testifying at the sentencing hearing for a man who had acted as his informant for more than a year, and then watching the guy's daughter practically collapse in the courtroom as the tough-on-crime judge handed her father ten years in federal prison, despite Nick's promises and the old guy's cooperation. Then he'd spent what was left of the day sparring with high-priced lawyers who were trying to paint him as a whack job as he'd testified in a related case, giving depositions, filling out the mountains of paperwork that followed the conclusion of every case like a tail follows a dog, and then, finally, on his way home, getting called in as an adviser to a hostage situation that had resulted in one of the hostages, a woman, being killed.

Just another day in the life of one of America's overworked, underpaid ersatz national police force, he knew. But still, the last thing he needed was to come in and hear his sister's voice on his answering machine.

"Some man called me tonight and said Keith's going to lose his job because of me. He said if I don't bring him copies of everything Keith has on some federal judge you guys are investigating, he'll tell the people in charge of security clearances that I'm a"—and here his sister's voice broke—"druggie."

"Oh, shit," Nick said, and dropped his hand to frown at the phone. That was their dirty little family secret, the one that he and Allison and her husband, Keith Clark—who also happened to be Nick's boss, head of the FBI's White Collar Crime Program—guarded like a leprechaun's pot of gold. If word of his sister's proclivities—she was an alcoholic who never met a drug she didn't like, although her high of choice was cocaine—got out, Keith would probably be fired. Can't have a federal law enforcement officer whose wife made him vulnerable to blackmail, after all.

Oh, wait, here was the blackmail.

"Can you come? As soon as you get this message. I need you so much. I don't know what to do. I know I shouldn't be so weak about . . . about things, but . . . you know, I can't help it. I'm scared, Nick. I'm so scared."

The beep ending the message interrupted the sound of her quietly weeping into the phone.

"*Goddamn* it, Allie." Nick slammed his hand down on the fake butcher-block counter. The counter wasn't all that sturdy—he'd been meaning to redo the kitchen since he'd bought the house five years earlier, but so far had never found the time—and everything on it jumped, including the water in the fishbowl. His two goldfish, Bill and Ted, gave him reproach-ful looks. Of course, the reproach in their little bulbous eyes could be because the box of fish food was sitting right there beside his hand, and he hadn't yet made a move to feed them. Bill and Ted—who were still on the excellent adventure that had begun two years ago, when he had met them at a carnival where he'd very misguidedly taken a woman and her six-year-old son on a date, only to have the kid beg for the fish, which Nick had won after spending about forty dollars on Ping-Pong balls to throw at their bowl, after which his date (the mother) had said she wasn't having nasty, smelly fish in her house and given them back to him, his lucky day—were sticklers like that. They wanted their two squares and a clean fishbowl. Other than that, they were dream roommates. They were quiet, they never had a bad day, and when he needed a listening ear, they were there.

As a reward for their patience, he pinched off some fish food, sprinkled it on top of the water, and as they greedily attacked the white flakes, he went back to the problem of his sister.

The first thing he did was try her cell phone. No answer. He considered calling her house, or his brother-in-law's cell, but if Allie hadn't worked up the nerve to tell Keith yet, that could be problematic. The message was less than half an hour old, which was about right because his cell had fallen out of his pocket and gotten crushed in the surge to subdue the hostage taker about an hour ago. A night owl, Allie never went to bed before one at the earliest, which meant she was almost certainly still up—somewhere. Doing something. The possibilities sent a shiver down his spine.

Shit.

"You are a pain in my ass," he said to the absent Allie, and turned on his heel, heading back out of the house and getting into his car. He would drive to her house in Arlington, some fifteen minutes away, and if she hadn't yet broken the bad news to Keith, he would stand by her while she did. If she had, if Keith was as livid as he was pretty sure Keith was going to be, he would stand by her through that, too.

Whatever it took. She was his sister.

Blood's thicker than water. He could almost hear his mother saying it as she stood swaying from too much booze in the doorway of one of the succession of trailers that had been their home when he and Allie were growing up. Usually when she said it she was sending him out after Allie, his beautiful, unstable, four-years-older sister whose own weakness for all kinds of chemical highs had manifested itself as early as middle school. He had been the stable one of the trio, the one who took a good, hard look at his hardscrabble life and vowed to do better, to circumvent an apparent family weakness for drugs and alcohol by not drinking, not getting high, not doing anything but working really hard, first for grades and later for money, so they could all have a better life. Unfortunately, his mother died while he was in college. But when he graduated, he kept his promise to himself: He took Allie, who'd already been through one husband, away from the squalid Georgia town in which they'd grown up, and moved her with him to Virginia, where he was just starting his career with the FBI.

For a while, things had been good for both of them. Buoyed by this opportunity for a new start, Allie had gotten a job and—as far as Nick knew, anyway—stayed clean. The thing about Allie was, when she wasn't high, she was a joy to be around, with a bright, effervescent personality that drew people to her like metal shavings to a magnet. She was also beautiful, a tall, slender, blue-eyed blonde with the delicate, elegant features of a model.

It was through Nick that Allie had met Keith, a fellow agent some years above Nick in the Bureau hierarchy. Nick had really, really hoped that their romance would be the saving of her. That because of her love for Keith, she would be able to leave her weaknesses behind. To his everlasting shame, he hadn't told Keith a word about her problems. How could he? She was his sister.

That was some fifteen years ago. Keith was family now, and to his credit had never once said to Nick, "Why didn't you tell me?" Because of course Allie, beautiful, fragile Allie, had worn down over the years. She had not been able to take the stresses of everyday life without what she called "a little help." Sometimes she went on an alcohol binge, sometimes she went on a drug binge, sometimes she did both. But between them, Nick and Keith had always managed to get her straightened out, to keep things hushed up.

Just like he hoped—no, *prayed*—they would be able to do this time.

When he reached the upscale Washington, D.C., bedroom community of Arlington, it was nearing midnight. His sister lived on a quiet street with big houses and well-kept yards, overhung with hundred-year-old oaks. When Allie and Keith had bought the house, they'd planned on filling it with children. The children hadn't happened so far, but Allie, at forty-one, had not quite given up hope.

At that time of night, the whole area should have been quiet and dark. But as soon as he turned into Allie's street, he was struck by the lights, the sounds, the hubbub of activity that, he realized as he drove closer, was centered around his sister's house.

"Oh, Jesus," he breathed, as the lights resolved themselves into the flashing strobes of emergency vehicles—cop cars and an ambulance and even a fire truck parked with its wheels on the lawn, which his sister would consider a big no-no—and the sounds turned into sirens and the activity to emergency personnel and neighbors and God knew who else swarming in and around the house.

Which had every single light in the place on.

His mouth went dry. His pulse raced. His heart started slamming in his chest.

He parked on the lawn because it was the only space available, and never mind that it would piss Allie off, then jogged toward the front door. Just the glass storm door was closed. The imposing carved-wood front door was wide open, allowing access to anyone who chose to enter.

Nick entered. Two swift strides down the entry hall, and he turned right into the spacious, tastefully decorated living room. There were a couple of uniformed cops standing around, a few people he took for neighbors huddled together, talking quietly, and some official-looking types in coats and ties that he was too agitated to even try to identify. His gaze immediately found Keith, who was talking to another uniform. This was a woman who was making notes on some pages on a clipboard as Keith spoke. A sweeping glance as he bore down on his forty-five-year-old brother-in-law told Nick that Keith was wearing the same suit pants and white shirt he had worn to work that day, although he had lost the coat and tie. His thinning medium-brown hair was rumpled.

Something bad had happened, that much was obvious.

"Keith. Where's Allie?" Nick asked without preamble as he got within speaking distance. His voice was loud, sharp. Everyone looked at him—the cop with the clipboard, the official types, assorted neighbors, his brother-in-law. Nick saw that Keith's snub-nosed, square-jawed, usually florid face had lost every bit of its color. His eyes were swollen and red-rimmed. The tip of his nose was red.

"Ohmigod, Nick," Keith groaned and covered his face with his hands. His shoulders heaved. With the sick feeling of just having taken a punch to the gut, Nick realized he was crying.

"Where's Allie?" It was a harsh demand. Panic flooded his system, making his fists clench, making him breathe too fast.

Keith sobbed. The cop with the clipboard and an official-looking type both moved toward Nick at the same time. From the expressions on their faces, he could feel bad news coming his way like a freight train.

But before they could get to him, he heard something else. The squeak-squeak-squeak of the wheels of a gurney. Nick pivoted and saw it being wheeled through the entry hall toward the door. There was a paramedic at either end maneuvering it. A white sheet covered it. Beneath the sheet, clearly, was a body.

A long, slender body.

Nick stopped breathing. He leaped for the gurney, ignoring Keith's plea to him to stop, ignoring the voices and hands that reached out to stay him. Before anybody could react enough to prevent him from doing what he absolutely had to do, he was beside the gurney and twitching back a corner of the sheet.

Allie lay there, her blond hair falling back away from her face to puddle on the white sheet beneath her. Her eyes were wide and glassy and fixed, and so badly bloodshot that he could see the redness at a glance. Her skin was ashen, her parted lips purple. There was massive bruising on her neck. . . .

A wave of cold sweat broke over him.

"Allie." His voice was hoarse. He knew, of course, that she wouldn't answer. It was clear at a glance that she was dead. *"Allie."*

"Sir!" One of the paramedics, outraged, pulled the little bit of sheet Nick was clutching out of his suddenly nerveless hand, draping it back over Allie's face. Then Keith reached him, along with the clipboard cop, hands on his shoulders, on his arms, restraining him, as the gurney started to roll again toward the door. Nick didn't move. He couldn't. He simply stood there and watched in stone-cold shock as his sister's body was wheeled out into the night.

It could have been a minute or it could have been an hour that he stood there. In the first aftermath of the terrible blow he had been dealt, time ceased to have any meaning. But finally he was able to face the unbelievable truth, finally he was able to think, to move, a little, and he turned to his weeping brother-in-law, whose hand still rested on his shoulder.

"Keith . . ." His voice was a croak. "What the hell—"

"She hanged herself." Keith sobbed mightily, then caught himself. "I came home and—oh my God, there she was. There was nothing I could do. She was already d-dead."

Nick felt his chest tighten as if a giant hand was gripping and squeezing his heart. It hurt. God, it hurt. He could scarcely breathe. His ears were ringing. His head felt like it was about to explode.

Allie's voice echoed through his mind: *I'm in bad trouble. . . .*

He couldn't tell Keith about it in front of a roomful of strangers.

"Come with me," he said to Keith, and took him by the arm. There were people everywhere, the house was full of people, so he dragged his brother-in-law out the back door, out onto the stone patio with its built-in party kitchen where Allie had loved to entertain.

Recalling that, his heart bled.

"She called me," he said to Keith when they were alone, and told him what Allie had said. The soft beauty of the night offered no comfort at all as he spoke. It was like a slap in the face in a way. How could stars still shine, how could flowers still perfume the air, with Allie dead?

"That's why then." Like himself, Keith seemed to be having trouble getting enough air. His shoulders were hunched, his head bowed. His voice was wheezy and thick. "God in heaven, Nick, that's why she did it. Because some creep threatened to blackmail her." He sucked in air. "Whoever he is, he's not going to get away with it. We're going to get him. And when we get him, we're going to nail his ass to the wall."

Nick pictured Allie's gray face on that gurney, and felt his gut clench.

"Oh, yeah," he said. "I'll find him. You can count on it. Whatever it takes."

It was a vow to his sister rather than a promise to Keith.

Then the first sharp stab of true grief punched its way through the shock, and he walked away from Keith and the patio and into the dark, where he vomited in the grass.

July 29, 2006

As last thoughts before dying went, it lacked something, and Katharine Lawrence knew it. Still, there it was: Her kitchen floor was filthy.

Lying on her stomach on the hard, cold tiles with her wrists duct-taped together behind her back, she was up close and personal with the slick, smooth expanse of glazed twelve-inch terra-cotta squares in a way she had never been before. That meant there was no missing the greasy smears on the surface, as if something oily had been recently spilled and not so carefully wiped up. Plus, there were small, muddy paw prints—the flat, round face of her Himalayan cat, Muffy, flashed into her mind—along with some dried blackish droplets that smelled like barbecue sauce, and a random assortment of unidentifiable scuffs, stains, and dirt.

For God's sake, didn't she own a mop?

"I'm going to ask you one more time: Where is it?"

The question was growled with cold menace some three feet above her head by a tall, muscular man in a black ski mask who leaned over her prone form. It was punctuated by a ham-like fist twisting hurtfully in her hair. The resulting yank on her scalp was nothing compared to the shaft of pain that shot down her neck as he brutally jerked her head back so that he could see her face, which, when it was not contorted with fear as it was just at that moment, was considered just a slightly crooked nose shy of beautiful. His gun—a big silver pistol—jammed hard against her temple. The impact of metal on fragile bone made her wince. The mouth of the gun was hard and cold, like death itself.

His eyes—hazel, close-set, with thick, black lashes that told her he was almost certainly dark-haired beneath the mask—were harder and colder.

As she met them, terror skittered down her spine like icy little mice feet. Her breathing quickened. Her heart, already thudding, accelerated until the pounding of her own pulse drowned out background sounds like the hum of the refrigerator, the soft hiss of the air-conditioning—and the quick footsteps of this guy's partner, who was searching the place room by room.

"I told you: There isn't one. It doesn't exist, okay? Whatever you may have heard, it's wrong."

There was nothing else she could say, even though she knew already that he wasn't going to believe her. He hadn't believed her before; he wouldn't believe her now. World without end.

His eyes darkened. His mouth, visible through a slit in the knit mask, thinned. Her stomach knotted with fear.

Would they kill her if they didn't get what they wanted? The thought made her want to throw up.

Yes was the despairing conclusion she reached as she considered the carefully calculated ferocity of the attack so far. There was a coldness to it, a purposefulness that told its own tale. She was as sure as it was possible to be that they—this man and his partner, both big, athletic guys dressed with eerie similarity in black T-shirts and sweatpants—had no intention whatsoever of letting her live.

Or Lisa either.

Lisa Abbott, her dear friend and former sorority sister, had, in the unluckiest of coincidences, selected this weekend to visit Washington, D.C., for the first time in the seven years since Katharine had moved there right out of college, armed with her spanking-new degree in political science and a head full of change-the-world ideals. Katharine had taken Muffy to a friend's for the weekend—Lisa was allergic to cats—then picked Lisa up at Dulles just after five. They had been excited to be together again after so long, gabbing away a mile a minute as they filled each other in on what was going on in their lives. They had stopped for drinks at Le Bar in Georgetown, had dinner around the corner at Angelo's, then gone clubbing. By the time they arrived back here, at her elegant two-story town house in the historic Old Town section of the D.C. bedroom community of Alexandria, Virginia, it was after midnight and they both had been more than a little sloshed. They had toasted their reunion with one more glass of wine, then gone to bed, not so much totally exhausted as totally wasted.

That was then.

Now Katharine at least was stone-cold sober, and Lisa lay about three feet away, facedown on the embarrassingly dirty floor with her wrists and ankles bound with tape just as Katharine's were. More duct tape covered Lisa's mouth. The airy, wrought-iron base of the granite-topped kitchen island separated them, but they could still see each other because of the structure's open design. Lisa's shoulder-length auburn hair spilled over her face so that all Katharine had been able to see of her expression since she'd been flung there was the terrified glint of her brown eyes. Lisa's silky yellow ankle-length nightgown was hiked to her knees, revealing the delicate trio of intertwined butterflies tattooed just above her left ankle. The ruffled hem fanned out around her tanned legs like the petals of some exotic flower. But at least the garment provided more coverage than Katharine's own night attire of tiny pink satin boxers and a matching knit tank. Lisa was an inch taller at five-foot-eight. Katharine was the more slender of the two, but Lisa was just as sexy with her well-toned, athletic physique. As Kappa Delts, the two of them had cut quite a swath through the Ohio State University frat boys once upon a time.

Even as Katharine stared fearfully into the cold, hazel eyes boring into her own, she was conscious of the sobbing rasp of Lisa's terrified breathing.

For four years we did practically everything together, and now that we're finally back together again, we're probably going to die together was the mournful thought that slid through Katharine's mind. *Oh, God, I don't want to die. Not like this. We're so young. Lisa just turned thirty, and I'm only twenty-nine. . . .*

They had everything to live for. Everything.

"Last chance: Where is the damned safe?"

Katharine cleared her throat desperately. "Look, I told you. There is no safe. The jewelry isn't here. It isn't mine. It was borrow—"

Katharine swallowed the rest of what she was going to say as he let go of her hair, took a step back, thrust his gun in the back waistband of his pants, and kicked her in the ribs. The action was carefully calibrated: hard enough to hurt but not hard enough to do any real damage.

Still, pain exploded through the right side of her chest, expanding outward in an instant from where the toe of his black sneaker connected with her bones. Katharine would have screamed if the pain had allowed it. Instead, she gasped, then writhed. Tears stung her eyes, overflowed to spill down her cheeks. She could feel their hot, wet tracks against her skin.

It hurt so bad—bad enough to stop her breath and cause a cold sweat to break out on her forehead. Jagged splinters of pain shot like superheated arrows into her organs, her muscles, her bones.

"So how's about we get real now?" His tone was still more conversational than threatening as he loomed darkly over her. Nevertheless, it was the most chill-inducing sound she had ever heard. After a single terrified glance up at him, she scrunched her eyes shut and went very still. "Where's the safe?"

Afraid to answer, Katharine did her best to block him out. She shrank into herself, shivering with pain and fear but otherwise not moving at all, feeling the prickle of perspiration as it sprang to life over her entire body. The ache in her side was still sharp enough to impair her breathing. Taking in careful little sips of air, she did her best to gather her wits. She was cold now, an icy, bone-deep cold that had nothing to do with the frigid tiles beneath her or the air-conditioning wafting over her sweat-dampened skin.

It was the cold of mortal fear.

The thing was, she was pretty sure that nothing she could say or do was going to make any difference in the end. But still she sought desperately to come up with anything, anything at all, that might turn the tide. . . .

"Answer me."

His fist clenched in her hair again, and she opened her eyes and cried out. Sharp needles of distress stabbed into her scalp as he jerked her head back. Her neck felt as if it would break.

"Where's the damned safe?"

He was close, frighteningly close, bending over her as he kept her head tilted up toward his and glared down into her face.

Their eyes met. The unmistakable menace in his drove fresh terror deep into her soul.

Her lips trembled. "There isn't one."

His eyes narrowed, hardened, until she couldn't take that brutal gaze a second longer. Pressing her lips together, swallowing convulsively, she closed her eyes again. For a moment, as she struggled to get her breath back, to move past the pain, she did nothing more than hang limply from the hand still locked into her hair. Her scalp tingled and burned from the pressure of his grip. Her neck ached. But even the most torturous physical sensation was nothing compared to the burgeoning panic that dried her mouth and made her pulse pound like she'd just run for miles, and turned her breathing into ragged little gasps for air.

Please, God, send help. . . .

Even with her eyes closed, she could feel his unrelenting gaze on her face.

"You know, I'm getting tired of playing around. If you don't tell me what I want to know, right now, how about I take a knife to your girlfriend there? Say, cut off a finger, or maybe her ear?"

Katharine's eyes flew open and locked on Lisa, who had suddenly gone stiff and still as a concrete statue. She didn't even seem to be breathing any-more, and Katharine might have thought her friend had fainted—except for the frightened flicker of her eyes.

"You wanna watch that? You wanna see her bleed? Is that what it's going to take?"

Katharine sucked in air and found her voice again. Or at least a sem-blance of her voice. What emerged was low and shaky, sounding nothing at all like her usual brisk, Midwest-infused tone.

"No," she whispered, sickened, her eyes never leaving Lisa. "Oh, no. Please. You've got to believe me, there isn't anything. . . ." Her voice caught as she saw Lisa start to shake. Fresh tears welled into her own eyes. Katharine had to force the rest out past the growing lump in her throat. "If there was a safe here, or any jewelry, or anything else of value that I could give you to make you go away, I'd tell you. I swear it."

His eyes glinted ominously. His mouth pursed. His gaze slid slowly and deliberately over her features.

Katharine trembled.

"You know, you're a real pretty girl. Maybe I should just leave your girl-friend alone, and start by carving my initials in your face instead."

Her stomach cramped like a giant fist had just closed around it.

"No." Her plea sounded pitiful even to her own ears. "No."

His threat was all the more horrifying because it was uttered in such a low, untroubled tone. Everything that had happened had been night-marishly quiet. Except for the single scared scream that had escaped her throat when he had first grabbed her, when she had opened her eyes one split second before he leaped on top of her to find a man creeping toward her bed through her darkened bedroom, there had been almost no noise. At least, no noise loud enough so that it was even remotely possible to hope that someone beyond these four walls might have heard and called the police.

She and Lisa, who had been sleeping in the town house's second bed-room, had been dragged down the stairs into the kitchen, flung to the floor, and roughly bound. Rape had been Katharine's immediate fear, but it hadn't happened. Sexual assault seemed to be the furthest thing from these men's minds.

What they were after, as they had made abundantly clear, was the contents of a safe that was supposedly concealed somewhere on the premises. In the safe, they seemed to expect to find hundreds of thousands of dollars' worth of jewelry. The normal burglar booty, like the plasma TV in the living room and the laptop in the den, didn't seem to interest them. Likewise, they'd left the jewelry that the women wore untouched. They had ignored Lisa's modest diamond pendant, and even Katharine's far more valuable diamond ear studs and the big oval-cut sapphire ring she had given herself for her last birthday, which ranked right up there as one of her very favorite birthdays ever.

Since bringing them into the kitchen, they'd mostly left Lisa alone. It was Katharine whom they had terrorized, Katharine whom they had questioned, Katharine whom they had roughed up, all in an attempt to get her to reveal the location of that nonexistent (so far as she knew, anyway) safe.

The thing was, they had known her name from the beginning. After the first fog of blind panic had cleared enough to allow her to think, that had chilled her to the bone. Clearly this was no random home invasion; it had been targeted specifically at her and carefully planned, although she got the impression that Lisa's presence had been a surprise to them. They had expected her to be alone.

From something else the thugs had said, she had gathered that they had seen the picture of her that had appeared last week in *The Washington Post,* the one that had caused her oceans of trouble even before this particular nightmare had begun, the one she hadn't even been aware had been taken until it had shown up in the paper. In it, she was dressed in a slinky white Dior evening gown and weighted down with what was practically a king's ransom's worth of eye-popping jewels, on her way to a dinner party at the home of one of Washington's top lobbyists. Apparently, the thug rumor network had it that those unbelievably valuable jewels, as well as other items of comparable worth, were kept in that mythical hidden safe in her town house.

As if.

The jewelry she'd been wearing in the picture wasn't even hers. It had been loaned to her for the occasion. Besides her ring and earrings, the only baubles she owned were the few little bits and pieces of nothing in the leather jewelry case on her dresser. Until late last fall, she had been living strictly on the salary of a federal government employee, which, if that needed translating, wasn't much. Certainly not anywhere near enough to enable her to acquire the kind of bling they thought she had.

That was what she had tried to tell them. Unfortunately, they refused to believe her even though it was the absolute, gospel truth.

While the thug who now had his fist in her hair had done his best to pound information she didn't have out of her, the other had gone on a rampage through her home. She had been beaten up to the sound of muffled thumps and thuds and crashes as the other man had torn the town house apart, flinging books from the shelves, snatching paintings from the walls, upending furniture, flipping over the expensive Oriental carpets that covered the highly polished hardwood floors. If her next-door neighbor, a doctor whose name escaped her mind at present, had been home, he might have heard something. But when she and Lisa had gotten home, the windows of his town house had been dark, and she knew that he was frequently away for the weekend. As for the junior congresswoman who lived in the town house on her other side, she was definitely back home in Minnesota until the end of August. There was a possibility that the lawyer couple who lived in the last of the row of four town houses might be at home—if they'd gone somewhere, they hadn't told her, but then again, why would they?—but even if they were there, it didn't seem to be doing anyone any good: So far, there had been no ringing telephone as a curious neighbor called to ask what was up with the middle-of-the-night commotion. Likewise, there had been no wailing sirens, no banging on the front door, no shouts to open up. As far as neighborly intervention was concerned, there was, in a word, nothing. If the doctor or the lawyers were indeed at home, they were clearly as oblivious to what was happening as the night-dark Potomac, which flowed sleepily past just across the cobbled street.

According to the clock on the black-fronted microwave, which was built into one of the exposed brick walls that were a feature of the recently redone kitchen, the time was one-oh-seven a.m. It was Saturday, July 29. Washington—at least, official Washington—was all but closed down for the summer. That meant that Old Town was thin of company just at present. Katharine's street, home to a number of the less important factotums of government, was at least half-empty. Her town house—the lovely historic one that had been totally remodeled, the one that came with a supposedly state-of-the-art security system, the one that was so pricey because it was in a good section of town, the one that up until about twenty minutes ago she had considered profoundly safe—was, on this steamy summer's night, as isolated as a cabin in the middle of a forest.

In other words, she and Lisa—poor, innocent Lisa, who had simply picked the wrong weekend to visit a friend—were on their own.

"Katharine. I don't want to hurt you or your friend." His tone was almost gentle. His eyes were not.

She took a shaky breath. Her voice, when it emerged, was stronger than before. "Then don't."

He blinked, slowly, like a sleepy turtle. Then, with deliberate movements that she couldn't miss, he reached into his pocket and drew out a knife. A silver knife, slim and innocuous-looking, about six inches long. No sharp edges visible, but she knew what it was at a glance: a switchblade.

Horror filled her. Her throat tightened as her gaze stayed glued to the knife. He had only to push a button. . . .

"You're leaving me no choice, Katharine, so this is on your own head. If you don't tell me where that safe is, I'm going to start carving that pretty face of yours up like a jack-o'-lantern."

Fearing what would happen next, Katharine's body tensed. Her mouth went dry. Her heart knocked against her rib cage. But there was only one answer she could give: the same one she'd been giving all along.

She shook her head in despair, indicating wordlessly what she then said aloud, *"There . . . is . . . no . . . safe.* Please, please believe that. Like I keep telling you, you're making a mistake."

There was a heartbeat's worth of dead silence.

"Stupid bitch," he said, and the very absence of emotion in his voice made it all the more terrifying.

"I'm telling the truth." Desperation made her voice shake. "I really am. This is just an ordinary rented town house. Why would there be a hidden safe?"

She heard the tiny click of the knife a fraction of a second before she saw the blade spring free of its casing. Light from the recessed fixtures overhead caused its honed edge to glint with wicked menace. It was, she could see, surgically sharp. Eyes glued to it, she drew in a deep, ragged breath.

"Using that won't help," she said. "I can't tell you what I don't know."

He leaned closer. His face was just inches above hers now, so close that she could see that his eyes were bloodshot and smell the faint scent of garlic on his breath. Then he smiled. A small, evil, terrifying smile. Suddenly light-headed, she was conscious of a strange rushing sound and realized that what she was hearing was her own blood roaring like a waterfall in her ears.

"There's a hidden safe here because your boyfriend put it here," he said.

2

Her boyfriend. Edward Barnes. A fit, distinguished-looking, soon-to-be-divorced forty-seven-year-old, who was in Amsterdam until Tuesday. They'd been seeing each other for the past thirteen months. He'd been her boss for the last four years. And—oh, yeah—he'd been the DDO—Deputy Director of Operations—of the CIA for two of those, taking her, his executive assistant, right up through the ranks with him, until now, when to all intents and purposes she, Katharine Marie Lawrence, former notorious party girl, was one of the most powerful people in the CIA.

Because she had Ed's ear. And now that his wife of twenty years, Sharon, had moved out of their Embassy Row mansion in the wake of that damned *Washington Post* photo, she had pretty much most of the rest of him, too.

Given that Ed owned the town house in which she lived rent-free, a perk of their relationship—a hidden safe suddenly seemed no longer completely beyond the realm of possibility.

Katharine's blood ran cold at the thought.

"I don't know anything about that. I just live here."

"Yeah." Sarcasm dripped from the syllable.

Almost gently, he pressed the blade to her cheek. As she felt the cold metal against her face, Katharine's breathing suspended. Her heart lurched. For a frozen instant horror paralyzed her. Then she realized that what she was feeling was just the smallest degree of pressure, no sting, no pain at all, and it hit her: only the dull edge touched her skin. He wasn't cutting her—yet.

"Please," she said. Her throat was so tight, it was difficult to get even that much out. Her heart thudded. Her stomach knotted. She could feel Lisa watching, see the frightened glint of her wide eyes. Her friend's horror was almost palpable. Then, despairingly because she knew it was useless, Katharine added, "Don't do this. Please don't."

"Where's the safe?"

Why wouldn't he believe her? What else could she say? Sticking with the truth—that she didn't know, that as far as she was aware there wasn't one—would get her hurt. Panic twisted through her insides like a coiling snake. Could she lie? she wondered desperately. But if she lied—if, say, she pretended to know the location of the supposed safe, just picked a site off the top of her head and said it was there—he would go look, and in just a matter of minutes, he would discover that she was lying. The thought of what he might do to her then made her dizzy.

But could it be worse than what he was getting ready to do to her now?

"Katharine?" His voice was so soft it was barely above a whisper. A silky, almost caressing whisper. He turned the knife over, resting the honed edge in the hollow beneath her cheekbone. Her breathing quickened. A scream bubbled up in her throat.

She dared not let it loose; he would cut her for sure then.

Fear tasted sour as vinegar in her mouth, but she forced the words through.

"If there was a safe, and I knew about it, don't you think I'd tell you?"

"Depends on how smart you are. For my money, you're not very smart. After all, you're fucking Ed Barnes."

Terror made it difficult to think, she discovered. Whatever she said,

whatever she did, the end result was going to be the same. He—they—
were not going to just go away. They were going to keep torturing her and
Lisa until they either found what they were looking for or were finally convinced that it didn't exist, by which time both women would probably be
dead. Since it was Saturday, it was unlikely that anyone would even miss
them until Monday, when Katharine didn't show up for work. When she
didn't answer the inevitable phone calls that would be placed to her home,
someone from the Agency would be dispatched to check on her. That
someone would show up at her door and not be able to get in and would
sooner or later call the police, and eventually her corpse and Lisa's would
be found right here on her grubby kitchen floor.

No. I'm not going to let that happen.

Determination stiffened her spine, had her gritting her teeth. She refused to just lie there and die.

There had to be a way out. She had to *try.*

Please, God, please . . .

Wetting her lips, she glanced up at him. "Look, I have money in the
bank. Lots of money." His eyes darkened. He frowned. *Oh, no.* Already
knowing he was going to refuse, she rushed on desperately. "Over a hundred thousand dollars. I'll give it to you. All of it. My ATM card's in my
purse. We can—"

"Yo, found it!" The exultant cry cut her off in mid-spiel. It came from,
she judged, the small den that, with the living room/dining room combination, kitchen, entry hall, and half-bath, made up the town house's first
floor. *It,* uttered in such a gleeful tone by the second bad guy, could only
mean one thing: the hidden safe.

Apparently it did indeed exist, because he'd found it.

Who knew? was her first lightning-fast reaction, followed almost immediately by a devout *Thank God.*

Even as the thoughts formed in her mind, the knife fell away from her
face. One second it was there, the next it was not.

She let out a deep, relieved breath.

"You're a lucky girl, Katharine."

Lucky or not, Katharine knew that this wasn't salvation. At best, it was only a brief reprieve. Her heart knocked against her ribs as her eyes locked with his for what seemed like an excruciatingly long moment. They were utterly cold; there was no pity for her there in those murky hazel depths. The hand that was still twisted in her hair shifted its grip.

He smiled at her.

Then, deliberately, with no warning at all, he slammed her head down. Her nose and forehead smashed into the tile with all the force of his arm behind it. The blow was so intense that she saw stars.

"*Uh.*" The pained cry came from her own throat, she realized fuzzily. Blood spurted from her nose; she could feel the warm, wet gush of it even through the whirlpool of dizziness sucking her down.

Letting go of her hair, he straightened to his full height.

"Be right back," he said, and left the kitchen with a dozen quick footsteps that echoed faintly as he crossed the hard floor. When he reached the dining-room carpet, the sounds disappeared, muffled by thickly padded wool.

Except for the sound of it, Katharine barely registered his leaving through the haze of shock and pain. Eyes closed, drawing ragged breaths in through her mouth, she lay as he had left her, stunned, while blood continued to pour from her nose. Maybe she lost consciousness, maybe not, but for a brief period she was aware of little beyond the gray cloud that fogged her senses and her own struggle to breathe through the gore.

"*Katharine.*" It was the merest breath of sound. Something touched her, something warm that jostled her left shoulder and leg. When she didn't respond, the touch came again, harder this time. There was something about it that felt urgent.

Not without a struggle, Katharine opened her eyes. Blood was in her mouth, salty and thick and warm, and the taste and oily sensation made her shudder. She lifted her head and spat it out. The kitchen swam in front of her, and she was immediately conscious of the crimson pool on the floor where her face had rested. Her nose . . . was it broken? It was still bleeding, she thought, but not as much now.

It hurt. Oh, God, it hurt.

"Katharine."

Her eyes had already begun to lose their focus again. Instinctively, she turned her head in the direction of that husky whisper. A flash of yellow snagged her peripheral vision, urging her on. Even as a new wave of dizziness washed over her and the rest of the kitchen went all blurry once more, her head completed that difficult quarter-turn and her eyes widened with surprise. Lisa was impossible to mistake. Her friend now lay next to her, turned on her side facing away, her yellow-nylon-sheathed back scant inches from Katharine's damaged face. It took a second—Katharine was still fuzzy—but then she realized that Lisa had rolled, scooted, wriggled, or by some other method propelled herself across the kitchen floor to her side.

Their eyes met over Lisa's shoulder.

"Get my hands free."

Lisa's slim, tanned hands, her fingertips unnaturally pale now from having been so tightly bound for so long, wiggled vigorously below the wide band of gray duct tape that was wrapped tightly around both wrists. Katharine frowned a little, blinking uncomprehendingly down at them. Then Lisa scooted another inch or so backward, thrusting her bound hands forcefully toward Katharine's face.

"My hands," Lisa hissed.

All of a sudden, it hit Katharine: Lisa was *talking*. Not easily, not well, but talking. The tape covering her mouth had come loose. *How?* Katharine considered, then realized that it didn't matter. The rectangular patch of industrial gray strips was still there, still glued to her upper lips and cheeks, but she was able to move her lower lip enough to form intelligible words.

"Use your teeth." It was an urgent whisper.

Katharine blinked again.

"Use my teeth?" she repeated, befuddled.

"Shh. Yes."

Katharine had forgotten to whisper. She realized that as soon as the words left her mouth, even before Lisa's face contorted viciously and her heels smacked warningly into the side of her thigh. Even as Katharine winced, reflexively jerking her leg back out of the way, Lisa glared at her.

"To get the tape off. Use your teeth."

This time Katharine remembered to whisper. "Oh. Okay."

But she still couldn't quite wrap her mind around what she needed to do. Her nose hurt so, like a tuning fork quivering with an agonizing sensation aimed directly at the pain centers in her brain. Her head throbbed, her ears rang, and every time she moved her head even the slightest bit, a new wave of dizziness assaulted her. Lisa wanted her to get the tape off with her teeth? That didn't quite compute, but Katharine obediently ducked her head in the direction of Lisa's hands. *Big mistake.* Pain exploded behind her eyes. Reality began to recede again. The ringing in her ears turned into an almost soothing buzzing sound. Suddenly the kitchen seemed to be shimmering around her like a mirage in the desert. There was nothing solid left in the world. . . .

"Katharine."

Except Lisa. Lisa, whose bound hands were bouncing up and down in the small of her back with unmistakable urgency. Lisa, whose bound heels were kicking her hard in the thigh. Lisa, who was directing a killer glare her way.

Lisa, who was doing her best to drag her back from the threatening mists of unconsciousness, even as Katharine longed to succumb.

"Katharine. You've got to do this, understand? Tear the duct tape around my wrists with your teeth."

The fierceness of the whisper penetrated the fog that was clouding Katharine's mind, sapping her muscles of their strength, turning her limbs to lead. Lisa's words finally registered, and Katharine deliberately widened her eyes and took a deep breath and fought for clarity. Then, before she could otherwise move or reply or do anything else at all, a loud thud from the direction of the den, followed by a string of vicious male curses, made her heart leap.

"You dropped it!" The roar rose accusingly over the cursing.

"Well, shit, it was heavy!"

Lisa, who'd been in the act of kicking her again, froze with her heels scant inches from Katherine's thigh.

Katharine froze, too.

Fear shoved out the last of the fog as realization burst on her like a bomb: They didn't have much time. The bad guys were still there, just a room away. They could be coming back for her and Lisa at any moment.

She *really* didn't want to be here for that.

"Do it." Lisa completed the kick.

Katharine still felt as if half her brain had turned into cotton candy, but now that she remembered what had happened and that both their lives were at stake, the other half of her brain, along with the rest of her, was definitely with the program.

If she and Lisa didn't get out of there soon, they were going to die. It was as simple—and as galvanizing—as that.

"Yes, okay," Katharine whispered.

Focusing required painful effort, but Katharine did it. She attacked the duct tape around Lisa's wrists with her teeth, ignoring the shaft of fire that shot through her excruciatingly sensitive nose as she accidentally brushed it against the warm firmness of Lisa's forearm. The pain was bad, bad enough to make her want to pull back and lie very still for a very long time, waiting for it to subside. However, death was worse. With that thought lodged at the forefront of her mind, Katharine ignored the pain and went after the tape with a ferocity born of desperation. Lisa kept her arms as stiff and still as possible, stretching them backward, straining against the tape with all her strength to take advantage of the tiniest rip.

There wasn't one. Despite Katharine's best efforts, the tape remained intact. It was gummy and acidic-tasting and just plain nasty. Getting any kind of purchase with her teeth was difficult. She kept hitting her nose on Lisa's arms. The resulting pain would have been disabling under any less dire circumstances. The appendage was as sensitive as an exposed nerve.

It was so damaged that she couldn't breathe through it; she had to gasp for air through her mouth. She was almost positive it was broken.

Not that the state of her nose mattered at all under the circumstances. They had only this brief window of time. . . .

"Hurry," Lisa breathed.

It seemed like hours passed. Days. Weeks. Months. But when she caught a glimpse of the microwave's clock, she realized that she was wrong. It was only one-fourteen. Impossible to grasp that only seven minutes had passed since she had last looked at those glowing numbers.

No matter how it felt, she couldn't have been chewing on the tape for longer than a minute or two.

"Don't do that," one of the bad guys snapped, loud enough so that Katharine jumped as if she had come into unexpected contact with a live wire.

"You got a better idea?" came the growled reply.

Heart pounding, Katharine quit with the tape for long enough to shoot a nervous glance over her shoulder toward the door. They sounded so close—terrifyingly close. Still, nothing more than the sliver of dining room that she'd been able to see before met her gaze: a corner of the glass-topped dining table, part of an upended gray-and-chrome upholstered chair, the painting of the single lily in a vase lying where it had been flung on the carpet. There was no sign of the men, thank goodness. They were in all likelihood still in the den; obviously, they had no idea what was happening in the kitchen.

Oh, God, how long until one of them decided to check?

Fright flooded like ice water through her veins as she arrived at the unavoidable conclusion: probably not very long.

"Hurry," Lisa breathed.

Oh, yeah. Recalled to herself, Katharine attacked the tape with renewed desperation. Her heart thumped. Her pulse raced. Her stomach twisted itself into a pretzel. At any moment—at any second—one of the men could come back into the kitchen.

Then she had no doubt at all that she and Lisa would die. After all, the bad guys had found the safe. They didn't need either of the women anymore.

Hurry. Hurry. Hurry. The word formed an urgent chorus in her brain.

"Where you going?" The raised voice belonged to the bad guy who had slammed her face into the floor. Even as she nearly had a heart attack, Katharine recognized it without a doubt. There was a roughness to it, a hint of New York or New Jersey street in the accent. He was clearly talking to his partner, who was just as clearly no longer nearby.

Oh, God, where was he? Her heart thumped like a piston in her chest as her every sense strained to find out. She couldn't tell; she could hear nothing, no footfalls, no sounds at all, to locate him.

Please, please, let him not be heading for the kitchen.

Panic gave her strength. She got a grip with her cuspids, ripped downward. Miracle of miracles, the tape tore. *Yes.* The moment was electric, and Lisa felt it, too, Katharine could tell by the triumphant clenching of her fingers. It was just the smallest rip, but it gave them hope, made success seem not so impossible after all. She kept at the tape like a terrier, the taste metallic in her mouth. Or maybe that metallic taste was blood. She didn't know, didn't care.

He could step into the kitchen at any second. . . .

Muscles straining, using short, sharp jerks that caused the tape to snap taut each time, Lisa tried to yank her hands apart as Katharine kept feverishly ripping at the layers of tape. Slowly, slowly, way too horribly slowly, it tore. . . .

Lisa forced her arms apart and suddenly her wrists were free. As Katharine, panting, let her head sag down onto the tile, their eyes met in a single brief moment of triumph. Then Lisa, loose strips of tape dangling from one wrist, jackknifed into a sitting position, yanked the tape from her mouth, and bent to claw at the tape around her ankles.

The sound of a flushing toilet answered at least one urgent question: the location of the second bad guy. He was in the powder room off the entry hall. For about half a heartbeat, knowing where he was even made Katharine feel better.

Then she realized that the kitchen could be his next stop. All he had to do was turn left and walk about a dozen paces straight down the hall. The arched opening that led from the entry hall into the kitchen didn't even have a door on it. He would be able to see them long before he reached it.

Lisa moved, and Katharine watched with her heart in her mouth as Lisa scooted on her butt across the kitchen floor. Katharine only realized her intended destination as Lisa grabbed the handle on the cutlery drawer and pulled it open. The soft slide of the roller mechanism sounded loud as thunder to Katharine's ears, and her heart pounded in answer as she shot a terrified glance at the door. The clinking of the cutlery as Lisa reached inside the drawer made her jump and brought her gaze flying back. A second later, Lisa's hand, which was still lost in the depths of the drawer, reappeared, triumphantly clutching a serrated steak knife. She sliced down with it, sawing with fierce sweeps through the duct tape binding her ankles.

"You wanna give me a hand with this?" the first bad guy called out. Katharine almost swallowed her tongue as she glanced around again: nothing.

"Thought I'd go ahead and take care of the ladies," his partner answered. Katharine's breathing suspended. She looked wildly back at Lisa in time to see her pull the tape off her ankles. "Get that out of the way."

Oh my God. He's coming to kill us. Right now.

From the sound of his voice, he was close. Way close. Steps away.

Panic broke over Katharine in an icy wave. Her whole body was suddenly bathed in a rush of cold sweat. Her heart kicked into triple time. Her stomach went into freefall. Her eyes locked with Lisa's, then widened in horror as Lisa stood up and she realized that Lisa was free—but she was not.

She could hear his footsteps, hear him coming toward them. . . .

Knife in hand, Lisa scrambled toward her, bent over her, sliced savagely at the tape around her ankles.

"We got plenty of time for that." The first bad guy sounded impatient. "Come here and help me with this first."

The footsteps paused for what seemed an interminable amount of time, then resumed in a changed direction.

Phew. Katharine felt as if she might collapse from relief.

The knife went through the tape around her ankles like it was tissue paper.

As the grip of the tape eased, Katharine frantically tried to pull her ankles apart, and suddenly she was free, too.

"Let's go," Lisa whispered. She grabbed Katharine's upper arm just above the elbow, propelling her to her feet, hacking at the tape around Katharine's wrists at the same time. The tape split, and Katharine tore her wrists lose from their sticky confinement. Coming upright so fast made her head feel as if it would explode. A knifelike pain from where she had been kicked shot through her side, making her fear that she had at least one cracked rib. Pins and needles attacked her blood-deprived arms as they moved. Sucking in air, she tried to run and discovered a terrible truth: Her legs did not want to work. Dizzy and weak, battling a sudden attack of nausea, Katharine forced herself into motion anyway, her legs heavy and her feet clumsy as she lurched crouching after Lisa, who was already darting away toward the far side of the kitchen. A small laundry room was located there, and in that laundry room was the back door.

Moonlight slanted through the not-quite-shut blinds on the two small double-hung windows behind the washer and dryer. The yellow glow of a streetlight in the alley beyond the small backyard and row of detached garages shone through the glass set into the top half of the door, making it fairly easy for them to see where they were going even though the laundry room light was off. Set into the wall just a few feet from the back door was the calculator-sized panel for the security system. The tiny light on it gleamed green, Katharine saw as she reached the door of the shadowy room seconds behind Lisa. Her thinking was slightly fuzzy, she knew, but that seemed to indicate that the system still worked. So why hadn't the alarm sounded when the intruders had broken in? Had she forgotten to turn it on? Or had they somehow known the code? Then she realized that it didn't matter. What mattered was that the panic button at the bottom of the control panel might still be functioning, too.

It was connected directly to the police department. All she had to do was hit that button and cops would be on the scene within minutes.

If it still worked, that is.

Flying across the room in Lisa's wake, she detoured slightly and stabbed the button hard just as Lisa reached the back door.

What she heard next made her forget about everything except the need for immediate escape: the quick slap of footfalls walking into the kitchen.

They sounded as loud as an alarm to her ears.

There was a split second in which her heart shot into overdrive. Her stomach clenched. Her blood turned to ice. Her eyes instinctively swiveled toward the rectangle of light that was the door to the kitchen.

For a terrible moment, nothing happened. Then . . .

"Hey! Where are they?" At first the man sounded confused, as if he thought he might just be overlooking his captives. A second later he managed to put things together and yelled, "They're gone!"

Their escape had been discovered.

"Shit. Shit. Shit."

The frantic breath of sound came from Lisa as she fought to open the back door, twisting the knob, tugging at it without result. Katharine heard it as she reached her friend, who cast a hunted look back over her shoulder.

"It won't open."

Frantic with terror, not understanding anything except the need to *get out that door NOW,* Katharine pushed Lisa's hands aside, grabbed the cold metal knob, turned, and pulled, too.

To no effect. The knob turned, but the door didn't budge.

Then Katharine understood.

The door was equipped with a dead-bolt lock that required a key to open. It had been designed that way to counteract the security risk posed by the window set into the top of the door. The key that fit the lock was at that moment hanging from a slender length of blue satin ribbon on the Peg-Board beside the dryer.

Some six feet away.

Her eyes flew to it, and then she leaped for it just as a man's tall silhouette appeared in the laundry-room doorway.

3

Trapped. *We're trapped.*

At that awful realization, adrenaline shot through Katharine's veins. Her heart gave a great leap. Her breathing suspended. Her pulse raced. If they didn't find a way out *now,* they were going to die.

"Hold it right there!"

The shout, coming as it did as she snatched the key from the Peg-Board and whipped back around with it, made the hair stand up on the back of her neck. This was the second bad guy, the one who had searched the place, Katharine realized from his voice. She could hear the other one coming, his footsteps a quick, continuous drumbeat of sound as they pounded across the kitchen.

Panic clutched at her heart. *Time's up.*

This guy's gun was in his hand now. He had pulled the weapon out from behind his back. She saw the moving glint of it as the light from the kitchen touched the metal. In a moment of dreadful clarity, she realized that he was raising it, positioning it, aiming at Lisa, whose back was turned to him as she tugged frantically at the door.

The door was locked. Struggling with it was useless. There was no way to get it open without the key.

"Lisa," she cried in terrified warning as she instinctively ducked down beside the dryer. "Look out."

"Shit."

Whirling, Lisa recognized her danger instantly. Katharine saw her spot the pistol, and the emotions that flitted in rapid succession over Lisa's face were as heartrending as they were impossible to mistake. Her eyes went huge; her mouth contorted. Her face turned ghostly white in the reflected light. Katharine could read her fear and desperation in every tense line of her body. Her hands came up in a classic defensive gesture. *"No . . ."*

Katharine was still looking at Lisa when she heard a peculiar whistling sound. *What?*

Her head was in the process of instinctively snapping around to try to ascertain what the hell that was when the answer became clear. Lisa squealed, the cry fraught with shock and pain. Katherine watched with disbelief as her friend was lifted off her feet and slammed hard against the door as if she had been picked up and thrown against it by an invisible hand. Behind her, the window shattered with a boom of exploding glass. The tinkle of glass raining down on the concrete steps and walk outside formed an eerie accompaniment to Katharine's horrified realization that Lisa had just been shot. The whistling sound—the gun was clearly equipped with a silencer—that she had heard was the bullet speeding past.

"Lisa," she screamed, too overwrought in that moment of extremis to remember her own danger. Surging to her feet, she darted toward her friend as Lisa's limp body slowly slumped to the floor.

Is she dead? Please, God, don't let her be dead. Her eyes are still open. . . .

"Bitch." The guttural expletive from the doorway was the only warning she got before a metallic *thwack* sounded right behind her.

Katharine's every sense refocused and went on red alert. A bullet had just smacked into the corner of the dryer. A bullet aimed at *her*. If she hadn't moved at that exact moment, she would have been hit. Her stomach knotted. Her skin crawled. With all need for concealment past now, she let loose with a scream that would have done a teen fright-queen proud, the sound tearing painfully out of her throat, echoing off the walls, never-ending. A lightning glance back over her shoulder revealed that the shooter was all the way inside the small room now. He was on the move, taking up a stance in the corner, positioning himself so that he had a clear shot at her as she hurtled toward Lisa—and the door. Another male silhouette—the second bad guy—filled the doorway where he had been.

"*Get her.*"

The shadowy figure that was the shooter grunted in answer as he crouched slightly, both hands steadying the gun as it tracked her flight. Cold sweat broke over Katharine in an icy wave. Her heart pounded out a desperate rhythm: She had to escape, had to escape, had to escape. . . .

There was no way out.

"*Goddamnit, shoot the bitch already!*"

As she waited with agonizing certainty for the bullet to slam into her back, time seemed to slow to a crawl. It was almost as if she had become separate from her body and was observing herself from a distance. It was, she thought grimly, the out-of-body experience from hell. She was still screaming, long, continuous riffs of sound over which she had absolutely no control. Her frantic shrieks ripped through the miasma of fear and violence and imminent death that shimmered like heat vapor in the small room.

Couldn't anyone hear?

No more than a couple of seconds could have passed. Terror sharpened her mind as it lent strength to her limbs and wings to her feet. In that instant of terrible clarity, as she raced toward the locked door and felt the tingle of a gun taking aim at her back, she already knew that she had no chance. There was no way she was going to be able to fit the key in the lock and get the door open before they shot her. She was as trapped in that small, dark laundry room as any cornered animal in a snare. At any instant now a bullet was going to rip its way through her trembling, sweating, cringing flesh and she would die.

Smack.

She stretched out, the key in her hand yearning for the lock that was less than a yard away, just as the bullet she'd been dreading sang past her cheek and slammed into the drywall beside the door frame with the sharp sound of a hand slapping flesh. Hard, dry grains of plaster blew back into her face, stinging her eyes.

"No, " she screamed. As her head snapped back in instinctive reaction, her frantic gaze fell on Lisa. Her friend's now-glassy brown eyes stared blankly up at her from the semi-sitting position she had slumped into. Black as oil in the near darkness, blood welled from Lisa's chest as she rested limply against the door.

She's dead. She looks dead. Oh my God, she's dead.

Above Lisa's head, the streetlight glowed brightly, a beacon.

Even as her forward impetus continued, even as she reached out for the knob and thrust the key desperately toward the lock, Katharine realized that she was no longer seeing the outside world through glass. Warm night air now mixed with the chill of the air-conditioning. Underlying the near-deafening shrillness of her own screams, she could just hear the ubiquitous chorus of cicadas—and the approaching wail of multiple sirens.

"Hey, what's going on in there?" a man's deep voice shouted from out-side. A blur of movement in the darkness beyond the door told her that someone was racing across the backyard toward the town house. Help was just seconds away—but that was still an eternity too far.

"Help! Help! Hurry . . ."

"Kill her!" came the roar from behind her.

This time the bullet was so close she could feel the wind of its passing in her hair.

There was only one chance of escape. Katharine took it.

I have to get out of here. . . .

Hurtling forward, leaping like she had never leapt in her life, she grabbed the doorknob and window frame for leverage and threw herself headfirst through the rectangular opening in the top of the door where glass had formed a barricade moments before.

For a mixed-up instant as she cleared the door and tumbled earthward, she got a glimpse of starry sky and the leafy branches of the young maple in the backyard swaying in the slight breeze, and the luminescent eyes of a neighborhood cat staring at her from beneath the neatly trimmed bushes that crowded against the detached garage.

Then she slammed hard into concrete, and the world went dark.

K atharine. Katharine, can you hear me?"

It was a man's voice, slow and heavy with the drawled cadences of the Deep South. The tone was authoritative. She must have been hovering on the verge of consciousness anyway, because when she heard it she opened her eyes.

Only to be practically blinded by the bright beam of a penlight shining directly into her face. Her eyes squinched closed again, fast. She took a deep breath, only to discover that she couldn't breathe. At least, not through her nose. When she tried, pain shot through her sinuses.

God, what was up with that? She was dragging in air through her mouth like a landed fish, she felt heavy and sluggish and totally out of it, and to top it off, she had the mother of all headaches.

"I'm sorry." He sounded genuinely contrite. "Look, the light's off. Can you open your eyes?"

Now that she had given up on the whole trying-to-breathe-through-her-nose thing, the pain in her sinuses merged with the pain in her head to settle into a dull throb behind her eyes. Unpleasant, but she would live. Anyway, there was something about that voice. It was deep and soft and compelling, and she wanted to obey it. Raising her lids cautiously, she did.

Everything was blurry, but she was immediately aware of a light-colored ceiling and walls and knew that she was indoors. Her surroundings were gloomy and gray, shadowy with the absence of any direct light, although there seemed to be enough light from some nearby source—a hallway, perhaps?—to allow her to see shapes, to see him. She was lying on her back on a bed, narrow and faintly uncomfortable, not her own. She wasn't lying flat, though: Her head and upper torso were elevated as the surface beneath her rose at a slight angle. His head dominated the center of her field of vision. His face was lean and tanned, topped off by a thatch of longish dark blond hair that waved back from his forehead. A profusion of curls flipped out untidily around his nape, but, with the light source behind him, she could not yet make out any details of his appearance beyond that. He leaned closer, peering down at her intently, blocking her view of the rest of the room. With his shift in position, the source of the light was no longer directly behind him, and she was able to see him a little better. He was frowning, she saw, and he wore glasses with narrow wire frames. The penlight, turned off now, was in his hand.

Even though his features were still slightly indistinct—that was the fault of her vision, she decided, as much as the absence of adequate lighting—she felt an immediate strong sense of familiarity.

Along with a little frisson of—something. Tension of some sort. Not a good kind of tension.

"Hi there," he said as their eyes met and held. There was definitely some kind of connection between them, but the harder she tried to latch on to it, the more elusive the memory became. Then, after the briefest of pauses in which he almost seemed to be waiting for something, he turned on the small lamp near the bed. Blinking in its sudden low-wattage glow, she realized that she was in a hospital room. It was all there, the heavily curtained windows limned with grayish light that managed to creep in around the edges, the dark TV affixed to the wall at the end of the bed, the banks of medical equipment, none of which, fortunately, seemed to be attached to her. Oh, wait, there was one narrow tube snaking out from the inside of her right elbow. Following it from where it emerged from beneath a strip of white tape up to the plastic bag half-full of clear liquid that hung from a shiny metal pole beside the bed, she realized that she was hooked up to an IV. *Not good.* Before she had time to think any more about the ramifications of that, he added, "Remember me?"

"Yes," she said instantly, because she did, absolutely, positively, no doubt about it at all. Then she got stuck again. Try as she might to pull his identity out of her subconscious, it wouldn't quite come.

But that little frisson of something was still there. *Was it . . . hostility?*

Blinking in consternation, she concentrated as his features came into sharper focus. What she registered first was an overall impression that here was a good-looking guy. His eyes, which narrowed as he watched her, were medium blue beneath the thin, rectangular lenses that didn't distort them in any appreciable way. There were crinkles at the corners of his eyes, which came partly from the sun but mostly, she thought, from the intentness with which he was regarding her. They were nice eyes, mild, intelligent, maybe a little reserved, set off by short, stubby, fair lashes and unruly slashes of ash-brown brows that formed thick, straight lines across his forehead. He had high cheekbones, a long, masculine, slightly off-center nose, a thin-lipped mouth, and an angular jaw with a stubborn-looking chin. He was tall, maybe six-one, although it was difficult to judge when she was lying on her back looking up at him, broad of shoulder, lean of build, probably in his late thirties. There was the faintest hint of stubble on his chin, more three-o'clock than five-o'clock shadow. He wore a limp blue oxford-cloth shirt with a slightly frayed button-down collar, no tie, open at the throat, with a white doctor's coat pulled on over it.

It was the coat that gave her memory the nudge it needed.

"Dan . . . Howard." The name popped into her mind on a wave of relief. "Dr. Daniel Howard."

Once she had the name, everything else fell into place. Of course, he was her next-door neighbor, the physician. He had lived in the adjoining town house since—when? Maybe the beginning of the summer. Not that she had seen a whole lot of him. She couldn't quite remember specific occasions, but probably they had introduced themselves once, then said hi whenever they happened to cross paths dragging trash cans to the curb and such. Had they had words at one time? Maybe his trash cans had blocked her garage, or her cat had walked on his car, or something? A minor dispute of that nature would account for the tiny flicker of antagonism, if that was indeed what it was, that had flared up inside her when she had first set eyes on him. Whatever, it couldn't have been too serious, because it was already fading away into the mists of her subconscious.

"That's right." Dan nodded, looking pleased, and she relaxed a little, as if pleasing him was important to her. Why that would be the case she couldn't imagine, though. Then, as the thought pricked at her, she wondered if she was shallow enough so that the answer was *just because he's a hottie*. Yeah, probably. That was also probably the reason she had been able to dredge up his name.

As she worked that out to her own satisfaction, she felt herself relaxing again.

"How are you feeling?" he asked.

"O-kay." She drew the word out, because what she really meant was okay, except for the headache and the impossibly stuffed nose and the small but sharp pain that shot through her chest whenever she moved and the nagging conviction that all was not right with her world, with which she was presently afflicted. It also didn't help that her voice sounded funny, all thick and nasally and not really like her voice at all. In other words, she was definitely *not* okay.

Not that she meant to say so.

"Good." He sounded pleased again.

"Where am I?" There was something wrong with her face. Or, more precisely, her nose. It felt weird. Thick and hot and, as she had previously discovered, totally congested. Swollen. Sensitive when she tried to wrinkle it, but not really—exactly—painful.

Just . . . weird. Sort of like the rest of her.

"Washington Hospital."

She absorbed that as she lifted a questing hand to her nose—her arms were bare, and she realized that she was wearing a blue hospital gown and a blue hospital gown *only* beneath the tan blanket and white sheets that covered her to her armpits—and discovered a bandage taped across it.

"My nose." Careful to keep a light touch, she felt the bandage, which pretty much covered her whole nose. Jeez, beneath the plastic the thing felt as big and shapeless as a baked potato. She only hoped there was a whole lot of gauze padding to account for most of the bulk.

"You got it smashed up pretty good." He seemed to be carefully studying her face. Then his eyes met hers again. "Not to worry, though. Once the swelling goes down, it should be good as new."

"When will that be?"

He shrugged. "A week or so, maybe. I'm more concerned about the blow to your head. How's that feeling?"

"I have a headache," she admitted.

"I'm not surprised. Other than your nose and the bump on your head, though, you don't have any significant injuries. Everything else is just random assorted scrapes and bruises. You're going to be just fine."

"You work here?" It seemed to her that she should know the answer to that. She knew his name, that he was her neighbor and a doctor. But she also felt like there was this big treasure trove of knowledge about him lurking somewhere in her subconscious that she couldn't quite access. She probably did know. She probably had Googled him or something once upon a time. After all, whether she had a boyfriend or not, she was only human. And he was cute.

"Sometimes. Not today, though. I'm here strictly because of you. When I got home last night, the first thing I heard was you screaming your head off. I ran up from the garage to see what was going on just as you came flying through the window. The police arrived about the same time, and an ambulance a few minutes after that. They loaded you up, and I came on into the hospital to make sure they were treating you right."

"Oh. Thanks." She thought that over for a minute. "You probably saved my life last night."

"Not a problem. That's what we good neighbors do." He smiled at her. It was a quick, wry smile that riveted her gaze. This she definitely remembered. She had seen him smile like that before. Had it set her heart to fluttering? Try as she might, she couldn't quite remember. But it was un-mistakably familiar.

He continued, "In case you're wondering, you should probably be get-ting out of here soon, maybe even as soon as later today."

"Today?" To her dismay, she drew a blank there, too. What day was it, anyway? Anxiously, she realized she couldn't recall. Here was some-thing she *definitely* should know—the date—but she didn't. The thought that she didn't know things she should was starting to really worry her. "Which is . . . ?"

"Saturday, July twenty-ninth." He glanced at his watch. "Six-forty-seven a.m."

The specter of a clock reading one-fourteen in glowing red numbers on a black background flashed into her mind, and she shuddered reflex-ively. She had the uneasy feeling that she was moving closer to some of that hidden knowledge, and that maybe she didn't want to go there after all. Whatever this thing was, she pictured it as something dark and im-mense and ugly hovering just out of the reach of her consciousness, like a middle-of-the-night monster a little kid just knew without looking was under his bed.

"Cold?" Dan asked, and picked up her wrist to check her pulse. It was only as she felt the warmth of his fingers against her skin that she realized that she was, indeed, cold. Freezing, in fact.

"A little," she said.

He released her wrist without comment and pulled another tan blanket, which had apparently been folded at the foot of the bed, over her, stretch-ing it all the way up to her neck and tucking it in so that her arms and shoul-ders were covered.

"Better?" he asked.

"Yes." The blanket was scratchy against the bare skin of her arms and neck, where it was pulled past the sheet, but the extra layer was welcome. "Thank you."

He gave a nod of acknowledgment.

There was no avoiding it any longer. For the sake of her own sanity, she had to know what was waiting for her there in the dark.

Her stomach tightened. She took a steadying breath. Her eyes met his. "So what happened? Last night? Why am I in the hospital?"

His expression changed ever so subtly. There was, she thought, a kind of wariness in the way he looked at her. The caution was subtle, but there. *Great.* She knew already that she wasn't going to like what she was getting ready to hear, and his expression just made her doubly sure. Her pulse accelerated with dread.

"You don't remember?" he asked.

She thought. And shook her head.

"Nothing?"

She frowned.

"Take your time," he said, watching her. "Relax. It'll come to you when you're ready."

She thought some more. Just as he promised, after a moment the fog began to clear and the images slowly began to crystallize in her brain. Terrible images. Frightening images. Even as they remained tantalizingly shadowy, her pulse began to race.

"There was a robbery—at my house. Some men broke in." Her mouth was dry from breathing through it, and she had to swallow before she could continue. "Two men, in black ski masks. They had guns."

"That's right." He nodded. His eyes never left her face. "What else do you remember?"

She had to concentrate hard to recover more details. It wasn't easy with her head throbbing and breathing an effort and the fog just waiting to descend again.

"They were after . . . some jewelry, which I didn't even have. I was asleep, and then I woke up, and there was a man in my bedroom . . ." Her heart lurched, her stomach clenched and her eyes widened with horror. "Oh my God! Lisa!"

Her gaze locked with his, silently asking him the question she couldn't bear to put into words. Before he even opened his mouth to reply, she knew from his expression that the news was bad.

"Is that your friend who was visiting?" He was stalling, she could tell, trying to gauge the impact of the truth on her.

She nodded as the terrible coldness that was raising goose bumps on her skin started to creep through her insides, too. "She's dead, isn't she?"

His eyes darkened, and she thought she saw a flicker of some emotion—sympathy for her?—there.

"Yeah, she is. I'm sorry."

"Oh, God. Oh my God."

Even though she realized that she had known, somewhere deep inside, about Lisa all along, his confirmation hit her like a fist to the solar plexus. Sucking in air through her mouth, she wrapped her arms around herself and closed her eyes as a great wave of dizziness broke over her. Her ears rang. Her throat tightened. Her pulse galloped. Lisa was dead. Lisa, bright, bold, always-smiling Lisa, had been horribly murdered right before her eyes.

She remembered everything now. She wished she didn't.

Tensing, Katharine waited for the tsunami of grief she knew was going to hit. She could feel it rushing toward her, feel the darkness of it, the weight. Then, suddenly, before it could reach her, she felt—different. Strange. As if she were suddenly far away, as if the awfulness of what had happened had been muted, as if it were now somehow coming to her over a great distance. She felt disassociated from the reality of it, as if it were a story she had seen on the evening news and was vaguely sad about but that really had no connection to her at all.

Yikes. Her thought processes might be a little warped at present, but they were not so warped that she didn't recognize that the way she was feeling—or, rather, not feeling—was wrong.

Abnormal, even.

She forced herself to open her eyes.

"Did she make it to the hospital?" Her voice was a croak. Even as she asked, ghastly images replayed in her mind: the two of them in the laundry room, the bullet slamming into Lisa, Lisa being thrown against the door . . . Yes, she remembered, all right. She just couldn't *feel* it. Not like she should.

His lips compressed. She could tell he didn't like what he had to say. "No. She was pronounced dead at the scene."

Blood gushing from Lisa's chest . . .

"I can't believe it happened." Despite the hideously graphic quality of the pictures in her head, her voice was surprisingly steady. She *knew* what had happened, knew the horror of it, knew that she had suffered a terrible trauma and a grievous loss, but once again that curious detachment intervened before her emotions could fully engage.

You're in shock, she told herself firmly. The realization was almost a relief. It explained so much. Shock was only to be expected. Shock was the norm in a situation like this. Shock would go away.

"It shouldn't have happened." Dan's voice had hardened, and his expression was grim. When their eyes met, he seemed to check for an instant at whatever he saw in hers, then added in a milder tone, "Hey, the reason we pay so much rent is because our neighborhood is supposed to be safe."

"Yes," she agreed.

The phone by the bed rang, making her jump.

Instead of answering, she frowned, hesitated, and automatically glanced at Dan. *Should I pick up?* Fortunately for her own dignity, she didn't ask the question aloud.

What is wrong with you? she demanded of herself even as the thing continued to ring and she reached for it. *Of course you should answer it. It's your damned phone. You don't need permission.*

Clearly the ordeal she'd been through had totally scrambled her wits.

"Hello?" she said into the receiver.

"Katharine? Is that you?" a voice boomed in her ear. It was masculine, and forceful, and something about the intonation told her that the speaker knew—or at least thought he knew—her well. Without waiting for her to reply, he continued, "What the hell happened?"

Unfortunately, the voice didn't ring a bell.

"There . . . was a robbery." She paused, wrestling with her memory banks, waiting for the voice on the other end of the phone to compute, for the speaker's identity to flash into her mind.

Nothing.

All she got when she concentrated was a worsening of her headache. Maybe the hospital had her doped up, she thought hopefully, glancing at the IV, and made a mental note to ask as soon as she got off the phone. That would explain why so many things she knew she ought to know were missing in action.

"What kind of robbery? Did they take anything? What'd they take?" There was a wealth of anxiety in the forceful voice on the other end of the phone.

Okay, she was still blanking. Before she answered any questions, she felt that it was important to establish who she was talking to. After all, *somebody* had tried to kill her last night.

For all she knew, it might even have been the person behind this authoritative voice on the other end of the phone.

"Um, who is this?" she asked cautiously, her gaze resting on Dan. He had turned away from the bed and was examining some beige metal box-like piece of medical equipment that stood unused on a stand beside the bed as he politely pretended not to listen.

There was the briefest of pauses on the other end of the phone.

"It's me, Ed." Impatience sharpened his voice. "Who the hell do you think? Katharine, *did they take anything?*"

Ed. Her boyfriend. Her divorcing, powerful lover. Of course.

The disconcerting thing was, even now that she knew who he was, she didn't recognize his voice at all.

E d," she murmured, seeking to mentally cement his name to the growl-
ing voice. Instantly his image appeared in her mind's eye: short, well-
groomed black hair just starting to go gray; heavy-lidded brown eyes;
meaty, triangular nose; full lips; a perpetually tan face with prominent
cheekbones and a square jaw. He was a hair taller than five-ten, an attractive, muscular man who liked to work out and had a closet full of expensive designer suits. And, good lord, he sounded like he was used to people
asking *How high?* when he said *jump*. Well, maybe he was just upset. She
concentrated, trying to remember what he'd asked. *Oh, yeah.*

"I don't know what they actually *took*," she said meticulously. "They
were after jewelry."

"Jewelry?" He sounded dumbfounded.

"That's what they said. I think they must have seen the picture in the
Post. You know, the one where I had on that set you . . ."

"Yeah, I know," he interrupted. The picture had caused him no end of
trouble, too. He'd been with her in it, of course, with his arm around her,

escorting her up some steps into the house. The magnificent necklace and bracelet and earrings she had been wearing had rightfully belonged to his wife, who was not yet his ex, and who had raised hell when she saw the paper. And, not incidentally, moved out of the house they were still sharing on a halfway-friendly basis and upped her financial demands. "What makes you think they were after jewelry?"

"I . . . I . . . that's what they said." She took a deep breath, trying her best to remember, to keep it all together. "They shot Lisa. She's dead."

There was the briefest of pauses.

"I heard. That's a hell of a thing." Another pause, and she could almost sense him fighting to rein in his impatience. Clearly, Lisa's murder was not, for him, the most important thing. Not that he knew Lisa. Unless her memory was failing her—well, it was, but still, she was pretty sure about this—he'd never even met Lisa. "I'm just glad you're okay."

"Well . . ." she began, meaning to tell him that she wasn't as okay as he seemed to think. But he interrupted before she could continue.

"Katharine. Who were they?" There was an urgency to his tone that made her grip on the receiver tighten.

"I . . . I don't know. Burglars. Thugs. They—"

He didn't let her finish. "Could they have been working for somebody?"

She didn't understand. "What?"

He gave an impatient *tcch*. "Do you think they were spooks?"

Katharine blinked, still all at sea. Then his meaning hit her. He was talking spooks as in the dark side inhabitants of the Alphabet Soup World they inhabited: CIA, FBI, NSA, DOD, NORAD, and at least a dozen more. *Spooks* as uttered by Ed meant covert operatives. The thought made her heart lurch. Her mind flashed back to the attack. Two men, dressed all in black, tall and muscular and all business, even when they were terrorizing her . . .

A chill ran down her spine. She didn't know why the possibility hadn't occurred to her before.

"I don't know. M-maybe."

"Damn it to hell." She could hear his teeth grinding. "What did they say? What did they do?"

Her stomach knotted. Her pulse revved up. An upsurge of remembered fear tasted sour in her mouth. She wet her dry lips.

"They said they wanted my jewelry. When I couldn't give it to them, they beat me up, then they tried to kill me. They sh-shot Lisa *dead.*"

"Tell me what happened. Start at the beginning."

Taking a deep breath, she did, although she gave him the edited version. She just didn't like talking about it, she discovered. And some parts, like the details of how Lisa had died, were just too raw right now. She needed time to process what had happened herself before she spelled it out for anyone else.

"Did they take anything? What did they take?"

The tension vibrating in his voice ratcheted up her own burgeoning agitation.

"I don't know. I didn't see. They were in the den . . . they found the safe. You never—" *Told me there was a hidden safe* was what she meant to say, but he cut her off with an explosion of curses.

"Did they get into it? Did they take anything? *What did they take?*" Ed practically screamed that last part, making her jump.

Bully. The thought popped into her mind unbidden, surprising her with its cool detachment. Did he always yell like that? The unsettling thing was, she didn't know.

She did know she didn't like being screamed at.

"I don't know." The sudden chill she felt was reflected in her voice. How many times did she have to say it? Her fingers hurt from gripping the phone so hard, and she shifted the receiver into her other hand, flexing her cramped fingers as she continued. "What was in that safe, anyway? *Was* there jewelry?"

She heard him inhale. The ensuing silence was as loud as a shout.

"Yeah," he said after a minute. "Along with some other things. Valuables. Cash. You know."

Yeah, she knew—knew that he was lying. It was there in his voice, plain as anything.

Don't call him on it. The warning sprang into her head as clearly as if she had heard someone say it aloud. Instinctively, she felt that her own interests would be best served by pretending to believe whatever he said.

"I'm coming home," he said abruptly, before she could reply. "Quick as I can get there. In the meantime, I'll send some people to you in the hospital. They'll watch over you. When you're ready to leave, they'll take you somewhere safe."

Somewhere safe . . . As his words sank in, her heart skipped a beat. That implied, unless she was mightily mistaken, that she wasn't safe where she was.

"Oh," she answered faintly, and realized that the thought of seeing him in the flesh sent butterflies swooping through her stomach. And not the good kind of butterflies. *Anxious* butterflies. *Fearful* butterflies.

"Love ya, babe," he said, and hung up before she could reply.

Katharine slowly pulled the receiver away from her ear. Her pulse raced, and looking down at her hand gripping the phone, she saw that her knuckles were white from holding on to it so hard.

"Is everything all right?"

She had forgotten Dan was there until he spoke. She glanced over to find that he was still standing a few feet away beside the medical equipment but was now openly watching her, and she wondered if her expression was as discombobulated as her thoughts.

He was a doctor. She latched on to that thought like a drowning man to a branch. She could tell him about the apparent gaps in her memory, about the odd sense of disassociation she was experiencing, about how generally *weird* she felt. About Ed, and not recognizing his voice, and her conviction that she needed to do what he said or the consequences would be—well, unpleasant. Dan might be able to help her, to explain it to her, to make it all make sense somehow . . .

Before she even had a chance to decide whether or not to say anything, a quick knock on the door made her jump and drove the issue temporarily out of her head.

Oh my God, could this be Ed's "people" already? The thought brought the hairs on the back of her neck to instant, prickling attention. Dan frowned, too, and glanced swiftly toward the door. Before either of them could get it together enough to reply, the knob turned and the door was thrust open.

"Morning, Miss Lawrence." Incongruously cheerful, a young black woman in green scrubs pushed a metal cart noisily through the door. "I just need to get a quick read on . . ." Her gaze fell on Dan, who had already turned back toward the bed and was grimacing sympathetically at Katharine. "Morning, Doctor." She wheeled the cart up beside the bed, transferring her attention back to Katharine and continuing her first thought as if she had never interrupted it. ". . . your blood pressure. Could I have your arm, please?"

Dan gave a small salute and mouthed *See you* as Katharine withdrew her arm from beneath the blanket and proffered it. By the time the nurse had the familiar black plastic sheath secured just above her elbow, he was gone.

"Relax, this'll just take a sec," the nurse said as Katharine blindly watched the band inflate. *Chill,* she told herself, to no avail. Relaxing even a little bit just wasn't in the cards at the moment. Her thoughts were in turmoil. She could feel her heart beating faster than normal. She felt jumpy, on edge, uncomfortable.

Frightened.

"Your blood pressure's a little high." Clucking disapproval, the nurse unwrapped her arm and tucked the cuff back into the cart. "You just rest for a while, and we'll check it again. Breakfast'll be around shortly."

"Thanks," Katharine said, and watched the nurse and cart trundle back out the door. Even with the door closed again, she could hear the muffled rattle of the cart as it headed on its rounds. The hospital was clearly waking up. People were moving around out in the hall. She could hear footsteps, voices, laughter. Someone being paged over a PA system. The light around the edges of her door seemed brighter, as if the wattage in the area outside the door had been turned up. The light behind the closed curtains was brighter, too, as beyond their shielding folds the morning took hold and the sun inched its way up the sky. Even the hum of the air-conditioning seemed louder, as if it were gearing up to combat the coming heat of the day.

A day that I'm lucky to be here to see.

The thought scared her all over again. It also filled her with an indescribable sadness, both for herself and for Lisa. One alive, one dead.

Why, why, why?

She tried to think, to sort things out a little, to impose some kind of order on the chaos that was her mind. But her thoughts raced and the images she needed to try to put any kind of coherent picture together melted away like sugar in a cup of coffee.

Giving up for the moment, she found the remote, turned on the TV—it was tuned to the Fox News Channel—and tried to follow the nurse's advice and rest. It was impossible. Her mind was in such turmoil that nothing the talking heads on TV said registered. The bed was uncomfortable, the blanket scratchy, the air-conditioning far too cold. Her mouth was dry, her head ached badly, and she couldn't breathe through her nose. And she still felt—weird. It was the only way to describe it.

Something was wrong: That was the firm conviction she couldn't get out of her mind. Something above and beyond the fact that she was in the hospital and Lisa was dead. Something—something—dear God, she didn't know what exactly, but *something*—that made her feel all shaky inside even as she tried to figure out what it was.

Ed's on his way. The thought was meant to be comforting, but her body responded independently of her mind: Her breathing quickened; her heartbeat sped up; her muscles tensed.

I don't want to see him.

The conviction of it surprised her. Had they had a fight? Not that she recalled, but . . . casting her mind back over her relationship with Ed was, she discovered, as impossible as everything else. Too much was missing. Only the bare bones were there, with the gaps between essential facts filled by blurry images that she couldn't quite pull together into a comprehensible whole, no matter how hard she tried.

I'm scared.

The thought popped fully formed into her mind. The fact that she was thinking it scared her even more.

Okay, she told herself firmly, *get a grip here. It's shock. It's temporary. Just breathe.*

Of course, that was easier said than done when she was minus a functional nose. But still, she tried.

Inhale, exhale. Inhale, exhale. In—

Quick, masculine footsteps in the hall outside her door broke her concentration. Her breath expelled in a snort that hurt her useless nose. Ignoring the instant electric jolt to her nose nerves, she froze, listening with mounting tension to the approaching footsteps. But they passed harmlessly on, and she sagged with relief. Then she started up the whole *okay, breathe* routine all over again.

After a few minutes she had to accept that it was a waste of good air. Her tension didn't abate one bit. Instead of finding comfort in the knowledge that people were going about their business in the hospital all around her, she found herself growing increasingly agitated by it. Who were these people? Did any of them mean her harm? That was pure paranoia and she knew it, but she couldn't seem to dismiss the possibility out of hand.

She moved restlessly, shifting positions in an effort to get comfortable, and the ring on her finger caught her eye. The sapphire was the size of one of her fingernails. The bright blue stone gleamed as she tilted her hand curiously toward the lamp; the diamond baguettes on either side sparkled. It looked almost impossibly glamorous on her hand, like nothing she could ever imagine herself owning—although her hand was glamorous, too. Staring down at her long, slim fingers, at her beautifully manicured, oval-tipped nails with their frosting of pretty pink polish, she felt like she was looking at a stranger's hand. It did not seem possible that hers could be so soft and well kept.

Almost cautiously, she touched the ring. The stone was hard and cold—
and big and valuable. Clearly very valuable. She had bought it for herself.
With money she had inherited. The knowledge popped into her head as a
solid nugget of certainty. It gave her hope that the fog in her brain might
be clearing away, but nothing else came. Not the name of the store she had
bought it from, or the memory of actually purchasing it, or anything at all
except those two small facts. As she probed her memory banks in a futile
search for more, she anxiously twisted the ring around and around on her
finger, then stopped when she realized something: The ring was loose. At
least a size too large, and maybe more.

Staring down at the ring, she realized that she was breathing in quick
little pants now that dried her mouth and throat.

Had she lost some weight lately? Her anxiety mounted as she realized
she had no clue. Or had she never gotten around to getting the ring sized?
Or did she just like to wear her jewelry loose? Any of those were possibilities. What made it frightening was that she just didn't know. Quickly
she raised her hands to the diamond studs in her ears: They were still there.
Still big and cold and valuable.

They didn't feel like anything that could possibly belong to her.

As she sat there fingering the heavy stones that were the size and ap-
proximate temperature of frozen peas against the soft warmth of her ear-
lobes, images from the night before swirled through her mind like outtakes
from a movie. A nightmarish shadow creeping through her dark bedroom.
A hard knee in the small of her back as her arms were wrenched behind
her. A voice demanding *Where is it?* over and over again. Two men, tall,
muscular, clad all in black, their faces hidden beneath knit masks . . .

Spooks. As she saw them again in her mind's eye, she wondered why
she hadn't instantly recognized them for what they were. The men who had
broken into her apartment, who had killed Lisa and tried to kill her, were
too fit, too well trained, too disciplined to be anything but cov-ops. Terror had probably kept her from connecting the dots at the time, but she saw
it quite clearly now.

And although she *knew* that they had been seeking jewelry, immensely valuable jewelry of the caliber she'd been wearing in that *Post* photo, knew it as in *this is an incontrovertible fact*, she could not actually remember them saying so.

So how did she know? Good question. Too bad she didn't have any other answer for it other than *I just do*.

What she did remember was them asking, "Where's the safe?"

The thought that she knew something without being able to remember exactly how she knew it made her break out in a cold sweat.

This is so not good.

Her hands dropped away from her ears, and the ring caught the light. The seductive blue gleam of the stone captured her gaze.

If confirmation of what she suspected was needed, there it was: Despite what she somehow "knew," plain, old-fashioned common sense told her that the intruders had not been after jewelry. If they had been, no way would this ring, and her earrings, have escaped their eye. Ergo, they had been after something else, something that they thought was kept in that hidden safe that Ed had never bothered to mention to her.

That Ed had deliberately not mentioned to her.

Her heart skipped a beat.

Ed knew what they were after, and he knew it wasn't jewelry. She had heard it in his voice.

Another flurry of loud footsteps outside in the hall made her suck in air and turn her face quickly toward the door. She tensed, waiting on tenterhooks, but they, too, passed on by.

When they were gone she went limp with relief, then simply lay there for a moment, considering. She was keenly aware of the pounding of her pulse, the tightness in her chest, the knot in her stomach.

Both times she had heard masculine-sounding footsteps approaching her door, she'd instantly concluded that they belonged to Ed's "people."

The people who were coming to watch over her and ultimately take her away with them.

Her brain—poor, gelatinous thing—seemed okay with that. But her body definitely was not.

In fact, every time she was faced with the imminent prospect of being tucked under the wing of Ed's "people," she about had a heart attack.

Hmm.

Maybe her body was trying to tell her something.

The sudden ringing of the phone nearly made her jump out of her skin. She sat bolt upright, the sudden movement jerking her IV. A quick, sharp pain shot through her chest and her head went all woozy and the room did a little unexpected shape-shifting. Heart pounding, breathing hard, she stared at the suddenly out-of-focus phone like it was a rattlesnake shaking its booty right there on her bedside table.

It was on its fifth ring before she got it together enough to answer it.

"Katharine?" This time she recognized the voice: Ed. "I just got off the phone with Starkey. He and Bennett are down in the hospital lobby right now, talking to a couple of cops who were asking for your room number at the reception desk. They're detectives, and they want to talk to you about what happened last night." There was the briefest of pauses. The volume of his voice dropped a degree. "Are you alone?"

"Y-yes." It was all she could do to keep her voice steady. For whatever reason, the knowledge that his "people" were on the premises set her nerves to jangling big-time. And never mind that she knew that, technically, she could be considered one of his "people," too. After all, he was her boss, her mentor, her lover . . .

Why did the thought make her go cold all over?

"Okay, listen: When you talk to the cops, I don't want you to tell them what I said about this maybe being some kind of insider job. No need to bring this circling back around to the Agency if we can help it. As far as public consumption goes—and that includes cops—this was a home break-in gone bad, plain and simple. They were after jewelry that they thought you had on the premises. Things got out of hand, and your friend got killed. Got that?"

Oh, yeah, I got it: You want me to lie to the police. But she didn't say it aloud. Once again, that big yellow caution light in her mind that seemed to be her primary reaction to Ed flashed on, bright as the sun.

"Whatever you say," she said. And didn't know whether to hate herself or congratulate herself for how meek she sounded.

"That's my girl." He sounded transparently relieved. "Anyway, now that I think about it, I feel it's quite possible the break-in may have been about that jewelry after all. There were some valuable stones in that set. Anyway, I'll tell Starkey to try to head them off at the pass if he can. But if he can't, you just stick to the jewelry scenario."

"Okay."

"I'm flying out of here in an hour. I should be back in D.C. late tonight. I'll see you then, or at the latest tomorrow morning."

"Okay."

"Love ya, babe," he said just as he had before, and hung up without waiting for her to reply.

Katharine was left to slowly put the receiver down. She felt as shaky as Jell-O in an earthquake. Her heart pounded so hard that she could practically feel it gyrating against her breastbone. Her blood thundered in her ears. Her muscles were tense, her breathing came quick and shallow, and— she discovered as she finally let go of the receiver—her hand shook.

She had to think, quick. Which wasn't as easy as it sounded. Her brain was definitely not firing on all cylinders. In fact, she had just enough reasoning ability left to realize that she couldn't depend on her reasoning ability at all.

Two men tried to kill me last night.

That was one thing she knew for sure.

Who were they?

Now *that* she didn't know. Except that they were probably spooks. Professionals. Covert-operations types.

Like the kind of men who routinely worked for Ed.

Ed, who wanted her to lie to the police. Ed, who knew perfectly well that whatever those thugs had been after, it sure as hell wasn't jewelry, no matter how hard he was now trying to make her think otherwise.

The thought of Ed made her tremble. The thought of his "people" made her want to crawl under the bed and hide. He spoke of Starkey and Bennett as if she should know who they were. But she didn't. She didn't have a clue.

But that was a problem for later. The problem of the moment was that they were on their way up to her room *now*.

And every instinct she possessed screamed *run*.

5

With her brain on the fritz, her instincts were all she had left. She had to go with them. But there was a problem: She was in a hospital bed hooked up to an IV drip. With assorted physical injuries. And a mental state that gave a whole new meaning to the phrase *dazed and confused*.

The thing was, Starkey and Bennett could come bursting through the door at any minute.

At the thought, panic assailed her, and that decided the issue right there. Without knowing more about what was going on than she did, she wasn't about to trust herself to them, no way, nohow. That being the case, she had to get herself gone, now, whatever it took. Hands unsteady, pulse pounding a mile a minute, doing her best to ignore the throbbing pain in her head and the lesser ache in her ribs, she threw back the bedclothes, swung her feet over the edge of the bed, and stood up.

"Oh, *crap.*" She said it aloud as her knees gave way.

If she hadn't managed to grab the IV pole for support, she would have gone down like a rock in a pond and it would have been all over right there. Fortunately, hanging on to the slightly wobbly pole was enough to keep her upright. Her head swam. Her ribs ached. Her legs continued to threaten to buckle. The room tilted dizzily before her eyes. Clutching the slender metal pole so hard that fluid sloshed in the plastic bag suspended from it, she locked her knees, stiffened her spine, and stayed on her feet by what was pretty much sheer force of will.

Whew.

So far, so good. At least she was standing.

Being tethered to the damned IV was an obstacle, that was for sure. But a glance down confirmed what she had suspected from the get-go from its unfortunate tendency to tilt: It had wheels. Four of them, to be precise.

Thank God for small blessings.

Moving carefully lest her knees betray her again, pushing the IV pole in front of her and using it as a support to help her stay on her feet, she shuffled toward the door as quickly as her protesting muscles would permit. The industrial gray linoleum was cool beneath her bare feet. A gust from the air-conditioning goosed her through the open back of her hospital gown. The thought of appearing in the open corridor with her backside flapping in the breeze was briefly daunting, but the alternative was far worse. She didn't know which floor she was on, but she did know that there were elevators to reach it. Starkey and Bennett could be on her floor even now, heading for her room. And if they weren't yet, they would be soon.

Her heart pounded at the thought. Her blood ran cold. Her breathing quickened. Forget hospital-gown embarrassment: She would run naked through Yankee Stadium in the middle of the World Series if it would get her safely away from them.

Only vaguely aware of the tingling of her skin as goose bumps sprang to life along her too-bare flesh, she took a moment she very much feared she didn't have to pause with one hand on the knob and press her cheek to the cool metal door, listening intently for any sound from the corridor. Holding her breath, jittery as a cat in a kennel full of dogs, she forced herself to wait and listen for at least a ten-count. To have Ed's "people" catch her in the act of fleeing her room would not, she felt, be a good thing. Better to skitter back to bed and try to delay her release from the hospital for as long as possible if that scenario seemed inevitable. But if she did that, she would to all intents and purposes be putting herself in their custody—which translated to "at their mercy." The thought made her throat contract and her stomach tie itself into a big, painful knot. Precisely why, she didn't know, but the fear she felt was unmistakable.

Chalk it up to those instincts of hers again, having their say.

Unfortunately, besides the hum of the air-conditioning and the pounding of her own heart, she couldn't hear a thing.

Maybe there was nothing to hear.

On that optimistic note, she pulled the door open a few inches, peering around it out into the hall. It was, as far as she could see, empty.

So go for it already.

Taking a deep breath, she did, stepping out into the beige-walled passage, pushing the IV ahead of her, wincing at the squeaky clatter of its wheels. It turned out, she saw with one quick wild glance around, that she was only two doors away from the end of the hallway—and a red exit sign marking a door that led, presumably, to the fire stairs. The nurses' station was perhaps fifty feet away in the opposite direction, opening off the middle of the corridor like a giant room without walls. At the nurses' station, a gray-haired man in scrubs stood with his back to her, talking with a brown-haired woman in white lab coat as he tapped an impatient finger on a manila folder that was spread out in front of them on the tall blue counter. A black woman in scrubs—presumably the same one who had taken her blood pressure not long before—pushed a rattling cart down the opposite end of the corridor. She, too, had her back to Katharine.

The elevators—there were four of them—were located in the wall directly opposite the nurses' station. Katharine knew, because even as her gaze touched on and identified the nurse with the cart, one of the elevators went *ping*.

Uh-oh, company.

Her eyes shot toward the sound, located the elevators, and then she watched in frozen horror as the doors of the second one from the left started to slide open, revealing a widening view of a man in a dark suit.

Her heart lurched.

Starkey. Or Bennett. She didn't know which, but then, it didn't really matter. Because behind him stood another man in a dark suit. Why she was so sure it was them she couldn't have said—okay, so maybe it was the whole hands-clasped-in-front-of-them, feet-planted-apart, wearing-sunglasses-in-an-elevator thing they had going on—but she *was* sure and the conviction was galvanizing.

I am outta here.

Grabbing her pole, lifting it right up off the floor so that the wheels wouldn't squeak and give her away, she turned and fled through the fire door.

As she had suspected, it led to an emergency stairwell. *Thank God.* She was across the landing and on her way down before the door had finished closing behind her. It was warmer in the stairwell, presumably because the self-closing doors blocked a lot of the air-conditioning. The cinder-block walls were painted a soft sage green. The handrail was smooth polished steel, cool to the touch and fortunately—because she was of necessity leaning heavily on it—very sturdy. The stairs were uncarpeted concrete. A flight of ten or so steps led from another landing above her down to where she had entered the stairwell, and in the slanted ceiling above her head there was evidence of more steps leading upward from that landing to the next floor. The flight of stairs she was chugging down led to another landing from which there was no exit, where the steps reversed directions and continued to descend, hopefully to a landing with an exit.

Faster. Faster. Faster.

Breathless with exertion, Katharine made it to the first landing and kept on going. It was tricky, because she was light-headed and her knees were unreliable and she had to plant the IV pole carefully on every step to keep it from rolling off and taking her with it to disaster. Sweating bullets, holding on to the rail for all she was worth, she cast numerous fearful looks behind her at the solid metal door, which thankfully remained firmly closed.

She was on step number four from the next landing—the one that, indeed, had an exit—when she heard the muffled slap of a quartet of leather-soled shoes approaching along the corridor from which she had just escaped.

Starkey. Bennett.

Her eyes widened. Her breathing suspended. She glanced desperately— and uselessly—up at the closed door. If it was indeed them—and she felt in her gut that it was—they should be in her room in a matter of seconds. How long would it then take before they worked out that she was missing? If she was lucky, they might think she was in the bathroom. . . .

Yeah, right. She might not remember much about herself, but she knew this: She was never that lucky. Anyway, the bathroom door had been open. She remembered seeing it standing ajar as she left her room.

Crap again.

It was a pain not having a functional brain. Coming up with a plan above and beyond *run* didn't seem like it was going to happen anytime soon. In that case, the only thing to do was to go with what she was already doing. Working the IV unit like a ski pole, supporting herself with the handrail on the other side, she feverishly swung on down the stairs.

"Hey—*nurse!*"

The shout from the hallway above made her jump, which was a bad thing in that it almost caused her to lose her footing and butt-bump down the rest of the steps. Only her grip on her trusty IV pole saved her. The voice was a man's, the tone imperative, as if he was used to being promptly attended to. From the take she got on the location of it, she was very much afraid that the speaker was yelling from the doorway of her abandoned room.

Yikes. She was willing to bet dollars to doughnuts that it was Starkey. Or Bennett.

The IV pole clattered onto the landing, and she was right behind it.

"Nurse!"

It was the same voice as before, but she didn't hear it nearly as well this time because the door to the next floor down was already swinging shut behind her when he bellowed.

On the other side of the door, she stopped because she didn't know what else to do. The overhead wattage was bright, and she felt frighteningly vulnerable in its relentless glow. Heart pounding, she took a second to get her bearings. The floor was crawling with people. A young couple, visitors from the outside from the look of their cutoffs and flip-flops, were just walking into a room only a few doors away. A nurse stood at the nurses' station writing something in a chart. Another one sat near the first, chatting on the phone. A man in scrubs conferred with a large group of what she presumed were a patient's relatives in the middle of the hall just beyond the nurses' station. Beyond them, two little kids turned somersaults down the length of the hall.

Fortunately, none of them so much as glanced her way.

Quick, what to do?

Go back in the stairwell and head down, making like a bandit for the great outdoors? In a hospital gown, with an IV pole for a buddy? *That* wouldn't be noticeable. *Oh, no, not at all.* Besides, any second now, Starkey and Bennett would start hunting in earnest for her. The thought sent a cold little thrill of fear racing down her spine. Would it occur to them that she might have taken the stairs? Unless they were idiots, she decided instantly, yes, it would.

Soon, the whole hospital would probably be put on alert. She didn't know what the protocol was for dealing with patients who'd gone missing, but she was pretty sure something would happen. And here she was, wandering the corridors in a flimsy little cotton gown that left her way overexposed, tethered by the arm to an IV unit that was as tall as a flagpole. Somehow, she didn't think she was going to be hard to locate.

The thought of being handed over to Starkey and Bennett—to say nothing of Ed—once they knew she had tried to run from them made her heart skip a beat.

She might not know much, but she knew what *danger* felt like when her body screamed it at her.

The nurse finished writing and slapped the chart closed. The sound made Katharine jump. Any second now, someone was going to glance her way. . . .

Move, a little voice in her head shrieked, and she did. IV pole and all, she shot across the hall, opened the door to the nearest room, and stepped inside, closing the door quietly behind her.

The light was off and the curtains were closed, though some light seeped in around them. Still, the room was dark and cool. Some kind of machinery whirred soothingly. The sound of heavy breathing brought her gaze to the nearest bed. It was, she saw as her eyes adjusted, empty.

"Who is that?" a querulous voice demanded from beyond the curtain that separated the room into halves. She had had a private room. This was a double, and clearly the empty bed had a roommate. "If you're here for Dottie, they just took her down to X-ray."

Katharine took a deep breath and found her voice.

"Uh, thanks," she called back. "If you don't mind, I'll just use the restroom while I wait for her."

"Help yourself." The voice was definitely female, definitely old, and definitely crotchety. "It's not like I can use it. I just wish. You ever tried to take a dump in a bedpan?"

Hoping the question was strictly rhetorical, Katharine made a noncommittal sound by way of a reply and rushed into the bathroom. Closing and locking the door behind her, she flipped on the light.

And froze.

She was looking at her reflection in the big plate-glass mirror that covered most of the wall over the sink. At least, she knew it had to be her reflection, because—a swift glance behind her confirmed it—there was no one else in the small, gray-tiled, steel-fixtured room.

The thing was, though, the woman looking back at her—the stranger with the poleaxed expression and the IV unit teetering precariously beside her—was no one she recognized at all.

Whoever this woman was, it definitely wasn't her.

You're *nuts.*

That was her first thought. Her second, as she stared wide-eyed
and openmouthed at what had to be her own reflection because there just
wasn't anyone else there in the bathroom whose reflection it could be, was
Holy crap, I've woken up in somebody else's body. Or something.

She had an unruly mop of curly auburn hair that cascaded around her
shoulders. Her skin was pale as milk. Her cheeks were full, her chin
pointed. Her eyes were deep-set, with thick, dark brown brows that gave
her expression a distinguishing gravitas that she had always liked. And she
was plumper, not plump but *curvier*, that was the word, than the waif in
the mirror.

Who was an impossibly thin beauty with a golden tan and shiny,
straight platinum blond hair that ended in feathery layers that reached
maybe an inch past her chin in front and was shorter in back. Right at the
moment, the 'do was a mess, with the ends sticking out every which way

and the back smashed, but she was pretty sure she was looking at a hundred-dollar haircut.

Or maybe even a two-hundred-dollar one.

The very thought of which boggled her mind.

I can't afford that. The thought popped into her mind out of nowhere.

The woman in the mirror apparently could. Along with a big ole sapphire ring and diamond ear studs that had to be at least a carat each and a pricey manicure and who knew what else.

This isn't me.

Heart pounding, staring horrified at the woman in the mirror who was—*duh!*—looking equally horrified as she stared back, Katharine broke into a cold sweat.

Whoa. Calm down. Breathe.

Okay, the bandage on her nose—which thankfully wasn't nearly as big or noticeable as it felt—kept her from getting a good look at that feature, but she definitely remembered getting her face smashed into her kitchen floor, so that was right. The bump on her forehead, too, had probably happened then, or maybe later, when she had flung herself out the window.

Which meant that she was definitely looking at the woman who had been terrorized and almost killed in her town house last night.

In other words, herself.

Get a grip. Who else could you be?

Her thick, dark brows were gone, replaced by elegant arches that were definitely lighter in color. But—and this was a biggie—her eyes were the right color: a soft, clear green. Very pretty, very distinctive. In fact, she had always considered them her best feature. She *remembered* them.

She blew out a sigh of relief.

See there?

With her lips still parted from that relieved sigh, she discovered her teeth. They were—she leaned a little closer to be sure—perfect teeth. Two rows of china-white Chiclets that gleamed at her when she pulled back her lips in a grimace to check them out.

Her heart started pounding again.

The thing was, she was pretty sure her teeth had never been that blindingly flawless. In fact, she distinctly remembered a tiny gap between her two front teeth.

What the hell is going on here?

Panic clogged her throat. Her heart stuttered alarmingly. She gripped the edge of the vanity tightly while the bathroom's reflection blurred behind her, trying to hold on to her sanity.

This is not me.

The thought was solid with conviction.

But it had to be her, because there was no one else it could be.

Am I dead? Did I die yesterday, at the same time as this woman maybe, and somehow miss the Heaven Express and wind up in her body?

Cold chills raced down her spine at the thought. *Cue the spooky music.* As she stared in growing horror at the woman in the mirror, she realized that she was breathing hard enough so that her throat ached, and she was going all light-headed and woozy and weak in the knees again. A little more shock to the system, she thought grimly, and she was liable to hyperventilate and pass out right there on Dottie and her crotchety roommate's bathroom floor.

"Katharine Lawrence, please check in at the nearest nurses' station. Katharine Lawrence . . ."

Booming over the PA system, the announcement was repeated twice. Katharine only needed to hear it once.

Her heart lurched. Her stomach dropped like she was on an elevator in free fall. The hair on the back of her neck leaped to tingly attention.

The hunt was on.

Okay, put the kibosh on the incipient panic attack. Whoever she was, whatever was going on with this whole body-switching thing, she was going to have to sort it out later. What she needed to do now was lose the IV, find some clothes, and get her newly skinny, newly blond ass out of the hospital.

Fast. Before the people who were looking for her found her.

Because no matter who she was, she still had the feeling that being found by them would be a really, really bad thing.

Her gaze lit on the tall silver pole looming beside her. New BFFs or not, there was no doubt about it: The IV had to go.

Wrenching her eyes away from the horror in the mirror, she looked down at her arm. And never mind that now that she knew it belonged to somebody else, she saw instantly that it was too tan, too thin, too elegant to have ever been hers. Later, she could freak out. Now, she just had to get herself—or whoever—out of harm's way. A piece of surgical tape secured the clear plastic tubing to her elbow. Beneath the tape, she knew a needle was inserted into her vein.

God, I hate needles.

This she knew. This was her. But this was also no time to be squeamish. Peeling off the tape, ignoring the churning in her stomach and the sweat that popped out on her forehead, she gritted her teeth and gently— *ouch*—pulled out the needle. A single drop of blood bubbled up in its wake. Fighting a battle with incipient nausea—obviously, she wasn't a big fan of blood, either—she grabbed a tissue and pressed it to the wound. After a moment, the bleeding stopped, and she threw the tissue away.

Yay. She was free of her best buddy the pole. Next up: clothes. Leaving the bathroom—

"Dottie, is that you?"

"Uh—she's not back yet."

She stealthily crossed to the closet and opened the door . . .

"Oh, I forgot about you. What're you, one of her daughters?"

"Yes."

. . . to find clothes. To wit, a short-sleeved blouse, dark, probably navy or black, with big pink flowers splashed all over it, and a pair of dark polyester slacks.

"Which one?"

"Uh, the oldest."

Ignoring the neatly folded panties and the bra laid out on the top shelf—

no way was she wearing another woman's undergarments, and, besides, the bra cups were so big and firm that they stood up on their own, rising like twin Mount Everests—she pulled the hospital gown over her head . . .

"Sandy?"

"Uh-huh."

. . . tossed it as far back along the overhead shelf as it would go . . .

"Well, that's good, 'cause I was wanting to ask you where you got that angel cake you brought in yesterday. It was *good.*"

. . . and hurriedly dressed in the absent Dottie's clothes. The blouse could have fit three of her inside it; the elastic-waist pants were instant low-riders. If she took a deep breath, she had a feeling they would be gone.

So don't breathe.

The PA system crackled to life again: "Katharine Lawrence, please report to the nearest nurses' station. Katharine Lawrence, we have an urgent phone call for you. Please report to the nurses' station immediately."

Her heart thundered.

Jesus. Move your . . .

"Sandy? The angel cake?"

"CVS." There were flat-heeled black shoes on the closet floor. Hurriedly sliding her feet into them—they were a little short and a little wide, but if she curled her toes, they'd do—she headed toward the door.

"CVS? They have a bakery?" The old lady sounded confused. As well she might, since CVS was a chain of pharmacies.

Oh, well.

"Some of them do." Katharine listened intently at the door, heard nothing, and gave it up. She needed to go *now,* while they were still hoping she was going to turn herself in to a nurses' station. "I think I'll just go check on Mom. See you later."

"Bring some of that cake next time, would you?"

"Sure. Bye."

Slipping through the door, she tried to look nonchalant. Which wasn't easy when her heart was beating a mile a minute and her pants felt like they might take a dive with each and every step and her cramped toes were already killing her. To say nothing of the fact that her legs felt about as solid as limp spaghetti and her head was swimming and the only way she was getting any air was through her mouth. The elevator was, she thought, her best bet, because the stairwell was too obvious and too easy to monitor. What she wanted to do was blend, blend, blend.

The hallway was even busier than before, which was a good thing, she told herself firmly. Smoothing her unfamiliar hair with her hands—she'd forgotten what a mess it was until she caught a glimpse of it in a shiny brass doorplate that read *staff only*—she kept her face averted from the nurses' station as she shuffled in the wake of an orderly pushing a man in a wheelchair toward the elevators. Not that they were likely to be circulating a wanted poster of her or anything—*yet*—but still her bandaged nose might, she felt, attract attention if, by some miracle, her hobbling gait did not. And attention was the very last thing she needed or wanted just at that moment.

No one paid her any heed. She joined about half a dozen people in front of the elevators just as the last one on the right went *ping*.

Holding her breath, pulse racing, she slid—unobtrusively, she hoped—behind the tall orderly for cover as the elevator doors slid open. Peeking warily around him, she huffed out a sigh of relief as she saw that the sole occupant was a blond teenage girl carrying a big bunch of flowers. She stepped out without more than a cursory glance at the group waiting to replace her, and walked away.

Katharine got on with the rest, crowding toward the back to make room for the wheelchair, just one of the group wedged in there. Looking studiously at the floor in case anyone was monitoring the security cameras with which she was almost positive the elevators were equipped, she rode down five floors to the lobby without incident, and got out.

There her nerve failed her. The lobby was a huge space with tall, dark-tinted windows and polished terrazzo floors. Modern seating groups consisting of black-leather-and-chrome couches and chairs anchored by area rugs in a red, gray, and black abstract design were scattered about. Escalators ferried passengers up to a mezzanine that offered a gift shop and a

McDonald's, according to the signs. An information desk was located directly in front of the elevator bank. Fortunately, it faced the entry and it was busy, with each of the three women staffing it occupied with her own little line of the lost or the clueless.

A pair of uniformed security guards, or maybe cops—it was impossible to be sure, because they were some distance away with their backs to her—idled near the main entrance, drinking from foam cups and chatting as they watched the comings and goings of the hospital's visitors.

Coincidence? Yes, probably. She was 99.99 percent positive that their presence couldn't possibly have anything to do with her.

Still, her heart picked up the pace again. No way was she going to chance it. Shrinking back into the shadows near the elevator bank, she took a quick, panicked look around.

And came up with plan B. It was pretty obvious, but still it was good to know that her shell-shocked brain hadn't totally deserted her.

Instead of going with the flow of the crowd and walking on across the busy lobby and out the twin revolving doors, she was going out a side entrance: the one promised by the small black sign affixed to the wall that offered *restrooms* and *exit,* and included a helpful arrow pointing the way.

It might be pure paranoia, she thought as she headed in the direction indicated by the arrow, but she had a pulse-pounding fear that they might already be watching the exits. She hoped there were not enough of them yet to cover all the ways out. In that case, the front of the hospital would be the most obvious place to wait and watch.

The question that gnawed away at her brain was, *Who, exactly, were "they"?* Ed's people? The men from last night? Someone else? And was there even really still a threat to her at all? She wasn't sure—she didn't know. She just had this overwhelming sense that she was in terrible peril.

That being the case, she was going to go with it.

The hospital wasn't a building, it was a complex, she saw as she left it. Tall, gleaming towers of industrial gray steel and glass were linked by a pair of glassed-in skywalks maybe eight stories up. Long, low buildings the size and general appearance of airplane hangars clustered at the base of the towers, and it was through the side of one of these that she exited. Emerging onto a sidewalk that ran alongside a small, nearly full parking lot, she stopped, momentarily blinded by the glare of the sun bouncing off dozens of windshields. Raising her hand to shield her eyes from the worst of it, she tried to get her bearings. The steady sound of stop-and-go traffic told her that there was a busy road nearby. The sky was a beautiful cerulean blue dotted with a handful of white clouds that looked like fluffy sheep. The sun, round and yellow as a tennis ball, hung just above the scalloped tree line that marked where the parking lot ended. The heat was palpable, wrapping itself around her like a thick, moist blanket. Already, at what she guessed couldn't be much past eight a.m., D.C. was sweating.

My hair'll be in ringlets by noon.

Oh, wait, it wasn't her hair anymore. She was now the possessor of an up-to-the-minute blond bob, and she had no idea what it did when confronted with steamy summer heat.

At the realization, her stomach cramped.

Steady, she ordered her rapidly unraveling nerves. *Don't panic. It's some kind of weird amnesia. It'll go away.*

If she lived long enough.

On that comforting note, she almost panicked again.

Okay, this whole amnesia thing has got to go on the back burner. First things first: Before you go to pieces, you gotta get somewhere safe.

Like where? The question twisted like a snake through her already holey brain even as she walked as rapidly as she could manage away from the hospital. Balancing on the sides of her feet to save her scrunched-up toes, she tottered across the glistening black macadam of the parking lot toward the narrow, quiet, tree-lined street beyond it. *Home,* was her instinctive answer, but then it occurred to her with a renewed sensation of disorientation that she didn't even know where "home" was.

A picture of the town house shimmered to life in her mind's eye. That was home. She knew it. But it just didn't feel right.

So what else is new? she asked herself in despair. *Nothing feels right.*

In any case, she couldn't go back there. Last night Lisa had been murdered there. She had nearly died there herself. The memories would be overwhelming. The police might still be there, investigating. The place had been torn up. There would be blood. . . .

Sooner or later, Ed's people would almost certainly come looking for her there. And for all she knew, they weren't the only people interested in her whereabouts. But no matter who was looking, that would be the first place anybody would check.

Think. You have to go somewhere.

Clothes: She needed clothes that were hers, clothes that fit, clothes that she could wear while going out and about without attracting undue attention. She needed underwear. She needed her purse, and her driver's license and credit cards and money. . . .

In the middle of the narrow strip of tired grass that separated the blistering parking lot from the shady street, she stopped dead.

She wasn't going home. She wasn't going anywhere.

She couldn't. She didn't have any way to get there. She had no car, no money, and nobody she could trust to call for help.

As she faced that awful truth, her heart started to pound. Her fingers curled into fists. Her . . .

"Katharine?" a man's voice called.

7

Katharine jumped what felt like a mile in the air, stumbling over her own cramping feet as she whirled to see a black Chevy Blazer pulling to a halt not ten feet away. It was leaving the parking lot, and had paused at the stop sign at the junction of the parking lot entrance and the street. The driver's-side window was rolled down. The man behind the wheel was looking her over with a frown.

Recognizing him, she felt a wave of relief.

"Dan!" Waving, she stumbled toward the car. He was the answer to a prayer. Her neighbor, the doctor. They might have issues about his garbage or her cat—okay, so she couldn't remember—but at least he didn't want to kill her. *That* she was sure about. Well, fairly sure. "Can you possibly give me a lift?"

"Sure." His eyes slid over her once more, and his frown deepened. But if that meant he was harboring reservations about doing as she asked, too bad, because she was already on her way around the car. Whatever the frown was about, it didn't stop him from leaning over to open the passenger door for her from the inside. Slipping into the black-leather seat, which was hot from the sun and which felt wonderful because of it, she closed the door and pressed the automatic lock button, which with an audible *click* locked the car up tight.

Just in case.

"Thanks." Giving him a quick, grateful smile, she cast a—she hoped— furtive glance back over her shoulder. A woman was walking out the same exit she had just used, and several people were now scattered throughout the parking lot, going their different ways, but none of them seemed to be in any way looking for or connected to her. They for sure weren't Starkey or Bennett, which was a major plus.

"Not a problem." If he was curious about what was going on with her, he didn't show it. His voice and expression remained untroubled. "Fasten your seat belt."

The Blazer started moving again, turning left onto the shady street with its tidy row of older, two-story brick houses across from the hospital as Katharine obediently fastened her seat belt. A slim young woman with a shiny dark ponytail and jeans pushed a stroller with a toddler in it along the sidewalk in front of the houses. A white minivan with a ladder on the top and some kind of lettering on the side rumbled past. Two prepubescent boys careened down the street on bicycles, heading straight toward them, and Dan swerved around them without comment.

With her seat belt secure, Katharine let her head drop back onto the warm, cushiony headrest with a silent sigh of relief. Against all odds, it looked like she had escaped.

From what? The question ate at her. She felt like she should know.

But she didn't. The harder she tried to remember, the more elusive anything beyond the present became.

"Where to?" Dan asked after a moment, which she spent working on remaining calm. Among other things, this involved doing her best to get her breathing and heart rate under control, staring sightlessly at the ceiling, and letting her feet slide unobtrusively out of those torturous shoes.

Good question.

Her head rolled toward him, and their eyes met as he stopped at the first intersection. He gave her a small, encouraging smile, and it registered once again that he was a really hot-looking guy. His glasses, which were perched firmly on his nose, added an air of abstracted intelligence, à la the absent-minded professor, to a face that was all lean planes and hard angles. There were lines around his eyes and mouth that reminded her that he had been up all night—on *her* behalf, which was certainly (probably) a plus in the can-I-trust-him department. His hair was really beautiful; grown out, she judged, those thick, dark gold waves would be the envy of many a woman. Since she had seen him last, he had lost the lab coat, and his limp blue button-down—it was short-sleeved in deference to the heat—revealed bronzed arms that were muscular enough that she felt safe in assuming that, his leanness notwithstanding, the good doctor regularly worked out. His hands, which were curled around the steering wheel, were large, tanned, broad-palmed, and capable-looking. The worn-out shirt was tucked into equally ancient-looking black dress pants that were belted around narrow hips. On his feet, she saw as she glanced down, he wore nondescript black wing tips, probably size twelve.

His work clothes, she presumed. Then another, really random, thought popped into her head: *Dr. McDreamy, look out.*

Dr. McDreamy? For a moment she was puzzled. Then, *Oh, yeah,* Grey's Anatomy. Her favorite TV show. *Yes.* She mentally pumped her fist as she realized that she remembered that, too. *That's a good sign, right?*

"Well?" he prodded patiently.

She made a face.

"I . . ." *I don't know* was what she had started to say. But it hit her then that she did know. Even with all the objections she could muster to it, there was only one logical, possible answer. "Home. The town house."

She added that last because referring to the town house as "home" felt strange. But if he thought her response was odd, he didn't show it. He merely nodded agreement.

The light changed to green, and his attention shifted back to the road as they turned right and the hospital receded into the distance. The tires swished, the air conditioner cranked out air that grew increasingly cold, and the mixed residential-industrial neighborhood in which the hospital was located was left behind as the Blazer pulled onto the Beltway, heading south.

Katharine didn't realize that she had been sitting in tense silence until he broke it, because she was busy making a mental list of everything she needed to grab from her apartment. The key was to get in and out as quickly as possible, before any of Ed's people—or anyone else—thought to look for her there. Presumably she had a car in the garage out back— yes, she did. She remembered it, she realized with another thrill of triumph: a champagne-colored Lexus that she had purchased with some of the same inheritance that had bought the ring and earrings. She would throw her things in the car and peel rubber out of there, then drive far, far away. . . .

On the run. But from what, exactly?

She didn't know. God help her, she just did not know.

"Nice outfit," Dan observed in a mild tone, glancing at her as he slowed to a stop at a red light. Blinking in surprise, Katharine realized that they had left the expressway and were now almost to Old Town. "Kind of a new look for you, though, isn't it?"

Startled by the interruption to her thoughts, she cast him a wary look. "Is it?"

"Sure."

He didn't seem to notice anything amiss in her manner, thank goodness. The light changed to green, and he accelerated, driving past an upscale new strip mall that had sprung up right on the outskirts of the carefully preserved historic district. Even so early, the morning traffic pulling in and out was steady, and she saw that the strip mall boasted a Starbucks. At the sight, her brain sat up and begged like a hungry puppy. She needed caffeine, she realized. Badly.

Down, girl. Later.

"So what kind of look do I usually have?" she asked cautiously. It wasn't just that she was trying to make small talk to keep the illusion of normalcy going, although there was that, too. It was more that, having just discovered that she had no idea what she usually wore, she was desperate to fill another hole in her knowledge of herself.

He shrugged. "I don't know. Sort of—more high fashion. Designer stuff, I guess. And your clothes usually fit."

She glanced down at herself. The primary color of the slacks and blouse was navy blue, she saw. The roses were hot pink. The material was some sleazy synthetic. The fit was—circus tent. Definitely not designer stuff.

"I borrowed this."

"Ah." He flicked another look her way. This one was definitely curious. "So, what are you running away from?"

That startled her into sitting bolt upright. A sudden, painful twinge in her rib cage immediately punished her for her impulsiveness.

"What do you mean?" Pressing a hand to her ribs, she tried not to look as rattled as she felt, but feared she did a poor job of it.

He shrugged. "Sneaking out the side door of the hospital, alone, under your own power, when not half an hour before you were in bed with an IV drip going and a nurse checking your vital signs. Wearing clothes that are obviously not yours. Casting furtive looks over your shoulder every few minutes. To me, it adds up to one thing: you snuck out of the hospital. So, I repeat, what—or who—are you running away from?"

Brain damage and caffeine deprivation were a bad combination, she discovered, especially when the emergency mission of the moment was to come up with a really convincing lie. In fact, she couldn't do it.

"So what if I say 'None of your business'?" she asked, narrowing her eyes at him challengingly. "What are you going to do, turn around and take me back? Do they have, like, hospital police who have to clear it before people can leave or something?"

He shook his head. "No, of course not. And you're right, it's none of my business. But the thing is"—his gaze touched on her hand that was still pressed to her ribs—"you still seem to be feeling pretty rough. Maybe you ought to let me take you back."

Her hand dropped and curled into a fist on her lap. "No."

His lips firmed with exasperation. "Look, whatever's going on in your life, you're probably better off in the hospital than running around out here on your own. You've been injured, and the experience you went through last night was pretty horrific. There might be something they missed, some kind of internal injury or trauma. For one thing, when I saw you coming across the parking lot, it looked like you could barely walk."

"That's because of the shoes. Mostly."

He glanced at her with incomprehension. "What?"

"The shoes. I borrowed them, too. They're too small."

His brows went up. "And you're seriously trying to tell me that that's what's making you stumble around like a zombie from *Night of the Living Dead*?"

"Yup."

He made a skeptical sound.

The ride suddenly became noticeably less smooth, and she realized that they had reached the centuries-old cobbled streets that marked the heart of Old Town. Originally settled as a river port in the seventeenth century, Old Town predated the capital by almost a hundred years. Just six miles south of D.C., it boasted quaint shops, narrow, tree-lined streets, and, at least in the summer, hordes of tourists. Restored gas streetlights stood sentinel on corners. Eighteenth-century buildings crowded together like soldiers standing solidly shoulder to shoulder. Black-painted shutters and wrought-iron window boxes enlivened the upper stories of shops and residences alike. Just at the moment, the window boxes were filled with bright purple petunias and brilliant red geraniums and delicate white Queen Anne's lace mixed with leafy green sweet-potato vines that spilled luxuriantly down aged brick walls. A goodly number of the streets had names that reflected the settlement's British roots, like Duke and King and Prince. Already, despite the early hour, the horse-drawn carriages that were favorites with the tourists were waiting for their first customers of the day in a patient line that snaked around Market Square. As the Blazer turned onto North Union Street, which ran parallel to the murky green Potomac, she saw that the first of the tour boats that ran all the way up to Mount Vernon and back was pulling away from the dock. A costumed tour guide, walking backward and gesturing animatedly, led a small group along the waterfront.

"You can trust me, you know," Dan said, drawing her gaze again. "If you're in some kind of trouble, maybe I can help."

For a moment, as that sank in, she stared blankly at his hard profile.

He makes me feel safe. I feel safe right now, with him, in this car.

Okay, then. That was her instinctive reaction. So far, she'd gone with her instincts every time. So, *should* she confide in him? Should she tell him that she was convinced that she was in terrible danger, although she didn't know why or from whom? Should she tell him about the horrible brain dysfunction that had left her feeling like she was trapped in another woman's body, with its accompanying memory loss and emotional numbness? He was a doctor; maybe he knew the answer; maybe he could explain it all to her.

Maybe he could fix it.

At the thought, she blinked with excitement. The thing was, she *wanted* to tell him. She wanted to trust him. He *felt* like somebody she could trust.

He'd come to the hospital last night on her behalf, and stayed with her until she woke up.

"Katharine? Will you let me help you?" He glanced her way and their eyes met. The thin glass lenses through which he looked at her didn't detract one bit from the surprising power of those gentle blue eyes, she discovered. Plus, his voice had a soothing quality to it that she found inordinately attractive. Maybe it was the southernness of it. Maybe it was its deep, rich timbre. Maybe it was . . . maybe it was . . .

Wait a minute. Whatever the hell it was, she refused to let it draw her in. Confiding in her neighbor the doctor might be a good thing. Then again, it might not.

The bottom line was, she didn't know him from Adam.

She didn't even know herself. The cold, hard truth was that she had no idea whom she could trust, and until she did, the smartest thing she could do was trust no one.

Including Dr. McDreamy here, with his compelling eyes and hot voice.

"Thanks, but I'm fine," she said, and managed to give him what she hoped was a bright smile.

He frowned. The Blazer pulled up at a stop sign, its turn signal clicking for a right turn, and she saw that they were at the junction of Union and Wilkes. The quartet of town houses in which they both lived was less than a block away, straight ahead on Union. The entrance to the alley that led to her garage was on Wilkes, right behind the parking lot of the Old Town Candle Shoppe, which was on the corner opposite. To reach the alley, and thus their garages, he needed to make a right turn, which explained the busily clicking signal.

"Uh, do you mind if we drive past the front first?" She was starting to panic again. The thought of returning to the town house made her go cold all over. Anything could be waiting for her there. The police might still be investigating; some of Ed's people might have already turned up. At the very least, she could be sure that reminders of last night's attack would be everywhere. . . .

He cast her a quick, searching look. "No, I don't mind. Listen, are you sure I can't take you back to the hospital? You taking off on your own like this just seems like a really bad idea."

There was quite a bit of traffic now, everything from cars to small paneled delivery trucks to motorcycles to bicycle-powered rickshaws, many of which were backed up at this three-way stop. A blue minivan turning left pulled out of Wilkes and curved in front of them. They were next. Dan silenced the turn signal and accelerated.

"I'm sure," she said as the Blazer went straight through the intersection. "Hospitals give me the heebies."

The great thing about that was, it actually felt true.

To their left, the busy boardwalk that ran alongside the green stretches of Founders Park and the marina had turned into a collection of funky shops and restaurants and art galleries that had sprung up in place of the old tobacco warehouses that largely had been torn down. Beyond them, generations of landfill, now overgrown with a carpet of carefully maintained emerald grass, sloped down to the river. On the opposite side of the street, the eighteenth-century look remained intact. Besides the candle shop, there was an antiques shop, a vintage clothing shop, and a toy shop, all housed in carefully restored Colonial-era buildings that had been pastel-washed in soft colors that made her think of those Valentine's candy hearts with the messages on them. Equally well-preserved private residences were shoehorned in next to the shops. Her tall, narrow town house, one of a quartet of attached brick row houses with fancy pedimented doorways and five (one was paired with the door) multipaned windows, was at the very end of the block. As they neared it, Katharine's heart started to beat faster. She was almost afraid to look.

But she did look, because she had to know.

From the outside, everything appeared as usual. There was no crime-scene tape, no sign of a police or any kind of investigative agency presence. All four gates were closed on the elegant wrought-iron fence that surrounded the front of the property and separated the long, narrow rectangle of grass into four tiny front yards. Most of the curtains on the twentysome odd windows fronting the street were closed, as they generally were in the mornings, to ward off the first brilliant rays of the sun as it rose directly in front of them. Her own yard was immaculate; not a blade of grass appeared to be out of place. The ankle-high row of bushy monkey grass lining her walk sported delicate white antennalike blossoms that showed no trace of having been disturbed. The four steps that led up to her black-painted front door were clear. On the stoop, the folded newspaper lay on the welcome mat. Everything appeared just as it would on any normal Saturday morning. It was as if the horror of the previous night had never happened.

It happened.

Katharine felt a pain in her hands, which had been resting on her lap, and glanced down to see that her fingers were curled into fists so tight that her nails were digging into her palms. Her breathing had quickened. Her pulse had sped up.

"You know, I just don't think this is a good idea. There's no way you

should be going back in there now. You shouldn't be out of the hospital."
A touch of impatience colored Dan's voice as he glanced her way. "Look
at you, you're shivering."

She was indeed trembling, and made a concerted effort to stop. The
Blazer was already slowing for another stop sign. Tearing her eyes away
from the town house, she glanced sideways and met his gaze. His eyes had
hardened, narrowed, and now glinted with purpose. Brain damage or no,
divining what that purpose was wasn't all that difficult: From his expression, it was fairly obvious that he meant to ignore her wishes and take her
back to the hospital.

There was something else, too: As long as he was driving, where they
went was his call. He could take her anywhere he wanted. Unless she
wanted to leap from a moving car, that is. And the thing about that was,
she was festooned with just about all the bumps and bruises she could take
for the time being.

That being the case, she decided to handle this the easy way.

The Blazer stopped at the stop sign. Like the previous one, it was a
three-way intersection, and busy.

She reached for the door handle.

"I think I'll just get out here." Opening the door as she spoke, she slid
out onto the pavement, steadying herself by the door handle for a moment as she tried to get the wobblies out of her legs. Luckily, Union had
only two lanes, which meant that that stepping out of the car put her approximately four feet from the sidewalk. She was in no danger of being run
down, at least.

"Hey! What are you doing?"

"Thanks for the ride," she said, still holding on to the door for support
as she dipped her head down to glance in at him. His eyes were wide with
surprise as they met hers, and she saw that he was off-center now, with his
torso leaning a little toward where she stood in the passenger doorway. His
right hand, which had been gripping the wheel, now rested on the console
between the seats. It occurred to her that that was the position it would

probably be in if he had grabbed for her but failed to catch her as she had exited the car. It looked like her instincts were spot-on once again. "See you around."

"Wait." Urgency quickened his voice, and he said something else, too, but she missed it as she closed the door and stepped resolutely away from the car. A car horn blared close at hand, making her jump. There were, she saw, four cars lined up behind him, and three each at the other two stops. He had no choice but to move, she knew, but still she was relieved when he did, with a resentful-sounding *whoosh* of tires.

Gritting her teeth with the effort it took, she moved off the street, stepping clumsily over the small drainage ditch and up onto the sidewalk, then walking back toward the town house as quickly as she could manage, which to tell the truth wasn't really all that quickly at all. Her ribs hurt, her head hurt, and her feet hurt. Plus the steamy heat seemed to sap what little strength remained in her muscles. She was operating on pure adrenaline, she knew.

When she glanced over her shoulder, the Blazer was far down the block.

She didn't know whether Dan would turn around and come back, but it didn't matter: She had no intention of going anywhere with him again.

Right now, she felt safest alone.

Shooting nervous little glances all around, she let herself in the gate and shuffled up the walk, her too-small shoes making small scuffing sounds on the herringbone-patterned brick. Already sweating from what felt like way too much exertion in the heat, she determinedly ignored the pounding in her head and the sick clenching of her stomach as she climbed the steps, skirted the paper—if she moved it, someone might realize she was inside—and reached for the doorknob.

It was only as she turned it and nothing happened that she realized that of course the door was locked.

And she didn't have a key.

She stared at the door, appalled.

There's a spare under the mat.

The little voice inside her head came out of nowhere. It felt foreign, as though it had originated somewhere outside of her body. *It doesn't feel like me.* The thought brought a rush of anxiety with it. But when she knelt down and checked, the little voice was right: A key was there. It was brass, substantial, and—when she fitted it into the lock—it worked.

Taking a deep breath, she consigned the whole out-of-body problem to later, when she wouldn't be quite so concerned with getting herself out of harm's way.

A quick glance around revealed no sign that she was being observed. The traffic in front of the house was still heavy, but the black Blazer was nowhere in sight. A teenage girl in a red Georgetown University T-shirt and denim mini walked her pug down the sidewalk. Faint strains of "What's Left of Me" spilled from the headphones she wore draped around her neck, making a surprisingly cheerful—considering the subject of the song—counterpoint to the sounds of squeaking tires and gunning engines as various vehicles took their turns at negotiating the intersection. An elderly couple in matching khaki shorts and straw hats went into the art gallery across the street. A man in a striped polo shirt and jeans and a little girl in a pink sundress emerged from the ice cream shop beside the art gallery and, licking away at their already melting cones, started walking in the direction of Founders Park.

If there was a threat in the vicinity, she couldn't find it. Sucking in a big gulp of hopefully fortifying air, she mentally braced herself for whatever she might find. Then she opened the door and stepped inside the house.

8

What struck her first was how cool the place was compared to the sultry heat outside. And how dim, with the lights off and the curtains—at least the ones she had been able to see from the street—firmly drawn. Closing the door behind her quietly, checking a second time, in a textbook illustration of hope over experience, to be sure that she had locked it, that the dead bolt that hadn't kept intruders out the last time was secured against them now, she paused for a second, listening. The house was quiet, hushed. She was *almost* sure she was the only person inside.

That *almost* was paranoia at work—she hoped.

But still, the alarm didn't greet her with its usual forty-five-second warning—and chance to silence it—before exploding into a cacophony of police-alerting wails.

For whatever reason, it hadn't gone off last night. Why should she expect it to be working properly now? And anyway, for it to work, someone would have had to have set it. Who, besides herself, knew the code?

The specter of two black-hooded figures rose terrifyingly in her mind's eye. Last night they had gotten in—somehow.

Her heart started to pound.

Get in and get out.

Slipping out of the punishingly short shoes, she picked them up—no way was she leaving such impossible-to-miss evidence of her presence right there at the front door—and padded barefoot across the slightly uneven planks of the age-darkened hardwood floor. The hem of the too-big polyester pants dragged a little, creating a soft swishing sound as she walked to the alarm's keypad, which was set into the wall only a few feet away. The blinking green light told her that the system was, indeed, not armed. The digital readout said *Call for service.*

Great. For whatever reason, the alarm was down. Had that been the problem last night? But the panic button had worked . . .

It didn't matter. At least, not right now. Taking a deep breath, she turned a shoulder to the keypad and proceeded on. The entry was a long hall that ran the length of the first floor, with all the living space to the right and Dan's town house beyond the thick dividing wall to the left. The hall ended in the arched door that opened into the kitchen. The ceiling was at least twelve feet high, and two small, antique-looking crystal chandeliers hung from it. About halfway down the hall, a simple, old-fashioned staircase that looked original to the building rose to the second floor, narrowing the hall before it reached the kitchen. The walls were real plaster, painted creamy white. An expensive-looking piece of modern art—stripes of horizontal colors in shades of red and orange and purple—hung over a wrought-iron, glass-topped console table. On the table was a pile of mail and a crystal vase full of gorgeous red roses. She was sure that their perfume must fill the air, but, courtesy of her damaged nose, she couldn't smell it.

Not that it mattered. She didn't allow herself more than a passing glance at the mail. She didn't have time to worry about why it was that she couldn't remember putting it there. There was a card tucked in among the roses, though, and that she couldn't resist. There were so many blanks in her memory—and now she couldn't remember getting what was really a magnificent bouquet. Who had sent them? Why? Or had she bought them herself, maybe in honor of Lisa's visit? Or . . . who knew?

The thing was, the lack of answers was starting to drive her crazy, and here was a quick-and-easy answer. Pausing just long enough to thrust a hand in the midst of the velvety blooms and pull the card out, she read: *With love from Ed.*

She dropped that card like it was hot. *Ed.* The very thought of him was enough to make her stomach knot.

He was the man she loved . . . and just thinking about him scared her silly.

Get going. There it was, what she was coming to think of as her guardian voice. She obeyed, turning away from the roses without another glance, padding swiftly for the staircase.

Her goal was to get what she needed and get out, quickly. Her malfunctioning brain could ponder what was going on with it when she was in her car and making tracks out of the city. With that firmly in mind, she didn't go into the living room but instead merely glanced inside as she passed its white-painted pocket doors, which were ajar. The walls were silvery gray; the overstuffed couch and the one chair she could see—a velvet tub chair to the right of the couch—were charcoal. The lamp beside it had a black wrought-iron base with a tweedy gray shade. It sat on a glass-topped side table. The cocktail table in front of the couch was wrought iron and glass, too, with a big, glossy book called—she couldn't see the cover, but she *knew*—*Rose Gardens of the South*. The Oriental rug was multicolored, with lots of ruby red.

The decor was beautiful, expensive, and in the best of taste, but unfortunately, she felt no kinship with it. This was not, she felt sure, *her* taste. Had she used a decorator? Or had Ed, who owned the place, had it done? Even as she reached the base of the stairs, though, something still more unsettling occurred to her.

It looks like nothing happened here.

Not a thing was out of place in the hall or the living room or anywhere else that she could see.

Her heart was thumping wildly now as she started up the steep, narrow stairs. Last night she had distinctly heard the living room being torn apart, along with the dining room and den. She couldn't help it—even though she knew she was better off not doing it, she had to glance inside the kitchen. Leaning over the polished oak handrail, she was able to see most of one end of the room. As far as she could tell, everything was in order. Even the one bar stool she could see had been restored to its proper place, which was pulled up to the wrought-iron-and-marble kitchen island. The last time she had seen that bar stool and its twin, when she and Lisa had made their break for freedom, they'd been shoved back against the cabinets.

Suddenly, she felt as if she were suffocating. Memories of the night before rushed back, compressing her chest, her lungs, making her gasp for air.

Not now. You can't think about that now.

Closing her mind to the terrifying images, she forcefully dragged her gaze away from the kitchen and continued on up the stairs.

Someone's cleaned up the house.

Who, though? She tried to quiet her galloping heart by reasoning it out. A housekeeper? The name LouAnn popped into her mind, along with a picture of a scrawny, fortysomething woman with short, graying brown hair and a lifetime's worth of wrinkles already etched on her face. LouAnn came once a week, on Mondays, she remembered, pleased with herself. But it was still early in the day, and what she had seen of the house looked pristine. She didn't remember much about LouAnn's work ethic, but she doubted that, even if the woman could have been persuaded to come in on Saturday, she could have accomplished so much in such a short time. So who did that leave? Ed's people? She might not remember them, exactly, but she remembered enough about them to know that they were frighteningly efficient. They might well have been hard at work restoring order as soon as the police finished up.

Maybe even before the police finished up. If there was something they wanted to make sure no one else saw . . .

Like any trace of whatever the intruders had really been after.

She was, she realized, literally sick with fear. The pain in her head was suddenly so bad it was almost blinding. Gritting her teeth against it, squinting up at the rectangle of light that outlined the window—it was fitted with a Roman shade, which was closed—at the top of the stairs, she hauled herself determinedly up the last few steps. Thinking too much, just like dwelling on the horror of the previous night, was an error. Her heart was beating like a rabbit's. She was breathing way too fast. Her palms were sweaty.

Okay, deep breath.

Reaching the second floor, she swiped her palms against her slinky-feeling pants. Then she turned and walked quickly back along the dim hallway toward the master suite, which consisted of a bedroom, a sitting room, and a bath at the front of the house. The rooms Lisa had used were slightly smaller and closer to the top of the stairs. The door to those rooms was closed; her eyes slid over it as she passed. No matter how much she was tempted to go inside, she would not, could not, stop. Not now. Not when time was of the essence . . .

Lisa's dead. Her things—a suitcase, her purse, her clothes—are in there. Someone's going to have to deal with them.

An upsurge of nausea caused Katharine to swallow convulsively. The image of Lisa's widening eyes as the bullet hit her sprang full-blown into her brain. It was as vivid as if it were happening again, right before her eyes.

Don't think about it. You can't think about it.

Not if she wanted to be able to function.

Firmly closing her mind to anything besides the present, she hurried down the hall. She was freezing, so cold she was shivering with it, and with every step she took, the weird out-of-body sensation she was experiencing grew worse.

The thing was, she knew her way around inside the house. She knew exactly where she was going, where everything was. She knew what the rooms looked like, how many bedrooms and bathrooms there were, even where the linen closet was located. (She had just passed it; it was in the mid-dle of the upstairs hall.) The house itself, the colors and furniture and ac-cessories, all felt familiar.

But they also felt wrong.

No way do I live here.

The thought rang with conviction. It also made her stomach cramp so hard she wanted to throw up.

Whatever the hell was going on, it was one more thing she didn't have time for just now.

Rushing into the spacious, expensively furnished master bedroom, she spared no more than a cursory glance for the profusion of stylish black-and-white toile that papered the walls, covered the twin windows in the form of luxurious, drawn drapes, was quilted into a bedspread custom-tailored to fit the queen-size bed . . .

Wait. The bed's been made. One more quick glance around confirmed it: *The bedroom's been cleaned up, too.*

Panic clutched at her heart as memory assaulted her again. The last time she'd been in this room, she'd been dragged from the bed . . .

Her skin prickled as cold sweat broke over her in a wave.

Flying to the huge walk-in closet—yes, she knew that it was the first door on the left just inside the bedroom, right beside the one that led into the sitting room—she pulled open the door, flipped on the light switch, and stepped inside. Then she stopped dead.

She was neat, meticulously so; at least, she thought she was. But her closet was a mess. Clothes had been pulled from their hangers and thrown in a heap on the floor. What looked like drawers full of lingerie had been dumped on top. The drawers themselves had been tossed about haphazardly.

Somebody searched my closet. She took a deep breath. *They did this last night, probably, when they were searching the house. Everything else has been cleaned up. Why not this?* The explanation was obvious: Either they were careless or they weren't finished.

The thought set alarms to jangling all over her central nervous system.

Jesus, get the hell out of here.

But in order to make good her escape, she had to get what she had come for. Five minutes, no more, and then she was out of there for good. Anyway, why did she feel so sure that the cleaning crew, whoever they were, posed a threat?

The answer to that was, she just did.

Calm down. A split second later, a corollary thought made the first almost impossible: *Hurry.*

Biting her lip, her heart pounding, she set the shoes on the floor—no way would they be noticed in this—then stumbled over a misplaced drawer as she grabbed for a black duffel bag that looked like it might have been used to travel to and from the gym.

If so, she realized grimly, she couldn't remember it.

There was lots of black in the heap, she saw at a glance, and lots of tailored jackets and skirts that she thought were probably suits. Right now, they weren't what she needed. Colorful, silky panties and bras were on top, and she grabbed random handfuls and thrust them into the bag, feeling no more familiarity with them than if they were new items she was grabbing off the sale table at Macy's. Then she rooted through the equally unfamiliar clothes, snatching up the simplest things she could find: T-shirts, a couple of casual skirts, white shorts, a pair of jeans. Weekend clothes. Everything else looked too formal, too pricey. She wore a lot of designer stuff, Dan had said.

Maybe so, but right at the present moment she didn't feel like a designer-stuff kind of girl.

The shoe rack had been left untouched, and she surveyed it with mounting dismay. Somewhere she must possess sneakers, or even a pair of flats, but they definitely weren't in sight. Heels were the name of the game. Dozens of heels. They ranged from four-inch leopard-print spikes to three-inch businesslike pumps to maybe an-inch-and-a-half casual sandals. In despair, she tossed a pair of black pumps into the bag and slid her feet into a pair of beaded turquoise sandals with kittenish heels.

They fit.

See?

Letting out a breath she hadn't realized she'd been holding, she took them off again. The idea of clattering around the house in noisy heels made her skin crawl even though she was almost positive that she was the only one there. Then she tossed the sandals into the bag, to be retrieved before venturing onto the hot pavement outside the house and, bag in hand, headed for the bathroom.

The bathroom was big, beautiful, all black and white tile to match the bedroom, with a marble Jacuzzi tub, a toilet that was set off from the rest in its own little enclosure, and a separate shower stall. She did what she had to do, then headed straight for the gleaming white porcelain sink. Seeing her terrifyingly unfamiliar reflection in the mirror that fronted the medicine cabinet was still a shock, but she didn't have time to panic, so she kept her eyes averted from it as much as possible. She hastily washed her hands, did her best to wash her face without getting her nose wet, and brushed her teeth. Then she opened the medicine cabinet and scooped the contents into the bag wholesale, pausing only to drag a small brush she found there through her surprisingly stiff-feeling hair and run a tube of tinted Chap-Stick over her dry lips. Closing the cabinet again, though, she couldn't help it: She had to look in the mirror. No magical transformation had occurred: However impossible it seemed, she was now a slim, tanned blonde with a bum nose and hair as straight as broom straw.

Could anybody say Invasion of the Body Snatchers?

The thought sent icy prickles of horror racing over her skin.

Later, she reminded herself grimly, and tore her gaze away. A quilted robe lay on top of a hamper behind the door, and she grabbed that, too, and thrust it into the bag. Made of heavy silk, smooth and luxurious, it felt like nothing that could possibly be hers.

The robe was jade green, she registered as she headed out the door.

One of my favorite colors.

Because it made her eyes look even greener than they were.

O-kay. How much evidence do you need?

A cheery little voice saying *Hello, moto* to the accompaniment of musical notes stopped her in her tracks just inside the bedroom. A phone, she realized after a few seconds in which her heart leaped for the ceiling. The sound made her cringe; muted as it was, it still seemed scarily, attention-grabbingly loud. It wasn't the bedside phone, though. That was right beside her, and the singsong voice came from farther away. Tracking down the sound, she discovered a slouchy black leather handbag tucked behind the nightstand on the side of the bed she'd slept on last night. The repeated *Hello, moto*s were coming from the purse.

It's not mine.

That was her instinctive reaction as she stared at the obviously expensive purse. But the phone inside kept on keeping on, and after a second she grabbed the purse anyway. The sound was making her frantic. She had to shut it up.

Of course, the annoying summons stopped just as she got the purse unzipped and was reaching for the phone. But even as she paused, on the verge of withdrawing her hand, she saw, along with the phone and various cosmetics and other assorted items including a set of keys, a wallet.

If the purse wasn't hers, and she felt strongly that it was not, this was her chance to prove it.

The wallet was Gucci. She recognized the distinctive design. Flipping it open, she found a shopaholic's dream: at least a dozen credit cards, including a black AmEx, in little leather slots; what looked like a substantial amount of cash in the pocket designed for it; and, in the plastic rectangle on the inside flap of the cover, a driver's license.

With her picture on it. Or, at least, a picture of the woman she saw when she looked in the mirror. The newly tanned, blond, and glamorous her. Along with her name, date of birth, and this address.

That's it, she told herself fiercely even as she dropped the wallet back into the purse, zipped it closed again, and headed toward the door. *You're you, damn it.*

The shoes fit, the robe color was right. The driver's license matched. Even the photograph on the nightstand that caught her eye as she was rushing out of the room was of her—the new, improved her—standing with a man she instantly recognized as Ed. Earlier, Ed had seemed to recognize her voice; Dan had recognized *her*.

She knew her way around inside the house. She had known where to find the spare door key.

There was no mistake: She was Katharine Lawrence, and this was her life.

So why, she asked herself as she slung the purse over her shoulder and, duffel bag in hand, hotfooted it back down the stairs, *did that just feel wrong?*

When the phone started ringing, I didn't recognize the ringtone and realize that it was my phone I was hearing. Then I had to hunt for the purse. I didn't know where it was, and I didn't recognize it, either.

The caveats hit her even as, aches and pains notwithstanding, she practically leaped the last few steps into the hall. For a moment she paused with one hand on the newel post, eyes widening, as she considered.

Hello, moto was pretty universal. In fact, she was almost sure that it was the default ringtone for that kind of phone. Probably the phone was new, and she hadn't personalized the ringtone yet.

Yes, but I still don't remember anything about it.

And if her purse had been found last night while they were searching the house, the bastards would have either taken it or dumped it and left it where it fell. But clearly the purse had not been found, because it had been tucked neatly out of sight, and nothing in it had been disturbed.

So if it was hers, why didn't she remember putting it there behind the nightstand?

There were lots of explanations, she assured herself, even as she recovered her wits enough to start moving toward the front door again. (Although the garage was her destination and the kitchen door offered the closest, most convenient access to it, no way was she setting foot in the kitchen again, she decided the instant the thought crossed her mind.) Maybe she was just a forgetful type. Maybe someone else had tucked her purse into that little hidey-hole. Maybe . . .

A whole long list of maybes was starting to unscroll through her head when the soft creak of a floorboard somewhere nearby refocused her attention like nobody's business. Her eyes widened. Her breathing suspended. Not just her ears but every fiber of her body strained toward the bone-chilling sound.

Nothing.

Other than the sounds of the house—the hum of the air-conditioning, the murmur of the appliances—she heard nothing more. Her gaze searched the hallway and as much of the adjoining rooms as she could see: still nothing. As far as she could tell, everything was just as it had been before. If there was anyone else in the house, she could neither see nor hear them. Probably, she told herself, what she had heard was just one of the usual creaks and groans of an old house settling.

But her instincts screamed at her: *Get out, get out, get out.*

Oh, yeah. I am so gone.

She was breathing again, shallow and fast. Her heart thudded so loudly that it was like having her own private drumroll crescendoing in her ears. Glancing warily around, with every sense she possessed now on red alert, she got a firm grip on the bag and rushed on whisper-soft feet toward the front door.

Her ears caught it first: footsteps racing across carpet; the rasp of quickened breathing. With her periphery vision, she saw a blur of movement as something big and dark and fast hurtled across the living room toward her.

Holy crap . . .

Whipping around to face whatever it was head-on, Katharine jumped back and crashed into the console table, screaming like death itself was after her.

Which, she confirmed seconds later as her brain registered what her eyes had already perceived, it was.

9

In that split second of shock before he was upon her she saw that the dark blur was actually a tall, muscular man dressed in a dark suit with a black knit ski mask pulled down over his face.

A spook . . .

Her heart practically leaped out of her chest. The tiny hairs on the back of her neck catapulted upright. The ski mask had holes cut out in it for the eyes and mouth, just like the ones last night's attackers had worn. In fact, if he wasn't one of last night's attackers, he could have been their twin.

Screaming like a siren, she tried to dodge, but it was too late. The purse slid off her shoulder; the duffel bag hit the floor with a thump. Scrambling sideways, banging into the console table again in her rush to get away, she was stopped by a huge arm hooking her neck in a brutal grab that yanked her back against his chest. Her feet went out from under her. She would have fallen if it hadn't been for his grip on her and her instinctive grab of his imprisoning arm. Behind her, mail spilled in a slither of paper. Water and flowers pelted her legs as the vase of roses toppled with a thud and a splash. Fortunately, the vase itself, after dumping its contents, came to rest on its side on the table without crashing to the floor and shattering around her bare feet.

"*Gotcha.*" There was a wealth of satisfaction in his voice—not a voice she recognized from last night, she registered instantly—as her feet scrabbled on the wet floor to regain their purchase. Terror washed over her in an icy wave as he used his choke hold on her throat to haul her upright. She felt his body heat, the abrasion of his clothes against her skin. He was big, strong, and probably close to twice her weight, she realized with despair, even as she gasped for air and her nails tore uselessly into the smooth cloth of his jacket. Still, she struggled to be free, squirming frantically and kicking back at his kneecaps with desperate force. He jerked his legs back just in time and the blows slammed into his shins, which did nothing more, as far as she could tell, than hurt her feet.

"Help! Help! Let . . ." *me go* was how the scream was going to end, but the words were still forming in her mind when his arm tightened viciously around her throat, choking off the words, choking her. Coughing, wheezing, she fought for air even as it hit her that this time there was no one to help her: She was on her own.

And after last night, she had to assume that he meant to kill her if he could.

Her fight-or-flight response went crazy. Adrenaline shot through her veins. Flight wasn't happening right now, not with the hold he had on her. But . . .

"Hold still."

The gun that he pressed to her temple was silver, she saw out of the corner of her eye, just like the one last night. And the cold, terrifying feel of metal against her skin was definitely the same. Talk about déjà vu all over again. She felt dizzy, sick.

Her nails released their death grip on his sleeve and her arms dropped. Heart pumping like a trapped bird's, terror racing like icy fingers down her spine, she forced herself to go perfectly still.

"Yes. All right." Her voice was low, hoarse. She had to force the words out past his constriction of her throat. But he clearly understood, because his grip on her eased fractionally.

"Fancy meeting you here," he said. "I thought I was going to have to search all by my lonesome."

She sucked in air. "For what? What do you want?"

"Don't give me that."

The arm around her neck tightened again, suddenly, violently forcing her jaw up and slamming her head back against his collarbone hard. Her feet went out from under her a second time, and he grabbed her around the waist to keep her upright. She barely had time to register that at least his gun was no longer pressed to her temple when he ducked his head so that his mouth was near her ear. The cotton hood felt smooth against her cheek and ear. His breath was warm against her skin. Struggling to breathe with his arm heavy across her throat, scrabbling to get her feet solidly back under her once more, she found herself looking at the ceiling, the wall, the vivid colors of the sunset painting to her left. On her right, she could see a good-sized portion of the living room as well as a sliver of the den, which, like the rest of the place, had been cleaned up. That sliver encompassed the desk, part of the fireplace, and the area above it where a painting of a sandy beach usually took pride of place. The only wrong note was that the painting was missing. In its place, a raw-looking rectangular hole about half the size of the painting gaped in the plaster. It took her a second, but then she realized that she was almost certainly looking at the spot where the safe had been.

If, as she assumed, the thugs last night had dug it out of the wall and taken it with them, then what was this guy looking for?

Stay calm. Try to think.

"Where is it?" There was an angry edge to her captor's voice that made her go cold all over.

"Wha-what—" His constriction of her throat made her break off to gasp for air. Her blood seemed to spike in her ears. What made the whole nightmare even more terrifying was the realization that she had absolutely no idea in the world what he was talking about. Her ignorance was not, as he seemed to think, a ruse.

Panic made her suddenly light-headed. *What don't I know?*

"I'm going to ask you one more time." His grip on her throat loosened again, presumably so that she could speak.

Now, her internal voice screamed even as her desperate, reaching fingers finally made contact with what they had been seeking: the newly empty vase. Curling her fingers around the cool, wet rim, she swung it up and over her shoulder in a frenzied arc, slamming it as hard as she could into his head.

"Oww!" Howling, he let go, staggering back as the gun dropped from his hand to go skittering away across the floor and the vase slipped from her fingers, hit the ground, and shattered with a *boom*.

Yes. That was all the opportunity she needed. Fueled by abject fear, she ran for her life. Leaping over the profusion of roses and water and broken glass like a champion hurdler, she bolted down the hall for the kitchen, screaming her lungs out all the way. It wasn't the route she would have chosen, but she had no choice because he stood between her and the front door, and even in his slightly stunned state she recognized that she had no chance of getting by him.

"You fucking bitch!" Murder was in his roar. A single petrified glance over her shoulder told her that he was already coming after her, barreling down the hall in pursuit like a linebacker after an opposing player with the ball. There was no sign of the gun. Clearly he hadn't taken the time to go after it. He was too eager to get his hands on her again.

Oh, God, please don't let him catch me.

Terror gave wings to her feet. Shrieking like a peacock with its tail on fire, she rounded the corner into the kitchen and raced across the cool, hard floor so fast her feet barely touched the tiles. Brick wall, microwave, kitchen island; she saw it all in a single wild-eyed glance. Heart pumping, panting with fear, she looked frantically for a way out. Heading for the back door wasn't an option, either, she realized as her gaze touched on the laundry-room door. Last night's debacle with the dead bolt was hideously fresh in her mind. Was it still locked? Was the glass still missing from the top of the door? She could maybe jump through it again—unless it had been fixed. It might have been fixed. She would be trapped. . . .

"I'm gonna make you pay."

He was only a few strides behind her now, his feet thundering over the tiles, his arms pumping like pistons as he narrowed the distance between them.

Her screams echoed off the walls as she made the only choice she could: circle through the dining room and the living room and back out into the hall, then try to make it out the front door before he caught her. Maybe she could even scoop up his gun, turn it on him . . .

Yeah, right, me and Dirty Harry and who else?

Escape was the best she was going to do, if she could even manage that. Cold sweat poured from her body as she careened toward the dining-room door, then realized to her utter horror that his long strides had almost closed the gap. He was right behind her. He was going to catch her. . . .

It was just a matter of seconds, she knew. Her shoulders hunched in terrified expectation. He grabbed for her just as she reached the threshold, his big, sausage-like fingers hideously white, like the fingers of a corpse. She shrieked again as that nightmarish hand brushed her shoulder and then, as she lunged away, grabbed the tail of the huge shirt that flapped behind her like a sail.

"No!" she screamed, trying to pull free, but he had a good hold and the synthetic material was strong. He yanked and she fell backward, landing hard on her butt on the kitchen floor. He overshot her, nearly tripping over her as her fall seemed to take him by surprise. Screaming desperately, heart pounding like a jackhammer, she at last succeeded in yanking her shirt free of his hold. Turning onto all fours, she tried to scramble away, to come upright again, to run . . .

The hard tile felt cold and slick beneath her hands. Her nails dug into the grout, her feet sliding uselessly on the slippery surface.

"Where do you think you're going?" There was a gloating edge to his voice as he regained his balance first, rushing her, grabbing at her, knocking her to the floor when she would have eluded him. She hit hard, sprawling facedown, then, realizing her danger, immediately tried to roll away, kicking and screaming like a steam whistle. To her horror, he succeeded in catching her right ankle. His hand was warm and terrifyingly strong but, she saw with a chill of repulsion, was also unnaturally white and felt plastic, inhuman. It was a second or so before she realized that he was wearing thin white surgical gloves.

"Leave me alone! What do you want?" On her back, she fought off her attacker with every ounce of strength she possessed as he tried to get a better grip on her. She could see his eyes, glinting at her through the slits in the mask. They were dark eyes, almost black in the dim light, and hard with menace. Despair lent a hysterical edge to her voice. "What do you *want*?"

"Shut the fuck up." He gave her ankle a vicious twist. She cried out with pain as she was forced to turn on her side. . . .

"Open the door!" The muffled shout was accompanied by a frantic pounding on the back door. Dan—she recognized his voice. It was the most welcome sound she had ever heard. "Katharine! Open the door!"

"Help! Help me! Help!" she shrieked, taking advantage of her attacker's momentary distraction to jerk her ankle free.

"Come back here, bitch."

Cursing, he came after her as she scooted against the base of the built-in island, pushing the bar stools out of her way, flattening her back against the swirling wrought iron, grabbing on to the cold metal twists for dear life. Knocking the bar stools aside with a crash, he ducked beneath the marble overhang, grabbing at her while she kicked and screamed her lungs out. His intent, she thought, was to scoop her up bodily and carry her away before help could reach her. If he succeeded in taking her out of the town house with him, she was toast, she knew. Terror and hope combined to give her what felt like superhuman strength as she clung to the wrought-iron island with both hands and kicked him away one more time.

"Dan! Help! *Help!*"

There was a tremendous crash from the direction of the back door, then another. "Katharine! Damn it to *hell!*"

"*Fuck.*" Her attacker aimed a vicious kick at her, which fortunately, because she saw it coming, she was able to dodge. He then turned and ran out of the kitchen. Even as she rolled out from under the island and staggered to her feet, she could hear his footsteps pounding down the hall.

Was he going for the gun? The thought galvanized her. She had to *move. . . .*

"*Katharine!*"

There was another crash, accompanied this time by the sound of splintering wood and a sharp bang as if the back door had been kicked open and hit the wall hard. Dan had succeeded in breaking in, she realized as she lurched desperately toward the laundry room on legs that felt about as sturdy as rubber bands. The washer and dryer and the hook that ordinarily held the back-door key and the patch of tile—eerily clean—where Lisa had died flashed into view, then Dan was there in front of her, having run inside. Chest heaving, taking up far more space than she would have thought, given his lean build, he looked about as wild-eyed and frantic as she felt.

"Jesus Christ, are you all right?" Dan grabbed her by the upper arms, his grip warm and hard and urgent, momentarily halting her frantic flight.

"There's a man. He has a gun," she gasped, throwing a terrified glance over her shoulder while doing her best to pull him with her toward the door.

"Go outside." He pushed her past him and ran on into the kitchen.

"Dan, no!" Katharine cried, looking after him, but it was too late, he was gone, and she was not about to go after him. She had come so close to dying twice now that she realized just how much she wanted to live. She wasn't putting herself in harm's way a third time, not if she could help it, not even for Dan, though he was endangering himself on her behalf.

She turned and ran.

A plywood panel had temporarily replaced the glass window in the door, she saw as she darted past it. The door itself, now splintered around the lock, stood wide open. Golden sunlight beckoned, underlined by a wafting influx of heated air. Heart pounding a mile a minute, she ran out into the wonderful, welcoming, life-affirming sunshine, flying down the steps, racing toward her garage.

It was only after she threw open the access door and discovered that her Lexus was *not there* that she remembered that the car's absence didn't matter anyway: The keys were in the purse, which she had dropped in the hall.

Unless she was planning to walk, she wasn't going anywhere.

Dear God, what do I do now?

How had she and Lisa gotten home? Had they taken a taxi? No matter how hard she tried, she couldn't quite remember. . . .

The last of the adrenaline was draining away. She could feel herself crashing, feel the weakness in her muscles, the wobblies in her knees, the pounding in her head even as she stood there gaping at her empty garage. Drawing in big gulps of air, she whirled around to look fearfully back at the town house just as Dan appeared, framed by the back door. He looked reassuringly normal, and she was conscious of a little burst of gladness that he hadn't been hurt. His gaze found her immediately, and some of the tension that had tightened his shoulders and mouth seemed to leave his body. Without acknowledging her beyond that one assessing look, he closed the damaged door behind him and came down the steps. His movements were calm and controlled. Clearly he'd found nothing he felt he needed to run away from. The intruder must have fled.

She sagged with relief.

Which was not to say that her attacker couldn't circle around to where they were, she cautioned herself as she felt the last of her strength ebbing. Or that someone else—Ed's people came instantly to mind—wouldn't appear. A thought occurred to her then: A bullet could come from anywhere. The killer didn't even have to be close. A quick burst of alarm set her pulse to racing again, and she glanced anxiously all around.

Where is he? Where did he go?

From where she stood, she could see only a double row of brick build-

ings and a seemingly endless line of small backyards. They were only one
backyard (Dan's) away from the cross street, but a tall honeysuckle hedge
backed by a six-foot-high brick wall ran from the far side of Dan's house
to the garages and beyond, permanently providing privacy from the street.
No one was coming at them from that direction. Looking the other way,
perhaps six fences down, a golden retriever paced. A man in a lawn-care
service uniform mowed grass. Until she spotted him, the roar of his mower
had been all but drowned out by the thundering of her pulse in her ears.
Still farther along, there was another tall brick wall where the residential
section of the street turned commercial, which meant no one was coming
at them from that direction, either. The lineup of garages cut her and Dan
off from the alley, and the town houses blocked them from the view of anyone on Union Street. They were, in effect, standing inside a rectangle of
brick walls, but still someone could get to them, someone could cut through
the narrow swath of green grass between their town houses and the quartet of nearly identical town houses next door, someone could sneak through
the small backyards, hopping fences, hiding behind bushes and trees—or
someone could turn sniper and fire on them from a roof, or a window, or
just about anywhere.

Her breath caught at the thought: If someone wanted her dead badly
enough, they didn't even have to get up close and personal to do it.

The idea was terrifying.

Wait, she told herself firmly even as her poor, tuckered-out heart
started to thud again. If the guy she had just escaped from had wanted her
dead, he would have killed her at once. He'd had plenty of time. Instead,
he had tried to force her to tell him where something was. What something?
She didn't have a clue. But that wasn't the point. The point was that he, and
whoever he was working with, thought she knew what it was and, more important, where it was, and he/they almost certainly weren't going to kill
her until either she told them where it was or they were finally convinced
she didn't know.

Great. From them she could look forward to being tortured before she died. From everyone else—assuming there was an everyone else, that this wasn't just a single group of bad guys, which she didn't think she could afford to assume—a quick and bloody death remained a real possibility.

She should be running right now, running for her life, she knew, but the problem was she was just so *tired*. Luckily, if her calculations were correct, for the moment she was probably safe enough. That being the case, running was going to have to wait at least until she got her breath back.

Wheezing audibly as she leaned back against the doorjamb, which was smooth with paint and warm from the sun and comfortingly solid, she watched Dan come toward her, walking quickly through the dappled sunlight past the small maple, which was still tall enough and full enough to partially shade the concrete path and part of the yard. His stride was long and athletic. His eyes were narrowed against the sun. As he drew closer, she saw that his mouth was grim. Suddenly, she was struck by another of those niggling flashes of familiarity. She had seen him striding toward her like this before. . . .

While she might not remember when, or how, or even remember him, exactly, some part of her somewhere deep inside indisputably did. The knowledge was both comforting and disturbing. She *knew* him, no doubt about it, but the details were missing.

Just like the details of her life were missing.

Am I having a bad day or what? The thought popped into her head out of the blue, surprising her. Then, when its truly ridiculous degree of understatement occurred to her, it almost—*almost*—made her smile despite everything.

"He got away," she said as Dan reached her. Her tone made it a statement rather than a question. She saw that he was carrying the purse and duffel bag she had dropped in the hall, and thought about straightening away from the door to take her things from him. But the truth was, she just didn't have the energy; she was too spent to move. It was all she could do to keep herself from collapsing in a little heap where she stood. "Thanks for bringing my things. I was just getting ready to leave with them when he surprised me."

He nodded. "There was just one guy? Was he one of the guys from last night?"

"I don't think so. In fact, I'm pretty sure not. His voice was different. His eyes were different. But he wore the same kind of black knit ski mask they did, and he had a big silver gun, like they did. He held it to my head." She shivered at the memory. "Pressed the mouth of it right against my temple."

His lips thinned. "So how'd you get away?"

"I smashed a vase over his head."

"The roses?" For an instant his expression lightened. "I wondered about those." He frowned again. "So was it another robbery attempt, do you think? What did he want? What did he say?"

She shook her head. "I don't know what he wanted. But he thought I did. He kept asking me where 'it' was."

He was frowning in earnest now. "What?"

"Like I said, I don't know."

The ramifications apparently occurred to him then, because he took a careful look around. "Okay, we probably need to head on into my house and call the police now."

"No." Her voice was sharp, her reaction instinctive. "No police."

Reasons why not came to her in jumbled spurts only after she spoke: Bringing the police in would delay her escape; they might call Ed, whose house it was, and he might ask them to hold her, which they would certainly do because of who he was; or while she was talking to the police, Starkey and Bennett might show up; or the police, or at least certain members of the police force, might even be involved in what was happening. The point was, she didn't know what was going on, didn't know who she could trust, and she wasn't prepared to risk her life to find out.

Besides, given that she was almost sure her attackers, both last night and just now, were covert-ops types, there was little the police could do. Ed and his ilk were way out of their league.

Dan was frowning at her. She realized she must have sounded pretty fierce. Her tone moderated slightly. "No police. Please."

His frown deepened. Her chin came up. She wasn't backing down an inch, and it must have shown in her face. Dan's mouth compressed. She could tell he wasn't happy about it, but he didn't press the issue.

Good man. Fast learner. She approved.

"You're bleeding." His gaze shifted. He was looking down at her feet.

She looked down, too, to discover blood on her right foot. It oozed out between her little toe and the one beside it, the bright scarlet blood garish next to the soft shell pink of the pricey pedicure she didn't remember getting. There were smears of blood on the concrete around her, and more smears on the walk, she saw.

"Oh." She lifted her foot to examine it, propping it against her knee. Sure enough, there was a cut near her toes. It was small, maybe half an inch long, barely bleeding now. At a guess, she would say she had cut it on a piece of the broken vase. The blood felt warm against her chilled skin, but there was no pain, which was probably why she hadn't noticed it. "It's nothing. No big deal."

"Are you hurt anywhere else?" His voice was perfectly even. But something about it made her glance at him in surprise. His jaw was tight, and there was a glint to his eyes that told her that this nice, gentle doctor was angry. On her behalf.

Which, actually, was kind of sweet.

"No. I mean, I may have a few more bruises, but nothing serious."

Letting her foot drop back to the ground, she took a deep breath and straightened away from the doorjamb. Her head swam, and that plus the pounding headache that had never really gone away made her unsteady on her feet. Dan, and the backyard behind him, seemed to tilt, and she took a staggering sideways step to recover her balance.

He caught her arm.

"You're just fine and dandy, huh?" The sarcasm in his voice was unmistakable. Her vision might not be totally clear, but it was impossible to miss the thinning of his lips. His hand felt warm and strong just above her elbow. If he hadn't been there, she probably would have just toppled over.

She took a deep, steadying breath and the world slowly righted itself on its axis.

"Basically," she said. He was watching her closely, and it didn't take a genius to figure out that maybe she wasn't looking so good. She pulled her arm free of his hold.

"I really am okay," she insisted, and stood perfectly still without swaying to prove it.

He didn't reply, but then he didn't have to: Skepticism was plain in his face.

The lawn mower shut off just then, and the sudden sound of not-so-distant traffic that replaced its steady roar served as a reminder that Starkey and Bennett—or anyone else—could show up at any moment. Hurting or not, exhausted or not, dizzy or not, she couldn't stand around just shooting the breeze. She had to get a move on. Her life might depend on it. The knowledge brought with it another microburst of energy.

Her eyes sought his. She wet her lips.

"Look, I hate to involve you in this any more than you already are, but my car's not here. Could you possibly give me a ride to the airport?" Her eyes narrowed on his face. "The airport, mind. Nowhere else."

She added that last as visions of being carted off to the hospital willy-nilly danced in her brain.

That was the plan she had come up with since discovering her car wasn't in the garage: Go to the airport, buy a plane ticket to somewhere, anywhere, just to throw them off, then hop on the Metro and disappear until she had time to recover her balance a little and think things through.

For someone whose brain was missing in action, she thought it was a pretty good plan.

Dan's eyes slid over her. He looked less than happy, and for a moment she thought he might be going to argue, probably in favor of the hospital. Or the police.

Then he shrugged. "Why not?"

Moving toward the access door to his garage, which was approximately ten feet farther along the brick wall, he glanced back over his shoulder at her.

"If you want to walk through your garage, I'll pick you up in front of it. That way you won't have to climb the fence." He had reached the fence, which was only about three feet high, as he spoke, and was already throwing a long leg over it.

"Oh. Good idea." A little belatedly she added, "Dan, thanks."

He merely nodded once in reply.

Moments later she was once again ensconced in the warm, cushiony passenger seat of his car as the Blazer, with Dan at the wheel, rolled away from the quartet of garages. With the brick wall blocking the end of the alley behind them, a succession of squat brick buildings on the right, and a tall wooden privacy fence running continuously on the left, it was like being in a tunnel, safe and protected. Katharine was busy sticking a Band-Aid, from the first-aid kit in the glove compartment to which Dan had directed her, over the cut in her foot. The purse was in the footwell at her feet. The duffel bag was in the backseat.

And all four doors were securely locked.

Just in case.

"So," Dan said as the vehicle bumped over the alley's uneven pavement and sunlight beat down through the windshield and the air conditioner blew rapidly cooling air into the vehicle's passenger compartment in a so-far vain attempt to counteract the ovenlike heat, "you want to clue me in on what's really going on here?"

Katharine looked at him. The temptation to confide in him, to pile her problems on his shoulders and see if he could help her figure them out, was strong. She *felt* she could trust him.

But . . .

Before she could explore that "but" further, the phone in her purse came to life, its cheery *Hello, moto* musical ringtone once again making her jump.

"You might want to get that," Dan prodded, as she stared down at the black purse like it was alive without making the slightest move toward it.

Hello, moto.

She glanced at him in surprise. "Oh. Right."

Of course, it was her purse, and her phone. She kept forgetting that. The call, therefore, was obviously for her. Pulling the purse up from the footwell, she fished inside for the phone, feeling a tense kind of anticipation.

It could be anyone. A friend, maybe, or . . .

"Hello, moto," it singsonged as she picked it up. It was one of those new black Razr phones, expensive as all hell, like everything else she apparently owned. It felt as unfamiliar in her hand as it sounded.

Staring down at it, trying to ignore the big, blue rock on her finger that was, at the moment, gleaming brightly in the sun, she watched a parade of numbers running merrily across the small display window.

A closer look revealed that a name appeared along with the number: Ed.

Her stomach clenched.

Hello, moto.

Ed was calling her. Her breathing quickened. Her heart started to pound. She felt like a rabbit with the hounds closing in.

Hello, moto.

She sat frozen, staring down at the cheerily chattering phone as her breathing suspended and the tiny hairs on the back of her neck stood on end.

Ed was calling. Oh, God, what should she do?

I take it you don't feel like talking?" Dan's voice was dry. Katharine realized that she was gawking down at the phone like it was a live grenade getting ready to explode in her hand. With her peripheral vision she saw that they had reached the part of the alley where parking lots and Dumpsters took the place of the row of garages. With no more brick walls to protect her, she felt suddenly, hideously vulnerable.

As if they—Ed's people, her previous attackers, whoever the hell "they" were—could see her now.

Sucking in air, she threw Dan a hunted look. "It's Ed."

She said it as if it explained everything.

The phone stopped ringing. She stared down at it, unconvinced, waiting. Her heart still pounded. Her pulse still raced. Her stomach twisted tighter—but the phone stayed silent.

"Ed Barnes? That's who you don't want to talk to? I thought he was your boyfriend."

Her head swiveled toward him. Her gaze focused on his face. She frowned, suddenly suspicious.

"How do you know who my boyfriend is?"

He arched an eyebrow at her. "Hey, I read the paper. There was a photo in it of the two of you a week or so back. It identified him by name, and said you were the 'mysterty woman' in his life. You're pretty photogenic, by the way. Him, not so much."

Katharine relaxed a little, her spine curving thankfully back into the seat. That damned picture again. Had everybody in the city seen it? Still, as an explanation, it made sense.

Dan glanced at her, his expression curious. "You talked to him in the hospital earlier, right? So why don't you want to talk to him now?"

She was too tired to try to think up a lie, and she hadn't yet decided whether or not she should tell him the truth. Her frown returned. This time, she directed the full force of it at him.

"You know, I appreciate the ride and all, but maybe you ought to mind your own business."

"Fair enough." His brow knit, and he held up a conciliatory hand. "Only trying to help."

A beat passed in which she felt bad for being rude to such a nice man, who had, moreover, saved her life at least once, probably twice. A man who was helping her to escape even as she was obnoxious to him.

Okay, so she was an ingrate. Lower than a snake's belly. A worm.

He glanced her way again, his expression tentative now. "I was just thinking that if you were my girlfriend, I'd be plenty worried. Seeing as how you disappeared out of the hospital like you did. Maybe you ought to think about calling him back and letting him know that you're alive, so he won't be siccing the National Guard on us or something."

Katharine's eyes widened. She hadn't thought of that. Much as she hated to admit it, Dan had a point. Ed had nearly infinite resources if he chose to employ them. Putting herself beyond his reach would be much easier if he didn't know that that was what she was trying to do.

"Good point," she said, and he nodded, then glanced at her expectantly.

Her hand tightened around the phone. As she looked down at it, steeling herself to do what she had to do, a tiny warning bell rang in her mind. For a moment she stared blankly at the phone's matte black surface as she tried to clarify just what, exactly, her subconscious was getting all hot and bothered about. The answer came slowly, but at least, thank God, it came.

"Can't they, like, trace cell phone calls or something?"

Dan threw her a quick look. "Only to the place from which the call was placed. For instance, if you called him back now and they traced it, all they'd find out is that you're close to home. Which, considering that you just got attacked there, someone already knows anyway."

Good point again. The problem she was having, though, was that she didn't trust herself to make a good decision. Real exhaustion was starting to set in. No matter how many times she blinked, or how determinedly she shook her head to clear it, it was hard to think clearly. She had a killer headache, her body hurt all over, and she was so tired that it was all she could do to stay upright in the seat. Add in the whole brain-damage thing, and she realized that mentally, she was flying blind.

"What would I say?" Her mouth was dry. "I don't want him to know that I'm running away from him."

It was more than she'd meant to tell him, but she needed a friend. And right now, in the people-she-could-trust stakes, Dan seemed to be the only game in town.

"Give me a minute," he said. "I'm thinking."

At least, Katharine registered, he didn't seem to be shocked. He appeared, rather, to actually be thinking the matter over as he drove. Reaching the end of the alley, the Blazer came to a stop at Wilkes Street. A delivery truck rattled past, inches away from the front bumper, followed by a seemingly endless procession of cars. More vehicles clogged the opposite side of the street. Pedestrians, including another tour group with a guide dressed as, if she had to guess, Martha Washington, crowded the sidewalks. The shops were open, the tours were under way, and the tourists, on this hot, sunny Saturday, were out in force. Being surrounded by so much activity should have been reassuring. Instead, Katharine felt terribly exposed.

Danger could be anywhere.

Dan made no attempt to pull out into traffic. Instead, he looked over at her. His expression was hard to read.

"You're going to tell him what just happened, right?"

Katharine thought about that. The thing was, she wasn't convinced that he didn't already know. "Yes. I guess. Only . . ." Her voice trailed off.

Dan looked at her keenly. "Only you think he might have had something to do with it. Which is why you're running away from him." It was a statement, not a question.

She hesitated only a moment before nodding.

"Wow," he said.

Her eyes narrowed. "That's not helping." Just to be sure he understood where she was coming from, she spelled it out: "I don't want him to know I suspect him. Otherwise, he'll guess I'm running away."

"Yeah." He grimaced thoughtfully. "You realize that the natural thing for you to do would be to tell him you were just attacked. It's what you would do if you *didn't* suspect him."

She blinked. That was so obvious she couldn't believe it hadn't occurred to her.

"You're good," she said.

"Okay, you could tell him, then say something like you're not up to talking to anybody right now. That you're scared, and torn up over your friend's death, and you just need to be alone for a while. That you're probably going to spend the night in a hotel."

Katharine's eyes widened slightly as she considered that. If Ed thought she was going to a hotel, he would start checking hotels. There were hundreds of hotels in the area. Even for him, with his resources, checking them all would take hours.

Hours she could use to find a place to hide.

"That's actually a really good idea." But still her fingers curled tightly around the phone. The idea of calling Ed terrified her, she realized.

"If you're going to call him, you want to do it now," Dan said. "While we're still close to home."

Katharine glanced at him and nodded. Right. So if Ed did trace the call, which he certainly could and probably would do, he'd have no more information than that she was at the corner of the alley behind her garage and Wilkes at the time she made it.

The Blazer was still idling. A big silver Suburban rolled out of the busy parking lot to her right and pulled in behind them. Time to move.

It was now or never.

Dan accelerated, turning right onto Wilkes, heading toward Union. Sunlight glared off the green-painted metal roof of the art gallery/ice cream shop/candymaker that they were heading toward, making Katharine squint. Beyond the two-story complex, the Potomac looked smooth as glass.

"How about we circle the block once?" Dan suggested.

Katharine nodded again. Gritting her teeth, she opened the phone, then realized that she had no idea what Ed's number was. For a moment, as she stared down at the tiny keypad, she was stymied. Then it hit her: Look at the call history. She did, punched a button, and the phone automatically dialed Ed's number.

As she waited for it to connect, her heart began to thud.

"Katharine?" Ed answered on the first ring. Good thing, too, because she was losing her nerve fast.

"Hi." Every muscle in her body had tensed. She was suddenly freezing, cold to the bone, so cold that she could feel goose bumps prickling to life all over her skin. She had to take a deep breath before she could continue. "I, uh . . ."

"Where are you?" he interrupted fiercely.

She ignored the question. "Somebody just attacked me. I went home, and he was in the house, and he grabbed me. He was looking for something, and he thought I knew where it was."

"*What?* What was he looking for?"

She ignored that, too. *Stick with the script.*

"I can't take this, you know? I'm scared to death. And I'm sorry, but I can't face talking to you or the police or anybody else right now. I just need to be alone for a little while. I—" As she spoke, her voice grew increasingly shaky. Ed cut her off without a qualm.

"Are you losing your tiny little mind?" He roared the question so loudly that she almost dropped the phone. Out of the corner of her eye, she saw Dan grimace in unspoken sympathy.

Wimp, she chastised herself silently. But still, her mouth was dry, and her heart raced, and the hand holding the phone shook, and there didn't seem to be anything she could do about any of it. Wimp indeed.

"You need to tell me where you are." Ed had his voice under control again, but from its strain, it was obvious that he was having to work to keep it that way. "Right now."

"I'm going to a hotel for the night," she continued doggedly. "I'll call you tomorrow."

"Damn it, Katharine, you . . ." He was getting louder again.

Before he could reach full throttle, she disconnected, closing the phone with a snap. Taking a deep breath, she sat there staring down at it. She was gripping it so hard that her fingers were white. Her pretty pink nails looked incongruously frivolous against the businesslike black.

I don't have pretty pink nails.

The thought was despairing.

"You did good," Dan said. Glancing over at him, she encountered a reassuring smile. She didn't smile back—a smile seemed beyond her capabilities just at present—but it helped to know that *he* could. It made her feel a little less like an escapee from the Twilight Zone.

The Blazer had stopped at yet another stop sign. Dan's attention returned to the road as he accelerated again. Katharine realized that they had completed their circuit of the block and were now heading away from the river, away from Old Town. A sign promised that Interstate 395 lay straight ahead.

Hello, moto.

Katharine gasped, nearly dropping the phone as it went off again in her hand. This time she didn't even need to see the name or number to know who it was: Ed.

A glance confirmed it.

Hello, moto.

Pulse racing, she stared down at the eerily unfamiliar phone as it jangled in her eerily unfamiliar hand. It was terrifying to realize that the call was coming from her eerily unfamiliar boyfriend, who might or might not be trying to have her killed for some unknown reason that had something to do with her eerily unfamiliar life.

Though he probably didn't know it, Ed's question had been right on the money: It was entirely possible that she was losing her—okay, she objected to the *tiny little* part—mind.

Hello, moto.

It was a good thing, she thought, that Dan was distracted by negotiating the corkscrew-like turn onto the expressway. Otherwise, there would be a witness to her quiet little meltdown in the passenger seat.

"Give it here." As soon as they were on the straightaway, Dan held out his hand for the phone. There was a quiet authority in his voice that had her obeying before she even thought about it.

Hello, mo—

The thrice-damned thing went abruptly silent as he pressed a button on the side.

"I turned it off," he said in response to her shell-shocked look. The merest hint of a grim smile quirked his mouth as he handed it back to her. "I would have thrown it out the window, but I figured you might want it again later."

"Yes. Thanks." The words came out on a gust of air as she released a breath she hadn't known she'd been holding.

So much for Ed. But turning off the phone didn't eliminate him—or his power, or his henchmen—from her life.

Oh, God, she was cold. So incredibly cold. If she wasn't careful, her teeth would start chattering.

"Put it in your purse," he said, and she did. Then she closed the vents, shutting off the flow of icy air that was exactly what she didn't need. Folding her arms tightly over her chest for warmth, she dropped her head back against the seat, closed her eyes, and tried to regain her composure. Dan drove in silence for a while, and she was grateful for that. The sound of traffic rushing by outside the window and the vibrations of the vehicle itself were surprisingly soothing. Gradually, her pulse rate slowed and her breathing steadied and her tense muscles relaxed. In fact, if she hadn't been so acutely aware of the direness of her situation, she might have succumbed to creeping exhaustion and dozed off. But she couldn't. They would be at the airport soon. Then she would be on her own. If she was going to pull this off, she was going to have to stay alert. She needed to be smart and strong and able to think fast on her feet—none of which seemed remotely possible just at present.

"We're almost there," Dan said. "I take it you did mean National?"

Katharine felt her stomach start to tighten again as she opened her eyes. Directly ahead, on one of the green signs that overhung the expressway, she read *Ronald Reagan Washington National Airport 1½ miles.*

"Yes." Her pulse was speeding up, too. Her head pounded. Her ribs hurt. Her knees felt weak. She had a bad taste in her mouth. The good news was, she was no longer chilled to the bone, although that was probably just because Dan had turned down the air-conditioning.

"So where you off to?" Dan asked.

She slanted him a look. No way was she telling him or anybody else her plan—just in case.

"Right. Mind my own business," he translated in a resigned tone.

"Sorry," she said.

He glanced at her. "You know, in my professional opinion, you might want to rethink flying off into the wild blue yonder for a day or two. Besides your physical injuries, which, granted, aren't all that severe, you've experienced some real psychological trauma. It's obvious you're not thinking straight. It's equally obvious that something bad's going down in your life. I would suggest that you take some time to regroup." His attention returned to the road. "Not that I'm poking my nose in or anything."

Katharine looked at him without replying for a moment. She watched the play of light and shadow over his face, and was once again struck by how familiar he seemed to her. He was only a neighbor, and to the best of her knowledge, she'd had only the most casual of relationships with him before today, but the truth was, her relationship with him didn't feel casual. It felt important, and solid, as if he were someone on whom she knew she could rely. Add in that hint of tension between them that she'd felt when he'd been looming over her bed when she'd first opened her eyes, and she suddenly wondered if, sometime in the past, he'd been more than just a neighbor. Asking him about the details of their acquaintance was an option, but if she did that, she would have to admit she didn't remember much. She wasn't sure that, until she had a better sense of what was going on, revealing her ignorance was a good idea. If someone was clever, it could, she realized, be used to manipulate her. Anyway, she was running out of time. They were rushing up on the exit, and once he let her out at the airport, he would be gone.

I'll be all alone.

The idea suddenly appalled her. Without him, she would be left to fight through this terrifying maze she was lost in on her own. She was so bone-tired, so confused, so frightened—she realized she couldn't face it.

Not just yet, anyway.

"Look, could we get some coffee?" she asked as the Blazer curved off the interstate toward the airport.

If he was surprised, he didn't show it. "Sure."

There was not, of course, a single Starbucks to be found in the blocks leading up to the airport. Dan pulled into a McDonald's drive-thru lane, ordered coffee, juice, and breakfast sandwiches for both of them, settled the drinks into the cup holders between them, then nosed into a parking space so they could eat. As soon as she got her hands on the coffee, Katharine pulled off the lid, stirred in a packet of Sweet 'N Low, and took an eager sip.

Coffee, minus its enticing aroma, lost something, she decided. Like its flavor. Still, she drank.

"Better?" he asked.

She nodded and watched as he attacked his Egg McMuffin with gusto.

"You don't suppose somebody could have followed us?" The thought occurred just as she was unwrapping her sausage biscuit with hands that she was dismayed to discover still shook a little, and she stopped what she was doing to glance nervously all around. The influx of even flavorless caffeine plus the prospect of food seemed to have perked up at least a few of her discombobulated brain cells, and all at once she wasn't so tired that she couldn't appreciate the danger she was in. The concrete jungle surrounding them boasted a furniture store, a Jiffy Lube, a Big Lots, a run-down strip mall, and a couple of low-rent apartment buildings. Lots of vehicles buzzing in, out, and all around. Lots of people in the vehicles. Pedestrians everywhere. She could feel herself tensing up again.

Bad guys could be anywhere.

Dan shook his head. "I don't think so. I kept a pretty good eye out, I think."

She blinked at him as he took another hearty bite out of his Egg McMuffin.

He chewed, swallowed, and grinned at her. "Hey, I watch TV. Besides, I figure since you're on the run, and I'm with you, that means I'm on the run, too."

She felt a flicker of remorse. "I'm really sorry I got you involved in this."

Shrugging, he polished off his sandwich with one last enormous bite. "I didn't have to give you a ride. If it comes to that, I didn't have to go to the hospital last night. Or pick you up in the parking lot this morning. So I'm at least as responsible as you." He washed the sandwich down with a swig of orange juice, then cocked an eyebrow at her. "You going to eat or not?"

The unconcern in his voice made her frown. She cast another nervous glance around. The parking lot was busy, with a lot of vehicles circling the drive-thru and pulling in and out of the parking spaces, and a lot of people entering and leaving the restaurant. Traffic on the street in front of them was steady and constant.

If someone was going to attack them here, there would be lots of witnesses.

"Whoever these people are, they mean business," she warned. "Last night they murdered my friend. If you're with me and they catch up with us, I'm pretty sure they won't hesitate to kill you, too."

"You let me worry about me, okay?" he said. "Eat."

There didn't seem to be much else to say, and since she was pretty sure that dozens of witnesses were the last thing that any bad guys worth their salt wanted, she gave up and took a bite of her sandwich.

After all, there would be plenty of time after he dropped her off at the airport when the bad guys could catch her all alone.

The thought almost gave her indigestion. Swallowing, she wrapped what was left of the biscuit back up again and stuffed it down in the sack. No matter how much she needed protein for energy, she had eaten all she could.

"Is that all you're going to eat?" he asked. His disapproval was plain in his tone.

"Yes." The narrow-eyed look she shot him dared him to comment further. He didn't. She took another swallow of the tasteless coffee, hoping for an invigorating shot of energy that didn't come. "Could we go, please?"

The idea of being on her own didn't appeal to her any more now than it had earlier, she discovered. But neither did the idea of sitting in a McDonald's parking lot, where anyone could spot them. Besides, what was the alternative? The answer was simple: There wasn't one. She was being hunted. She might not know much, but she knew that as well as she knew the sun rose in the east. She had to run while the chance was there.

If they caught her . . .

Her heart started to accelerate at the thought.

"Sure thing."

She could feel the tension building in her neck and shoulders as he reversed out of the parking space, then drove toward the exit with only a single stop to deposit the remains of their meal in the trash. Her headache was back, a dull throbbing behind her eyes, and she was so tired she felt boneless. Though she'd been hungry, the sausage biscuit now felt like a rock lodged in her stomach. The coffee had left a bitter taste in her mouth.

"Can I make a suggestion?" Dan pulled out into traffic as he spoke.

Looking carefully around, she saw nothing that appeared out of the ordinary. Still, she felt her stomach twist a little tighter around the rock. They would reach the airport access road in just a matter of minutes. She breathed deeply, trying to summon up every last iota of strength, determination, and clear thinking that remained to her.

Her eyes swung toward him. "What?"

"Forget flying anywhere today. I have a cabin a couple of hours out of D.C. A fishing cabin. We could go there. You could take a shower, change your clothes, get some sleep. Maybe we could even try to figure this thing out. Then, if you still want to get out of Dodge, I could take you to the airport first thing tomorrow."

She stared at him. The prospect of a shower and sleep and some time to think was tempting. The thought of not being left on her own until she'd had the shower and sleep and some time to think was nothing short of dazzling.

Wait. Be careful.

"You're putting yourself in terrible danger for me," she said slowly, trying to put all the puzzle pieces together before she made a decision. Her eyes never left his face. "Why?"

He glanced her way, met her gaze.

"I'm a nice guy?" he offered with a flicker of a smile.

Her lips compressed. The twinkling blue eyes, the wry curve of his lips—she knew them. She *knew* them.

What she didn't remember was in what context, exactly.

"How do I know I can trust you?" Her tone was wary.

This time, when he met her gaze, he wasn't smiling at all.

"You don't, I guess," he said. "But you can."

Maybe she wasn't *entirely* convinced. But she was persuaded. Her gut trusted him. And Dan was all she had.

"So, airport or not?" His eyes were on the road again. Traffic was heavy, stop-and-go, with lots of people entering and exiting the highway. Up ahead, a sign announced the turnoff to National. "Your call."

Tomorrow, after she'd showered and slept and thought, she would be in a much better place, much stronger physically and, hopefully, mentally, too. If she carried through with her plan now, there was the possibility that she would make a mistake from sheer exhaustion. It was even possible—and she felt a thrill of horror at the idea—that Ed might have seen through her lie about the hotel. He—or someone else, the someone who was behind one or both attacks, if it wasn't Ed—might be one jump ahead of her and already have people watching the airport. Airports. Metro stations. Amtrak stations. Bus stations. All public transportation facilities. With her car missing—and maybe Ed or whoever had had something to do with that, too—public transportation was her only way out of town, and he would know that.

Galloping paranoia? Maybe. But maybe not.

In that case, though, the best way out of the city was by private car. Which she was in.

"Not," she said. "The cabin sounds good. Thanks."

"Not a problem."

He didn't smile, but he did seem to relax slightly. Some of the tension left his shoulders. His grip on the wheel eased. His expression seemed lighter somehow. Katharine, too, felt a lessening of stress now that the decision was made. Taking a deep breath, she allowed her head to drop back against the seat—the warm leather supporting her tense neck felt amazing—closed her eyes, and tried to relax, too.

Unfortunately, her mind refused to get with the program. It raced hither and yon, trying to make sense out of everything that had happened, then, when that proved impossible, trying to make sense out of something, anything.

But she couldn't.

The thought formed out of nowhere, solidified, then twisted through her mind like a particularly nasty little worm: Was good-neighbor Dan just a little too good to be true?

Her eyes popped open, and without lifting her head, she turned her gaze toward him. They were back on the expressway now, heading west on I-66, and traffic was humming along, heavy as usual. A semi went flying past, and she could feel the vibration of it shaking the SUV. Through the windows she could see blue sky bisected by the vapor trail of an airliner. Arlington National Cemetery went by on the left, and she realized that she recognized the grassy acres of trees and monuments instantly, even at speed and from a distance, even before the sign identifying it flashed into view. Funny that she should know things like where Arlington was, and that it was possible to hop on the Metro at Reagan National Airport and disappear, and even that this degree of traffic was normal for Saturday on this expressway, and yet know practically nothing else.

Not about herself. Not about him.

He'd said she could trust him. Of course, once upon a time Ted Bundy had probably told women the same thing.

But nevertheless—sort of, kind of—she did.

She thought.

Maybe.

"Okay, I'll bite." He glanced over at her, met her gaze—until that moment, she hadn't known that she'd been staring at him, apparently like a frog at a fly—and frowned. "Want to tell me why you're looking at me like I've suddenly grown two heads?"

Y ou're not wearing your glasses."

The fact had just occurred to her. They were, she saw at a glance, folded into his shirt pocket. Without them, his slightly professorial air was lost. He looked less abstracted, and more like a man who could handle a little physical action.

Which, under the circumstances, was probably a good thing, even if it was slightly disconcerting.

"Oh." Looking self-conscious, he patted his shirt pocket. "They're here. I took them off when I was trying to slam my way into your house. Don't worry, I don't need them to drive. They're mostly for close work." He threw her a quick look, then pulled the glasses from his pocket and dropped them down into the pocket of the driver's-side door. "Is that why you were staring at me?"

"Actually," she said in dulcet tones, "I didn't realize I was. It must have been because I was just remembering the first time we met."

His brows went up. As he glanced her way again, she saw that he was now expressionless.

"Were you, now?"

She waited. His attention returned to the road. He didn't say anything else. She frowned.

"I was trying to think how long ago that was," she prompted. She thought her casual tone was nicely done.

He shrugged.

Great. Now he turned into a man of few words.

"How long ago was it?" she probed a little more pointedly.

"A while."

"So tell me about it." If there was a slight edge to her voice now, she couldn't help it. She was tired and scared and hurting, and being subtle required a lot of effort. Plus, it didn't appear to be working particularly well.

He glanced her way again. This time he looked wary. "What? The first time we met? Why?"

Because I need to know, dammit.

"It's like telephone, you know, the game where one person whispers something to another person, and then it goes on down the line, and by the end the story's usually totally different?" Good one. She almost believed herself. "I want to see how well our memories match."

"You're kidding, right?"

"No, I'm not kidding." Okay, now she was sounding downright grim. *Lighten up, girlfriend.*

"To tell you the truth, I have no idea."

She tried not to sound as outraged as she felt. "You don't remember?"

He looked a little guilty. "Hey, it's been hectic all over lately. What, did I say or do something that's etched into your consciousness for all time? If so, I apologize."

"Never mind," she said sulkily, and subsided into silence again.

So much for plumbing the depths of his mind for clues about her past.

Clearly it was going to be more complicated than she felt able to deal with just yet.

"You know," he said after a minute or two, "I've been thinking: Are you sure the man who jumped you today couldn't have been just a garden-variety burglar? Maybe he heard what happened last night on, say, a police scanner or something, and thought your house would be empty in the aftermath and decided to seize an opportunity."

"I'm sure." Her tone was sour.

He glanced at her. "How? How can you be sure?"

"I just am." She sighed. "He was wearing a suit, for one thing. An expensive suit, black or navy blue—it was kind of gloomy in there, and everything happened so fast, it's hard to be sure of the exact color, but dark—with a white shirt and a dark tie. Not your typical burglar gear."

He shrugged. "I don't know. Maybe dressing like that makes it easier to break into a house in a nice neighborhood without anyone suspecting what you're up to. You've got to have another reason for thinking he was something besides a burglar. A nice suit by itself doesn't cut it. So, what else you got?"

"He had a big silver gun just like those guys last night. He knew who I was. He was looking for something specific. Believe me, he was *not* a burglar." Okay, she sounded testy. So sue her.

"All right, he wasn't a burglar." Dan now seemed ready to accept her judgment on that. "Do you remember anything about him that would help you to identify him? Any identifying marks or scars, for example?"

She shook her head. "None that I saw."

"You get a look at his eyes? What did they look like?"

"They were dark. Really dark. Almost black. And kind of small."

"Race?"

"I think he was white. Dark-complected but white. Or maybe Hispanic. Not black."

"Hair?"

She shook her head. "I didn't see it. It was hidden by the ski mask."

"Size? How tall was he?"

"Six feet, probably. And muscular. He was in good shape. Like the kind of guy who might work for Ed."

"You think he was CIA, huh? That's reassuring." Dan's voice was dry. "Good to know we've got the Feds on our tail."

Hearing him say "we" and "our" didn't really make her feel any safer, but it was vaguely comforting to see that as far as he was concerned, they were in whatever they were in together. At least, if they got caught, she wouldn't have to die alone.

Then something else occurred to her.

"Wait a minute. How do you know Ed's with the CIA?"

He looked at her. "The *Post* photo, remember? The caption said he was, like, Director of Operations or something."

"Oh."

A beat passed.

"You see anything else?" Dan asked. "What about his hands?"

A vision of thick, dead, white fingers flashed into her mind. She barely kept herself from shuddering.

"He was wearing gloves. Surgical gloves. Look, what does it matter? It's over. He's gone. And as far as I know, there's no Facebook for spooks."

He shot her a glance. "Spooks?"

She huffed out an impatient breath. "That's what they call the covert-operations guys."

"You think this guy was one of them?" He paused, seeming to have a little trouble getting his tongue around what was coming next. "A spook?"

Jeez, her head was hurting again. "Like I said, does it matter?"

"Maybe. There's a lot of traffic around us. No telling who's in any of these vehicles. I just thought it would help if I could kind of eliminate people like that guy in the minivan there, say, from suspicion."

Katharine raised her head high enough to see a tan Dodge Caravan rattling along in the lane beside them. The driver, bald and pudgy, was looking in his rearview mirror as he yelled at the quartet of kids strapped into the back.

"Him you can safely eliminate." She let her head drop back down against the seat.

"He was just an example. You see what I'm getting at here."

Reluctantly, she did. She had a feeling her heart would have picked up the pace again if she hadn't been so totally wiped out.

"You think we're being followed?"

He shook his head. "I *don't* think so. But I've been wrong before."

"Wonderful."

"So, you see anything else on this guy that struck you as memorable? What about his feet? What kind of shoes?"

She had a momentary flashback to a kick slicing through the air.

"Black," she said. "Dress shoes."

In her mind's eye, she was back beneath the kitchen island, fighting for her life as the foot flew past her face with scant inches to spare. It seemed so real suddenly that she could almost feel the breeze. At the time, noticing his footwear hadn't been her primary focus. Plus, she'd gotten only a glimpse, but . . .

She frowned. "There was something on the sole—a logo. It was round and—" Her eyes suddenly went wide. "Oh, my God. The floor. The floor's wrong."

"What?" Dan looked at her with incomprehension.

She barely noticed. Mentally, she was still there, clinging to the wrought iron, her right side battened down against unyielding terra-cotta tiles.

"The tiles are wrong. They're . . ." Her voice trailed off for a moment as rising panic threatened to choke her. "They're too small."

"*What?*"

Katharine didn't even register that he had spoken. She was frantically replaying everything that had happened in the kitchen earlier today in her mind, and comparing it with what had happened there the previous night.

Last night she had been nose to nose with a floor sadly in need of a mop. Beneath the grime, the terra-cotta tiles had been smooth, cold, and hard as brick. In her mind's eye, she could see them perfectly: stone-colored grout lines marking out straight rows of twelve-inch squares.

Today she had fallen on that same floor. She had scrambled across it on all fours. Her hand had been palm down across one of the tiles, her nails scratching against the stone-colored grout as the heel of her hand was abraded at the same time by the roughness of yet another line of grout. In other words, her hand had actually been longer than the tile. *Because the tile itself couldn't have been more than six inches square.*

Today, the entire kitchen floor had been a sea of smooth, cold, hard-as-brick *six-inch* terra-cotta squares.

Her mouth dropped open in horror.

"What?" he said, watching her. "What?"

"The floor's wrong." Her voice was faint. The interior of the SUV seemed to be closing in around her like a big, black fist. She felt as if she were trapped, suffocating. Suddenly, it was hard to breathe. "The tiles have changed. How could the tiles have changed?"

"*What?* You're not making any sense."

"Something's wrong." She felt like she should be screaming the words, but instead her voice was barely audible. Her vision went all blurry; her heart began to thud. Her head throbbed like it would explode. "Oh, God, something's really, really, wrong."

A wave of dizziness swamped her.

For the tiles to have changed was impossible.

"Just so you know, you're starting to scare me here. You've gone white as a sheet. I need to know what you're talking about if you don't want to get rushed to the nearest emergency room, pronto."

Katharine got the impression that the Blazer was speeding up. Either he was putting the pedal to the metal, or the world outside the SUV had suddenly turned into a kaleidoscopic blur of color and sound. The hospital—he was threatening her with the hospital again. Still, she couldn't get those six-inch terra-cotta tiles out of her mind. They were wrong, wrong, wrong . . .

She sucked in air.

Get a grip. Chill.

"I don't need a hospital." She took another deep breath. "It's just . . . oh my God, Dan, I think I'm losing my mind."

"Well, that's reassuring," he said dryly after a moment passed in which, busy trying to convince herself that she'd somehow gotten it wrong about the tiles, she didn't say anything else. Katharine became vaguely aware of an abundance of green whizzing past the windows, and realized that the Blazer was banking around a steep turn that could only, from the amount of foliage surrounding them, be an exit.

"No hospital." Her voice was stronger. She tried to focus exclusively on the here and now. As far as the floor was concerned, her mind had to be playing tricks on her. She realized that. No way could the floor really have changed. But each image was so real. The twelve-inch tiles. The six-inch tiles. In the same kitchen, only hours apart. She almost moaned, but bit the sound back when she realized that it would probably send Dan over the edge.

They were on a straightaway again. Katharine realized that they had left the interstate behind for an only slightly less busy four-lane highway. Clustered around the intersection where they found themselves was a collection of fast-food places, cheap motels, and gas stations.

"What are you doing?" she asked as he pulled into a Stop-N-Go Mart that looked like a shoebox made of equal parts concrete blocks and glass. An ancient blue Ford pickup and a newer white Infiniti were at the pumps out front. A beefy farmer type complete with overalls did the honors for the pickup. A blond, stylish, fiftyish woman was filling the Infiniti. Both looked harmless. More cars were parked in front of the store. Their passengers were, presumably, inside.

"We're going to stop here for a few minutes and watch who comes off the expressway after us. And in the meantime, you're going to talk to me and tell me what the hell is bothering you so much about a floor."

The Blazer pulled on around the store and stopped near the restrooms, which were located on the side of the building well away from the gas pumps. At the far edge of the pavement, back behind a trio of lurking Dumpsters, two empty picnic tables had been set up in the grassy strip between the parking lot and the Taco Bell next door. A raggedy-looking elm provided them with patchy shade.

Dan turned off the engine and got out, slamming the door behind him. Then he came around to Katharine's door and opened it. The all pervasive sound of traffic immediately filled her ears.

"Come on," he said. "Get out."

Complying, she discovered, wasn't all that easy. With the best will in the world, she didn't seem to be able to make her muscles work. When she simply looked up at him without doing anything else, he made an impatient sound under his breath, then leaned in and unfastened her seat belt for her. His upper arm brushed her breasts, and she was suddenly very aware of the contact, and of how firm his biceps were. Her brow knit; that tiny jolt of awareness was impossible to mistake for anything else—and the most disconcerting thing about it was that it felt so hauntingly familiar. He was close, so close she could see the texture of his bronzed skin and each individual hair in the stubble darkening his jaw, and a tiny, comma-shaped scar near the corner of his left eye. He must have felt the weight of her gaze, because he glanced at her and their eyes met. The reassuringly mild blue of his eyes was no longer quite so mild, she discovered, nor quite so reassuring. Instead, his eyes had taken on a glint that made them look harder and more purposeful.

"Come on." Straightening, he held out his hand to her. If he was feeling anything approximating the jumble of conflicting emotions that had just hit her, he gave no sign of it. "I want to get where I can see the road. If we sit at the picnic tables, we can watch everything that's going on around here without being noticed. Unless someone knows precisely where to look, they won't spot us."

She took a deep breath. The worst of the shock seemed to be receding—as long as she didn't think about those damned tiles. Even letting the smallest memory of her kitchen floor into her mind threatened to send her world tilting on its axis.

Because no matter how she spun it for herself, there was no reconciling the difference in the size of those tiles.

Stop. Don't go there. You'll make yourself crazy.

The thing was, though, she was very much afraid it was too late: She already was.

"How do you know that?" Katharine put her hand in his simply because his was there in front of her and resisting required more effort than doing what he wanted. His hand closed around hers, warm and strong, and she allowed him to pull her from the car. Only when she was on her feet and the steamy heat was wrapping itself around her like a hug did she notice how cold she was. Goose bumps covered her arms. She had to grit her teeth to keep herself from shivering. Her legs felt unsteady. Taking a step sideways, she leaned against the side of the Blazer for support. The blacktop was hot beneath her bare feet, and getting hotter by the second. Shifting uncomfortably from foot to foot, she was suddenly thankful for the too-long hem of Dottie's pants. If she hadn't discovered the insulating properties of little puddles of rayon just when she did, she would have been doing her own personal version of an Indian war dance right there beside the car.

"I've stopped here before. It's on the way to the cabin."

He dropped her hand as he closed the door behind her, then pressed the button on his key ring to lock the vehicle. She knew that was what he did, because she heard the beep, but she really wasn't paying much attention because she was trying so hard not to compare mental images of the tiles.

There has to be an explanation. . . .

"Katharine."

Startled out of her near panic by the forcefulness of his tone, she looked at him in surprise. He was standing right in front of her, arms folded over his chest, giving her the kind of look that made her think he had probably said her name more than once. Meeting his gaze required that she look up, and as she did so, she registered just how tall he truly was: The top of her head barely reached his chin. His eyes were narrowed against the sunlight, she saw, and his mouth looked surprisingly grim.

Again, she was struck by that disconcerting sense of déjà vu. Had she stood with him like this before?

Where? When?

"Hmm?" she murmured distractedly, her eyes searching his face. Every feature was familiar, but she could recall no details at all about any interactions they might have had prior to this morning. She knew him—and yet she didn't.

Weird. Weird. Weird.

Her heart started to thud.

"Can you make it?" His tone was impatient.

He meant could she walk to the picnic tables. Katharine blinked a couple of times in an effort to clear her mind, then nodded, again because any alternative was bound to be more trouble than simply agreeing with what he wanted her to do. As she straightened away from the Blazer, she was suddenly aware of how bad she really felt. She was dizzy, weak-kneed, and tired to the bone. Her head hurt and her stomach churned and she was freezing despite the blazing heat that was multiplied tenfold by the intensifying effect of the blacktop. But the worst thing of all was knowing that she had lost it.

Absolutely, totally, without a doubt lost it. Because what other explanation could there be?

She was a skinny blonde named Katharine Lawrence. And those tiles had to be the same.

"Careful," he warned when she started hotfooting it (literally) toward the grass and almost tripped over her borrowed pants in an effort to keep her feet off the sizzling pavement.

She didn't bother to reply. Awkwardly joggling from foot to foot took concentration, especially when stopping was not an option unless she wanted fried feet.

"Jesus Christ," he added in a resigned undertone, coming up behind her. He swung her off her feet and into his arms before she had any idea of what he meant to do. "Don't you have any shoes?"

"Hey," she protested as she grabbed on to his shoulders for support. They were wide beneath the limp blue shirt, sturdy and well-muscled, and the arms cradling her were sturdy and well-muscled, too. "There are some in the duffel bag."

"Here's a radical thought: Maybe you should try putting them on your feet."

"Next time I have a few spare minutes when nobody is trying to kill me, maybe I will." Her tone was tart.

That made him smile. His eyes crinkled and his mouth quirked at the corners, and he flicked a glance at her.

"Point taken."

With her arms wrapped around his neck, she had an up-close-and-personal view of his profile. It wasn't classic, precisely, but it was handsome and manly, and the crooked smile struck a chord deep in her memory bank: She'd seen him smile like that before, she was almost sure, but again, no details surfaced to back up the feeling. The sun beat down on them, gleaming off the unruly dark gold waves of his hair, deepening the tired lines around his eyes and mouth. He was looking tense, and with a little wake-up call of surprise, she saw that he must be almost as scared and jumpy as she was. Driving a getaway car for a woman running for her life was almost certainly not something he did every day. Getting pulled into the thick of a murderous (possible) government conspiracy likewise must be new to him. She hadn't thought of it like that before, but now that she did, she saw that he was really being a mensch about everything. More than a mensch, in fact: a hero. *Her* hero.

Which, paranoid, ungrateful creature that she was, immediately struck her as suspicious.

"So-o," she said on a long, drawn-out note, her arms around his neck tightening a little as he passed the Dumpsters, stepped over the concrete berm, and started walking across the grass to the picnic tables with her, "why are you being so nice to me?"

He flicked her another one of those sideways glances.

"I'm a nice guy, remember?"

The glimmer in his eyes was a twinkle, she discovered. It grew more pronounced as she frowned at him.

"Right," she said, clearly unconvinced.

He laughed.

The odd thing about it was, his teasing didn't completely eliminate her suspicion, but it did make her relax a little. The old adage about looking gift horses in the mouth popped into her mind, and she decided it was an old adage because it was true. Anyway, the bottom line was that she felt safe with him. She did not feel at home, exactly, in his arms, but she didn't feel like she was being manhandled by a stranger, either.

"You can put me down. We're on grass," she pointed out.

"Too late now: I've already thrown out my back."

That crack she considered unworthy of a reply. He carried her easily, like she weighed nothing at all, and she had a moment there when she found herself almost admiring his strength until she realized she probably didn't, now that she was a skinny blonde with big jewelry and perfect nails and *brain damage.* That last thought was so upsetting that she barely even registered anything else until he set her down with something less than grace on the picnic table's bench. The molded plastic was surprisingly comfortable, she discovered. The heat was still palpable, thick and enervating as the inside of a steam room, but a delicate, lacy patchwork of shade from the elm spread over the area like a shadowy doily, sheltering it from the direct rays of the sun, making the temperature oh, say, ninety in the shade.

To her poor, frozen self, the sauna-like heat felt good.

"Okay, so why don't you start by explaining to me why you think you're losing your mind over floor tiles," he said, settling in beside her, his long legs just brushing hers and his forearms resting comfortably on the tabletop. He spared her only the briefest of glances as he spoke. Instead, his eyes fixed on the overpass with its ramps that curved down past a background of leafy forest to the road they'd just left. There was traffic, she saw, as she followed his gaze, lots of traffic coming off the near ramp and going up the far ramp and pulling in and out of the surrounding businesses and zipping along the highway in front of them. But none of the various vehicles caught her eye, none of them appeared to be searching for anyone, and besides, unless someone was right on their tail, she was pretty sure there was no way anyone was going to be able to find them in such a busy place. They were the proverbial needle in the haystack. Realizing that made her feel a tiny bit better. Or at least safer.

His words brought the competing images of her kitchen floor from last night and today forcibly to mind. There was no mistake: No matter how she tried to reconcile the two, they were indisputably different. The question became, then, how much should she tell him? Should she keep the changing tile sizes to herself? Only total surprise had made her blurt out her discovery like that in the first place. But the thing was, she couldn't figure out what was happening. If she kept trying, her brain would burst.

The tiles made no sense.

With her elbows resting on the table, she dropped her face into her hands and closed her eyes.

"You're going to think I'm insane."

"That's presuming I don't already." The dryness of his tone brought her head back up again. She narrowed her eyes at him, and he made an impatient sound. "Come on, spit it out."

Her stomach tightened. Her toes curled into the soft carpet of grass. Her hands clenched convulsively.

"Last night," she said carefully, "Lisa and I were tied up on my kitchen floor. I was on my stomach, with my face as close to that floor as it could possibly get. *I saw that floor perfectly.* And it was made up of tiles that were twelve-inch squares." She paused, wetting her lips. "Today, when that man was chasing me, I fell on the kitchen floor. My hand landed on one of those tiles. Not only did I see it, but I felt the size of it. That tile—all the tiles—were six-inch squares. Same kitchen, same kind of terra-cotta tile. But the size of the tiles changed."

His attention had shifted from the traffic. His eyes bored into hers like twin lasers.

"That's not possible," he said.

That's what I keep telling myself. But believe me, it's the truth."

"You must be mistaken."

"I'm not mistaken."

"Hallucinating, then. Or . . ."

As his voice broke off, she gave him a warning look.

"Or nuts?" she finished for him, too sweetly.

"Yeah. Something like that."

"Thanks," she said with no small degree of bite. "You're being a big help here."

"What kind of medication did they have you on in the hospital?"

That was a good question. "Actually, I wondered that, too."

"You don't know?"

"How would I know? I was unconscious, remember? I was the patient. You're the doctor. Don't *you* know?"

Their eyes met and clashed. He frowned.

"I wasn't there in the capacity of your doctor. I didn't prescribe the medication, I didn't administer it, and I don't know what it was. I could check, but that doesn't help us right now."

Again with the "us." Okay, for that she was willing to forgive him a certain amount of insensitivity.

"Could they have given me something that maybe causes hallucinations?"

"Maybe." He paused, seeming to think the matter over. "But it's pretty far-fetched to imagine that it would cause you to hallucinate about the size of the tiles on your kitchen floor. I mean, what a thing to hallucinate about."

Just remembering what else she was possibly hallucinating about made her head hurt. It was too much—she couldn't keep it to herself any longer. With her mind on overload, she needed help.

There weren't even any options to consider. Dan was it.

"That's not all." God, her head was pounding. She pressed her cold fingers to her temples in an effort to calm the relentless beat. "The thing is, I don't seem to"—here she hesitated, searching for the right word— *"know* myself."

He stared at her for a moment.

"Just for the record, I'm not a damned shrink. And is there some particular reason why you feel the need to *know* yourself right now?"

It was difficult, she discovered, to sustain soul-destroying angst in the face of total obtuseness. Her hands dropped to rest on the table, her spine stiffened, and she glared at him.

"I'm not talking about lacking an inner understanding of my psyche. I'm talking about not recognizing myself." There was a definite caustic edge to her voice. "Physically, I mean. The person I see when I look in the mirror is not me. At least, it's not who I think I am."

"What?" He looked at her like she had suddenly grown two heads.

"I'm not blond, okay? I'm not skinny like this. I don't have perfect teeth, or a perfect manicure, or own big sapphire rings or diamond earrings." She touched the sapphire ring as she mentioned it, then as she glanced down at it and saw its big, bright, obnoxious sparkle, started anxiously turning the too-loose bauble round and round on her finger. "Look, it doesn't even fit. It's too big."

He glanced at the ring, then back up at her.

"Katharine—"

"That's just it." Her voice shook. She stopped twisting the ring and clasped her hands together instead. "I don't think I'm Katharine. I don't feel like Katharine. I feel like I've been dropped down into some stranger's life."

By this time her pulse was racing and her breathing had quickened. She had his total attention now. There was an arrested expression in his eyes, and his gaze was fixed on her face.

A beat passed in which they simply stared at each other.

"You took a pretty hard blow to the head," he said finally.

"I know," she said. "I'm hoping it's that, or the medication they gave me. The other thing is"—she sucked in much-needed air—"I seem to be missing a lot of memories. I mean, for example, I recognized you when I woke up in the hospital this morning, but I can't seem to remember things like how we met."

"Ah." Comprehension suddenly dawned in his eyes, and she knew he was recalling her earlier fishing expedition into that very topic.

"Ed, too. I mean, I know about Ed, who he is, that he's my boss and that we're . . . involved, and I can picture him and all that, but when he called me, I didn't recognize his voice. And the only thing I feel when I think of him is distrust. No, fear."

His brows knit, and he looked as if he would say something, but she forestalled him by rushing on.

"Somebody's looking for something, and they think I know what it is and where it is, and I don't. Somebody tried to kill me, and I don't have a clue who, or why." She swallowed. "I don't seem to feel anything. Emotions, I mean. Like Lisa. She was one of my closest friends. She got k-killed in front of me." She closed her eyes. "I know that, but I can't seem to feel it. I don't feel the grief I know I should be feeling for her. And—and that gorgeous, expensive town house. It isn't me. I didn't decorate it. It's not my taste. Those aren't my things. *I don't live there.* And now the tiles. I know it seems stupid, but this thing with the tiles is just the last straw."

"I can see where it might be," he agreed, and she felt his gaze on her face. Then he added, "Try not to worry about it too much. Whatever it is, we'll sort it out."

That "we'll" was the most comforting thing he could have said. Her eyes opened, and she rewarded him with a small, unsteady smile. His gaze slid down to her mouth, then rose to meet her eyes again. His expression was suddenly impossible to read.

"All I can think of is that this has to be some kind of weird amnesia," she said. "But . . ."

Her voice trailed off despairingly, and to her dismay she could feel her eyes starting to well up. She tightened her lips as she felt them begin to tremble. The thing was, she never cried. Or at least, the old her didn't. But this was the new her, and it had been a really bad, horrible, no-good day.

Watching, his eyes hardened. His lips tightened. His expression went from unreadable to—what? Unsympathetic?

"Yeah, well, don't let it throw you," he said. His attitude had changed in an instant. He was distancing himself from her. She could feel it. His voice was almost brusque. Maneuvering his legs out from beneath the picnic table, he stood up and looked down at her with a frown. "Come on, time to go. If there was anyone following us, we would have spotted them by now."

She had been so wrapped up in pouring her troubles out to him that she had completely forgotten that they were watching for a possible tail. Her eyes widened and her gaze shifted, sweeping the parking lot, the highway, the adjoining businesses, the ramps. Vehicles of every description were swarming all over the place like busy little bees. If it had been up to her to keep track of who was whom and what was what, she would have failed miserably. Fortunately, it hadn't been up to her.

"Oh. Right."

His change of tone was so abrupt that it was disconcerting. It also—

although she didn't like admitting it, even to herself—hurt her feelings a little. Clearly, the guy wasn't up to dealing with weeping women. Which actually worked for her, now that she thought about it, because she had no intention of crying, anyway. The only thing crying ever did for anybody was make their nose all stuffy, and she was way ahead of the game there: She already couldn't breathe through her nose. She'd had herself under control again as soon as she had felt the threatening tears.

But she still didn't appreciate his attitude.

Sliding her legs out from beneath the picnic table, she stood up. Her head swam and her knees threatened mutiny, but she wasn't about to let any further weakness show. Chin up, shoulders squared, she started walking determinedly toward the car.

He followed without a word.

When her bare sole hit the blistering blacktop, she marched on without so much as an outward wince.

Step, *sizzle,* step, *sizzle,* step . . .

"Oh, for God's sake," he said, and came up behind her and scooped her up into his arms without another word.

Even as she grabbed on to his shoulders, she glared at him.

"Nobody asked you to pick me up."

"Yeah, well, try wearing shoes and I won't have to."

"Just for the record, I wasn't going to cry back there."

"Never thought you were."

"Oh, right. You got all distant and broke off the conversation because you thought I *wasn't* going to cry." Her arms curled around his neck simply because there was nothing else for them to hold on to. His chest felt all warm and solid against her, and his neck provided a strong anchor for her arms, and if she hadn't been so ticked off at him she would have almost enjoyed the ride. But she was ticked off: *He* was the one who had encouraged her to unburden herself, after all. Then her innate sense of fairness, unwanted and inconvenient, kicked in. "Look, I realize you don't have to be doing any of this, and I'm grateful. If you want, we can turn around here and you can take me back to the airport. I'll be just—"

He shot her an exasperated glance and interrupted before she could finish. "Drop it, angel eyes, would you please? You know damned well I'm not going to leave you on your own."

As that registered, she went perfectly still in his arms. She could feel him tensing, feel his arms hardening around her, feel the expansion of his chest as he drew in a long, deep, not-as-discreet-as-he-probably-had-hoped breath.

Their eyes met.

"*What* did you just call me?" she asked.

It wasn't much—barely more than the flicker of his eyelashes. But it told her that he hadn't meant to say it, that his words had caught him by surprise as much as they had her, and that in the few seconds since he had spoken, he had been anticipating her response with trepidation. Except for that telltale flicker, though, his expression was impossible to read. His eyes revealed nothing at all. His mouth was unsmiling, maybe a little hard. Otherwise, his face was blank.

"I don't know. What?"

Why wasn't she surprised that he was opting to play dumb?

"Angel eyes?" she repeated in a testing way. There was something about it—something that seemed to reach deep into her subconscious. *Angel eyes* . . .

"Oh, that. Look, it just came out. Don't go making it into a big deal."

"Have you ever called me that before?"

He glanced away.

"Maybe. I don't know. You think I pay attention to things like that?" He heaved a sigh, then met her gaze again. The mild blue eyes looked mildly rueful. The hardness had left his mouth. His arms around her even felt less constricting. "All right, I confess. You got me. It's just something I call women sometimes, okay? Nothing personal at all."

Her gaze was both skeptical and searching, and he looked away again. She was just starting to think that perhaps that whole looking-away thing was totally significant when the arms holding her shifted without warning. As she felt her body dip, she instinctively tightened her grip on him. An

instant before she heard the *beep* that was him unlocking the door, she realized that they had reached the Blazer.

Okay, maybe he had been looking toward the SUV.

"If you need to use the restroom . . ." Breaking off delicately, he glanced
toward the ladies' room. At the same time, he managed to get the door open
without setting her on her feet, which required a significant juggling act
on his part.

"I don't." Even while she was hanging on to his neck for dear life, she
was still studying his face.

He nodded acknowledgment without meeting her eyes. Then he
dumped her into her seat, like, she thought, a sack of very hot potatoes,
closed the door on her—she could almost feel his relief—and walked
around behind the Blazer and out of her sight.

She was left with the impression that he wanted to put the whole subject of what he had just called her behind them.

Angel eyes . . .

The memory remained tantalizingly elusive, but she was sure—well, almost sure—it was there. But the harder she tried to capture it, to assign the
words their proper time and place and context, the more it seemed to slip
away. It was frustrating. No, worse, it was maddening. Vaguely, she heard
the rear driver's-side door open, but beyond glancing over her shoulder to
make sure it was Dan and not some murderous bad guy who had opened
it, she paid scant attention. Her head dropped back to rest against the seat
as she desperately racked her brain, searching, searching, searching for the
key that would unlock all the hidden details of her past . . .

Without result.

But her instinct, that same gut feeling that had sent her racing out of the
hospital in advance of Bennett and Starkey, that had warned her to play nice
with Ed, that had kept her one step ahead of whatever was going on so far,
was niggling at her again.

Angel eyes had struck a chord. She was almost—and *almost* was the operative word, because she couldn't be one hundred percent positive—sure
that someone, somewhere, had called her that before. If that was true, then

logic dictated that the odds-on favorite had to be Dan. Unlike darling, or sweetheart, or baby, for example, *angel eyes* was not a generic endearment.

As a matter of fact, it would seem uniquely fitted to someone whose best feature was clear green eyes.

Hmm.

So far, she'd taken Good Neighbor Dan on trust coupled with a vague memory of him as her next-door neighbor, and a certain feeling in her gut. Maybe that wasn't very smart.

The driver's door opened, and Dan slid in beside her. She was just shifting her newly suspicious gaze his way when the pair of sandals she had taken from the town house landed on her lap.

Momentarily sidetracked, she glanced down at them in surprise.

"You might want to put them on." His tone was dry. "I need to run in here for supplies. And I don't think leaving you alone in the car is a good idea. Unless you disagree, that means you're coming in with me."

She glanced at him, glanced down at the sandals, and then, as he drove around toward the front of the store, slipped them on one at a time in a silent act of agreement. Under the circumstances, with visions of silent assassins dancing in her brain, she wasn't a big fan of staying in the car alone, either. As she had noted before, the sandals fit. Of course, they were basically thongs with heels. Tricked-out, expensive-looking thongs with dangling turquoise beads and supple leather straps, but nothing that was too exacting as to size.

They were pretty shoes, feminine shoes, frivolous shoes—but she had no sense that they were her shoes.

If the shoe fits, does that make me Cinderella?

That was the semihysterical question that flitted through her mind as she stepped inside the store with Dan right behind her. Walking into so much air-conditioning was like walking into a solid wall of cold, and by the time he grabbed bread and milk and chips and whatever else it was he was grabbing off the shelves, she was freezing again. Her arms were crossed tightly over her chest and her teeth were locked together to prevent them from chattering as she kept a wary eye on their fellow Stop-N-

Go shoppers. A heavyset guy in a green T-shirt and unfortunate plaid shorts, a harried mother with two children begging loudly for candy, a couple of teen boys picking soft drinks out of the cold case—if these folks were Feds, Alphabet Soup World was in bad trouble. In fact, the only person in the store who looked in the least like he could possibly fit the covert-ops bill was—Dan.

The thought occurred as, having paid cash for the Extra Strength Tylenol that was her sole contribution to their booty, she moved away from the counter to wait for him. Standing several feet behind him as he was paying for the groceries, she watched him pull his wallet out of his back pocket and fish several bills out of it, which he then handed to the orange-aproned clerk, who was a plump, thirtyish woman with a bad blond perm. The movement made his shoulders flex, and as the cash register flew open with a jingle of coins, Katharine was suddenly struck by how broad his shoulders really were. Her gaze swept him, and her eyes widened.

For all his leanness, the guy was built. The reason she hadn't picked up on it before was probably because up until now she'd basically had frontal views of him, which meant that she had focused primarily on his face. Now, seeing him from the back, she realized that his limp cotton shirt did little to camouflage a torso that was a classic vee. The shirt was tucked into loose black dress pants that rode low on his hips, courtesy of an ancient-looking black belt. His hips were narrow, his butt small and tight and hard-looking, his legs long and muscular. And—and this was the kicker—just like the putative covert-ops guys in her town house, he was wearing black dress shoes.

In other words, Dr. McDreamy was total spook material.

Except for the hair. Covert-ops guys went in for buzz cuts, not dark gold waves that curled around their shirt collars.

Katharine frowned.

"You all come back now, hon," the clerk said, handing over some change.

"I will," Dan promised genially, tucking the bills into his wallet and shoving the wallet into his back pocket again. Gathering up the groceries and casting a quick look around to make sure she was still with him, he headed for the door.

Katharine followed, but not so closely that she didn't see the clerk giving him an appreciative once-over as he pushed through the door.

As he opened her door for her, then put the groceries into the back of the Blazer, she collapsed back into her seat without a word. Closing the door, fastening her seat belt, she stared unseeingly out the windshield, blind to the big silver ice machine not a yard in front of her nose, blind to the brightly colored banners advertising milk at $1.19 a gallon and Little Debbie snack cakes at four for a dollar that were plastered to the big plate-glass windows, blind to the comings and goings of customers passing in front of the SUV.

One question consumed her to the exclusion of all else: Was she being dumber than a rock here?

He was built like a spook, he'd been Johnny-on-the-spot ever since she'd opened her eyes on this hellish day, and he'd called her "angel eyes."

She knew this guy, yes, but what, exactly, did she know?

The sound of the motor turning over coupled with a rush of tepid air shooting out of the vents refocused her attention in a hurry. Dan was already sitting next to her; he had started the Blazer. A growing panic made her heart begin to race. If she had any doubts about who and what he was, now was the time to act on them. While they were here, in this well-traveled area, she had options. Not great options, but options. She could call a taxi. Or hitch a ride. Or, well, if one of those two didn't pan out, she could probably think of something else. But once the Blazer was on the road again, she realized, her choices dried up. Dan would once again be the only game in town. And by his own admission, he was taking her to a cabin—a cabin that was probably out in the back of beyond . . .

Could anybody say "jumping out of the violent spook killer pan into the sneaky cov-ops kidnapper fire"?

"Wait. Stop," she ordered. "Hold it right there."

With one hand already on the gearshift, he looked questioningly at her.

"I want to see some ID," she told him firmly.

H is eyes widened. *"What?"*

    "You heard me. I want to see some ID."

Once again, he was looking at her like she had grown a second head.

"You want to see some ID?" His tone was incredulous. "You mean, like, my driver's license? That's ridiculous. You *know* me."

She shook her head. "I already explained it to you. I don't even know myself right now, much less you. At least, not for sure. It's like I'm trapped in one of those house-of-mirrors things they have at amusement parks. Everything's so confused in my head that I can't be sure what's real and what isn't. So my new motto just became trust . . . but verify. And by verify I mean I want to see some ID."

"You're joking."

"Nope."

A beat passed in which they exchanged measuring looks. Her chin was up, her shoulders were squared, and her hand was curled in her lap and ready to make a grab for the door handle. If he started to drive away, all bets were off: She was leaping for the pavement.

"Fine." He took his hand off the gearshift, and she huffed out a silent little breath of relief. Unbuckling his seat belt, he reached into his back pocket and produced his worn-looking brown leather wallet, which he passed to her. "Knock yourself out."

Ordinarily, she was probably squeamish about going through other people's private possessions. *Probably* was the operative word there, because, of course, she couldn't quite remember. But this was not ordinarily. This was potentially life or death. *Her* life or death. She opened that wallet without a qualm and found herself staring at a clear plastic window with a driver's license in it. Pulling the license out, she held it up and closely examined the small picture.

She didn't even have to glance at the genuine article sitting beside her to know that it was the same man.

Her attention shifted to the identifying information: Daniel Webster— *Webster?*—Howard; DOB 11/16/67 (which, she calculated quickly, made him thirty-eight years old); height, 6'1'; weight, 185 lbs.; address, 1215 Union Street, Alexandria, VA.

Okay, so that checked out. With a quick glance at him, she looked at the names on the credit cards: Daniel Howard, Daniel W. Howard, Dan Howard. There was even an insurance card with his name on it, and another from the state medical association, complete with the age-old physician symbol.

"Satisfied?" he asked sardonically as she restored everything to its proper place and handed his wallet back to him.

"Yes. Sorry."

She had the grace to feel a little ashamed of herself. Apparently, he really was Good Neighbor Dan, that *angel eyes* slip notwithstanding. Maybe she was just imagining it felt familiar. Maybe she was just imagining this whole thing. Maybe it was all a dream, and when she woke up she would marvel at how real it had all seemed. Maybe . . . maybe . . .

To hell with maybe. She was suddenly too tired to think about it—any of it—anymore.

"So are we on for the cabin or not?" Having restored the wallet to his back pocket, he refastened his seat belt as he spoke.

"Yes." Even her voice sounded exhausted now. Under the circumstances, there was really no other decision she could make. The cabin was the best available choice. "By the way, thanks for offering. And for everything else."

"You're welcome." If there was an acerbic note to that, it was only a very slight acerbic note. He might not be totally thrilled to have his identity and motives questioned, but it seemed that he understood.

"You really are a nice guy, aren't you?"

"So I've been telling you."

"Yeah, well, maybe that takes some getting used to."

"In that case, maybe you ought to start thinking about running with a different crowd."

Good point again. "Maybe."

The Blazer was in motion now, and a moment later they swung out of the parking lot, joining the stream of traffic heading west. A mile or so down the road they left the fast-food places and motels and gas stations behind, and the traffic thinned out. A few miles farther down the road, and they and a big green farm tractor trundling along in their lane were the only vehicles left in sight.

Dan whizzed past the tractor.

"Did you get any water? Or anything I could take a couple of Tylenol with?" she asked once they were safely back in their lane again.

"No water. Orange juice. Milk. Soda. How bad's your head?"

"I'll live."

Turning to reach into the backseat, she snagged an orange Fanta from one of the plastic bags. Then she retrieved the Tylenol from her purse, where she had tucked it away, and swallowed two capsules. The fizzy orange soda was sweet and tangy and cold, and she realized as she drank it that this particular brand was a favorite of hers.

Then the ramifications hit, and she almost choked on the mouthful she was swallowing.

How had he known that? *Had* he known it? Or was it just one more mind-bending coincidence?

"What now?" he asked, on a long-suffering note. It was only as he glanced her way and their gazes met that she realized she was staring at him.

"I like orange soda," she said.

His attention returned to the road. "Good. So do I."

Her eyes remained fixed unwaveringly on his face. "*You* like orange soda?"

"Didn't I already say that?" His lips thinned impatiently. He flicked another glance at her. "Is there some sort of significance to this that I'm missing out on here?"

She wavered. After all, millions of people probably liked orange soda. That he should buy some wasn't exactly remarkable. Was it?

Jeez, was she getting totally paranoid or what? Either she trusted the guy or she didn't. She couldn't keep bouncing back and forth between the two like a ball in a tennis match.

Her gut said trust him. Her brain said—who the hell knew what her brain said? It was hard to tell with scrambled brains. So she was going with her gut by default.

"No," she said, realizing that she was way too exhausted to even begin to make sense of the labyrinthian possibilities that not trusting him presented. "I was just wondering, is all."

He grunted by way of a reply, and that was the end of that.

Ten minutes later, Katharine realized with relief that the throbbing headache that had plagued her all day was largely gone. With her head resting back against the seat and her lids drooping with weariness, she watched tall, green fields of corn and shorter green fields of soybeans and the occasional herd of cows or sheep stream past the window. The great thing about a nearly empty two-lane highway was that it was pretty easy to be sure they weren't being followed. Soon she lightened up on the whole looking-over-her-shoulder thing, and even Dan glanced in the rearview mirror less and less frequently. For a while they traveled alongside the C&O canal, and she caught a glimpse of one of the long, mule-drawn canal boats, complete with costumed driver and loaded with tourists, as it maneuvered through a lock. Then the canal branched north, curving through a vast expanse of forest, and she lost sight of it.

"You know, I've been thinking about it," Dan said as they passed through the tiny town of, according to the sign, Witt, which was really nothing more than a cluster of houses grouped around a four-way inter-section, "and I think what you're experiencing here may be some form of post-traumatic stress disorder."

"What?" She frowned at him. "I thought that was just for, like, combat veterans."

He shook his head. "Any kind of traumatic event can bring it on. What you experienced last night certainly qualifies. Impaired memory is one of the symptoms, and so is emotional detachment. Lack of trust is in there somewhere, too, I'm pretty sure. I'd have to look it up to be certain, but I think you fit the criteria pretty well."

Katharine thought about that for a moment. This feeling she had that she wasn't herself, that she didn't look like this, that her possessions weren't hers, was just—perception, she realized. It was possible—no, even likely, because what was the alternative?—that the problem lay with her mind. Likewise, the recurring lack of trust she was experiencing toward people like Ed and even Dan himself might well be the result of some kind of disordered thinking. She had nothing concrete with which to back up any of that. Everything was based on her perceptions, every reaction on her instincts.

Except for one thing.

"So how does that explain the tile?" she asked. Her head was starting to hurt again, as images of the different-sized tiles took possession of her mind. "I felt that floor. I couldn't have imagined that." Then, her confidence shaken, she added in a near whisper, "Could I?"

"I don't know." Dan shot her a glance. "I'm not an expert on this. But at least for right now, post-traumatic stress disorder is the best explanation we have."

He was right, and she knew it. There were loose ends—like the tile—but the general theory fit the facts. Anyway, she wanted so much to believe in a simple, logical explanation for why she saw a stranger every time she looked in a mirror. Post-traumatic stress disorder was an answer she could deal with.

"How do you cure it?"

"Talk therapy generally helps, I believe. And medication."

"Great." Her tone was borderline despairing. But, she told herself, it was still better than the best alternative she had been able to come up with—that somehow she had been caught up in some otherworldly mix-up and was trapped in another woman's life.

There was no medication for that.

"Sometimes it even gets better on its own," Dan added, on a more cheerful note. "Who knows, you may wake up tomorrow and be perfectly fine."

"From your lips to God's ears." Katharine gave him a small, wry smile. Then she took a deep breath and allowed her head to drop back against the seat again. Despite the Tylenol, her headache was back in spades.

The farther they went, the more rural the scenery became. Clapboard farmhouses and ranch-style brick houses and the occasional trailer set well back from the road became the order of the day. Barns and black-painted board fences dotted the landscape, which was emerald green and rolling as far as the eye could see. In the distance, the smoky blue peaks of the Appalachian Mountains formed a towering western horizon that looked like jagged teeth biting into the sky. The sun soared overhead, round and yellow as an egg yolk stuck smack in the middle of an upside-down blue bowl, and everything—plants, animals, and humans alike—seemed wilted by its heat.

Even though she was in an air-conditioned vehicle, Katharine felt wilted, too. If she'd been just a little less anxious, she would have fallen asleep. But she couldn't quite stop with the occasional quick glance out the back windshield. Distrust and detachment and a weird inability to recognize herself might be all in her head. The fact that someone was hunting her definitely was not.

If they were being followed, though, it had to be by a crow. She was as sure as it was possible to be that nothing any larger was on their tail.

By the time they turned off onto a hard-packed gravel road and started bumping through a forest so thick with old-growth maples and oaks and elms that their entwined branches formed a leafy canopy that blocked out the sun, she realized that thinking about his cabin as being in the back of beyond had most likely been an understatement. There was nothing around but woods. The thing was, she was almost too tired to care. Her eyelids were so heavy that she could barely keep them open. It had been a while since either she or Dan had spoken; he, too, seemed tired and engrossed in thought.

"Here we are," he said, after the Blazer had lurched through the tenth pothole in as many minutes.

Stifling a yawn, Katharine sat up, stretched a little, and looked around.

She saw instantly—because it was the only building in sight—that he was referring to a small, one-story log cabin with a rusty-looking metal roof supported by four narrow wooden posts that overhung a low-slung porch. It was set in a grassy clearing that, because of the position of the sun, was half sunny, half in shade, with the cabin being split down the middle between the two. Beside the single step leading up to the porch, a gnarled mountain laurel, its dark green foliage heavy with purple blooms, grew. There was an outbuilding that could have been a small garage a little way behind the house. The yard was overgrown and dotted with dandelions, and, like the house, gave off an air of general neglect. It was obvious at a glance that the place was infrequently used.

Looking at it, Katharine was irresistibly reminded of the movie *Deliverance*. She wouldn't have been a bit surprised to hear distant strains of "Dueling Banjos."

What have I gotten myself into?

Gravel crunched beneath the tires as Dan turned into the driveway and stopped beside the house. He cut the engine and got out. She sat still for a moment, eyeing the cabin and its surroundings with caution.

Either you trust the guy or you don't.

He opened her door for her, and she got out.

"So where do you fish?" she asked a moment later as she stepped up onto the porch, which was made of wide planks that looked older than dirt. Dan was right behind her, the duffel bag slung over his shoulder, the groceries in their white plastic bags in his hands. The fact that there was not another residence in sight, that she had not, in fact, seen another dwelling since they had turned off the highway, loomed larger in her mind with every step she took. As far as she could tell, the cabin was completely isolated, which meant that she and Dan were on their own.

Not that she felt nervous about that or anything.

"The Shenandoah River runs about a half-mile back that way." He nodded toward the left of the house. She looked, but all she could see were trees and more trees. She listened, but if the telltale gurgle of water was present, it was drowned out by other, competing, nature sounds. Besides the rustle of plastic and their own soft footsteps, all she heard were birds and bugs. "I keep a runabout on a trailer out in the garage. When I want to fish, I just hook it up and off I go."

When Dan stepped past her to unlock the front door, which lacked a window and was, like the rest of the cabin, made of weathered wood, it swung open with a protesting creak.

Stepping into the house with some trepidation, Katharine was relieved to find herself in a clean and functional, if somewhat dusty, living room. The floor was scuffed hardwood with an oval braided rug in shades of tan and brown laid down on top of it. The walls were generic white. There was an orange tweed couch with a tan velour recliner beside it, both of which had seen better days. A dark wood table with a brass lamp on it sat between the two. A matching coffee table in front of the couch and an out-dated TV (it had rabbit ears on top of it) on a metal stand in the far corner completed the décor. There were no pictures and no personal items. No knickknacks at all.

"Do you get out here much?" she asked, her gaze touching on a cobweb in a corner.

"Not as much as I'd like." Dan shut the door, and gloom enveloped them. Katharine realized that the curtains—they were a limp white and hung behind the couch, which was placed in front of the big front window—were closed. "When I can."

He walked past her, heading, she assumed, for the kitchen, which was separated from the living room by a half-wall. The top row of cabinets was visible from where she stood.

"Make yourself at home," he said over his shoulder.

She did, by following him into the kitchen. Her head hurt, her legs felt wobbly, and she was so tired she could barely think, but still she thought it was a good idea to get the lay of the land, so to speak. The kitchen was small, ugly—green laminate counters atop mustard-yellow cabinets, harvest-gold refrigerator and stove that looked decades old, faux wood linoleum floor—and dark. He dropped the duffel bag on the floor, deposited the groceries on the small rectangular wooden table that, along with two chairs, took up most of the floor space in the middle of the room, then pulled open the thin white curtains above the sink.

The window was clearly protected from the direct light of the sun, because sunlight did not pour in, but the room was suddenly light enough so that she could see dust motes in the air.

"You know, maybe this wasn't such a good idea," Katharine said uneasily, glancing around. All thoughts of Dan as an unknown quantity aside, it had suddenly occurred to her just how very vulnerable they would be if they *had* been followed. This place looked about as sturdy as a Cracker Jack box. Whoever was after them could kick the door down with impunity. If that happened, there was no one around to help or hear.

Dan was putting milk and lunch meat in the refrigerator, which, she saw, except for a bottle of ketchup and some pickles, had been previously empty.

He flicked a glance at her and shook his head. "There you go with those trust issues of yours again. You're safe here, I promise."

"This has got nothing to do with trust issues. It's just . . . what happens if they find us?"

"Nobody's going to find us." He put the last of the perishables in the refrigerator and shut the door. "We weren't followed, because I kept an eye out. That's why I took the most backward route known to man: If anybody had been on our tail, I would have seen them. Anyway, there's a security system—I usually don't set it because it goes off every time there's a thunderstorm, which is a pain in the ass to deal with from out of town—which is wired into the sheriff's office. They're closer than you think, and they're usually here within just a few minutes after the thing goes off. Besides, I've got a gun."

Her eyes widened. Her pulse kicked up a notch. A vision of the kind of big silver handgun she had become way too familiar with over the last twenty-four hours materialized in her mind.

"You've got a gun?"

"Yep."

He moved, opened a drawer beside the stove, and reached inside. When his hand resurfaced, it was grasping a slender black pistol—she thought it might be a .22—that had clearly seen better days. It was not, by any stretch of the imagination, a government-issued weapon. The pride with which he looked at it was telling: No spook worthy of his name would be caught dead gloating over a gun like that.

Perversely, the sheer inadequacy of the weapon made her feel better. It assuaged most of the rest of her residual suspicion that he might be something other than what he seemed.

"Good to know," she said, forbearing to point out just how useless that thing would be if they actually had to fight off the murderous-minded goons who had twice invaded her house. The fact was, if they were found, they were toast.

At this juncture, when she was so tired she was practically swaying on her feet and with her mind less than functional, all that was left to do was pray they weren't found.

"Hungry?" he asked, laying the pistol down on the counter with a casualness that would—if she hadn't had more important things to worry about—have made her nervous about his trustworthiness with a weapon. "I make a mean baloney sandwich."

Katharine shook her head. "Just tired."

She was, in fact, exhausted, which in its own twisted way was a good thing: Exhaustion, she was discovering, had a wonderfully dulling effect on fear.

"You look it. You probably ought to sack out for a while."

She nodded. "Sounds good."

"Bathroom's down the hall on the right. The bedroom's just past it. There's only one, but it's all yours. Come on, I'll show you."

Hefting the duffel bag, he led the way toward the back of the house and showed her where everything was. Not that he needed to, because it was a very small cabin, just the living room and kitchen at one end and the bedroom, bathroom, and a utility room at the other. He pointed out the closet where a bunch of mismatched towels were stacked alongside rolls of toilet tissue and a couple of unopened bars of soap, then headed back toward the front of the house.

"Yell if you need me," he said over his shoulder.

Katharine nodded from the bedroom doorway where she was standing, then stepped inside, closed the door, and looked around.

The bedroom wasn't a great deal larger than the double bed that nearly filled it. The bed was strictly utilitarian, consisting of a mattress and box spring on a frame that had been pushed into the far corner of the room, probably to provide as much floor space as possible. A cheap pine nightstand with a blue ginger-jar lamp on it stood beside the bed. A scarred oak chest against the wall beside the closet door constituted the rest of the furnishings. Like the living room, the walls were generic white. The long, narrow window was covered by another pair of the cheap white curtains, which were carefully drawn. No attempt had been made at decoration: A blue velour blanket had been pulled over the top of the bed, hiding everything, including the pillows, and that was it.

Dan had said that he'd changed the sheets right before he'd left the last time he'd been there, so the bed was clean and ready to go.

She was so tired she didn't even care.

But before she crawled into bed she had to have a shower. She felt so grungy she couldn't stand herself. The terrible, lurking suspicion that there might still be dried blood on her from last night was something she couldn't shake.

The thought made her stomach twist.

Carrying everything she needed with her, she went into the bathroom. Various noises from the kitchen located Dan for her just before she closed and locked the door; he was probably eating the baloney sandwich he had offered her.

Stripping off Dottie's clothes with relief, and turning the water on full-blast, she stepped into the tub, pulled the plastic shower curtain closed, and let the blessedly hot water sluice over her. Washing her mind-bendingly straight, coarse hair without getting her nose wet proved tricky, but she did her best, closing her eyes and tilting her chin back as the shampoo rinsed away down the drain. Steam from the hot water even had the added benefit of opening her nasal passages a little, so that she could actually get a whiff of the Irish Spring soap with which the cabin came equipped, as she rubbed its lather into every square inch of her skin she could reach.

It was in the course of doing this that she made two appalling discoveries: number one, she had had a Brazilian wax, and number two, a small red heart with an arrow through it was tattooed on the left side of her abdomen just above her bikini line.

Holy crap.

Either of these on its own was enough to totally freak her out. Both of them together made her go all light-headed and weak-kneed. She sat down abruptly on the edge of the tub while the shower curtain billowed around her and the hot water continued to rain down on her legs.

The idea of herself with such a blatantly sexy crotch was mind-boggling. As far as she knew, she had never had such a thing done to herself in her life. But the tattoo was even worse: She knew, *knew*, that she would never willingly get a tattoo.

She was needle-phobic.

Hyperventilating was not a solution, she told herself sternly even as she caught herself starting to succumb to it.

The reality was, she was now a skinny blonde with expensive belongings, a bikini wax, and a heart tattoo. It might be a new reality for her, but it was reality all the same.

Post-traumatic stress disorder was supposed to explain this?

I don't think so.

Okay. Succumbing to panic was useless, as she had already discovered. Until she was able to get her mind around these new additions to her person, the best thing to do was simply not think about them.

Or anything else.

Just go through the motions.

Forcing herself to her feet, she rinsed off the last of the soap, turned off the taps, got out of the tub, toweled herself dry, and used the blow-dryer she found on the wicker caddy in the corner to blow her (new) hair dry. Then she pulled on panties and a T-shirt—pretty, über-feminine white lace panties and a snug white T-shirt with a pink heart in the center of it, both of which fit reasonably well, and neither of which seemed like anything she would ever actually buy— wrapped herself in her robe, and staggered into the bedroom.

There she immediately fell into bed, burrowing under the covers, closing her eyes, doing her best to keep her mind a blank.

When that didn't work, she tried counting. Numbers, not sheep.

By the time she reached twenty-seven, she was out like a light.

Sometime after that, she began to dream. Dark dreams, scary dreams. In them, she was running for her life. . . .

Suddenly she found herself observing what looked like a shabby office. The details were hazy, but she knew it was night, and the room she was looking into was dark except for a small amount of light filtering in through what she knew was a door to her left, although she couldn't see it; a wall protruding into the room blocked her view. Her vision sharpened, focused, and she realized that she was in the scene, too, in a second room that was connected to the first by an old-fashioned wooden door that stood open. She was sitting in a hard, wooden chair facing that open door. She was actually tied to the chair, tied hand and foot, and gagged, too.

She was terrified. Her heart was racing. She was sweating, shaking. Something terrible was about to happen, she knew.

Looking around, searching for what it was that was scaring her so, she saw the shadowy outline of metal file cabinets and a serviceable metal desk and chair lining the wall near her. Behind the desk was a closet. Its door was partly open, and she saw that there was a mirror on the inside of the door. In the mirror she could see her own reflection.

She had masses of curly auburn hair that cascaded over her shoulders. Her skin was so pale it looked ghostly in the dim light. She was shapely, curvaceous, stacked . . .

A terrible dread filled her.

There was a man in the other room now. No, two men, shadowy figures whose features were concealed from her. She watched them through the open door. One forced the other to his knees. The man who remained standing had a gun in his hand, and he was pressing the mouth of it into the curve between the other man's shoulder and neck. He was screaming something—she could hear him but couldn't make out the words—and the man who was on his knees was now crying.

She was screaming, too, she realized, but no one could hear her, screaming silently because she loved the man on his knees, the man who she knew was about to be killed. Fighting to be free of her bonds, of the chair, she drew the attention of the man with the gun. He smiled at her—she saw that quite clearly—and she knew he was evil, knew he was going to pull the trigger in the next second and murder this person whom she loved, and there was absolutely nothing she could do to stop it.

Then the gunman's head exploded, just exploded into a ball of pink mist and gore, and what was left of him dropped to the floor at the same time as the kneeling man collapsed. He, too, keeled forward, sprawling face-first on the floor, his body limp in a running river of blood.

Even as silent screams of horror ripped through her body, another man stepped into the opening between the two rooms. He was in a shooter's stance, facing her, and in his clasped hands was a big silver gun. He was tall and formidable and aiming right at her. . . .

A shaft of light touched his features, illuminating them.

Jolted awake, Katharine opened her eyes, looked straight into the face of the man she'd just seen aiming a gun at her in her dream, and screamed to wake the dead.

14

W hat is it? What's wrong?" he demanded.

His hands—strong, warm hands—closed around her bare upper arms. She could feel their imprints like a brand on her chilled skin.

Her startled-awake eyes met his—hard blue eyes, caught in a shaft of indirect light—and she exploded out of the warm cocoon that had sheltered her, coming bolt upright into a sitting position as another scream, jagged and raw and searing in its intensity, tore of its own accord out of her throat.

"Jesus Christ." He winced. His hands tightened on her arms.

"Get your hands off me. Let me go."

"It's all right."

"No." Panicking, she began to struggle, trying to break free of his hold without success. She was trapped, he had her trapped, there was nothing she could do, she was helpless and at his mercy and, as she already knew all too well, he had no mercy.

"Damn it to hell." He gave her arms a little shake. His fingers dug into her skin. He was close, too close, leaning over her, his face just inches away from hers, and there was nothing, absolutely nothing, she could do about it.

He owned her.

This time her cry was one of distress. It was softer, more piteous, as she recognized her plight. He had her fast; unless and until he was ready to let her go, she would never be able to break away.

"I'm not hurting you." He must have misinterpreted the sound she had made as one of pain, because his grip on her arms loosened.

"Let me go."

Succeeding in jerking her arms free of his hold at last, she scrambled over a soft surface—a bed, she was on a bed in a dark room illuminated only slightly by that grayish shaft of light—until a corner trapped her. Whirling to face him, she crouched, squeezing back against walls that felt cold against her bare thighs, at bay on the bed, knowing him for her enemy.

"Keep away from me, " she warned.

He cursed again, under his breath, and straightened. She could feel his eyes on her, although she could not see his features at all now that the light was directly behind him. He was silhouetted by the grayish rectangle of light, an open door with light coming through it. He looked big and strong and formidable standing there blocking the door, blocking the light, and she shrank back into her corner, staring at him with huge eyes.

"You had a nightmare."

His voice with its slow drawl was meant to be soothing, she thought. But it did not soothe her. Instead, it touched something deep inside her, some buried memory, some forgotten association, and in response her stomach knotted with anger and fear.

"Who *are* you?" It was a strained cry torn straight from her heart. Even as she said it, she knew the answer, knew who he was, knew all about him, but . . . but . . .

In the same instant that she reached for it, the knowledge all went away. Vanished, *poof,* just like that, like a puff of smoke blown to oblivion by the wind.

"Katharine. It's me. It's Dan."

A light came on, momentarily blinding her. Wincing, she turned her face away from the source. He had turned on the lamp beside the bed.

Dan. As his name registered, her eyes adjusted to the light and she was able to look at him directly. He stood beside the bed, his hair rumpled, his eyes heavy-lidded and tired, the lines in his face more pronounced than she remembered, the stubble on his jaw discernibly heavier. He was wearing only his loose black pants, minus the belt, which meant that she could see about an inch of blue pin-striped boxers as the pants clung to his hips for dear life. His chest, and his feet, bare.

It appeared that, like her, he had been asleep.

"It's all right. You're safe."

That voice again. Oh, God, she knew that voice, knew it well, but the context was impossible to dredge up. Sucking in air, she cast a quick, furtive glance around, trying to get her bearings, trying to get a handle on what was happening. It was clearly night. She could see the darkness of the world outside through a sliver between the imperfectly drawn curtains. There was a steady drumming sound, insistent and rhythmic, that in her agitation she was only just now becoming aware of. It must be raining. The sound was rain hitting a tin roof.

All at once, she knew where she was: in the bedroom of his fishing cabin, crouched on his bed, wedged tightly back into the farthest corner of it as a matter of fact, staring at him like a trapped wild thing. Her heart pounded. Her pulse raced. Her breathing came fast and hard.

"You were having a nightmare," he said again.

A nightmare. She blinked, remembering, seeing it all again in lightning-fast replay. Her eyes sought and held his.

She had seen him, almost as clearly as she was seeing him now, in her dream. But the self who had been there with him in her dream had not been the skinny blond she was now. It had been the real her, the authentic her, the self she knew in her heart and soul she truly was. And he had been pointing a big silver gun at her.

Good Neighbor Dan my ass. Distrust permeated every fiber of her being.

She didn't know what was going on, but she did know this: She had to get away from him. She had to get out of there.

Until she figured out what was happening, she was going solo.

But he stood between her and the door. He was bigger, stronger, far more ruthless. To get away from him she had to be smart.

"A nightmare," she repeated, as if she were slowly accepting it.

He nodded. "Must have been a bad one."

His eyes were hooded and dark as he watched her with the same kind of calculation a predator might turn on its prey. Meeting his gaze, she managed—at least, she hoped she managed—to look merely worried and bewildered.

"I . . . don't really remember." She suddenly became aware of the chill breath of the air-conditioning caressing her legs, and realized that she was wearing only the scanty lace panties and snug tee. Wedged back in the corner as she was, with her legs bent almost double and her hands pressing into the mattress beside them, there wasn't a whole lot of her that he could see, she hoped. But still, it was too much. "I screamed, didn't I?" Shaking her head ruefully, she willed her wired body to let go of the flight impulse for the moment. Letting out a deep breath, she sank down on her butt, drawing her legs up in front of her and wrapping her arms around them for modesty's sake. "I can't believe I did that. I'm sorry I woke you."

"No problem." He was still watching her carefully. "In fact, I'd be surprised if you *weren't* having nightmares."

"Post-traumatic stress disorder," she said, nodding wisely.

"Exactly." He sounded pleased at her acceptance of this as the cause of her symptoms. His eyes searched hers. "Can I get you a drink of water or something?"

"You know, if you don't mind, I think I'll take you up on that offer of a baloney sandwich. How about I get dressed and meet you in the kitchen?"

Some of the tension left his face. "You like mayonnaise?"

She nodded.

"Tomato soup?"

She nodded again. It actually did sound good. She had missed supper. Lunch, too. Her stomach growled, right on cue.

"You got it," he said, and she rewarded him with a tremulous smile.

His eyes slid over her in one last assessing look, and then he turned and left the room. She got a good view of his bare back and registered just how heavily muscled his shoulders and biceps really were. Wide and powerful-looking, his shoulders tapered down to a narrow midsection and an athletic-looking butt, she saw with a sweeping glance as he walked out of sight.

She frowned thoughtfully.

Although she'd been too upset to pay any attention earlier, she had a sudden flash memory of his chest: It was wide and muscular, with well-developed pecs covered by a light smattering of dark brown hair above tight, toned abs.

In fact, his leanness was deceptive: This was the physique of a well-honed machine. For a moment longer she stayed where she was, trying to get her thoughts in order, to sort things out, to come up with a plan.

The bottom line was, she had seen Dan in her dream. In the midst of horror and carnage he had appeared, pointing a big silver gun at her. And she had been her auburn-haired, curvy self, the self she saw in her mind's eye.

Coincidence? Maybe. The result of scrambled brains, or post-traumatic stress disorder? Maybe.

But maybe not.

Her gut was screaming in favor of the *not.*

Uncurling herself from the cramped position she was in, sore muscles protesting every move, she clambered off the bed. Closing the door—it didn't have a lock—she pulled jeans and a bra from the duffel bag. She dressed quickly—the jeans were a little long, a little tight, but, once she rolled them up at the ankles, doable; the bra was nude stretch nylon that, because of the nature of the material, molded itself effortlessly to her perky what-she-guessed-were-B-cups—even as she tried to come up with a plan. Trading the white T-shirt for a plain black one (the harder to see in the dark), she gave the kitten-heeled sandals a jaundiced look—if she had to run, they would be worse than useless—and left them off. Anyway, under the circumstances, walking around the cabin in her bare feet would probably seem more natural. Then she opened the purse, extracted her driver's license, credit cards, and cash, and stuffed them into her back pocket. Running a brush through her hair, she smoothed a slick of tinted, strawberry-flavored lip balm over her dry lips and stuck the tube in her front pocket.

That was it. That was all she could take with her. Everything else she had arrived with would have to be left behind.

The plan? Ditch Dan.

Exactly how she was going to accomplish that she didn't know. Wait until he was asleep and run for it? Hope he decided to take a really long shower and run for it? Bop him over the head with something and run for it?

The thing was, running for it was the key. And the more she thought about it, the more urgent the need to take action became.

He had promised to drive her back to the airport tomorrow so that she could, as he supposed, catch a flight out.

Ain't gonna happen, was the verdict she arrived at. Either he was hoping to talk her out of it or he had some means in mind to prevent it. Or maybe he meant to try the first, and if that didn't work go with the second.

In any case, if she was going over the wall, she needed to do it tonight. The sooner the better, as a matter of fact.

Taking a deep, steadying breath, she opened the door and stepped out of the bedroom.

Except for the glow coming from the kitchen, the short, narrow hall was dark and full of shadows. Over and above the sound of rain drumming against the roof, she heard voices, faintly, which shook her for a moment until she realized that they must be coming from the television. As she reached the doorway that led into the living room, she saw at a glance that the TV was indeed on with the volume turned low. Light from the kitchen spilled over the half-wall so that the living room was almost as brightly illuminated as the kitchen itself.

The doorway that led into the kitchen was a couple of feet to her left. Through it she could see a slice of space that included part of the kitchen table, which sported two paper plates with two white-bread sandwiches—one sandwich, presumably baloney, on each—with a bag of Lay's potato chips in the middle of the table. A slight rattling sound was unexplained. She assumed that Dan, who was out of her sight, must somehow be the source of it. The merest hint of a yummy tomatoey smell told her (a) that her nose was once again minimally functional, and (b) he was indeed making tomato soup.

Another rumble from her stomach reminded her that she really was extremely hungry.

Once again she glanced into the living room, undecided as to the next best step. Her goal was to get away. To do that, the first thing she needed to do was lull Good Neighbor Dan into thinking that nothing had changed: She still trusted him.

Even though she most emphatically did not.

Too many things just didn't add up. Who he was and what he was up to she didn't know, not for sure. But . . .

His car keys lay beside a cell phone—presumably his cell phone—on the coffee table.

As soon as her brain registered that, her eyes widened. Her pulse quickened. Her breathing suspended. Her gaze fixed on the keys, riveted there, while all sorts of thoughts ran through her mind. There was no doubt about what set of keys it was: She had seen him insert them into the Blazer's ignition too many times for there to be any mistake.

All she had to do was pick up the keys, go out the door, get into the Blazer, and drive away.

For a moment the simplicity of it stunned her. Without the Blazer, he wouldn't even be able to give chase.

The sharp, unmistakable clang of tinny metal on tinny metal made her start. Glancing sharply toward the sound, she realized that she could see Dan in the kitchen. He was standing at the stove with his back to her, under a round wall clock that said it was just a little after ten-thirty, stirring a metal spoon around inside a ratty-looking aluminum pan that was steaming over a gas burner alive with a flickering blue flame. He was still shirtless, and the size and style of those flexing back muscles reinforced her conviction that he wasn't what he wanted her to think.

Okay, so maybe up until now she had been dumb as a rock. People could change.

It was clear that he had no clue that she was nearby, watching him.

Carpe diem—seize the day. Even as the words popped into her mind, her heart started to pound. This was it: her chance. Casting another assessing glance at Dan, she went for it, moving stealthily toward the coffee table, her bare feet soundless on the tightly woven cords of the rug. Pulse racing, practically holding her breath lest he should look around and spot her, she picked up the keys carefully, so carefully that they wouldn't jingle and betray her. The noise from the TV provided a cover; so, too, did the patter of the rain and his efforts in the kitchen. Holding the keys tightly in her fist, she moved away, all the while shooting lightning glances in Dan's direction. He continued to stir the soup, oblivious.

It was only a few steps to the door. Reaching it, she cast a nervous glance over her shoulder to find Dan, still at the stove, pouring milk from the carton into the soup. With her heart now thumping so loudly that its thudding in her ears was all she could hear, she took a deep breath and went for it, turning the knob, so quietly, pulling open the door inch by careful inch, praying that it wouldn't creak, and then when the opening was wide enough, slipping through it out into the cool, damp darkness of the porch.

By that time, her heart was pounding so hard she was surprised it didn't burst through her chest. The muted roar of the rain sounded loud as a NASCAR track in her ears. Did he hear it? How could he not hear it—or smell its earthy scent as it poured in through the opening? A quick, scared glance back revealed that he gave no evidence of being aware that anything was amiss. In fact, he was once again stirring soup.

Taking a deep, steadying breath, she silently eased the door shut behind her.

There was, she told herself, no reason to panic. She figured he wouldn't even start to wonder where she was before the soup was done. First he would call her, then go check the bedroom, then search the cabin . . .

She ran like a spooked rabbit anyway. The Blazer was parked no more than thirty feet away. Heart pounding, pulse racing, every nerve ending she possessed terrifyingly attuned to the house she was leaving behind, she tiptoed to the edge of the porch and then bolted, flying off the porch into darkness that would have been absolute except for the light filtering out through the tightly closed living-room curtains, running through the driving rain, her bare feet slipping and sliding over the already-soaked-to-flatness grass. She was wet to the skin almost immediately. Warm, drenching water ran down her face, got into her mouth, her eyes, which she had to blink to keep clear. She had the keys in her hand, pointing them at the car, punching the button that she knew, from the tiny beep and flare of light that accompanied the urgent jabbing movement of her thumb, had already unlocked the door, when all hell broke loose behind her.

The electric screech of an air horn split the night.

The noise was so loud, so terrifying, so totally unexpected that she jumped in fright and would have screamed, too, if she hadn't managed to swallow the sound at the last second. Surprise caused her head to whip around so fast that she nearly gave herself whiplash. Huge-eyed, goggling at the cabin, which was now practically vibrating on its foundation with the force of the noise it was emitting, she realized something appalling: She had forgotten about the alarm system, which was now going off like an air-raid siren behind her.

It must, she calculated as she reached the Blazer and jerked the driver's door open, operate on about a forty-five-second delay. When the code was input within that time frame, nothing happened. If it wasn't—well, Rip van Winkle himself couldn't sleep through the result.

There was no way he now didn't realize she was gone.

Adrenaline exploded through her veins. Her heart went into overdrive. Every tiny hair on her body catapulted upright. Throwing herself into the driver's seat, glancing up at the cabin what felt like every other second, she slammed the door behind her—no need to try to be quiet now—then hit the button locking all the doors and jabbed the key at the ignition at the same time. But she couldn't get the key to fit in the damned little slot.

What if they weren't the right keys?

Panting with the urgent need to hurry, hands shaking, she tried again, more carefully. This time the key went in. Almost bouncing in the seat with apprehension, she stepped on the accelerator—not too hard, because she didn't want to risk flooding the engine—and turned the key. The Blazer roared to life. The headlights, which must have been set to automatic, came on, their brightness terrifying as they cut through the darkness, unmistakably blazing her location to the world. They illuminated rain, trees, half a dozen sets of small animal eyes shining at her from the undergrowth . . .

The horrible deafening screech of the alarm was abruptly silenced.

That was so not good. *He's coming. . . .*

Her breathing suspended. Her stomach heaved. Throwing the Blazer into reverse, she stomped the gas. The *thuckety-thuckety* sound of tires spinning uselessly in the mud filled the air.

Oh my God, the car's stuck.

The door to the cabin flew open. Light spilled out. Dan appeared in the aperture, backlit by the glow behind him. She could see nothing of him beyond his shape, hear nothing beyond the pounding of her own heart and the wet slap of her uselessly rotating tires. But she knew, without having to see his expression, without having to hear a shout or curse, that he was coming after her.

And he did, almost instantaneously, racing across the porch and hurdling to the grass, pounding through the rain toward her, gesticulating, obviously yelling something that she couldn't hear—just as the tires found purchase at last and the Blazer shot backward toward the road.

15

Punching the gas for all she was worth, she drove like a bat out of hell. The Blazer careened backward, almost overshooting the road, while she spun the wheel hard to the left in an effort to avoid smashing into the fortress of trees on the other side. Looking frantically over her shoulder as she reversed, she lost sight of Dan. Even as the tires bit into the gravel of the road, even as she braked and reached down to shift into drive, she looked wildly around for him.

She couldn't find him.

Heart pounding like a jackhammer, breathing like she had been running for miles, she strained to see any hint of movement through the darkness.

Besides the faintly illuminated shape of the cabin, which was about the length of a football field away now, and the bold swath of silver rain and shiny wet gravel and brown tree trunks and green foliage caught in the beam of her headlights, her surroundings were cloaked by night. Dan could be anywhere, she realized with a rush of cold fear. He could be racing up to her door even as she had the thought. He could—and here her breath caught—be nearby, assuming that shooter's stance she remembered from her dream, aiming his gun at her. He could . . .

The bottom line was, he could be anywhere doing anything, but she didn't have to wait around to find out what it was.

Killing the headlights in the fond but probably futile hope of making the Blazer harder to locate, she put the pedal to the metal and did her best to peel mud out of there. The Blazer made a gallant attempt to answer, lurching forward, tires crunching as they chewed up the ground beneath them. The result was a slow, sideways slither, and she realized to her horror that underneath the top layer of gravel the road had turned into a sea of mud. Leaning forward as if to urge the car on, holding on to the wheel for dear life, she gritted her teeth and sucked in air and ordered herself not to panic. Then she did her best to ignore her runaway pulse and eased up on the accelerator.

It was too late. Even as she fought to get the fishtailing vehicle moving forward again, the right rear side smashed into a tree.

The sharp crunch of crumpling metal caught her by surprise. The accompanying shuddering jolt knocked her against the driver's door. Unhurt, still holding on to the steering wheel for dear life, she wrenched around to see what she had hit. In the same quick, indrawn breath, she registered that it was a massive oak and that the Blazer was still drivable.

Go, go, go.

Jittery as a teenager with a fake ID in a bar full of cops, she tried to peer out every window at once. *Where is he?* Every instinct she possessed urged her to stomp the accelerator clear through the floorboard. But that, she knew, would only worsen the problem. Cursing under her breath, pulse pounding so hard it was difficult to concentrate over the frantic thudding in her ears, she reined in her surging adrenaline and gently, gently, eased down on the damned pedal.

Please, oh, please . . .

The Blazer surged forward, held its ground strongly for a moment, then rocked back against the tree again with a scraping of metal on rough bark. *Oh, no.* Holding her breath, praying for all she was worth, she gently pressed the accelerator toward the floor once more.

This time the sickening *thuckety-thuckety* sound of wheels trapped in mud was her only answer.

Heart racing, stomach churning, she faced the horrible truth: She wasn't going anywhere. The Blazer was stuck. She might be able to rock it out, but she didn't have time. Dan could catch up with her at any second.

There was no choice. Unless she wanted to be caught there in the Blazer like a raccoon in a trap, she had to run for it.

But where to?

That, she told herself even as she killed the engine, was another one of those problems to be worked out later.

Jerking the keys from the ignition, she pushed the door open and scrambled out into the steamy night. The muddy gravel beneath her feet felt warm and squishy. In the typical fashion of summer showers, the rain was easing off now—now that it was too late to do her any good, she reflected bitterly. A few fat drops hit her in the face; more plopped into standing puddles that formed gleaming black pools on the road. The moon, a silvery crescent, peeked out from beneath the blanket of thick, gray clouds, unexpectedly illuminating everything—including herself and the Blazer. *Of course.* Closing—not slamming, on the off-chance that Dan was deaf, blind, and stupid and was thus somehow not aware of the Blazer's location and fate—the door, she punched the lock button on the key ring.

It repaid her for her cleverness by responding with a beep and an acknowledging flash of light.

Crap.

Breaking into a ragged run, she took off at a slant through the trees. Except for the whole beep-and-flash thing, locking the door had been a good idea, she told herself defensively. If he wasn't able to get the door open, trying to determine whether or not she had locked herself inside was bound to eat up some time. Anyway, once she was well away from the Blazer,

given the darkness and the vastness of the space she had to hide in, she figured she would be almost impossible to find.

With that in mind, she ignored the weakness in her legs and the light-
headedness that made thinking a chore and the various aches and pains
that should have slowed her down, and determinedly kept on chugging over
the thick, wet carpet of fallen leaves that covered the ground. There beneath the trees, only a few fine drops reached her, and those, she suspected,
were falling from the canopy. Mist rose from the ground, ephemeral as a
chiffon veil, as stray beams of moonlight filtering down through the trees
shone through it. The air was thick and humid, and she was sure the earthy
smell of damp vegetation must be strong, although she caught only the
merest whiff of it. The soprano piping of tree frogs mixed with the
whirring of insects to form an incessant background chorus. Small pairs of
eyes, luminescent as stars, gleamed down at her from high up in the trees.

As long as they stayed up there, she decided, hunching her shoulders
instinctively in case something should decide to take a flying leap, it was
all good.

"Katharine?" Dan's voice cut through the darkness like a knife, its
sharpness only slightly blunted by distance. He was at the Blazer, she was
almost sure from the direction of the sound. She imagined him rattling the
door handle, trying to peer inside.

"Damn it, where are you?"

The question was yelled into the night. Her heart gave a great leap.
Glancing instinctively back—he was standing in front of the Blazer, one
hand on the hood as he stared in her direction (she was sure she was right,
although it was too dark to allow her to see anything except the moonlight-
limned shape of him)—she almost smacked into a low-lying branch. She
managed to dodge it but lost her footing and went down on one knee. It
made painful contact with a rock.

She cried out. The sound wasn't loud, and it was almost certainly
muffled by the little creature chorus and the spattering rain and the rush
of the wind ruffling through the leaves high overhead, but it was sharp

and high-pitched and it made her cringe even as she forced herself to get up and go on.

Please, God, he didn't hear.

But when she glanced back, he was gone. The Blazer was still there, so she knew she was looking in the right place, but he no longer stood where he had a moment before. There was nothing now in front of the Blazer but the empty darkness of the road that, because it was open to the moonlight, was a lighter shade of black than anything else around.

The discovery that she could no longer see him gave her the willies.

She wasn't far enough away yet. Not nearly far enough away to be safe. Panic gave her a renewed burst of speed. Chest heaving, gulping in air, ignoring the new pain in her knee and her old pains alike, she fled through the trees. The ground began to slope downhill, and the wet slickness of the leaves made the footing tricky. Fortunately, there was very little undergrowth. Except for the places where gossamer ribbons of moonlight slanted through, it was dark as the inside of a cave. She dodged through dozens of closely spaced tree trunks poised like silent, immovable sentinels that were visible only because their solid columns were a shade blacker than the surrounding woods.

Then two things happened at once: She emerged into a small, moonlit clearing, and a hand grabbed her arm.

Her heart leaped. Her adrenaline surged. Her pulse went off the charts.

She screamed. She couldn't help it. It was such a shock, she hadn't heard him coming, hadn't heard a thing above and beyond her own labored breathing and the hurried slap-slap of her own footsteps in the wet and, of course, the whole woodland chorus. But here he was, Johnny-on-the-spot again, lunging out of the darkness, catching her arm.

She whirled, screeching, to face him—and her foot slipped out from under her and she went down.

"What the hell . . . ?" he began, catching her other arm as well to break her fall, only to break off abruptly as he went down, too, when she grabbed at him instinctively for support and he lost his footing right along with her. *"Shit."*

When they hit the ground, smacking into the cushiony carpet of leaves at the same time and sliding a little, they both ended up on their sides facing each other, but she was quicker. Even as he lay there cursing, she retained the presence of mind to roll away and try to scramble to her feet.

The leaves were slick as ice beneath her bare soles; they slipped and slid beneath her, making a speedy getaway impossible.

"Oh, no, you don't." Lunging upward, he grabbed at her, his fingers scrabbling at the back of her T-shirt and then hooking in the waistband of her too-snug jeans, yanking her back, yanking her down. Then, when she hit on her stomach and instinctively rolled, he heaved himself up and over her, shoving her onto her back. Before she could move, he came down on top of her with all the subtlety of a truckload of wet cement. Her breath expelled with an emphatic *ooph*. "You're not going anywhere."

He had her pinned in place. He was too big, too heavy. She stood almost zero chance of getting away now, she knew. Heart racing, pulse pounding, painfully sucking in as much air as she could squeeze into her squashed lungs, she still fought for all she was worth.

"Get off," she cried, shoving at his shoulders. He was still shirtless, she realized, and his skin was warm and damp and smooth beneath her hands. His shoulders were wide enough to almost completely block her view of the roiling night sky; his muscles felt solid as stone walls. Wriggling like a fish on a hook, she beat at him with her fists and jerked her legs up between his in a heartfelt but ultimately futile attempt to knee him.

"Damn it, stop it." He batted her fists away, then grabbed for them and missed, but did manage to put an end to her attempts to knee him by the simple expedient of trapping both her legs beneath his.

"*Get the hell off me.*" By this time she was practically breathing fire.

"No."

At this brutally simple response she went nuts, heaving and kicking and punching at him while he cursed and dodged and warded her off as best he could. Ducking his head, he hid his warm, bristly, unwelcome face in her straining-to-avoid-his-touch neck—then, in a lightning attack, caught her wrists at last and pinned them on either side of her head.

"No," she cried, but it was a waste of breath and she knew it. She could struggle all she wanted to: She wasn't going anywhere.

Exhausted, she lay still at last. She was breathing hard and so was he. The heat from his body radiated through her wet clothes; his weight pushed her down into the leaves. Now that it was safe, he lifted his head and looked down at her. Their faces weren't more than six inches apart, and she realized that there was just enough moonlight so that she could see him fairly well. Their eyes met. His were dark, narrowed, impossible to read. But from the set of his jaw and the line of his mouth, she got the definite impression that he wasn't in the best of tempers.

Well, goody, goody, she thought, because neither was she. Being forcibly pinned on the wet ground beneath approximately ten tons of overmuscled man was making her feel more than a little pissy.

"Coward," she spat, quivering with outrage, and gave one more try at jerking her arms free even though she knew it was a waste of energy. His fingers were long enough to wrap easily around her wrists, and strong enough to snap said wrists like twigs. His body was solid and heavy as a fallen tree atop hers. She was mad as hell about being manhandled. She was apprehensive about being caught, and about finding herself so completely at his mercy. She was worried about what he was going to do now, about what was going on here that she didn't understand, about her whole weirded-out life in general. But she was not, she discovered with dawning interest, actually physically afraid of him. "Let me go."

"What the hell is the matter with you?" His voice was a furious growl. His eyes glinted down at her as they moved over her face. "Why on earth would you just take off like that?"

"What, am I supposed to be some kind of prisoner now? I wanted to leave, so guess what—I left."

"You stole my car. Hell, you wrecked it!" He sounded genuinely upset about that. "You were trying to run away from me. Why?"

"Oh, I don't know," she said through her teeth. "Maybe I have a problem with being lied to."

"*What?*"

He was looking at her like she'd grown an extra head again. By this time, she was getting pretty damned tired of being looked at like that. He might be dangerous, but not, she thought, to her. He hadn't hurt her so far, and she was as sure as it was humanly possible to be, given her current cognitive limitations, that he wasn't going to.

That being the case, she decided to lay her suspicions on the line and see what kind of reaction she got.

"You're not a doctor. You know it, I know it, so admit it."

His response was not what she had expected. No guilt, no anger, no shocked confession. No tensing of his body, no glancing away. He simply stared at her for a moment, then rolled his eyes.

"Jesus, are we back to that again? You *know* me, remember? You're my next-door neighbor. You even checked my frigging ID."

She narrowed her eyes at him. "Yeah, and you know what I think, now I've had time to think about it? I think it was fake. I think everything you've told me about yourself so far is bullshit."

His brows twitched together. His face tightened. "Katharine . . ."

"I'm not Katharine," she gritted out. Then, more slowly, her eyes never leaving his, she added, "And I think you know it. You do, don't you? Don't you?"

"*What?*" His tone was incredulous. The look he was giving her said she was completely, around-the-bend loony tunes. If she'd had her hands free, she would have decked him. Because she wasn't. She *wasn't.*

At least, she was pretty sure she wasn't.

But then, he wasn't reacting as he should have if she was hitting the nail on the head, either. Maybe the guy was a consummate actor. Or maybe he really didn't know anything.

Or maybe she was just totally, completely wrong and soon the men in white coats would be coming to haul her away.

All in all, the third possibility was the one she liked the least.

"Why don't you tell me what's really going on?" Despite her best efforts to keep her cool, there was a note of rising hysteria in her voice. "Who do you work for? Are you CIA?" A hideous thought occurred, and her heart lurched. "Holy crap, do you work for Ed?" Her lips parted as she sucked in air.

The thought was terrifying, and it must have shown in her face because he gave a quick shake of his head.

"No. Hell, no. Of course I don't work for your boyfriend, or the CIA." His eyes searched hers. His voice was grim. "There was a reason why you ran out like that, and I want to know what it is."

"Maybe I just got sick of the company."

"It's something to do with that dream you had, isn't it? You were fine up until then."

She broke eye contact as the memory of the nightmare made her stomach clench, and started struggling to get free again.

"Let me up."

"Not till you tell me."

She stopped struggling—it was useless, and she knew it—and glared up at him. "You want to know about my dream?" Her tone was belligerent.

"Yeah, I do."

She hesitated. Just remembering the nightmare set her teeth on edge. The emotions had been so real, so intense, and what ultimately had happened had been so horrible. . . . Even now, with the images flickering only faintly on the edges of her brain, she felt a rising tide of terror, anger, loss. . . .

Wetting her lips, she tore her eyes from his, glancing around in an effort to reassure herself that this—this steamy wet night, this sexy, suspicious man crushing her into the ground with his weight—was the reality and the other was the bad dream.

Where they were, near the edge of the clearing, darkness surrounded them on all sides. The pale slice of moon was just visible when she looked up, playing peek-a-boo among the racing storm clouds, lightening the night to the thick gray of twilight and then, as it ducked behind the clouds again, plunging them into near total darkness once more. Branches stretching out like bony fingers far overhead provided some protection from the intermittent sprinkles that still fell. Under her back, the ground was soft and spongy beneath its layer of wet, slippery leaves.

She was wet to the skin, and with the gusts that were now swirling through the trees, she would have been cold, she thought, but for him.

Everywhere they touched—and that was just about everywhere—she was toasty warm.

She glanced back up at him, and their eyes met.

"You can trust me, you know." His voice was very quiet.

"Said the spider to the fly."

"Tell me about the dream."

Maybe, she thought, if she did, he could explain it. Or explain it away. Whatever. But she suddenly wanted—no, needed—to share it, to hear what he had to say about it.

She took a deep breath. "It was night. I was tied to a chair in a some kind of an office. An old-fashioned-looking office, with metal file cabinets against the wall and wooden desks. I looked like I feel I should, like the me I always think I am until something reminds me, with wavy auburn hair and pale skin and a few more curves, you know? The office has two rooms, and I can see into the second. There are two men in there, just opposite the door. One is forcing the other to his knees with a gun shoved right in the place where his shoulder and neck join. He's going to kill him, I know."

The more she talked, the more vivid the image in her mind's eye grew. It was almost as if she were right there in the midst of the dream again. By the time she broke off to try to put some distance between the here and now and the horror flick running in her head, her breathing was ragged.

"Go on." His voice was grim.

She flicked a look up at him. All right, this was definitely the here and now. The moon outlined his wavy hair in silver rather than gold. She could feel the heat of his body, feel its solid weight pressing into hers, hear the rasp of his breathing, see the shadowy lines and angles of his face and the dark glint of his eyes. Considering that she'd been running from him, he'd caught her, and he now had her pinned to the ground and all, it was probably stupid of her to feel safe. But she did.

"Then something happens—I guess somebody I can't see shoots the man with the gun. His head just—explodes." She shuddered at the memory. "He and the other man—and I don't know who the other man is, but I know he's someone I care a lot about—just sort of crumple to the ground, dead, and there's this rolling river of blood."

By this time her eyes were closed, squinched shut as she tried her best to block out the memory—no, the dream. But it didn't feel like a dream, it felt real, and therein lay the problem: She was hideously, horribly afraid that somehow, some way, it was real. Or at least it had once been real. She could feel him looking down at her, but she didn't open her eyes. The images were way too close, way too vivid, and she was having to work way too hard to push them away. Her heart pounded, her pulse raced, and her stomach had long since curled itself into a pretzel. She was even a little nauseated.

"Scary dream," he said, with absolutely no intonation at all. "I can see why you woke up screaming."

She opened her eyes and looked at him. It was a long look, penetrating, almost accusing.

"There's more."

"So let's hear it."

"You were in it." Her tone was tense, her gaze suddenly wary. All at once she was cold, despite his all-encompassing body heat, and she shivered a little. *Maybe,* a little voice inside her head whispered, *you're making a mistake here. Just because you feel safe with him doesn't mean you are.*

He blinked once, almost lazily, like a cat. "Me?"

There was, she thought, a certain grimness about his mouth. Or was that merely an illusion cast by the shadows that danced over them as the moon ducked beneath the clouds again and the creaking branches overhead swayed in the wind?

Jesus, who knew? All she knew was that she was trusting her gut on this—and she could only pray she wasn't wrong.

Dumb as a rock was not exactly the epitaph she had always dreamed of.

She took a deep breath. Her eyes locked with his. "After somebody blew that man's head off, you appeared in the door between the two offices and pointed a big silver gun at me."

There. It was out in the open. Holding her breath, she searched his eyes, his face for a reaction.

For a moment he didn't say anything. He simply looked down at her, his expression—what? Thoughtful? Worried? Angry? She didn't know. It was too dark. His face was impossible to read. She could feel the rise and fall of his chest against hers, and thought that perhaps he was breathing a little faster than he had been when she had started talking. His shoulders flexed, as if, she thought, he was trying to work some tension out of them. His fingers moved; his hands were still warm and strong on her wrists, but his hold was perhaps a little looser now. His body was heavy, pushing her into the wet, spongy ground, but she discovered to her own surprise that she no longer minded at all.

That strong sense of familiarity she always felt in his company was back. Whoever and whatever he was, she thought, she *knew* him. Which meant, of course, that he knew her, too. The sheer surprise of that corollary thought made her stiffen and frown at him. She felt like a blind person trying to make her way in a sighted world.

"Who *are* you?" she whispered, her eyes glued to his face. She was breathing hard, still shivering a little, trying not to let herself get totally unnerved. The answer was something she both needed and dreaded to hear.

In response, his eyes slid over her face and his mouth curved into the smallest of rueful smiles.

"Looks like I'm the guy you see in your dreams now, angel eyes," he said.

Angel eyes.

Even as that registered, even as it resonated and found its home deep inside her, even as her eyes widened and her heartbeat quickened and her brain scrambled to latch on to the elusive memory that was *right there,* he lowered his head and touched his mouth to hers.

16

The electricity generated by that soft, almost tender kiss was so strong it practically ignited the air. She froze for an instant, absorbing its intensity, letting it scorch through her. He kissed her again, his lips teasing over her mouth, barely there yet nevertheless managing to make her heart stutter, make her loins clench.

She shouldn't want this, shouldn't want him, and she knew it. But she did.

He let go of her wrists at last, sliding his hands up along her palms to clasp hers, stretching her out, keeping her trapped beneath him while still pressing those soft little kisses to her mouth. She didn't turn her face away, didn't resist or reject him—didn't want to, even though with the tiny part of her brain that was still rational, she knew she should. Instead, her fingers twined with his and her body arched up under his and her eyes closed. She burned with wanting him. Her heart beat in slow, thick thuds. Her body tightened with quivering anticipation. But still she tried to keep her head, keep some kind of control, reminding herself that she was lost in some nefarious game that she didn't understand, and he was part of it, too, she was almost sure. And he was probably dangerous and she certainly didn't trust him and . . .

It didn't matter.

He slid his tongue along the line between her lips and her bones melted. Just like that.

And she gave up on the whole trying to think thing and made a tiny little sound under her breath and wrapped her fingers around his—and kissed him back.

He let her take the lead then, let her kiss him, and she pressed her lips to his long, mobile mouth with hungry intensity, plying his lips with hers, her pulse accelerating until she could hear it drumming in her ears. Her heart pounded fast and strong. Her body tightened and burned.

His lips were dry and warm and firm, and she had wanted to kiss them for so long that now that it was finally happening she couldn't seem to get enough of the feel of them against hers.

I've wanted him forever.

How she knew that she didn't know, but she did. That was the one rock-solid thought that surfaced through the steam clouding her brain. Breathing erratically, clinging to his strong hands like she would fall for a thousand miles if she didn't, she pressed her tightening breasts up against his chest and licked into his mouth and let go of everything except this moment and the way she felt with him. His mouth was hot and wet and exciting and she couldn't get enough of it. . . .

That's when he broke the kiss, lifting his mouth from hers, sucking in air.

"Jesus." His voice was low, husky. "This is a mistake."

But if that's what he thought, he wasn't making any moves to do anything about it. His fingers were tight on hers, his body hard as he pressed her down into the leaves. He was breathing way too fast. She could feel the rapid rise and fall of his chest against her breasts. Opening her eyes, she saw that his mouth had gone all grim and his jaw was taut and his eyes were narrowed and glinting down at her through the moonlight. A dark flush rode high on his cheekbones. Their faces were so close that she could feel the warm brush of his breath against her cheek. So close that all she had to do was lift her head a few inches to touch her lips to his again.

But for some obscure reason that she didn't even try to make sense of, she didn't do it. She wanted *him* to kiss *her*. She wanted him, not her, to be the one to lose control. She wanted him to be wild for her.

Like, she discovered to her chagrin, she was wild for him. So much so that she was practically on fire with it, making sexy little moves beneath him even though he was no longer responding at all, curling her bare toes deep into the wet leaves.

There was no doubt that he wanted her. His body was aroused. She could feel the physical evidence of it against her with absolutely no possibility of mistake. In fact, every muscle in his body felt rigid. But all of a sudden he wasn't doing anything about it. Instead, he was holding himself perfectly still, apparently engaged in some kind of inner battle that she could only guess at.

"Let me go then," she said, the words a challenge.

His eyes slid over her face, stopped at her lips, lingered. Her mouth went dry. Her heart raced like she had been running for miles. Of its own accord, her chin tilted up just the smallest fraction. Her lips parted in silent invitation.

His eyes gleamed hotly down at her.

"You make it sound easy." The wryness in his voice was matched by the slight curve of his mouth.

Before she could even start to puzzle out the whys and wherefores of that, his head dipped and his mouth was on hers again.

The carnality of the kiss made her dizzy. His mouth moved on hers with a fierce, hot urgency that made her go all soft and shivery inside. She forgot everything but him as passion exploded between them like an incendiary device. He slanted his mouth over hers and slid his tongue between her lips and pushed a thigh between hers and in general pretty much succeeded in rocking her world. He knew what he was doing, knew how to tantalize, how to thrill, and he had her near mindless and panting and moving urgently against him in response. Her body quaked and her breasts swelled and her back arched as she kissed him back with escalating desire.

"I want you," he whispered as he let go of her hands at last to wrap his arms around her. They were strong and hard as they pulled her closer yet. His hands felt big and warm through her wet T-shirt as they splayed across her back. Heart pounding, pulse racing, still kissing him for all she was worth, she slid her hands with sensuous pleasure over the smooth, satiny skin of his shoulders and back. His skin was warm and faintly damp with rain and, she thought, perspiration. The underlying muscles were toned and strong and so unmistakably, blatantly alpha male that her insides turned to jelly even as the few tiny, remaining functional synapses in her brain fired feebly.

All this mind-blowing sizzle was coming from somewhere, and never mind that he knew how to kiss and knew his way around a woman's body. That wasn't it—or, at least, that wasn't all. There was a pent-up quality to it, an aching, abiding need that made her think what was happening had been a long time coming.

Who are you?

The question flared in her brain again, but then his hand found her breast and every last vestige of rational thought she possessed vanished in an avalanche of fiery longing. Her breath caught. Her throat went dry. Her heart threatened to slam its way out of her chest.

Murmuring her pleasure into his mouth, she wrapped her arms around his neck and threaded her fingers through the silky curls at his nape and clung for all she was worth.

The only thing she knew for sure about him, she thought hazily, was this: She wanted to get naked with him in the worst possible way. And right now that was all that really mattered.

His hand burned through her wet T-shirt, causing her nipple to tighten and butt up into his palm while heat rocketed through her body. Arching up into that caressing hand, kissing him as if she'd die if she didn't, she barely noticed when his caressing hand froze and he suddenly stiffened.

Then he pulled his mouth from hers and lifted his head.

"*Shit,*" he said, even as, with deliberate sensuousness, she ran her lips along the bristly, faintly salty line of his jaw.

This was sufficiently surprising that her eyes blinked open and she quit kissing him. The moon had clearly retreated behind the curtain of clouds again, because their surroundings were dark with shadow. As far as she could tell, the rain had stopped completely. The wind was blowing harder than before. Although they could barely feel it, deep in the sheltering woods as they were, she could hear the rush of it through the leaves high overhead. The woodland chorus trilled insistently on.

He was breathing hard. His body, hot and hard with desire for her, covered hers almost completely. His hand rested heavily on her breast, cupping it possessively.

But suddenly his attention was elsewhere.

"What?" she asked. He was, she saw, staring back the way they had come. Lying on her back as she was, she couldn't see what he was looking at without doing some serious damage to her neck, but from the hardening of his jaw and the grim set of his mouth, something was up. Her heart still pounded. Her body still quaked. Physically, she was definitely still with the program. But all of a sudden she remembered that the world—at least, *her* world—was fraught with uncertainty and danger.

And he was looking through the woods like some of it had just landed on their doorstep.

He flicked a glance down at her just as her arms unwound themselves from around his neck.

"We've got company." His tone was abrupt. His hand left her breast and he eased himself off her.

"Who?" Her voice was sharp with fear. Looking around, she saw nothing but darkness and trees.

"Come on."

He was on his feet now, reaching a hand down to help her up. She took it, scrambling up beside him, suddenly cold to the bone as she followed his gaze to find herself looking at—two round, bobbing lights, each about the size of a baby aspirin. Flashlights. On this side of the road, coming at them through the trees. The pale beams cut through the night-dark forest in slow, sweeping strokes, illuminating trees and foliage and the shiny, wet leaves that seemed to cover every inch of ground.

Watching them come, she started to shiver. Her instincts screamed *run,* but Dan wasn't moving. Her hold on his hand tightened, and in response his fingers curled tightly around hers, and he pulled her protectively close to his side. Breathing hard, heart racing, she leaned against his muscular warmth, clutching his hand as if it were a lifeline. Her eyes were all on the oncoming flashlights—until it occurred to her that Dan wasn't moving or making any kind of potentially defensive preparations. Motionless as the thick tree trunks around them, he was just standing there watching the flashlights—and whoever was holding them—approach. His face could have been carved from stone.

"You know, don't you? You know who they are." Her eyes were wide as they met his. Her voice was shrill with the beginning of panic. She sucked in air, grabbed his arm, shook it. *"Tell me the truth."*

"You don't need to be afraid." His voice was low and soothing. His arm encircled her waist, pulling her up against his chest. His hand came up to slide along her cheek. As she stared up at him, aghast, he dropped a quick, hard kiss on her mouth. "I won't let anything happen to you. Trust me."

"No," she said, almost frantic now as she realized that the flashlights were only yards away. Her pulse pounded. Her stomach clenched. The taste of fear—sour as vinegar, as she had recently learned—was in her mouth. "I don't."

A single wild look around told her that she was almost out of time. She could see the tall, dark silhouettes of the men holding the flashlights now. Clearly, this was her last chance to run. She pushed at his chest in a desperate attempt to free herself, only to realize that he had her fast.

He wasn't going to let her go.

"What are you doing?" she cried even as she struggled to free herself. Terror dried her throat, set her heart to pumping wildly. "Dan—"

"It's going to be okay," he said.

And then the men reached them, and it was too late.

When Katharine awoke the next morning, it was almost ten. She was feeling much better. Stronger, calmer, more at ease with herself and the world. Examining her reflection in the bathroom mirror of her room in the Embassy Suites Hotel, where Dan had driven her last night by mutual agreement after explaining to the two men from the sheriff's department who'd been behind the flashlights in the woods that the burglar alarm had gone off by accident, she was even able to reassure herself that the reflection looking back at her was indeed her. Now she remembered the drastic diet that had whittled away her curves, remembered getting her teeth fixed and her hair colored and cut. She even remembered making weekly visits to Mystic Tan to keep herself from looking so unfashionably pale. If yesterday's lapse had been some kind of weird amnesia, well, at least it had been temporary and easily cured.

A good night's sleep had worked wonders. It had allowed her to see that her fears had been nothing more than the product of a blow to the head coupled with the terrible trauma she had suffered. Having a dear friend murdered in front of her in combination with being attacked and terrorized (twice) in her own home would be enough to send most anybody off the rails.

But now she was back, restored, whole. She could even breathe better through her nose, although she meant to keep the bandage across the bridge in place until it was thoroughly healed.

She showered, blew her hair dry, put on her usual makeup, got dressed in a turquoise tank and a pretty summer skirt that she retrieved from the duffel bag, and slid her feet into her elegant sandals. Straightening her ring, which was too loose because of her weight loss, she touched her ears to make sure the diamond studs were still in place. Then she fished her phone out of her purse and made a quick phone call. She got voicemail and left a message, then disconnected. The room came equipped with a tiny kitchenette, which included a coffeepot and packets of coffee. She made herself some.

Then, cup in hand, she sat down to wait.

It didn't take long.

The knock on her door was sharp and imperative. Calmly she rose from the chair by the window, picked up her purse and the duffel bag, and crossed the small suite to the door. After a quick, careful look through the peephole, she opened the door and smiled at the two men waiting for her in the green-carpeted hallway. It was a good feeling to realize that she remembered them now. They were CIA case officers who, unlike most of those in the bloated Agency hierarchy, reported directly to Ed and acted, basically, as his errand boys. Her relationship with them was professional rather than friendly—she thought they might disapprove of the fact that she was sleeping with the boss—but she'd seen them on the average of several times a week for the past two years. Tom Starkey was closest to the door and, apparently, was the one who had done the knocking. In his early thirties, he was about six feet tall, broad-shouldered and fit in a navy blue suit, white shirt, and red tie, with a square-jawed, handsome face, a buzz cut that looked like it would be medium brown if it ever grew long enough to actually have a color, and a faint bulge beneath his jacket that, Katharine knew, was the shoulder-holstered pistol that he was never without. A couple of steps behind him stood George Bennett, maybe five years older and half an inch taller, with darker brown hair and a paler complexion but otherwise looking enough like Starkey to be his brother. It was the suits, Katharine thought, that made them look so much alike. Bennett was wearing a navy blue one, too, and a white shirt, although his tie had subtle stripes. Short-haired, well-built men in suits tended to lose their individuality if you saw enough of them.

Clearly, since that was the case with her, she'd been a resident of Alphabet Soup World for too long.

"Morning, Ms. Lawrence," Starkey said, as politely as if he had not spent the past twenty-four hours searching frantically for her, which she knew, without anyone having to tell her, he had done. Ed would have been upset at her disappearance. When Ed got upset, Starkey and Bennett got busy. They had undoubtedly borne the brunt of his displeasure as well.

"Good morning," she answered. Neither of them had so far cracked a smile, and she understood from that that she was far from being their favorite person at the moment. Well, so be it. She had done what, at the time, she'd felt she had to do.

Even though now she knew how unnecessary all that panic had been. Starkey took the duffel bag from her and closed the door.

"This way," Bennett said, and she followed him without even asking where they were going while Starkey brought up the rear. Because, the thing was, where they were going didn't really matter. By coming back, by making that phone call, she had placed herself in Ed's hands, and Starkey and Bennett were there as extensions of Ed. They were taking her where Ed had told them to take her, and she found she really didn't need to know more than that.

Ed was her boyfriend. She could trust Ed.

Her room was on the third floor. They rode the elevator down, and then the pair of them waited like watchful nannies while she checked out.

"Mr. Barnes is in a meeting," Starkey informed her as he settled her into the backseat of the big black Mercedes waiting beside one of the hotel's side entrances. "He said to tell you he'll be with you this evening."

Katharine nodded, and he closed the door on her. He and Bennett got into the front seat. Starkey drove. The tires swished and the air-conditioning hummed, but besides that there was no other sound. None of them spoke as they pulled away from the hotel, which was an older specimen of the chain located in Garfield Heights, in the seedy section of Southeast Washington. The hotel was near the Navy Museum, which was a major tourist attraction, but it was surrounded by run-down apartment buildings, cheap ethnic restaurants, and discount stores, with a few pockets of restored older homes providing glimpses of the block-by-block revitalization that was under way.

She had chosen the hotel, she remembered, because it had allowed her to pay cash. Using her credit cards would have, she feared, brought Ed down on her within the hour. And she had needed the time to be alone, to think, to sleep.

The sleep had, of course, done her a world of good. Her disordered thinking had completely gone away. She was herself again.

In minutes they were on the freeway heading into D.C. Looking toward the city, what Katharine saw was an ocean of gray: wave upon wave of concrete and steel. The skyline for as far as she could see was a staggered grid of buildings. Although it was not yet noon on Sunday, and Washington tended to be a churchgoing town (politicians, with voters to please back home, were big on public worship), traffic was heavy as usual, primarily because of all the tourists. As they crossed over the Anacostia River, Katharine looked down at its glassy green surface to see that the boats were out in force: small sailboats, colorful as songbirds, tacking in a zigzag pattern to catch any available breeze; cabin cruisers zipping along under their own power, trailing white ripples of wake; barges loaded with cargo, chugging steadily upstream. The sky was bright Tiffany blue. The clouds were white and feathery. The only trace of last night's rain was the rise in the humidity. The heat was positively swampy, Katharine thought as Starkey pulled into an underground parking garage beneath one of the anonymous high-rise apartment buildings that were a feature of the central part of the city, found a spot, and parked. But she didn't have long to experience it. They walked a few yards to an elevator, which whisked them skyward. They got out on the twelfth floor. It was a narrow, thickly carpeted corridor lined with widely spaced doors. When they reached the third door on the left, Starkey produced a key, unlocked it, and swung it open, gesturing to Katharine to precede him inside.

She did, walking into a small vestibule that opened onto a moderately sized living room. There was a big window wall opposite the entrance. The drapes were open, flooding the room with light. Besides that, the living room was basically a square box furnished with a big striped couch in shades of gold and cream and brown with matching gold tub chairs on either end. A landscape in a simple gilt frame hung over the couch, and a big plasma-screen TV dominated the wall opposite. Cream wall-to-wall carpet extended throughout the apartment, which had a single bedroom, a bath and a half, and a small but well-equipped kitchen with a dining alcove off it. Katharine saw all this as she followed Starkey, who was carrying the duffel bag, into the bedroom.

"Whose apartment is this?" Katharine asked as Starkey put the duffel bag down. "Is it Ed's?"

He shrugged. Katharine realized that she wasn't going to get an answer. If he even knew, he would consider it Ed's business, to reveal or not as he chose. Starkey and Bennett were unimpeachably discreet—and unimpeachably loyal.

"There's food in the kitchen," Starkey said as he turned to go. "Or one of us can go get carryout, if you want. The thing is, Mr. Barnes told us that we weren't to leave you alone." He gave her a reproachful look. "We can't protect you if we aren't with you."

Katharine nodded. She really didn't want Starkey and Bennett as enemies, so she figured she better start mending fences. "I know. I understand." She tried to inject some remorse into her tone, although it took a surprising amount of effort. Emotionally, she discovered, she was still feeling a little bit of a disconnect. "Look, I'm sorry I ditched you and Bennett at the hospital. I think, after everything that happened, I must have been a little bit out of my head."

"It was a bad scene. Right at the beginning, we were afraid you'd been kidnapped. Until you called Mr. Barnes."

"I never thought of that," she said. When Starkey's only response was a sour look, she gave it up and added, "You know what? I *am* hungry. And I don't feel like cooking."

"How about hamburgers? Or tacos?"

Actually, Starkey seemed a tad less unfriendly than before, so maybe her little speech had helped, Katharine decided. They often ate fast food around the office, where the hours tended to be long and the three of them were often among the last to leave, waiting as they were for Ed. Although they very rarely waited together. Starkey and Bennett had their sphere, and she had hers.

"Tacos," Katharine voted, and Starkey nodded and left her alone.

After he came back with the food and they ate, Katharine returned to the bedroom, which was tastefully decorated with another gilt-framed landscape over the queen-size bed, and taupe walls and curtains. Curious, she opened the curtains to reveal a sweeping view of the apartment building across the street. Looking between it and the under-construction highrise next to it, she caught a glimpse of the Convention Center, and that helped orient her. She was just off New York Avenue, probably on K or L Street. She didn't know why, but it made her feel better to know approximately where she was.

She sat in the small gold velvet armchair beside the comfortable-looking bed with its gold spread, and pulled her phone out of her purse. In her mind burned a list of things she needed to do, and she mentally checked them off one by one as she did them. First she called Sue Driver, a mutual friend of hers and Lisa's, and listened to her exclamations and condolences while begging off telling her anything on the grounds that it was too upsetting to talk about, before finally managing to ask when the funeral was to be. Armed with that information—it was scheduled for Tuesday—she called Cindy Parrent, the friend who was watching Muffy, and asked her if she could possibly keep the cat until Wednesday. Then she made arrangements to fly to Cleveland, Lisa's hometown, the next day.

By that time, the pounding headache that she thought had vanished along with her irrational fears was back. Swallowing an Extra Strength Tylenol from her purse with a drink of water from the adjoining bathroom, she looked in on Starkey and Bennett—they were watching football in the living room and apparently having a good time, although their faces went carefully blank as soon as they spotted her in the doorway—and thought about taking a nap.

But the idea of falling asleep didn't appeal to her. Sleep brought dreams with it, and some dreams, she thought vaguely, could be scary. Instead, she needed something to occupy her mind.

So she curled up in the armchair, picked up the remote from the chair beside it, and turned on the small TV tucked into the tall white armoire opposite the bed. *CSI* reruns were on the first channel that popped up. There was nothing graphic—yet—but the thought of watching an autopsy or worse made her stomach churn. Hurriedly, she started flipping through channels, and finally settled on *Full House* reruns. TV didn't get much more mindless than that.

Despite her determination not to, she was just about to doze off in the armchair when the door to the bedroom was thrust forcefully open. Startled wide awake, she sat up abruptly as Ed, natty as always in a charcoal-gray designer suit, white shirt, and black tie, his black hair slicked carefully back, strode into the bedroom, stopped short at the sight of her, and planted his fists on his hips, a furious expression on his face.

I've been going out of my mind worrying about you," he yelled, while Katharine winced at both the blast of anger that was so loud it completely drowned out the TV and the idea that Starkey and Bennett were overhearing it. She could just picture them smirking in the next room: Ed took them to the figurative woodshed often enough. They would be glad it was her turn. "Where the hell have you been?"

Remember, Ed is always right. Anything to please Ed. Be submissive. Supportive. Agree with everything he says. Go along with anything he suggests. Your job is to keep him happy.

The parameters of her relationship with Ed spooled through her mind in an instant. She knew this relationship, knew that he was the dominant partner and she was very much subordinate. She had been following those rules for years. She could follow them a little longer.

Even if, somewhere deep inside, they made her just a little bit mad.

"I'm sorry," she said in a conciliatory tone. He was still glaring at her, his heavy-lidded brown eyes dark with rage, his square jaw taut with it. "I didn't mean to worry you. So much happened that . . . I guess I just freaked out."

"You ran away from the hospital." There was a wealth of anger in his tone. "Starkey and Bennett were on their way up to you, and you just took off. Why would you do a thing like that?"

"It was because of the police. I just couldn't handle talking to them right then. I . . . wasn't thinking straight."

He slammed the door behind him as she spoke and strode quickly toward her. It was amazing how threatening a five-foot-ten-inch, stockily built man could look when he was pissed, she thought. Her heart gave an unexpected lurch—*I'm afraid of him*—then quickly settled back into its normal, natural beat as the words *You're in love with him* superseded her first instinctive reaction.

. . . in love with him; in love with him: The words formed an echo in her brain, beating in her head in tandem with her pulse, overwriting anything and everything else.

Smiling, she rose from the chair to meet him.

"Don't run away from me again." His tone was terse, but when she obediently shook her head no, some of the aggression left his expression. Reaching her, he caught her up in an embrace, wrapping his big arms around her, pressing his meaty lips to hers. He kissed her thoroughly if not all that expertly, but she responded with appropriate enthusiasm.

His tongue's thick as a salami. He tastes sort of like salami, too.

The thought, with its accompanying surge of revulsion, was quickly swamped by a rush of others: *He's handsome, sexy; he's been your boyfriend for more than a year; you're in love with him.*

. . . in love with him; in love with him.

Still, when he let her go, what she felt was relief.

Just to be safe, she sank back down in the chair. The bright glow of the late-afternoon sun was reflected off the dark windows of the building opposite, and the light pouring in through the window beside her was intense. It must have bothered Ed, because he cast an impatient look out the window, then moved, closing the curtains with a quick tug on the cord.

Even as the curtains swished shut, Katharine was conscious of a vague feeling of—what? Vulnerability? Claustrophobia? Isolation? Something unpleasant and confining, as if she had been suddenly cut off from her last connection to the world.

A shiver ran down her spine. Now that the only illumination was the blue glow of the TV—Michelle was cracking the *Full House* family up, but Katharine was no longer even remotely interested—the room suddenly felt cold. Reaching out, she turned on the lamp beside the chair to combat the sudden gloom, then picked up the remote and clicked the TV off.

"So where the hell have you been?" Ed stood looking down at her, fists on hips again, a frown beetling his brow. He was looming above her, his posture intimidating. *Deliberately,* she thought.

Katharine's stomach contracted. Her pulse raced. After the men from the sheriff's department had gone, she and Dan had agreed that it was best that Dan be left out of the story of the day's events entirely. Anyway, she knew that if Ed should learn that she had actually exchanged a heated kiss with her well-meaning neighbor, however befuddled her thinking had been at the time, he would go ballistic with jealousy. And the thought of Ed in a jealous rage made her shudder, not only for herself but for Dan. So for both their sakes, she already knew she was going to lie about much of the previous day's odyssey, and even had what she was going to say all planned out. But still, the prospect of lying to Ed made her nervous.

If he caught her at it, the consequences would be bad, she knew. The key, then, obviously, was to lie very, very well.

"You know where I was: the hotel." Her tone was utterly calm and collected. "I called you from there."

His eyes never left her face. "How did you get there?"

"You mean after I barely survived being attacked for a second time in my own home?" She deliberately threw that out there in hopes that it would distract him, and the conversation would thus move on to what was, as far as her telling the truth was concerned, solid ground. "I took the Metro."

"That simple, huh?" He shook his head. "I can't believe Starkey and

Bennett weren't able to track you down. They must be losing it." His face softened fractionally as his eyes moved over her. His gaze touched on her bandaged nose, her bruised forehead, and she could see him registering that she truly had been hurt. "You've had a bad time, haven't you? I'm glad you're okay, babe. And I'm sorry about your friend. But our priority right now has to be to find these people."

She threw another distraction at him. "Do you have any leads?"

Watching, she thought it was like shutters had slammed closed over his eyes. They went suddenly opaque.

"A few," he said evasively. "Believe me, I'll find them. And when I do . . ."

She shivered inwardly at the threat he left unfinished. Boyfriend or not, Ed had a ruthless, violent side that she, personally, wouldn't want to run afoul of. With all the resources of the Agency at his disposal, she had no doubt at all that sooner or later he would run the perpetrators to earth. Then they might, or might not, actually make it alive into the justice system and eventually into a courtroom. She was betting on the *might not.* Courtrooms were messy, public places where way too much sensitive material came out. She had little doubt that Ed's preferred way of handling what he no doubt considered a private matter would probably be to make the offenders just disappear.

As in, *bang bang.*

"So walk me through what happened after you ran away from the hospital. Did you go straight back to the town house?" He was watching her carefully. His thick, black brows were almost touching over his nose.

Katharine thought, *He's suspicious.* And her heart began to pump a little harder.

"Yes."

"How did you get there?"

She had to fight the desire to take a deep, steadying breath. The way he was watching, he would notice, she knew. And it would give too much away.

"Taxi." That was the lie she particularly hated to tell, because it could be checked. But it would take a while, if he even bothered. She hoped—no, prayed—that he wouldn't bother. In any case, she would be flying to Cleveland early in the morning, and she was pretty sure he couldn't check it before then. And then she would have a two-day respite before she had to face him again.

"So you left the hospital, took a taxi to the town house, and got jumped by an unknown assailant who was looking for something, although you have no idea what." His eyes narrowed. His jaw tightened. "Then you call me. You tell me what happened, you *don't* tell me where you are, and you hang up on me. I'm not happy about that, babe."

Just like taking a deep breath, wetting her lips was probably out, too.

"I'm sorry. I was scared and upset. I wasn't thinking straight. And I called you today from the hotel, just like I said I would."

"You put me through a hell of a night."

"I'm sorry," she said again.

His eyes bored into hers. His lips pursed. That he was still angry with her was obvious. It was also obvious that her perceived transgressions weren't the most pressing thing on his mind.

"All right, I'm gonna let that go. For whatever stupid reason, you opted to go it alone, hopped on the Metro, and went to the hotel where Starkey and Bennett picked you up. Is that right?"

Katharine looked him straight in the eyes. "Well, I rode around on the Metro for a while trying to think what to do, but otherwise that pretty much sums it up. You have to remember, I was upset."

"We found your car at the Bayou Room, by the way." It was a nightclub on King Street in Alexandria. *Good to know.* "I know you'll be relieved to know that it's safely back in your garage. I assume you and your friend had too much to drink and took a taxi home from there?"

Katharine nodded, although she really didn't remember that part. But she did remember that she and Lisa had gotten pretty sloshed.

"So then, since you didn't have a car, how did you get from the town house to the Metro station?" He shot the question at her. He knew as well as she did that the chance of walking out the door and immediately hailing a taxi in Old Town was about as good as the chance of finding the pot of gold at the end of the rainbow. Basically, it wasn't going to happen.

But she was prepared. "I walked."

She could see him mentally calculating the distance between the town house and the nearest Metro station. It was, as she had already determined, a fairly long way but doable. From his expression, he came to the same conclusion.

In other words, for now at least, her story had passed muster.

"All right, get up." His tone was brusque.

She looked up at him in surprise.

"Get up," he said again. Reaching down, he slid a hand around her elbow and practically hauled her to her feet. "We're going back to the town house now and you're going to walk me through everything that happened. I want to hear every detail. I want to know every move those assholes made. I want you to tell me every word they said. *Every word*, do you hear me?"

Katharine went cold all over at the prospect. Instinctively, she tried to pull free of the hand gripping her elbow. "Oh, no. Please. I just can't face it right now. My head hurts and—"

His face was hard as he looked at her. "You already cost me a day with your damned stupid stunt. I mean to find those jokers, and I mean to do it soon. I can't let the trail grow any colder than it is already."

Go along with anything he suggests.

She never wanted to see that town house again. But she quit trying to free herself. Instead, she deliberately relaxed the arm he was gripping way too hard and nodded.

"Okay, Ed," she said softly.

The next few hours were torturous. With Starkey and Bennett in tow, they went to the town house. The decor still felt alien, Katharine registered as they walked inside, but at least it was a familiar kind of alien now and it didn't freak her out. What did freak her out was that the scattered roses and broken vase were gone, and the entryway was once again pristine.

Katharine found this so unnerving that she had to ask about it.

Ed snorted. "I had people clean it up. Until I get a handle on what's going on here, you think I'm going to leave things for the cops to go through? It was bad enough that our people got in here late the first time. The local yokels were already all over the place before our people came in and secured the scene. By that time, what we basically ended up doing was cleaning up after their investigation." He cast a dark look at Starkey. "I'm not happy about that."

"We got here as quick as we got word," Starkey protested.

Ed snorted.

Glad to know that there was a logical explanation for the town house's uncanny ability to appear as if nothing bad had ever happened in it, Katharine reluctantly took Ed and the others on through to the kitchen and laundry room. A few small bullet holes remained in the walls, although the bullets themselves had been removed. And there was a crease in one corner of the dryer that had come from a bullet, too, she knew. The back door had been replaced with a new one. When Ed theorized that the second intruder had come in through the previous door, which they had removed from its hinges and were going over in the lab with a fine-tooth comb because its lock had been broken, Katharine didn't correct him, although she knew better. She only hoped Dan had not left fingerprints on it, or that his prints weren't traceable. Leaving Dan out of this was way more important than setting the record straight.

Katharine didn't like to think what Ed's reaction would be if he were to find out about Dan. It made her go cold inside.

Every time she looked down at the kitchen floor, her headache spiked. At her first glimpse of it, her heart had started to pound: The tiles were indeed six-inch squares. But even as she walked Ed through the attack that had killed Lisa, told him everything she could remember, pointed out the place where she had crouched beside the dryer and the spot in front of the door where Lisa had died, she kept seeing in her mind's eye the twelve-inch terra-cotta squares that she remembered from that night.

The question that kept pounding away at her brain was: *How could the floor have changed?*

It puzzled her so much that she even asked Ed, in what she hoped was an offhand manner, if the tiles had been replaced in the Saturday-morning cleanup, maybe because they were damaged or bloodstained?

He looked at Starkey.

"The tile wasn't damaged, and there wasn't that much blood. We just had it mopped," Starkey said.

Okay, time to let the subject drop. The thing was, though, mopping couldn't change twelve-inch squares to six-inch ones, and that seemed to be what had happened here. But if worrying about it was going to provide her with the answer, it would already have happened, so she tried to force the discrepancy out of her mind. Despite her best efforts, though, it gnawed at her: The image of those twelve-inch squares just wouldn't go away.

That wasn't the only thing that gnawed at her. Although deep inside she remained convinced that the original attackers had been after something other than jewelry when they had been searching for the hidden safe, she never said so. Every time she went over what Lisa's killers had said, what they had done, for Ed, she stuck to the fiction that she thought they had been looking for the safe for the valuable jewelry from the *Post* photo that was supposedly inside. *Why? Instinct?* She couldn't have said for sure. All she knew was that some internal censor in her brain kept her from making her true opinion known. The other troublesome thing was, Ed *knew*. He knew they hadn't been after jewelry. She could see it in his eyes, hear it in his voice. But he pretended that he thought the jewelry was the motivation for the attack.

It was like they were both playing a game. Only he didn't know she was playing. And she knew that she couldn't let him find out.

The thought that he might find out scared her.

As far as the second attack was concerned, he seemed as genuinely baffled as she was.

By the time ten o'clock rolled around, they had been at it for more than four hours, with only a short break for takeout Chinese. Katharine was exhausted and sick to her stomach. Her head pounded. She was emotionally wrung out, and cold to her soul.

More than she had ever wanted anything in her life, she wanted to get away from that town house—and Ed. He was relentless, picking away at everything she said, wringing every tiny detail he could from her, then demanding more.

Finally, Ed finished with her, and she was able to go upstairs and pack some clothes to take with her to Cleveland. Even her closet had been semirestored—the clothes were hung up again, although haphazardly—so it didn't take her long. Black was the order of the day, and she found a small garment bag hanging in the back of the closet to pack everything in. After that was done, she steeled herself and walked into the spare bedroom.

The bed was made, the closets and drawers and bathroom emptied. Not a trace of Lisa remained. Standing there looking around the room where Lisa had gone to bed happy only two nights before, she knew she should be feeling a great wave of grief for her murdered friend. But she didn't. What she felt was—empty.

Her memory might be back, but her emotions were still on the fritz.

But still, she meant to do what any loyal friend would do and see that Lisa's belongings got safely home. Only there were no belongings there.

"What happened to Lisa's things?" she asked when she came downstairs again. The three men stood in the living room together, and from the look of it, Ed was giving the other two orders. Ed shut up and they all glanced around at her as she walked toward them with the garment bag hanging over her shoulder.

It didn't take a genius to realize that she wasn't supposed to overhear.

"I had them packed up and sent on to her family." Ed nodded at Starkey, who took the garment bag from her. Ed hadn't objected when she had told him that she meant to go to Lisa's funeral, as long as she took Bennett with her, as he had something he needed Starkey to do. Katharine hadn't argued. She suspected that the reason he was so willing for her to go was to keep her from talking to the police, who were investigating Lisa's murder and the break-ins, for as long as possible. Maybe even until they gave up on trying to talk to her, and the crimes got put on the back burner, which tended to happen fast around D.C., where there was so much crime. "I thought that would make it easier on you. You ready to go now?"

Katharine nodded, and he slid a proprietary hand beneath her bare elbow. It was overwarm and a little sweaty, and when he rubbed the pad of his thumb caressingly over her silky inner arm, her skin crawled. Still, she didn't pull away, and his hand stayed where it was as he escorted her out the door and along the shadowy walk to the Mercedes, which was parked at the curb. Starkey and Bennett followed silently. It was a beautiful, warm summer night, with the star-studded sky and the fingernail moon reflected in the black waters of the Potomac. The ornate, historically correct street-lamp on the corner gave off a gaseous yellow glow. The soft murmur of the river was punctuated by the slap of small waves against the riverbank as a lighted dinner boat loaded down with tourists disappeared upstream. Strains of music and the sounds of revelry from the boat were still barely audible. All the nearby businesses were closed, which meant there was very little traffic. Only a few pedestrians strolled the sidewalks, most of them on the other side of the street as they branched out from the restaurants around Waterfront Park, which glowed faintly white in the distance from the strands of Christmas-tree lights that marked its entrance.

As Starkey opened the rear door of the Mercedes for her, Katharine dared a quick glance at Dan's town house: It was dark.

Where is he? The question popped into her brain unbidden, and immediately her headache ratcheted up. She couldn't think about Dan now. It was too dangerous. She had to concentrate on being with Ed.

She slid into the back and scooted across the smooth leather seat, and Ed got in beside her. The inside of the car was dark and shadowy. Katharine caught a whiff of a cigarette aroma that she hadn't noticed earlier, and realized that her sense of smell was coming back by degrees: Ed abhorred cigarettes, and if the smell had been at all strong, he would have refused to ride in the car.

As Starkey—who was driving—and Bennett got into the front seat, Ed's hand settled on her knee.

Looking down at his fleshy hand with its pale, pudgy fingers, Katharine had to battle an urge to push it away.

But she didn't. She let it stay where it was, gritting her teeth as it lightly, almost absentmindedly caressed her knee.

And thanked God that she was wearing a long skirt.

They were headed, Katharine knew, back to the apartment, which Ed had told her the Agency sometimes used to house visitors. He hadn't offered to take her home with him to his Embassy Row mansion, probably because he didn't want to hand Sharon any more ammunition in his already tense divorce negotiations, and she was thankful for that. But when they pulled into the underground garage again and, instead of getting into his car, he rode the elevator up with the rest of them, Katharine began to get a bad feeling about his plans for the rest of the evening.

She was his girlfriend. He probably meant to sleep with her. As she realized that, every muscle in her body went tense.

Desperately, Katharine tried to remember what sleeping with Ed was like. No luck. She could conjure up no memories of that at all.

Probably a good thing.

Still, she knew they had been sleeping together for thirteen months. More than a year. Clearly, she enjoyed sleeping with him, or she wouldn't do it. Anyway, she was a big girl, right? How bad could it be?

You got a Brazilian wax. Your sex life must rock.

Her stomach knotted. A shiver of distaste ran down her spine. No matter how many positive thoughts crowded into her brain—*You're in love with him; he's sexy; your job is to keep him happy*—she kept remembering that salami taste.

And those pudgy fingers.

I can't do it, she thought, panicking for real as, instead of entering the apartment with them, Starkey and Bennett stayed in the hall. Only Ed followed her inside.

"Make me a drink, would you?" he asked, loosening his tie as he walked toward the couch. "Everything you need's in the kitchen."

Katharine looked at his broad back in despair. His favorite drink was a martini, and she knew just how he liked it, but still she had to force herself to obey. Walking into the small galley kitchen, she realized that her hands were shaking. The cabinets were, indeed, well stocked. As she found what she needed, she watched out of the corner of her eye as Ed pulled off his tie and shrugged out of his coat. Clearly, he was getting comfortable, settling in for the long haul.

Mind racing, she took as long as she possibly could to make the drink. Could she plead the age-old feminine excuse of a headache, which in her case had the advantage of being absolutely true? How about exhaustion? Bubonic plague, anyone?

"What's up with that drink?" Ed called to her impatiently. He'd turned on the TV and was flipping through the channels.

Her heart lurched. Her stomach churned.

Time's up.

"On its way," she answered with false cheeriness.

I can't do this, she thought again as she picked up the martini. Her hand trembled so badly that the liquid sloshed in the glass. The thought of what was likely to happen when the drink was consumed made her want to run screaming for the hills.

Think, think, think.

But besides coming right out and saying *Not in this life, pal,* she couldn't think of anything else that was guaranteed to work. And given Ed's nature, even such a blunt rejection might not be enough. In fact, she suspected that he would react to it very, very badly.

Exiting the kitchen on legs that were by now pure jelly, she walked slowly toward the couch, casting a speculative glance at the door to the hallway on the way. Starkey and Bennett were probably still right outside. If she bolted, they'd catch her, and Ed would be pissed, and her situation would suddenly become so much worse. Anyway, she couldn't run. She shouldn't want to run.

This guy was her boyfriend.

Anything to please Ed.

But not this. Not this.

He wasn't watching her; his attention was all on the TV.

"Here you go." Her tone was bright. A smile was pasted to her lips. Her heart beat like a trapped bird's.

"Thanks." He took the glass from her, patted her ass in thanks, then spared her a glance. "You're not having one?"

"I left mine in the kitchen," she lied, then turned and fled back to the kitchen and another few minutes' respite. Gripping the edge of the counter with both hands, watching him through the wide rectangular doorway that separated the kitchen from the living and dining areas as he sipped at the martini—"It's a little dry, babe"—she felt like vomiting. She was that nauseated, that panicky.

Then she had an epiphany.

She would flood the bathroom.

The one adjoining the bedroom. Stop up the toilet good and tight, then flush, flush, flush until water was pouring over the bowl.

Lots and lots of water. A torrent, if she could manage it. Noah and his ark would be right at home.

Yes.

At the very least, Ed would have to call in Starkey and Bennett. If she did it right, it would be a job for a plumber.

And she meant to do it right.

As God was her witness, there would be no getting it on for anybody in that bedroom tonight.

With her courage in hand—and a couple of small dry sponges she'd spotted under the sink tucked into the waistband of her skirt to start the planned activities off right—she started for the bathroom.

Ed looked around at her. He was already, she saw, more than three-quarters through his drink.

"Come 'ere, babe," he said, and patted the couch beside him invitingly.

She smiled at him. It was one of the hardest things she had ever done in her life, but she did it.

"I'll be right back. Just give me a minute to freshen up."

He seemed to accept that, because he grunted and his attention returned to the TV. She was hurrying across the bedroom when his cell phone began to ring.

His ringtone was the *William Tell* overture. *That* she hadn't known, either.

"Barnes here," he answered, and then she didn't hear him say anything more because she had reached her destination and her pulse was pounding like a kettledrum in her ears.

Closing and locking the bathroom door behind her, wishing vainly for a chair or something else large and unwieldy to wedge beneath the lock for insurance, she turned an assessing eye toward the toilet.

It sat in its corner, gleaming white, innocently doing what toilets do, which is nothing, with no inkling of what she was getting ready to do to its innards. Pulling the sponges out from under her skirt, she moved toward it.

What sounded like a fist banging on the door stopped her in her tracks. She whirled, a sponge in each hand, her heart leaping into her throat.

"*Babe.*"

Eyes wide, pulse racing, she stared at the white-painted panel.

"Y-yes?"

"Got to take off. Something's come up. I probably won't make it back tonight."

Her breath left her body in a near silent *whoosh*.

"Okay," she called.

"Love ya, babe."

"Uh . . . me too."

The tension left her body like air escaping from a balloon. Her knees went weak with relief. Sinking down on the edge of the tub, a sponge still clutched in each hand, she listened to his retreating footsteps until she couldn't hear them anymore. Then she dropped her forehead to her knees.

It was the phone call, she thought, that had done it.

Talk about saved by the bell.

S he cried at Lisa's funeral. The lily-draped coffin, the grief etched onto the faces of Lisa's parents and two sisters, the weeping of the hundreds of mourners packing the church, wrung her heart. With Bennett—introduced as "a friend from work"—stone-faced beside her in the pew, she wept like her heart would break. As the minister said, it was so, so sad that such a promising young life should have been cut so brutally short. And that it had happened because of her absolutely killed her.

Afterward, as she mingled with Lisa's family and friends, some of whom were her own friends, too, from college, she was still so overcome with sorrow that she could barely talk.

Which was just as well, because she couldn't remember anyone there.

She felt like she had been beamed into an alternate universe. Some of the faces—a handful of Kappa Delts—she vaguely recognized. Everyone else, even women of her own age who came up to her and hugged her and wept on her shoulder, women who clearly recognized her and knew her, were strangers to her. She could recall nothing about them at all.

Not that anyone caught on. She hugged and cried where appropriate, and made small talk where appropriate, and in general conducted herself just as she would have if she had belonged there. But she didn't. She *didn't.*

It was a terrible, surreal feeling.

Her brain damage was back.

By the time she—and Bennett, her silent, stoic shadow—boarded the plane that would take them back to D.C., she was worn out with the whole thing. But she had come to two conclusions: Whatever was happening was clearly connected with her work and Ed, and, hey, she didn't need the job that badly, and her boyfriend now creeped her out. Time to lose the job and the guy. And, she needed to see a doctor. As in a psychiatrist, to see what was up with her head.

Because something was clearly very wrong with her.

When the plane touched down at National, Starkey was there waiting for them. Katharine took one look at him and felt like she was suffocating. Her chest constricted, and she had to work to keep her breathing even. Her nails dug into her palms with the effort she made to stay calm.

Her mind was going a thousand miles a minute. She kept her expression carefully serene.

As she got into the back of Mercedes, which Starkey had brought to pick them up, and Bennett closed the door behind her, she felt like an animal caught in a trap.

If she never saw either of them—or Ed—again, it would be way too soon. The problem was, she knew as well as she knew the sun would rise in the morning that they wouldn't just let her say *buh-bye* and walk away.

Whatever it was that was going on here, she was in way too deep for that.

"I want to go to the town house," she said clearly from the backseat when they were on the access road and it became obvious, as Starkey, who was driving, changed lanes in anticipation of turning right, which would lead into D.C., that they were probably heading for the apartment again. "I need to get some fresh clothes."

Starkey and Bennett, in the passenger seat, exchanged glances. Bennett shrugged. Starkey glanced in the rearview mirror at her.

"Sure," he said, and changed lanes again. Minutes later they were heading toward Old Town.

According to the clock in the dashboard, it was eight twenty-one p.m. by the time the Mercedes nosed into one of the parking spaces beside the garages that were allotted for visitors. On a Tuesday in August, though, that meant that Old Town was still thronged with tourists. It didn't get fully dark until almost ten, and the long, golden evenings were the best time of the day. The temperature had, as was usual as night approached, dipped from sweltering to pleasantly languid. While the main thoroughfares were crowded with visitors, the alley and backyards around the garages were full of neighborhood people barbecuing and playing with their children and walking their pets and taking out trash. The cheerful sounds of happy people at play made her unhappily aware of how very on edge she felt. The scent of grilling meat—her sense of smell was definitely back—hung in the air. Katharine realized that she was hungry. Her last meal—airplane food—she had left almost untouched.

Food, however, was not on the agenda for the moment. Fishing in her purse for her garage door opener, Katharine opened the overhead door, walked through the garage past her car—*thank God it's here*—and up the walk toward her back door. The backyards nearest to her own were empty. A squirrel in the maple tree chattered, presumably at the barking golden retriever down the block. Starkey and Bennett formed a solid wall of silent suits behind her. Unable to help herself, she cast a quick look at Dan's town house. The curtains were closed. There was no sign that he was at home.

Her head started to pound. She was not supposed to think about Dan.

Unlocking the new back door, refusing to allow her mind to stray from the present to Lisa's death in front of the previous door, she walked on across those accursed tiles and headed toward the stairs.

"I'm going to take a shower before I do anything else," she said, pausing at the bottom of the stairs to look at her expressionless twin shadows, who were right behind her. By this time, she was thinking of them as wardens rather than bodyguards. "Why don't you sit down in the living room and make yourselves comfortable? I'll be down when I've changed."

The two exchanged looks. Starkey shrugged, and then they both headed toward the living room. Barely suppressing a relieved sigh, Katharine climbed the stairs. Forget taking a shower: She'd already had one that morning. Forget changing clothes, too: She didn't have that kind of time. Anyway, the black Armani pantsuit she was wearing with a white T-shirt and pumps worked fine. Shed the jacket, and she was casual. Keep it on, and she could go anywhere. It was a nice, versatile outfit to run for her life in.

Because that was what she meant to do. If she stayed, at the very least she was going to have to deal with Ed. He wasn't going to be happy when she dumped him, but that was just too bad. She knew something had changed with her, knew her mind wasn't where it had been even a week before, but then she supposed a brush with death tended to do that to a person. In any case, her personal relationship with Ed was over.

No way was she ever, under any circumstances, sleeping with him again. The very idea made her want to heave.

Once she gave Ed the boot, her job was probably history, too. Certainly, he would no longer want her as his personal assistant. Anyway, the idea of spending even one more day sucking up to a powerful man—any powerful man—was less than appealing. She wanted more than that from life.

Plus, there was the whole somebody-was-trying-to-kill-her thing. Without Starkey and Bennett—who would be gone with Ed—she was vulnerable. She didn't kid herself about that.

They'd come after her twice. What was that saying about the third time being a charm?

The simple, obvious solution was to do what she had meant to do from the first moments after she had regained consciousness in the hospital: get in her car and drive far, far away.

She grabbed a clean set of underwear and a fresh, pale blue T-shirt from her bedroom, stuffed them and her shoes—clattering around in heels was never a good idea when one was trying to sneak out—in her purse, and crept back down the stairs.

The TV was on. She could hear it. She could even see its reflection in the glass fronting the sunset painting in the entry hall. The reflection wasn't clear enough to allow her to make sure Starkey and Bennett were plopped on the couch in front of it, but she had to assume they were. Holding her breath, heart tripping like a drunken frat boy, her stomach tightening with every step, she made it all the way down to the entry hall and sidled around the newel post, her eyes glued to the living-room door. The TV was loud; they were watching a baseball game. That was good. With every nerve ending she possessed on high alert, and the sounds of a TV crowd cheering for God-knew-what filling her ears, she crept toward the kitchen, her bare feet soundless on the hardwood floor. She saw at a glance that the kitchen was empty, and scuttled across it like a crab on hot sand. Slipping through the laundry room, her heart in her throat now, she risked a quick glance back over her shoulder—nothing—and eased open the back door. Every click and squeak was as excruciating as a shout.

Nothing happened. Nobody came. Closing it behind her—*carefully, carefully*—she fled down the steps and along the walk to the garage, her keys already in her hand, casting fearful looks over her shoulder all the way. The soft, golden evening and happy sounds and good smells were lost on her now. Every bit of her focus was on getting away.

Almost there.

Heart racing, breathing far too fast, she opened the access door to the garage, closed it behind her, raced to her car, and got in, locking the doors behind her. With a quick exit in mind, she had left the overhead door up. Hands shaking, she put the key in the ignition and turned the engine over.

Then she was outta there.

Oh my God, I made it. I made it.

There were too many people out and about for her to gun it like she wanted to. The alley was too narrow, the pavement too uneven. The kid hitting a tennis ball against the side of a garage down the street did not deserve to be roadkill. Neither did the little old lady struggling to push a wheelbarrow loaded with plants to her neighbor's yard. She might be sweating despite the blasting air conditioner, her hands might be gripping the steering wheel so tightly that her knuckles showed white, but still she had to keep only light pressure on the accelerator.

At least until she got out of the damned alley.

When at last she reached Wilkes, she had to wait what felt like forever for a break in the traffic, and then, pulse racing, biting her tongue in an effort to stay calm, she shot out through the tiny hole in the slipstream and turned left toward the expressway.

And made it about half a block before getting stuck in traffic.

The narrow, cobbled street was packed. Katharine saw that a bright red local bus was making its leisurely way along, stopping at various shops to let some people off and others on. The line of traffic caught behind it, which included her, was moving at a snail's pace—when it moved. A lot of the time it didn't. There was no way to pass; the other lane was equally busy. And the sidewalk—yes, she even considered driving up on the sidewalk to get around—was full to bursting with shoppers, folks sitting at small, round tables scarfing down pizza in front of tourist fave Ye Olde Pizzeria, and a ghost walking tour. She knew that was what the moving clump of approximately thirty people was, because the costumed guide was holding up a sign.

If traffic didn't start moving soon, she thought, she would have a heart attack, and then she could be one of the ghost tour's featured attractions.

Her pulse raced. Her stomach twisted itself into a knot so tight it was almost painful. But there was nothing to do. Her only option was to just sit there, crawling forward as conditions permitted. She didn't even honk her horn.

Then the whole line of traffic came to a stop, for a good cause this time as the bus, swinging wide, slowly, ponderously turned right at the intersection at the top of the hill.

There was a sharp tap on the window beside her head.

She almost jumped through the roof. Her head jerked around, and to her horror she found herself looking straight at Bennett, who was glaring at her through the glass.

19

K atharine almost had a mini–nervous breakdown right there.
Busted. Oh, God, think fast. What to say?

In that instant, while she was still gaping at Bennett, while her heart was doing calisthenics and her pulse was shooting up through the stratosphere, her mind went into overdrive. She could refuse to roll down the window, and as soon as the cursed bus got out of the way—which would, hopefully, unclog the traffic—put the pedal to the metal and scoot on out of there.

With Starkey and Bennett behind her, and the rest of the Agency pretty much at Ed's command, the chances of getting away without being tailed and/or actually stopped were just about nil.

She could jump from the car and try to lose herself among the crowds, even in a pinch appealing to shopkeepers, tourists, everyone and anyone to protect her from the big, bad men who were after her.

Who just happened to work for the CIA. Who would flash badges if necessary and blather something about her being taken into custody for her own protection.

The shopkeepers and everybody else would give her up like she was contagious.

Same with calling the police. The Agency outranked them. Even if she talked them into shielding her for a little while—by offering to talk to the detectives, say, about Lisa's murder—Ed would soon get her back. She would be foolish to allow herself any illusions about that.

That left Dan. Her good neighbor had helped her before. But . . . but he was a doctor, and no match for CIA.

Just thinking about running to him made her head pound.

Anyway, she had agreed to leave him out of this. If Ed ever found out about his existence, Dan would be in danger.

Katharine faced the horrible truth: She was on her own. This was like her own personal episode of *Survivor*: She had to outwit, outplay, outlast.

Bennett tapped on the window again, harder than before. Now his face was scrunched up into a ferocious frown.

Game on.

Rolling down her window, she had no trouble coming up with a ferocious frown of her own.

"What?" she snapped.

His eyes widened slightly. Her tone had taken him aback, she was pleased to see.

It took a couple of seconds, but he recovered. "You trying to ditch us again?"

"You're damn right I'm trying to ditch you. I've had one or both of you with me for the last three days. You know what? I need some space." The bus was out of the way at last. Traffic—*Thank you, God*—was beginning to move. She started to roll up the window again. "Go away."

"*Wait.*"

Bennett stuck his hand in the window, preventing her from rolling it up all the way. She thought about continuing regardless, but making him truly angry, which crushing his fingers was almost guaranteed to do, would be stupid. The car was moving now, slowly, as successive vehicles took their turn at the stop sign, and Bennett walked along beside her, his hand folded over the top of the glass.

The scowl she gave him was fierce. "I said *go away*."

"But . . ." The ferocious frown had been replaced by a look of confusion. "Where are you going?"

"If you must know, to get my cat. Look, I'll meet you back at the town house in about half an hour, okay? I just need to be by myself for a little while to clear my head." She cast him an irritated look. "And by the way, I'm rolling up the window."

"But . . ."

This time, as she stepped on the accelerator, she kept her finger on the window button. Bennett snatched his hand back, then just stood there in the middle of the street, frowning after her as she took her turn at the stop sign at last. The black Mercedes was, she saw, some six cars back. She had never even seen it coming.

Taking a deep breath, trying to will her heart to slow its frantic pounding, she drove through the intersection like the coolest cucumber around, and watched in the rearview mirror as Bennett turned and scurried between the opposing lanes of traffic until he reached the Mercedes. Slapping a hand on its hood, presumably to warn Starkey of what he intended to do, he darted in front of the car, opened the passenger-side door, and ducked inside.

At that moment, Katharine crested the rise and was, briefly, out of sight. The Beltway on-ramp was close, she knew. The discreet sign with its accompanying arrow at the side of the road made that clear. Wistfully, she thought about just ignoring the Mercedes behind her, pulling onto the expressway, and roaring west, as far as Saint Louis, maybe, or even California. Forget this nightmare: She could start a whole new life.

But she knew Ed would never let her go. Not like this. If she went, she would have to have enough time to get well away, and then she would have to hide. The thing to do, then, was outsmart him. She would continue to act all huffy and fed up with the lack of privacy—not that it was much of a stretch—and in the meantime she would go pick up Muffy and see if, maybe, Cindy wanted to visit for a while. Like several hours. Maybe even order in pizza and watch a movie or something. The thing was, tomorrow was Wednesday. A workday. Under the circumstances, *she* had taken the week off, but Ed was still going in, and when he was working he was in the office every weekday morning by seven. Probably he wouldn't want to stay up as long as she was planning to stay out.

If she could just avoid a showdown over their relationship tonight, tomorrow might provide her with another chance to get away. As long as she kept her cool and didn't let anyone suspect that escaping was what she was trying to do.

Traffic wasn't a whole lot better on the other side of the intersection, she found to her dismay, and a moment later discovered the reason: POTUS—the president of the United States—was on the move. Police cars, lights flashing, blocked the street as the presidential motorcade, flags flying, rolled past on South Alfred Street.

Just another Tuesday evening in and around the capital.

Glancing in the rearview mirror, she saw the Mercedes top the rise. *Okay, forget trying to give them the slip.* She was definitely going to get her cat. The problem was that she couldn't remember where her good friend Cindy lived.

Having brain damage was starting to get very, very old, but there didn't seem to be a whole lot she could do about it. Luckily, the solution occurred to her almost instantly: Cindy's phone number was programmed into her phone. If she input the number into the Lexus's GPS system, it would come up with the address and direct her there, too.

Muffy, here I come, she thought, and reached for her phone. A few minutes later, with the GPS's mechanical voice directing her, she left Old Town behind for its more modern surroundings. Cindy, it turned out, lived out toward Franconia in a fifties-era subdivision. The houses were sturdy brick or stone ranches; the lawns were small and dotted with such child-friendly amenities as aboveground swimming pools and plastic playhouses and swing sets, and children were everywhere.

Although she could conjure up a vague picture of Cindy in her mind, that was all she could do. She knew that they were good friends, but she couldn't remember anything else about her. Not what she did for a living, not how long they had known each other, not whether Cindy was married or had a family.

The realization made her stomach tighten.

Cindy's house was the third one from the left on Woodland Street. It was a modest brick ranch with a fifties-era picture window, a small front stoop, and an attached garage. As Katharine pulled into the short driveway that ended at the closed garage door, she glanced back the way she had come. Sure enough, there was the Mercedes, just turning down the street.

Katharine realized that her palms were sweaty. Her heart rate was up. Knowing that Starkey and Bennett were following her on Ed's orders was really starting to put her on edge. Turning off the engine, she shed her jacket and put on her shoes, then, in T-shirt and slacks, headed for the front door. En route to the house, she had tried giving Cindy a call to let her know that she was on her way, but the answering machine had picked up. Still, she could see through the open front curtains that the TV was on—a cartoon was playing—so she felt fairly confident that someone was home.

"Hi," she said to the man who opened the door in response to her knock. He looked to be in his early thirties, average height, a little on the stocky side, with short, tobacco-brown hair and a round, jovial-looking face. He was wearing khaki shorts, a blue Orioles T-shirt, and flip-flops. A big-eyed, blond-haired toddler in a diaper and pink T-shirt peeked up at her from behind his legs. "Is Cindy home?"

"She's at the hospital," the man said. "Lindsey's finally having that baby."

From the way he just opened the screen for her to enter, she presumed they knew each other. At a guess, she would say that she was looking at Cindy's family, her husband and little girl. Also, he clearly thought she knew all about Lindsey, whoever that was, and her baby, when the truth was she didn't have a clue.

"Finally," she echoed, figuring she was pretty safe with that. The living room was creamy yellow with lots of chintz. A pink baby blanket and pillow were on the couch. A half-full baby bottle sat on the oak coffee table.

"Oh, listen, I heard what happened with you. Man, I'm sorry. That kind of thing's why we moved out to the burbs."

"Thanks. Yeah, it was bad."

As he closed the door behind her, Katharine got a glimpse of the Mercedes pulling to a stop across the street. She felt herself tensing. Her pulse kicked it up a notch. Her stomach did the full pretzel. With Cindy at the hospital for who knew how long, the prospects of staying at her house for hours to avoid Ed didn't look good. In fact, she was clearly going to have to come up with plan B.

"You here for your cat?" His eyes slid away from her as if he had spotted something. "Oh, wait, there it is. I gotta tell you, Cindy loves that thing."

Katharine looked, and there in the doorway that led into a hall that presumably led to the bedrooms stood Muffy. Almost the size of a beagle, the cat was a puffball of fluffy white hair that nearly reached the floor. Ears, paws, tail, feet, and flat, round face were charcoal-gray. From the midst of all that gray, a pair of china-blue eyes stared at her.

"Hi, Muffy," she achieved by way of a greeting. The strongest emotional reaction she felt upon seeing her pet was surprise that the thing was so big. But of course she had known that. She had just forgotten, was all. Just like she had forgotten so many other things.

Her throat threatened to close up at the thought. Knowing that chunks of her life were missing was really starting to get to her.

"The carrier and food and everything's in the kitchen," the guy continued cheerily. He plopped down on the couch, and the little girl climbed up on his lap. A moment later, the child was settled cozily in the crook of his arm with the bottle in her mouth and the pink blanket over her while they both watched TV.

Katharine realized that she was expected to just help herself.

Okay, then.

She walked toward the cat, who waited until she had almost reached it to turn around and stalk away, tail held haughtily high. It led the way into the kitchen, which was small and cheerfully cluttered. Near the back door was a tan plastic pet crate: obviously Muffy's carrier. Two small ceramic dishes nearby held dry cat food and water. A yellow bag of Meow Mix, its top rolled so that it was clear the bag was only about a quarter full, sat on top of the crate.

Katharine cleaned the dishes, then picked up the food and the cat carrier and placed them both on the counter. She put the dishes inside the carrier, which still left plenty of room for the cat. All things being equal, she decided not to take a chance on carrying Muffy outside in her arms, or letting him—her . . .

With a quick widening of her eyes, Katharine realized that she didn't know whether the cat was a male or a female. Jesus, how could she forget a thing like that about her own pet? Her breathing came a little faster as she chalked up one more inexplicable hole in her memory.

This is so not good.

Okay, so she had a cat of undetermined gender. That was not the point. The point was that she didn't want to let Muffy ride loose in the car. There was too much potential for disaster.

With everything in readiness, she looked around for the cat.

Muffy was crouched under the oval-shaped maple table, looking up at her through the chair legs.

"Here, Muffy. Here, kitty."

That earned her a disdainful swish of a tail.

"Come on, Muffy," she tried again, going down on all fours and stealthily—at least, she was trying to be stealthy, although with the cat watching her every move stealthy didn't seem to be happening—scooting the chair Muffy was crouched behind out of the way. "Here, kitty, kitty."

As soon as Katharine reached toward it, the cat bolted, hightailing it for the bedrooms, nails scrabbling over the hardwood floor in its haste.

"*Dammit.*" Katharine stared after the cat. Clearly Muffy hadn't been pining away with longing for its owner to come back.

"She's probably under our bed," Cindy's husband called from the living room as Katharine got to her feet. "That's where she goes when Sammy Lou here chases her."

Katharine took a deep, calming breath.

"Thanks," she called back.

She had learned two things, Katharine thought as she found the master bedroom and surveyed the large bed, under which her cat presumably lurked: Cindy's daughter was named, or nicknamed, Sammy Lou, and Muffy was a she.

Good to know.

The bedroom had cream walls, oak furniture, and a rose-and-cream gingham spread over the king-size bed. It also had a dust ruffle that reached clear to the hardwood floor. Katharine had a thought, and closed the door behind her. Then, crossing to the bed, she dropped to her knees and lifted the simple white ruffle. Muffy was under there, all right, crouched right in the middle. Those blue eyes fixed on Katharine's face, shining balefully at her through the under-the-bed gloom. Taking a stab at reading cat body language, she interpreted that look to mean that Muffy was not particularly pleased to see her.

Well, guess what? The feeling was starting to be mutual. If it hadn't been for Starkey and Bennett out there waiting to see her emerge with her pet, she would have let the animal visit with Cindy's family for a while longer.

But Starkey and Bennett were out there, which meant she needed the cat.

"Here, kitty," Katharine tried again, infusing her voice with as much enthusiasm as she could muster. "Come here, Muffy."

Muffy twitched her tail, but that was the only part of her that moved. Katharine extended an arm in her direction, saw that that wasn't going to get the job done, cursed under her breath, and dropped to her stomach. Then, thankful for the hard smoothness of the floor, which made the job easier, she started sliding under the bed.

For the first time, she was truly glad she was now so skinny. Otherwise she wouldn't have fit. The bed couldn't have been much more than a foot off the floor.

Unmoving, eyes gleaming even brighter than the ring on Katharine's hand, the cat watched her scoot toward it. Then, when she was within inches of being close enough to grab it, Muffy took off, scrambling for the far side of the bed.

"No, " Katharine cried, and lunged after it like a crocodile after a duck. She caught it, too, her fingers raking through inches-thick fluff and hooking around—*yes, hooray!*—a collar that had been hidden in all that hair.

Shouldn't I have known about the collar?

Muffy promptly turned around and hissed at her with all the venom of a cobra, and Katharine let the whole I-am-losing-my-mind thing go as she went eyeball to eyeball with a totally ticked-off cat.

"It's okay, Muffy. Good girl, Muffy."

Hiss or no hiss, Muffy wasn't getting away. Luckily, the cat showed no propensity to actually attack. It made like a dust mop with claws, staying belly to the floor and trying to dig in for traction as Katharine grabbed hold with her other hand, too, and pulled the cat toward her. Keeping one set of fingers locked around the collar just in case, Katharine inched her way back out from under the bed, pulling Muffy, who dragged her claws over the wood every inch of the way, with her. Finally, they were both out from under the bed, and, grimacing at the necessity, she picked the cat up.

Muffy promptly hissed at her again.

There was an identification tag or something dangling from the collar, a longish gray plastic rectangle almost hidden in all that fur, and Katharine was tempted to check it out, to make sure her name was on the tag and she really was the cat's owner.

Because Muffy seemed to remember her even less well than she remembered Muffy.

But she didn't bother, because she knew already what the tag would say: Muffy was hers.

Apparently, they had some owner-cat bonding issues.

Sighing, Katharine tentatively petted the cat, who hissed right on cue, carried her to the kitchen, and stuffed—there was no other word for it, because Muffy resisted valiantly—her inside her carrier. Then, with Muffy glaring angrily out through the metal grate, she picked up the carrier—it was heavy—and the bag of cat food and headed toward the front door.

"You got everything?" Cindy's husband asked as she walked back into the living room. He was whispering, because Sammy Lou had fallen asleep in his arms.

"Yes, thanks. And tell Cindy thanks," Katharine said.

He nodded, and Katharine quietly let herself out the front door.

The first thing she saw was that it was full twilight now, with the kind of soft, gray dusk that happened only in summer. Lights had come on inside the houses. The smell of freshly cut grass hung in the air. Fireflies blinked like tiny white Christmas lights all up and down the block. Cicadas sang. Other insects whirred. Noisy children played hide-and-seek a couple yards over, and a woman stood on a porch toward the end of the block, yelling for somebody named Eric. Presumably, Katharine thought, a mother summoning her son home.

The second thing she saw was that the Mercedes was still parked in front of the house across the street.

Okay, time to come up with plan B.

Problem was, she couldn't seem to think of anything right at the moment.

Eyeballing the black bulk of the waiting car, feeling Starkey and Bennett watching her although she couldn't see them through the tinted windows, she warded off an attack of the shivers and quickly loaded Muffy and the cat food into the backseat before sliding into the driver's seat herself. Starting the car, turning on the lights, she reversed down the driveway, then headed for the top of Woodland Drive. From there she turned north toward Old Town.

She never made it. A car emerging from a side street pulled out in front of her just before she reached the next stop sign, the last one she would come to before entering the outskirts of Alexandria in fifteen minutes or so. From the stop sign on in, it was pure windy country road. Gorgeous during the day but, she had to admit, a little spooky at night. Of course, with Batman and Robin on her tail, at least she didn't have to worry about random kooks and carjackers.

Lucky me.

At first she didn't notice the car in front of her particularly. What she did notice is that when she stopped behind it, waiting for whoever was driving it to look both ways at the stop sign and then proceed, it stayed put.

Besides that car and the Mercedes behind her, there was not another vehicle in sight. The intersection was clear, and yet the car—it was black or navy blue, some kind of large, dark sedan—didn't move. It was full night now, and the warm lights of the subdivision had been left behind. Except for three sets of headlights stabbing through the darkness, illuminating grassy berms and a tangle of scrub trees and one another, the area was dark as pitch.

There was not, Katharine registered idly as she glanced around, trying to see what the holdup was, a moon tonight.

Bam.

The explosion was so sudden, so shocking, so unexpected that Katharine screamed and jumped. Her heart leaped, and her head swiveled instinctively toward the source of the sound. She was just in time to watch round pellets of glass rain like a downpour of diamonds into her backseat.

Her back passenger-side window had just shattered. Katharine was still registering the seemingly impossible truth of that when a hand—a man's hand, wide across the knuckles and tanned—and dark-suited arm thrust through the opening and pressed the button to unlock the front passenger-side door. Just as quick as that.

Get out of here.

Her instincts screamed it, but it was too late. Even as she looked frantically forward, even as her leg muscles tightened in preparation for shifting from the brake to the gas and stomping that thing through the floor, she realized that the car in front of her had her blocked in.

In the same instant, the front passenger door opened and a man slid into the seat beside her, closing the door behind himself.

Starkey.

Her heart was just starting to ease off on its frantic thudding, and she was just getting ready to heave a sigh of relief when she saw that he had drawn his gun.

It was pointing at her.

Her jaw dropped. Her eyes rounded. She stared at him in disbelief.

"Mr. Barnes wants to see you," he said.

20

W hat the hell do you think you're doing?" Katharine yelled. She slapped her palms against the steering wheel for emphasis. "You just broke my window!"

Starkey's expression never changed. It was pure stone face from the moment he slipped in beside her. "I said, Mr. Barnes wants to see you."

"Well, good for Mr. Barnes." The car up ahead still wasn't moving. Its taillights glowed at her through the darkness like a pair of evil red eyes. Not that it mattered: For the time being, they were going nowhere. "You can go ahead and get out now. You're not riding with me. And I'm sending you a bill for the window."

"I don't think you understand the situation. Mr. Barnes told me to bring you to him. Any way I have to." He made a small threatening gesture with the gun, which was black and businesslike-looking and pointed straight at her in a very menacing way.

"Oh, you're scaring me now." She glared at him. "Get out of my car."

Out of the corner of her eye she saw a flash of light, and even as she frowned at Starkey she realized that a man had gotten out of the passenger side of the dark sedan that was blocking her in and, in fact, was at that moment crossing in front of her car.

"You don't want to drive, you can ride in the back with him." Starkey nodded at the man who was by then looming up outside her window. She went cold all over as she realized that the car in front of them was there specifically to assist Starkey and Bennett in escorting her to Ed. Apparently, he was no longer prepared to take a chance on her giving them the slip. A single glance through the glass at the newcomer told Katharine that he was one more short-haired guy in a suit. She was really starting to hate the type. "And believe me, you don't want to ride with him."

The guy pecked on her window. Using the passenger-door controls, Starkey rolled it down. This guy was older than either Starkey or Bennett, in his late forties maybe, with a blunt-featured, heavy-jowled face that made her think of a bulldog.

"Everything under control?" he asked Starkey.

"Who are you?" Katharine demanded, determined not to lose control of the situation even though adrenaline was starting to race through her system and her pulse was starting to pound. This, she was beginning to feel, had the potential to be bad.

The man smiled at her, his eyes, which were small and brown, crinkling at the corners. Something about that smile made her skin crawl.

"Name's Hendricks, Miss Lawrence. Carl Hendricks. Pleased to meet you."

Katharine couldn't say the same, but she did manage a curt nod.

"Drive or ride?" Starkey asked.

Okay, getting away from them didn't seem to be a possibility at the moment. At least driving would give her some options.

"I'll drive."

Starkey nodded at Hendricks, who opened the back door, flooding the interior with light.

"What's this?" He was talking about the cat carrier, which was in the seat behind Katharine.

"My cat," she said, at the same time as Starkey said, "Cat."

"I like cats. Oh, he's a big one. Pretty, too." Hendricks moved the carrier over to the adjoining seat. There was a crunch as it came to rest, and Katharine realized that it was now sitting on pebbles of glass. Hendricks got in and closed the door. The interior light went off again. "Hey, kitty. Nice kitty."

Through the rearview mirror, Katharine saw him stick his fingers through the grate at the front of the carrier, presumably with the intention of petting the nice kitty. The response he got was a virulent hiss, and with a muttered curse, Hendricks quickly snatched back his hand.

Despite everything, Katharine almost smiled.

The car in front of them got under way at last, turning left toward Alexandria. Starkey nodded to Katharine, and she followed suit. Behind them, the Mercedes, with Bennett driving, brought up the rear. By her count, it was four case officers—if Hendricks and whoever was driving the other car were, indeed, case officers—to one personal assistant—namely, her. The odds of getting away anytime soon weren't looking good.

"Where are we going?" Katharine asked, trying to sound more confident than she felt.

Starkey shrugged. "You'll see."

Not a reassuring answer.

"Just for the record, I don't appreciate this."

"So take it up with the boss."

Therein, Katharine feared, lay the problem. Clearly Ed had okayed the use of force to bring her to him, or this wouldn't be happening. Despite Starkey's gun, she didn't really fear him or Bennett. But Hendricks— Hendricks was new, and not in a good kind of way. Something about Hendricks worried her. Then it hit her: He didn't look like a CIA case officer. He wasn't fit enough. And there was an undefinable something about him. . . . For a moment, she couldn't quite put her finger on it. Then she realized: He wasn't professional enough.

So who and what was he?

Her hands were tight around the wheel and the pit of her stomach felt like it was in free fall as she drove through the dark Virginia countryside, considering that question. A breeze had come up, blowing into the car, ruffling her hair, and carrying the scent of crops and the occasional bug with it. The sound of it rushing past the broken window filled the silence as no one spoke. She was virtually blind to the fields of corn and tobacco undulating like rustling black oceans on either side of the road, to the occasional lighted crossroads, to the slash of headlights as oncoming traffic appeared and then passed them by, leaving them alone in the darkness once again.

It occurred to her that, in general, Ed was not averse to operating outside the box.

Maybe Hendricks was part of what was outside the box.

The thought gave her cold chills.

And she realized that, all the happy talk in her head notwithstanding, she was afraid of Ed.

Just as the bright lights of Alexandria appeared tantalizingly on the horizon, the sedan in front of her turned left at a crossroad, heading away from the city. When Katharine looked longingly in the opposite direction, Starkey told her to follow the sedan. They were not, it seemed, going home—or any place where she might be able to crash the car into a lamppost, say, and reasonably expect people to gather around to help.

For another twenty minutes or so they drove north on back roads while Katharine's tension increased like steam building inside a kettle. In the back, Hendricks was murmuring, presumably to Muffy, who made no audible response. They passed a sign reading *McLean, 2 miles* that got her hopes up. The vast complex that was CIA headquarters was located there, and she guessed that must be their destination. Which, all things considered, was a good thing. There would be armies of people around. Nothing too bad could happen there.

Instead, just at the edge of town, so close to people that she could see the golden arches of McDonald's right down the road, the sedan turned into a used-car lot just ahead. *Big Jim's Pre-owned Cars* was spelled out in giant neon letters arching over the entrance. The neon wasn't lit, which

Katharine presumed meant the lot was closed. It was, after all, nearly eleven by then. But big halogen lights glowed down on the rows of cars, each of which, as far as she could tell, had its price painted in white on the windshield. The term *junkers* came to mind as her gaze ran over some of them, but that wasn't what was worrying her.

A used-car lot didn't seem like a place she wanted to go.

Her stomach lurched. Her hands tightened on the wheel. Her gaze shot to Starkey.

"A used-car lot? You've got to be kidding me," she said. By this time, the attitude in her voice was pure bravado.

"Pull in." His eyes were hard on her face. His mouth was tense and unsmiling. She could sense Hendricks leaning toward her, sense the threat he represented. Doing anything other than what she was told was not an option: If she didn't, her situation just became much worse. At this point, she could still take the high ground, claiming that she had left only to go fetch her cat. None of them—not even Ed—were mind readers. They had no way of knowing that she had ever intended anything else.

Whatever was coming, she was just going to have to try to bluff her way through it.

Her heart started knocking in her chest. It was an effort to control her breathing, make it seem normal. The key, she thought, was not to reveal the slightest hint of fear.

Although she was scared to death.

She pulled into the car lot, and at Starkey's direction followed the sedan past the small, trailer-like sales office toward the rear. The wheels bounced over uneven pavement that, once the sales lot was passed, turned to gravel. A squat brick building sat in the shadows at the far end of the lot, with an open field ending in a line of scraggly trees stretching behind it. More trees formed a narrow strip of woods on either side of the building, which had three big white garage doors and a smaller, people-sized door in front and, over them, in more unlit neon letters, a huge sign that read *Service*.

A handful of cars were parked in front of the building, cars without prices on their windshields. Of course, the sign did say *Service*, so it was possible that that was exactly what the cars were there for. But she didn't think so.

Looking around, Katharine felt her throat go dry. There was no chance that they'd stopped here because somebody needed to get, say, an oil change. She could practically feel the bad vibes emanating from the building.

The sedan pulled up at the end of the line of cars. Starkey indicated that she should park beside it.

She did, turned off the car, and got out, standing there all alone for a moment, her heels sinking into the gravel as she took a deep, she hoped calming, breath and cast discreet looks in all directions. Despite this place's location on the outskirts of town, from where she stood there was nothing to be seen except dark fields and trees behind and to the sides of the building, and, in front of it, the deserted used-car lot. They were totally isolated, a speck of nothing beneath the vast dark sky.

In space no one can hear you scream. The words popped into her head out of nowhere. They applied, she realized, to this place, too. And she was as sure as it was possible to be that it was no accident.

By then, Starkey and Hendricks were getting out of the car. Another short-haired man in a suit exited the dark sedan just as the Mercedes, tires crunching, pulled in beside them. Katharine spared the Mercedes no more than a glance as Bennett cut the engine and got out, too. Instead, she took another long, assessing look at the building. It was boxlike and unremarkable, a nothing place, like hundreds of thousands of other boxlike brick buildings the world over. The faintest hint of white light showed under the garage doors. Someone was definitely inside—Ed, most likely, and probably other people, too.

Swallowing hard, she had to battle the sudden urge to turn and run. But Hendricks stood right behind her, practically breathing down her neck, and Starkey was coming around the front of the car toward her. Bennett was moving in from the right, and the fourth man stood waiting, apparently for them to head his way, on her left. They would catch her in a heartbeat if she tried.

And she would lose the whole presumption-of-innocence thing she had going on, which was the only defense she had against whatever was coming.

Her throat was dry, and her heart was beating far too fast.

"Let's go," Starkey said. He reached for her arm, but she jerked it sharply out of his reach and he didn't force the issue. Head held high, she started walking toward the building, with Starkey beside her and Hendricks bringing up the rear.

A piteous meow reached her ears.

"Muffy," she exclaimed, stopping dead and glancing over her shoulder. "What about Muffy?"

This time, Starkey did grab her arm, his fingers digging in just above her elbow. Katharine glared at him, but she didn't try to break free. She didn't want to not succeed, and then end up as his de facto prisoner.

"The cat?" He was already urging her forward again. In response to the pressure on her arm, Katharine reluctantly began to move. "The cat'll be fine."

"Yeah, don't worry," Hendricks said. "I like cats."

Somehow, Katharine didn't find this reassuring.

Starkey fished his cell phone from his pocket with his free hand, and they stepped onto the concrete walk that ran the length of the building. He pressed a button, and she could hear the call being dialed.

"We're here," Starkey said into the phone a moment later, then listened briefly before continuing with "yes" and—pause—"right now."

Then, as they reached the building, he clicked the phone shut, put it in his pocket, and punched a code into a keypad next to the people-sized door. There was a beep and a click. Then Starkey turned the knob and they entered.

The interior of the building looked like—big surprise—an extra-large garage. There were three work bays, complete with car lifts and banks of tools. A red Jeep sat in the far bay, its hood up. The other two were empty. Overhead, rows of fluorescent lights gave off a white glow. The floor was smooth concrete. The walls were gray-painted concrete block. A rattling hum filled the air, courtesy of the huge industrial fan mounted in the far corner. It apparently was designed to pull in fresh outside air through the small, rectangular windows located near the ceiling. But none of the windows was open, and the result was that while there was a breeze strong enough to stir her hair, the temperature was nearly as warm inside as out and the air smelled stale.

"What is this place?" she asked Starkey, who was already steering her toward a metal door to her left. He shrugged. Not that it mattered. Even as she asked the question, she had a feeling she already knew the answer: The car lot was an Agency "front," a place where they could take care of business away from the eyes and ears of the couple thousand people who worked at headquarters. The car lot, and maybe even the garage, might well be operated as legitimate businesses. No one would raise an eyebrow at lots of people and vehicles coming and going at all hours of the day and night. But somewhere on the premises—downstairs, she assumed, because the door Starkey opened led to a set of stairs that went down—Agency business would be conducted. The kind of business that was best taken care of, to put it in Agency parlance, "off the reservation."

The rattling fan would make an excellent source of masking noise—the kind of noise that kept conversations and other sounds from being picked up by the increasingly refined surveillance equipment that could, if not thwarted, listen in on a private, low-voiced discussion in a closed room from inside another building a quarter of a mile away.

The thought made her blood run cold.

"Hey, you think maybe I could get a good deal on a used car?" Hendricks asked in a jocular tone. "My girlfriend's kid's getting ready to turn sixteen."

Nobody answered. For everyone but Hendricks, the mood seemed to be growing more tense by the second. They were all walking down the stairs now, their feet making hollow clanging noises on the metal treads, which had no risers, so the concrete floor at the bottom was clearly visible with every step. Katharine was in the lead, moving with care because the stairs were steep and her legs were jelly, with Starkey, who had been forced to let go of her arm because of the narrowness of the stairwell, right behind her. Bennett and Hendricks followed in that order, with the newcomer bringing up the rear. The stairwell was fully enclosed, with doors at both the top and bottom. The outside wall of concrete blocks was cool and slightly damp—she knew because she rested her hand against it as she descended, since there was no handrail; the inside wall was metal sheeting. Only a single bulb hanging from a cord at the top of the stairs provided illumination; its position caused their own elongated shadows to precede them. The air in the stairwell was stagnant and smelled faintly of mildew.

By the time they reached the bottom of the stairs, Katharine's heart was pounding. Her pulse raced. Her stomach had tied itself into a knot. She eyed the closed metal door in front of her with trepidation. What was on the other side? She had a feeling she didn't want to know. When Starkey reached around her to turn the knob and push the door open, it took every bit of courage she could summon to walk through the opening with her shoulders back and her head high. The others were right behind her.

They stepped into what looked like a modern office. Down here the walls were a smooth beige drywall; the floor was covered with plush gray wall-to-wall carpet. A quartet of beige-and-gray metal desks marched in a row against the wall opposite the door. Each was outfitted with its own computer and telephone, and had a comfortable-looking desk chair pulled up to it. A fake rubber plant—at least, Katharine thought it was fake; it looked way too shiny and healthy to be real—stretched toward the acoustic-tiled ceiling in the far corner, beside a door that led into some inner offices. A large framed map of the earth took pride of place on the wall through which they had entered. Beneath it was a long couch in bright Carolina blue, with a coffee table complete with magazines in front of it.

Katharine was just noticing that the air-conditioning worked almost too well—at least, she preferred to think that the goose bumps that were prickling to life along her arms were caused by the air-conditioning—and that the rattling from the fan upstairs was faint but still audible, when, at the far end of the room, the door to what was apparently an inner office opened and Ed stepped out.

Her heart lurched. Her throat closed up. Her hands started to curl into fists at her sides until she became aware of the involuntary movement and stopped it.

She might be afraid of Ed, but she wasn't stupid enough to let him know it.

"Hey, babe," he said, just as if they were meeting under the most ordinary of circumstances, as he walked toward her. "Sorry I had to bring you all the way out here."

He was minus his suit jacket, but everything else—white shirt, long-sleeved despite the heat, red power tie, navy pin-striped pants—was immaculate. His black hair was perfectly groomed, and he looked as wide awake as if it were eleven a.m. rather than p.m.

"Was kidnapping me really necessary?" Deliberately keeping it light despite the fact that her pulse was racing and every nerve ending she possessed was screaming, she smiled at him as he approached and accepted the peck he dropped on her cheek with apparent equanimity. "Starkey"—she cast Starkey, who was standing just slightly behind her, his hands clasped in front of him now, a reproachful look—"broke the window on my car."

"We'll get it fixed." Ed looked at Starkey, who remained impassive, slid a glance over the other three men, and wrapped a hand around Katharine's elbow, drawing her with him as he started back the way he had come. The touch of that moist, meaty hand almost made her shudder. It took iron control not to. "See, I need your help. There's something I want to show you."

Okay, Ed seemed fine. As far as she could tell, he wasn't angry, he wasn't menacing, he wasn't hostile. So why did her heart threaten to pound its way out of her chest?

The only answer she could come up with was instinct.

The door led into a narrow hallway that ran the length of the building. Doors opened off it. Ed opened the second door to the right and stood back to allow her to precede him inside.

It was a gentlemanly gesture, and she might have felt more favorably about it if she'd had any real choice.

Her first impression of the room she walked into was that it was some kind of a lab. It was small with a dark gray linoleum floor, and it smelled faintly of alcohol. The walls were white, the lighting stark and recessed. Long stainless-steel counters ran along three sides of the room. There was medical equipment—a tray with syringes and gauze, a box of surgical gloves, small labeled vials of liquid—and stacks of files and a computer on the counters. Two bright-blue molded plastic chairs were pushed neatly beneath them. Another computer sat on a desk in the middle of the room. There were two comfortable-looking black leather office chairs, one on either side of the desk.

A man rose from the chair behind the desk and came toward them. He was a small guy, not much taller than she was herself, and wiry. Early fifties maybe. His gray hair was cut close to his head, and his eyes were gray, too, behind a pair of bifocals. His features were delicate, his pale skin wrinkled. He was wearing black pants and a white open-necked shirt with a blue doctor's smock zipped up over it.

"I'm Gene Pettinelli," he said, nodding at Katharine. "I'll be doing the testing."

Her eyes widened.

"Testing?" Instinctively, she looked over her shoulder at Ed. He had closed the door behind him, she saw. Of the four men who had followed them down the hall, only Starkey and Bennett had entered the room in their wake. They were now positioned behind Ed on either side of the door. Hendricks and the other man were probably waiting in the hall.

"I've got some pictures I want you to look at," Ed said. "It may be that some of the assholes who broke into your town house are among them."

Pettinelli was gently leading her toward the chair behind the desk.

She kept casting alarmed glances back at Ed. "But . . . I didn't see their faces. I wouldn't recognize their pictures if I saw them. I—"

"If you would just sit here," Pettinelli interrupted politely, pulling the chair behind the desk out for her.

Without thinking about it, Katharine sat. Every bit of her attention was focused on Ed, who was watching her with his fists on his hips and an in-

scrutable expression on his face. Looking at pictures didn't sound bad—
not nearly as bad as what she had been expecting—but something about
the setup, the atmosphere, the smell, something was giving her the willies.

"You probably saw more than you think," Ed said. "Little details that
you wouldn't consciously remember, maybe."

"Pardon me," Pettinelli murmured, leaning in front of her. Katharine
only realized that the chair came equipped with a seat belt and he was fastening it around her when she heard the *click*.

"Wh-what?" she stuttered, looking down in disbelief at the webbed
black belt that was now clasped around her waist. Bullets of adrenaline shot
through her system. "What is this? What are you doing?" Her eyes were
huge as they flew to meet Ed's. Her voice sharpened with the beginnings
of panic. *"Ed . . . ?"*

"Pettinelli here is going to test your body's reactions to some pictures."
Ed spoke as if what was happening was the most normal thing in the world.

"Even if you don't consciously remember something, your body may
well respond to a familiar stimuli in a telling way," Pettinelli said.

Her arms were on the armrests. Glancing down, she was just in time
to watch as he fastened a pair of webbed restraints around her forearm,
one near the elbow and one near the wrist. Her arm was thus secured to
the chair.

It wasn't uncomfortable, but . . .

"*No.*" Her eyes shot back to Ed's face as she sheltered her left arm protectively in her lap, hunching her shoulders forward, glaring at him. "No,
I don't want to do this. I'd rather just look at the pictures normally first,
and then—"

"This is quicker." Ed's expression never changed. His eyes as they met
hers held no affection for her, no sympathy, no softness of any kind. "And
more accurate."

"If you would just put your other arm on this armrest," Pettinelli said.
He reached out to grasp her wrist, his fingers cool, his hold very tentative
and respectful. A heartbeat passed in which Katharine realized that she had
no choice, none whatsoever. Her arm was going to be strapped to that

chair with her cooperation or without it. Taking a deep breath, trying to control the panic that curled through her stomach and tightened her throat, she gritted her teeth and let Pettinelli do what he would with her arm.

"This won't hurt," he promised her as he slipped little blue rubber cups on the ends of the ring, index, and pointer fingers on her right hand. Thin, black wires ran from the cups to a black metal machine that rested beside the computer on the desk. He scuttled around to the other side, sat down, and spoke to her across it. "I'll just show you some pictures on the computer screen, and you tell me whether any of them look familiar. And your body will tell me, too, of course."

Ed stood behind Pettinelli, arms folded over his chest, watching her with a frown on his face. Katharine could no longer even look at him. Her damp palms curled around the edge of the armrests. It took every ounce of willpower she could summon to keep her cool.

She had no choice but to go through with this.

Breathe, she ordered herself fiercely.

Slowly, rhythmically, she did. *Inhale, exhale . . .*

"Here we go," Pettinelli said. "Don't talk unless you recognize someone. Just look."

The screen, which had been dark, came to life. There were pictures of men on it, head shots with their names typed under them. At first glance she thought they might be mug shots. Then she realized that they had been taken from what looked like ID badges from Alphabet Soup World. Six to a row, five rows per screen. Call it spook-a-vision.

She scanned the first screen, then the second, without consciously recognizing anyone. Gradually, she started to relax; all this drama had been in aid of this exercise in pointlessness. The intruders had been wearing masks and all she had seen were their eyes, as she had explained to Ed so many times that she had lost count. Under the circumstances, the head shots were useless. She would have had an easier time identifying them from statistics like height, weight, and build.

When she finally did come to a head shot she recognized, it was right in middle of the third screen and she was so used to scanning quickly through the pictures that she nearly skimmed right over it. But even as her eyes started to slide past, the familiar face registered on her brain. Blinking, she looked again.

There in front of her was a picture of Dan. His hair was cut ruthlessly short, there were no glasses anywhere in sight, and he was minus the Malibu tan.

But there was no mistaking him.

The only thing was, the caption under his picture read *Special Agent Nick Houston, FBI.*

Even as she looked at it, her head began to hurt.

21

There! We got something! You recognize somebody?" Pettinelli was so excited he was practically bouncing in his chair. Glancing around, he said to Ed, "We got something!"

The screen wavered before her eyes. Her headache turned into a splitting pain that felt like it was cleaving through her brain. She felt dizzy, disoriented. Trying to focus her eyes made her stomach roil, so she gave up and closed them. Letting her head drop back to rest against the back of the chair, she took deep breaths as cold sweat broke over her in a rolling wave.

Not Dan. Nick . . .

"Who? Who is it?" Ed was beside her, grabbing her upper arm, shaking her. "Tell me who it is."

My God, she thought with a quick rush of panic that cut right through the horrible pounding in her head, she had to think. Her own reaction as much as the machine had given her away. She couldn't tell them, though, not the truth. She summarily rejected the possibility. Every instinct she possessed urged her to protect Dan—no, Nick.

Nick . . .

The headache was so bad it was making her sick.

"Which one?" Ed demanded, his face so close to hers she could feel the heat of his breath on her cheek. His fingers dug painfully into her arm. *"Which one?"*

Opening her eyes required a huge amount of effort, but she did it. The room swam, and she found herself briefly blinking at half a dozen computers floating in a fuzzy circle above the desk. Then she sucked in air, gritted her teeth, and clutched the ends of the armrests so tightly that her knuckles turned white.

The revolving computers coalesced into one sleek, gray machine sitting solidly on the desktop.

"I think—him," she said, and instinctively started to point, although with her arms strapped to the chair, pointing wasn't going to happen, as she quickly discovered. "Fourth row, second picture from the left."

Sorry, she said mentally to the guy, who was a square-jawed military-looking type with an aquiline nose and a dark crew cut. He was identified under his picture as *Special Investigator Frank Rizzo, DOD.*

"Him?" Ed had turned to face the screen and now tapped Special Investigator Rizzo's picture.

"I can't be sure," she temporized, doing her best to ignore the fogginess clouding her brain. She didn't want to be responsible for anything horrible befalling a—as far as she knew—perfectly innocent man, but she couldn't think of anything else to do but point out *someone.* "But . . . the eyes look familiar." She let her head drop back against the chair again, and closed her eyes. Her heart thumped against her ribs. Her pulse raced. Her head pounded. "Oh, God, I think I'm going to be sick."

This had the virtue of being perfectly true—nerves had her stomach churning like a washing machine—as well as providing an urgent reason for them to release her. After all, they wouldn't want her to upchuck all over their chair, would they?

"Okay, show her the rest," Ed said.

"I need to take a break." Katharine opened her eyes and clutched the ends of the armrests, trying to stay cool and focused for long enough to at least persuade them to let her get out of that chair. The knowledge that she was trapped in it was starting to give her claustrophobia, big-time. She feared she was going to totally wig out if they didn't let her go soon. "Please. I'm going to throw up."

Every time she thought about Nick—*Yes, Nick, that fit, he wasn't Doctor Dan, he was FBI agent Nick*—she got an attack of what felt like vertigo that was so bad she literally thought she might pass out. She couldn't process what she had just discovered, not here, not hooked up to this damned machine, not with the eyes of Ed and Pettinelli and Starkey and Bennett all focused on her.

"Later." Ed's tone was dismissive as his gaze shifted back to the computer. "Look at the screen."

"Please," Katharine said again, and she thought Pettinelli might have thrown her a sympathetic glance, but she couldn't be sure because her attention was focused on Ed, who clearly had no sympathy for her at all.

He glanced at her and his eyes narrowed.

"Look at the screen," he barked, and she did, because it didn't seem like she had any other choice if she ever wanted to get out of that chair. She looked while her stomach churned and her head pounded and nausea threatened, but the machine didn't register anything through four more screens of head shots because she didn't see anyone else she knew.

Why is Nick masquerading as Dan? The question swirled relentlessly through her brain, making her temples pound and causing shooting pains behind her eyes that made staring at the computer screen positively painful, without finding any sort of workable answer.

"That's it," Pettinelli said when the screen went dark again. She blinked, relieved. He, too, sounded glad that it was over. He stood up, his fingertips resting on the desk. "That's all of them."

"Can you please let me out of this chair?" Katharine asked through stiff lips. Her muscles felt weak and shaky, and she thought they might need more blood circulating through them. She was still a little dizzy, a little disoriented, and she clutched the arms of the chair for dear life.

"In a minute." Ed didn't look at her. Everyone else in the room ignored her, too. "You have the video loaded, right?" He was talking to Pettinelli. "What do I have to do to play it?"

"Just hit this button," Pettinelli said, and Ed walked around to the other side of the desk to look where he pointed, then nodded in comprehension.

"Thank you, Mr. Pettinelli." Ed's tone was dismissive. "You can go on home now."

He gave Starkey a significant look and Starkey moved at last, opening the door.

"This way, Mr. Pettinelli," Starkey said. "If you'll get your things, we'll walk you out to your car."

Pettinelli hesitated, glancing at Katharine.

Don't leave me.

The words sprang into her mind, but they took too long to form and she ended up not saying them out loud. In any case, asking him to stay would do no good, she knew, and would only anger Ed. Panic was bubbling up inside her again, sharp and urgent enough to poke holes through the confusion she couldn't seem to shake, and it quickened her breathing and made her heart race. There was something ominous, she knew, in the fact that she was still strapped to the chair while Pettinelli was told to leave.

But she couldn't think of anything to do about it.

"Mr. Pettinelli," Starkey said. Pettinelli turned and walked out of the room without so much as another glance at her. Starkey and Bennett followed, closing the door behind them so that she was left alone with Ed.

"I want out of this chair," Katharine said, her voice louder and more insistent. She wasn't screaming yet, but she soon would be. Not that it would do any good. Meeting Ed's eyes, which were hard and flat as river stones, she felt her blood turn to ice in her veins and went still.

There was real menace in them. She'd seen him look that way before, but never at her.

"Watch." He leaned over the computer and stabbed a button with his finger. The screen flickered to life.

It took Katharine all of about a second to realize what she was watching. The video was black-and-white, silent, and grainy but clear enough. There she was, dressed in Dottie's oversized clothes, walking gingerly across the hospital parking lot in her too-tight shoes, stepping into the grass, face lighting up as she turned to the black Blazer that pulled into the exit road in front of her. Then she was hurrying toward it, hobbling a little, saying something to the man whose face was now clearly visible in the driver's window—*Dan.*

No, Nick. Unmistakably Nick.

Even as she watched herself climb into the passenger seat and watched the Blazer drive away, her head started to swim again. Bits of memories, fragmented as pieces of torn photos, came spiraling to the surface. Nick scowling at her, Nick walking toward her, Nick smiling.

Nick. Not Dan. But how did she know Nick?

"That came from a security camera at the hospital," Ed said. She looked at him, her vision a little unfocused, still trying to sort fact from fiction and integrate the past with the present, and registered the anger in his face. His voice was silky-soft. Dangerously soft.

This was bad, she realized. Her heart lurched. Her stomach dropped clear to her toes. The sour taste of fear was sharp in her mouth. Her chest heaved as she took a deep breath.

He came toward her, gripped the arms of her chair, and pulled her around to face him. The blue caps popped off her fingers to hang dangling from their thin black wires. The chair's casters squeaked over the smooth linoleum. Her heels dragged helplessly along. One of her shoes loosened, fell off. The seat rocked as the force of the forward motion pressed her back against the smooth leather. For a moment, one stupid, hopeful moment, she thought he was getting ready to unbuckle the restraints that held her to the chair.

Then he straightened.

"You lying bitch."

Without warning, he backhanded her across the face. Pain exploded across her cheek. Her head rocked to the side under the force of the blow.

She cried out in pain and shock. Her cheek stung. Her eyes watered. Her mouth fell open in disbelief.

"Ed—"

She got no further. He hit her again, slapping her face so hard that the chair went scooting sideways, causing her face to burn and ache, bringing more tears to her eyes, making her ears ring. She was helpless, unable to get up, unable to get away, unable even to lift a hand to ward off another blow.

"Why?" she cried, blinking up at him through welling tears. "What did I do?"

"Don't play stupid with me." He was breathing hard. Though her vision was hazy with tears, she saw that his face had turned scarlet with rage. "You sold me out, didn't you? I knew there was somebody on my tail. I knew it. The signs were all there, these last couple of months. Things out of place, somebody logging on to my computer when I was out, the tinny sound the phone gets when somebody's listening in. I knew I wasn't imagining it. It was you all along, wasn't it? You're working as an informant for the goddamned FBI."

"No!" Katharine shook her head, desperate to convince him of the truth. Fear tightened her stomach, her throat. "No, Ed, it's not true! I—"

"Don't lie to me." He took a hasty step forward, grabbed the arms of her chair, and pulled her to him, sticking his face right in front of hers. His eyes were black with fury. His jaw worked with it. He was so angry he was practically spitting in her face. "What do they know? What did you give them?" His voice crescendoed until he was shouting in her face. "I want to know what you gave them."

Her heart knocked against the walls of her chest. "Nothing. Nothing. I didn't give them anything. It isn't true."

"How long have they known? How much do they know?" Veins bulged in his temples. His heavy brows met over the bridge of his nose. "Did you find out what I was doing and go to them, or did they come to you?"

"Neither." Her voice was high-pitched, shaking. She was practically pushing the back of her head through the back of the chair in an effort to put as much distance between them as she could. "I didn't sell you out, Ed, I swear to God."

"They were trying to get enough on me to take me down before I knew anything was up, weren't they? Thank God I found out in time." He sucked in air through his teeth. "Were they the ones who broke into your house? So they could get their hands on the things I was keeping in the safe without me suspecting what was really going down?"

"*No.*" Katherine shook her head, desperate to convince him of it. "No, it's not true. None of it's true."

But he didn't believe her. "You traitorous bitch, don't you know I have enough shit on everybody in the whole damned government to make this go away? *Poof,* like a puff of smoke. But it won't go away for you. You're going to tell me everything you gave them, everything you know, and then you're going to die."

He pushed her away from him abruptly, so that her chair went careening back until it crashed into the edge of the counter. As her head was flung forward by the jolt, Katharine grabbed onto the seat arms for balance, her eyes burning with tears that were brimming over now, her cheeks stinging, terror forming a huge, cold knot in her chest.

"Ed, you have to listen to me!" she cried even as he strode for the door. "I'm not working for the FBI! I'm not working for anybody! If somebody sold you out, it wasn't me. I swear it. *I swear it.*"

"Hendricks," he roared, sticking his head out into the hall, completely disregarding her words as he flung open the door. The man appeared almost instantly, leading Katharine to believe he had been lurking outside. He was puffing away on a cigarette, and the fact that Ed ignored it told her how absolutely beside himself he was: Ed hated anyone smoking around him. Behind Hendricks was his shadow, the other man whose name Katharine had never learned. Hendricks's gaze slid over her as he entered the room, and he lowered the hand holding the cigarette to smirk at her.

Her heart pounded like it was trying to beat its way out of her chest.

Her mouth was so dry she had to swallow before she could get another word out.

"Ed . . ." she begged. "Please listen."

"I want to know everything she knows," Ed said to Hendricks, ignoring her completely. "*Everything*. I'll meet you at the Plantation in—what?   say, three hours. That should give you plenty of time."

"Don't imagine I'll need a third of that." Hendricks looked her over appraisingly.

"I didn't do it," Katharine cried, knowing time was running out. Adrenaline rushed like speed through her veins, and she jerked at her arms, trying to free them from the restraints without success. Every instinct she possessed screamed *run*, but there was nothing she could do. "I'm not working for the FBI."

Ed turned to her, his expression savage.

"You know what Hendricks here does?" There was not one scrap of feeling for her in his eyes, she saw as their gazes locked. "He's an independent contractor for us. His specialty is, he gets people to talk. Real tough guys beg for the chance to sell out their mother before he's done with them." His gaze swung to Hendricks. "What was it you did last week, Hendricks? Peel the skin off some guy's face like it was a grape?" He looked at Katharine again as Hendricks nodded confirmation. "Did you know a person can still be alive with no skin on his face? And talk and cry and everything? Pretty gruesome, though."

Katharine's stomach turned inside out.

"Oh, God, Ed, no. Please. You're making a mistake. It wasn't me!"

Her frantic pleas fell on deaf ears. He was already walking out the door, only pausing to say "Three hours" over his shoulder to Hendricks, who nodded.

"Ed, no!" Katharine screamed, desperate. Her life was on the line, she knew. "Please, please listen!"

The door closed behind him with a click that reverberated loud as a gunshot through her head. Her heart pounded. Her pulse shot through the roof. She jerked vainly at her arms again and tried to open the lap restraint by heaving against it. The chair scooted across the floor, but the straps held.

She was trapped in the damned chair.

Her gaze shifted fearfully to Hendricks. She could feel tears tracking down her cheeks, the salt in them stinging the abused flesh.

Hendricks walked up to her, slowly, shaking his head, puffing away, his skin gleaming under the overhead light. A thin, gray finger of smoke floated behind him. The smell of the cigarette hung in the air.

"Well, good golly Miss Molly, who woulda thought we would end up like this, you and me?" he said to her in an affable tone. "It's a shame, but there you are."

As Hendricks reached her chair, the other man approached on her other side. He was probably in his forties, too, but he had hair, light brown, in a regulation military cut that did nothing for his round face and puffy blue eyes. His complexion was florid and he had a little goatee, and, all in all, looked almost as scary as Hendricks.

"Shame," the second man echoed, his eyes running over her. She watched him warily. Her skin crawled at the expression on his face. She felt boneless suddenly, as if fear had turned all her muscles to jelly, and her heart threatened to beat its way out of her chest.

"This is Lutz," Hendricks said by way of an introduction. He pulled the cigarette out of his mouth, contemplated the glowing tip for an instant, then put it down on the back of her hand and ground it out.

Katharine screamed.

Hendricks grinned as he lifted the cigarette away and flicked the spent butt into a waste can.

"She's got a real girly scream. I like that," he said to Lutz, tapping another cigarette out of the pack he pulled from his shirt pocket and lighting it. Sweating and gasping, sick from the burning pain in her arm, able to smell her own scorched flesh in the air, Katharine watched in terror as he put the fresh cigarette between his lips and took a drag.

"We ain't done a woman in a while," Lutz agreed.

Watching that glowing cigarette, Katharine panted and flinched and trembled.

Get a grip. You can't fall apart. They're going to kill you if you can't think of a way to stop them.

She took a deep, shaky breath.

"Look." Her voice was unsteady as she fought to regain some semblance of composure, of control. "You don't have to hurt me. I'll tell you anything you want to know right now."

Hendricks took another deep drag on the cigarette, then pulled it out of his mouth.

"I know we don't have to hurt you," he said, and smiled at her. "But it's fun."

This time he moved slowly, grinning and watching her terrified face as he touched the cigarette to her arm just above her wrist, only inches from the first burn.

Katharine screamed again. The searing pain rocketed through her nerve endings to her brain. The scorching smell wafted to her nose. When he lifted the cigarette away at last, tears were streaming down her face.

"All right, let's go," Lutz said, sounding bored. "They're probably waiting to turn out the lights."

"That would be us," Hendricks replied, but they both got to work unbuckling the straps holding Katharine to the chair.

When she summoned up the wherewithal to ease off her other shoe and get her feet solidly under her, when she would have exploded out of the chair, doing her best to break free of the two of them and bolt through the door even though she knew she had no chance, absolutely no chance, of making it, Hendricks forestalled her by grabbing her wrist just as the lap belt was undone, yanking her up out of the chair and at the same time twisting her arm hard behind her back.

The pain was excruciating.

"You give me trouble, I'll break it," he told her, and she believed him.

They frog-marched her out of the building, which now appeared to be deserted. On Hendricks's say-so, Lutz turned out the lights behind them. When they emerged into the breezy warmth of the night, Katharine saw that the Mercedes was gone.

She was all alone with Hendricks and Lutz.

The knowledge made her heart pound like it was trying to beat its way out of her chest.

"We'll go in her car," Hendricks said as he shoved her toward it. The gravel dug into her bare feet, but she barely felt it. Her arm felt like it was being wrenched from its socket. And she was deathly, deathly afraid. "Barnes told me to get rid of it, and gave me a set of keys. When we're done, we can catch a ride back here for ours."

If Lutz said anything, Katharine missed it because they had reached her car by that time and Hendricks shoved her into the backseat, then climbed in beside her while Lutz got into the driver's seat.

Muffy greeted her with a *meow* as her carrier was jostled when Katharine slid over. She picked up the plastic crate, cradling it on her lap, with some thought of using it as a weapon or at least protection. Something. Anything.

It was pathetic, she knew, but it was the only thing she had.

"Hi, cat," Hendricks said, and stuck his fingers through the grate, which was pointed toward him. Muffy hissed.

Smart cat.

"Just so you know," Hendricks said as Lutz started the car and began backing out, tires crunching over the gravel. "If you give me any trouble, if you try to escape, the first thing I'll do is put out your eyes."

He smiled at her as he said it. She believed him. Shivers of horror prickled over her skin. Her shoulder ached. The burns on her hand and arm throbbed. Her cheeks felt swollen and numb. But the worst thing, positively the worst thing of all, was the absolute icy fear that coursed through her veins. Unless she could somehow think of a way to save herself, they were going to hurt her horribly. And before the night was over, she was going to die.

Her breath was coming in ragged little pants.

Get calm, she ordered herself. *Think. Try.*

"You know," she said in the calmest voice she could muster, turning her head and looking Hendricks in the eye, "I have money. A lot of money. How much would it cost for you to just let me go?"

They were on pavement now, passing the rows of for-sale cars, rolling inexorably toward the road. It was dark in the car, but not too dark that she couldn't see his expression. He was interested, she could tell by the way his eyes flickered. She could feel Lutz looking at her through the rearview mirror as the car paused at the junction between the car lot and the road.

"Where you got it?" Hendricks asked.

She had to take a deep breath before she answered, but she tried not to let him see. "In the bank."

"Suppose we mosey on by the bank on the way to where we're going and you withdraw all that money and give it to us? Then we can have the money and still have fun."

Katharine was just opening her mouth to explain to him how that wouldn't work for her, when his door and Lutz's door both flew open unexpectedly and they whipped around with startled cries. Her eyes were still widening in shock, she was still in the process of registering dark-covered arms, and hands gripping pistols, thrusting into the car, when her own door was yanked open and her arm was roughly seized.

She screamed, jumped, tried to yank free of this new threat—then saw Hendricks's scalp explode into the front seat. To her stupefied horror, he had just been shot in the head.

I t's all right, it's me, it's me," her captor shouted in a rapid-fire burst of words as Katharine was hauled shrieking from the car, which was now slowly rolling forward. "Jesus, quit screaming, would you please?"

But she couldn't, she was on autopilot, the terror and horror of the last few hours amped up a thousandfold by the new terror and horror of seeing bloody murder committed right in front of her eyes, by the rawness and extremity of her fear for her own life. In the front seat, she saw Lutz slump over out of sight, his blood spraying the dashboard and windshield. Her bare feet hit rough, warm pavement, and the night sky tilted crazily overhead as she stumbled forward, out of the car. Muffy's crate, which was on her lap, slid toward the ground and would have crashed into it if she hadn't retained the presence of mind to grab the handle as it fell. Out of the corner of her eye, she saw two black-garbed men push the bodies of her erstwhile tormentors farther inside the car as they, too, jumped into the vehicle. It stopped moving, and she guessed that the man who was now in the driver's seat had stepped on the brake.

"Get rid of them and the car," her captor ordered, his hand still tight on her arm, keeping her on her feet, keeping her knees from collapsing and smacking into the ground, even as he pulled her away from the car. Another scream was tearing out of her throat of its own accord when she recognized the voice, recognized him, saw that it was Dan, no, Nick, yes, yes, Nick. *Thank God for Nick.*

Nick dressed all in black, with a black watch cap over his golden head.

He had come for her, and the frantic beating of her heart began to slow by infinitesimal degrees.

The scream died in her throat.

"I'll take her with me and we'll all meet up at Gardens Park," he said, dragging her around behind his Blazer as she heard grunts of agreement and slamming doors and tires gripping pavement as her Lexus and a black SUV peeled out of the car lot, heading away from McLean. In the meantime, Nick had opened the front passenger door and was in the process of thrusting her inside the Blazer when the cat carrier smacked into his legs.

A vicious-sounding hiss came from the carrier.

"What the *hell?*" He took the plastic crate from her while bundling her the rest of the way inside.

"C-cat," Katharine managed, although she was shaking all over now and breathing so fast that she knew she was in imminent danger of hyperventilating. "Don't leave it."

He muttered something—she thought it was probably a curse—as he closed her door, but an instant later the door behind her opened and the carrier landed on the backseat. A glance over her shoulder found Muffy's eyes, as big and round as hers felt, shining balefully at her through the darkness. It was enough to tell that the cat was unhappy, but all right.

Nick's door was yanked open and he dropped into the front seat, closing it behind him. It was only then, when she registered that he didn't have to start the car, that she realized it had been running all along.

"Put on your seat belt," he said, his eyes raking over her, and when she didn't move because she just couldn't, her muscles wouldn't work, he cursed and leaned over, securing it for her. He pulled the watch cap from his head and tossed it in the back, running his fingers through his hair. She saw the gleam of metal on his chest as he moved, and realized that he was wearing a shoulder holster that was almost invisible amid so much black. His pistol was shoved into it.

Then the Blazer was on the move, peeling rubber as they headed in the opposite direction from the others.

"Wr-wrong way," she pointed out through chattering teeth as she lay back in the seat and tried to get some kind of equilibrium back.

"We're not going where they're going," he said, slowing down as they passed through the jumble of lights and buildings that was all she managed to absorb of McLean. She was cold, icy cold, freezing to death, so cold that she would have wrapped her arms around herself if she wasn't absolutely too spent to move, and she knew it wasn't from the air conditioner because it wasn't even on. She was shivering, long, tooth-rattling tremors that she knew were caused by shock.

"Why . . . not?"

He cast another glance at her as they turned right at a deserted intersection on the other side of McLean, and she saw from the roadside sign that they were heading for the Beltway.

"Because I don't want them getting their hands on you again." His voice was hard.

"Who?"

He shook his head. "That's something we probably ought to talk about later."

She looked at him with a frown, but since the only illumination was a reflection from the headlights that were slashing through pine-covered knolls as the road twisted and turned through them, plus the faint light from the dashboard instruments, it was impossible to tell anything about his expression except that it was grim.

Still, his profile was limned against the darkness outside the window, and she recognized the curve of his brow, the line of his nose, the jut of his chin. The hair was wrong, long and wavy where always before it had been cut ruthlessly short, but everything else was right: the breadth of his shoulders, the lean, muscular strength of his torso, the powerful length of his legs. His hands were curled around the steering wheel, and she recognized the broad palms and long fingers, too.

Nick. Definitely Nick.

A wave of relief washed over her that was so strong it made her dizzy. She was safe, finally, with Nick.

"What took you so long?" she asked shakily, then to her own surprise burst into tears.

"Shit. Fuck. Damn it to hell and back." She could feel his gaze on her even though her own eyes were closed as she fought to keep the tears contained. "I know this has been bad for you. Would you please not cry?"

Her eyes popped open. Uncontained now, more tears rolled down her cheeks. "You'd cry too if you'd just been burned with a cigarette and told somebody was going to peel your face off and . . ."

"I know," he interrupted, real pain for her in his voice. The Blazer was climbing now, emerging from the darkness into a burst of light, and she saw the big halogen expressway lights at the top of the entrance ramp and realized that they were curving onto the Beltway, heading toward Maryland. "We had eavesdropping devices on, we heard everything. It nearly killed me listening to it, but there was no way to get in. It's a secured Agency site. You'd practically have to have a nuclear bomb. Anyway, with Hendricks and Lutz there, I knew they were going to bring you out. The kind of dirty work they do, they have a specialized facility."

"The Plantation." Katharine drew a deep, gasping breath that wasn't quite a sob. Tears still spilled down her cheeks, but they were slowing down and she was pretty sure the worst of the onslaught was over. She sucked in more air and tried to will the flow to stop.

"Yeah. What they do there isn't—wasn't—pretty."

"You killed them." The memory of Hendricks's scalp sailing into the front seat, of Lutz's blood spraying the windshield, made her shudder.

"Yeah, well, you gotta do what you gotta do. And sometimes people deserve to die. Those two made a nice living out of torturing people, sometimes to death. The world's a better place with them gone."

"If you hadn't gotten there in time . . ." The thought made her dizzy all over again.

He threw her a quick, frowning glance. "There was no way I wasn't going to get there in time, so you can just put that thought out of your head. I've had somebody with you every step of the way. Since you left the cabin. Listening, watching, looking out for you. We're real good at clandestine surveillance, you know? You remember that phone call Barnes got, the night he brought you back to that apartment you were staying at after you'd been to your town house? That was us, telling him that one of his informants had just been picked up by the Kremlin. We knew he'd rush out of there, and figured you'd probably be glad."

Katharine's eyes widened as she remembered.

"Oh, yeah," she said, in a massive understatement. "I was glad."

A rest area was coming up, and she glanced at him in surprise when they pulled off into it. There were trees and big overhead lights and a small brick building with a glass front that housed restrooms. A semi was parked in the first of the two parking areas, and a couple of cars were parked in the second lot, in front of the building. Through the glass, she watched a middle-aged couple disappear into the restrooms inside.

"Is this is a good time for a pit stop?" Katharine asked doubtfully, wiping the last traces of tears from her cheeks with careful fingers. Her cheeks no longer throbbed, but the salt from the tears still made them sting a little.

His quick grin made her dizzy. She remembered—she remembered—another day when he had grinned at her like that. They were in a house, she saw in a flash, in a kitchen, and she was yelling at him to go away and she took off her shoe and threw it at him and he ducked and it missed, slamming into some cabinets—and then he grinned at her, just like that. She blinked, trying to make sense of it, trying to put it into some kind of context, but then her head started to hurt so much that she couldn't think at all and the memory was lost as quickly as it came.

Pressing a hand to her head, she was trying to ignore the pain while fighting to recapture that elusive memory when he pulled into a shadowy spot well away from the other cars, turned off the engine, and unfastened his seat belt.

"Do you trust me?" he asked, fishing something from his pocket and then turning toward her with it. It was, she saw, a pocket knife.

That redirected her focus in a hurry. Her eyes widened as she looked from the knife to his face. A whole jumble of additional memories burst like flashbulbs in her brain, too fast for her to make sense of any one of them but leaving her pretty sure about the sum of the whole.

"Are you kidding me, Doctor Dan? No."

This time his grin was slower dawning but just as disarming. "Fair enough. You need to do what I tell you anyway."

"What?" Her tone was wary. She eyed the knife.

"Bend over and wrap your arms around your knees and hold on tight." The grin was gone. His mouth was looking grim again.

She was, she thought, rightfully wary. "Why?"

"Because you've got a locator device embedded in your back and I need to dig it out before they find us."

Her eyes went wide with horror. "Ohmigod."

"Yeah."

He didn't look any happier about it than she felt, and Katharine quashed the whole litany of protests and questions that ran through her brain in favor of taking a deep breath, unfastening her seat belt, and doing what he said.

If there was a locator device in her back, it had to come out. If Ed hadn't yet scrambled an army to look for her, it was only because he didn't yet know she had escaped. As soon as he did, he would. Anything was better than ending up in Ed's hands again.

And despite everything, including what she had just said, she found she did trust Nick after all.

Sort of. Kind of. Maybe. Well, at least about this.

"It's tiny," he said, as she hugged her knees for all she was worth and turned her face away and squinched up her eyes tight. "And it's right under the surface. They tried to put it where it would be covered by your bra strap, so it wouldn't show unless somebody did a complete strip search."

"Oh, God," she moaned, her arms tightening around her legs as he pushed up her T-shirt and the back band of her bra.

"I'll be as quick as I can." Pause. "There it is."

She felt his finger lightly touch her back on the left side and flinched as if he'd stabbed her.

"Nick . . ."

"Steady."

His left arm came down across her shoulders, long and heavy and confining, doing his best to hold her in place.

"Don't move," he warned, bearing down on the arm, and she squinched her eyes shut even tighter and hugged her thighs and gritted her teeth.

And flinched for real as she felt the sharp blade of the knife touch her flesh before digging in. She cried out, jerking reflexively, heard him say "Don't move" again in a fierce tone and forced herself to be still, sucking in air, holding her breath, locking all her muscles so she wouldn't move. The pain was sharp and intense, cold metal jabbing through skin and muscle accompanied by the sensation of welling warm blood. Her warm blood. She went all light-headed as a wave of cold sweat washed over her and her stomach roiled. But she didn't move again.

"Got it," he said just when she thought she might be going to pass out, and the knife lifted away from her. His arm across her shoulders went from pressing her down to giving her a quick, comforting hug. "I'm sorry I had to do that. You okay?"

Nodding, Katharine stayed where she was, her head resting on her knees, breathing hard.

"Watch your head."

She was so dizzy she didn't really comprehend what he was doing, but she heard him open the glove compartment, then heard other assorted small noises, too, and moments later felt the slight abrasion of what she thought must be a gauze pad sliding over her back, presumably to wipe away the trickling blood. Then he pressed something—she assumed it was another gauze pad—firmly against the small wound. He was obviously using the contents of the glove compartment's first-aid kit to treat the injury he had caused her, and she slowly, slowly felt the worst of the dizziness begin to subside.

"You okay?" he asked again, sounding worried.

With the dizziness almost gone and the cold sweats and roiling stomach disappearing with it, she was able to take stock. The wound really ached only a little. It didn't hurt nearly as much as the throbbing burns on her arm and hand.

"Yes," she said, opening her eyes and turning her head so that she faced him. She was still bent over, with her head on her knees and her arms around her legs, but she felt as if she might be able to straighten up soon. He was leaning close, so close that all she could see of him was his black-clad middle, as he gently dabbed ointment on her back. She heard paper rip and felt him sticking what she guessed was a Band-Aid to her skin. Then he carefully pulled her clothes back down for her. Surprisingly, even having her bra band on top of the Band-Aid didn't really hurt.

"That's my brave girl," he said.

She was still absorbing the possible implications of that when he got out of the Blazer, closed the door, and disappeared. Frowning, she waited for an increasingly restive moment and then began to feel the first stirring of panic. Where had he gone? She was sitting up to look when he slid back into the SUV.

"Where did you go?" The shrill edge to her voice reflected her anxiety.

"See that car over there?" He was looking pleased with himself, she saw. The merest hint of a smile curved his mouth, and his eyes were more relaxed than they had been all night. He fastened his seat belt as he spoke and started the car.

Looking where he indicated as he reversed out of the parking space, she nodded. It was a sporty white BMW. The driver was, presumably, in the restroom.

"I taped the locator device to the back bumper. Wherever that car goes, they'll follow. Until they figure it out. Should take a few hours, anyway."

Katharine blinked at him. They were already heading down the curved access ramp that connected with the Beltway.

"Good idea," she said. She was working hard to get her body to chill out, to get her breathing and heart rate and pulse under control. But she suspected that there was so much adrenaline in her system now that it would take her a while to get unjuiced. She felt wired and wrung out at the same time.

"I thought so." He glanced her way. "Put on your seat belt."

She did, glad to discover that her muscles were once again minimally functional. Then, as they pulled out onto the Beltway again, she leaned back—gingerly, testing the new wound in her back to see how sensitive it was, and was relieved to discover that it was hardly sensitive at all—and let her head drop down against the top of the seat. She then rolled her head to the side so that she could look at him.

"Nick," she said experimentally. The name felt right and familiar on her tongue.

"Hmm?"

The Blazer merged into traffic, just one more set of headlights among dozens zooming away into the dark. She felt—almost—relaxed.

It was because she felt safe with him.

"You lied to me." Her tone was severe.

He shot her a glance. His lips quirked. "No more than I had to."

"Doctor Dan," she said witheringly. Then, frowning as the larger problem occurred to her, she asked, "Why didn't I recognize you right away? I couldn't have hit my head *that* hard."

A beat passed.

"I was under cover," he said at last. "It was safer for you not to recognize me. I let my hair grow and scrounged up some glasses. Which I kept forgetting to wear, by the way."

Katharine thought about the hair and the glasses: When it came right down to it, they hadn't mattered. He might not look like an FBI agent, but he still looked like Nick. Her eyes widened as she suddenly realized something: Every time a memory of him that predated the moment when she had woken up in the hospital and seen him leaning over her as Doctor Dan popped into her mind, she immediately experienced a pounding headache. And with the onset of the headache, the memory was gone.

The shoe dropped.

"You people have done something to me, haven't you?" There was a note of horror in her voice as she stared at him, aghast. "Haven't you? To my mind."

He shot her a glance. Headlights from oncoming traffic, which was separated from their side of the Beltway by a grassy median, swept through the car, briefly illuminating his face. His expression was guilty. She pursed her lips angrily.

"No more lies," she warned.

He sighed. "Some of your memories were temporarily blocked. You agreed to it."

"What?" She sat bolt upright in the seat, glaring at him, and never mind her exhaustion or the half-dozen assorted pangs and pains that shot through her body. "You blocked my memories? How?"

"I didn't. The Bureau has a lot of resources, including people who know how to do things like that."

"What did they do?"

"Calm down," he said, which had the completely predictable effect of making her want to scream—or clobber him with the nearest solid object. She did neither, clenching her fists and narrowing her eyes at him instead.

With the part of her brain that was still capable of noticing such things, she realized that they were preparing to leave the Beltway. Glancing up automatically, she saw that the sign they were getting ready to pass beneath before curving off onto the exit ramp read *Silver Spring*.

"I think it was a combination of hypnosis and drugs," he finished in response to her tell-me-the-truth-or-die look.

The resulting moment of silence was electrically charged.

"Hypnosis and drugs?" she echoed, outraged. A vague memory stirred, making her head hurt—not the debilitating pain she experienced when memories of him before the hospital tried to surface, but still significant twinges—yet she persevered. The heat of his lips on hers—*wince*—flashlights bobbing toward them through the woods—*wince*—utter terror, followed by a strange, almost zombie-like calm. She spluttered with indignation as the picture came into focus for her. "The sheriff's deputies—in the woods—after you kissed me. They weren't there about the alarm. They weren't frigging deputies. They were your people. And they were there to mess with my head!"

He grimaced. Seething, she interpreted that to mean he was guilty as charged.

"I think the word they used was 'reprogram,' " he said, too calmly. "Certain memories were leaking through that were making things difficult for you. You were starting to freak out, remember? You weren't any good to us like that, and you were a danger to yourself. Once they got you calm and comfortable again, you were okay to be with Barnes."

"*To . . . be . . . with . . . Barnes.*" She spaced the words out dangerously. "That's what this is all about, isn't it? You used me to get to Ed."

"You agreed to do it," he said, his voice even. He shot her a look. "Anyway, there's no point in getting all bent out of shape now. It's over. You're out of it."

That was so disingenuous that she felt her blood pressure rise.

"I want my memories back," she said through her teeth. They were at the bottom of the ramp now, and she got a vague impression of an intersection with gas stations and convenience stores.

"You'll get them back," he promised, merging right. "It's completely reversible. The investigation should be wrapped up within the next twelve hours or so, and then we'll fix it."

The look she sent him scorched the air.

"You mean fix *me*, right?" Another thought occurred, and her breath caught. "Ed was right, wasn't he? I *was* an FBI plant. I just didn't know it."

"Something like that." His lips quirked, just barely but enough so that she could see the beginnings of a smile and react badly. "See why not knowing what you were up to was safer?"

"You're not laughing," she said, with a warning note.

"No." His tone, and his face, went suddenly totally serious. "I'm not laughing. Too many people have died, or been hurt, because of this. It's time it was over."

"What's *it*? What are you investigating?" She sensed him hesitating. "Damn it, I'm part of this. I have a right to know."

"Yeah," he said. "I guess you do. Barnes has been blackmailing people. With all the surveillance the Agency conducts, he has dirt on just about everybody in Washington. And he's using it, too, to manipulate people into giving him what he wants."

"What does he want?" she asked, suddenly noticing that they were no longer on a major road, but rather a narrow residential street lined with small leafy trees and boxy apartment buildings.

"Different things. Sometimes money. Sometimes for other government entities—like us at the Bureau—to back off on certain investigations. Sometimes career advancement. Notice how fast he's climbed the ladder over there? Blackmail buys a lot of promotions."

"Oh my God," she said. "Are you sure?"

"Oh, yeah. The bottom line is, he wants power. We've been investigating him for almost a year now. We probably could have gone on a little longer, but now that he's figured out we're on to him, it's over. He'll be under arrest in the next few hours." He pulled into a small parking lot beside a four-story brick apartment building, found a parking space near the door, and cut the engine. "There are a few loose ends still left to tie up, but we've basically got everything we need to put him away for the rest of his life."

The fact that they were parked did not escape her attention. The building in front of them was squat and unpretentious, just like all the other buildings on the block. A few scattered lights shone through the small casement windows that marched in well-ordered rows across the front and sides, but there was no one around. The lot was a little more than half-full of mostly older vehicles of various descriptions, with a Dumpster at the far corner and a single yellowish light on a pole beside it that left most of the parking lot in deep shadow. A niggle of apprehension—just a niggle, because she was with Nick, after all—raised its head. The way things stood, any sort of unknown quantity worried her.

She was, she could tell, experiencing serious trust issues.

"Where are we?" she asked, glancing warily around. "This isn't the FBI equivalent of the car lot, is it?"

"What, don't you trust me?" That slight, maddening quirk of his lips was back. It told her that he was finding this amusing again, despite everything.

"No," she said. "I damned well don't. And you're going to have to drag me kicking and screaming from this car if you don't give me a straight answer about what this place is."

He looked at her for a moment without saying anything. There was just enough light for her to see his face. The infuriating curve of his lips was gone. He wasn't smiling now. His jaw was hard and his eyes had a steely glint to them.

"You want it straight? Fine, here it is: Barnes wants you dead. Some elements of the Bureau want to bring you in for 'safekeeping.' Whoever broke into your town house might well still be interested in getting their hands on you, too. In other words, for the time being you're Miss Popularity, and not in a good way. This is a place for you to hide out until it's all over. I rented it a couple of days ago, as soon as I knew I might have to pull you out. Only one other person knows about it besides me. If we'd gone with my guys back there, you would be a bone of contention right now. People have different ideas about things. Maybe you would've ended up back at some facility with them trying to erase your memory of this altogether. Or maybe . . . well, who knows? I just think it's best to get you out of the way and keep you out of the way until nobody cares about you anymore."

She felt a small thrill of alarm. "You mean, you're not in charge of what happens to me?"

He grimaced. "I am, at least in theory. But now that we've hit pay dirt with Barnes, some of the higher-ups at the Bureau are honing in. I don't feel like I can guarantee that things will go my way on everything, and I don't see any reason to take chances with you." A glimmer lightened his expression. "You ever heard possession is nine-tenths of the law? That's the principle I'm operating under here."

He got out as he finished, and Katharine, who was now perfectly willing to go inside the building, unfastened her seat belt and opened her door. As she swung her legs out, he was there beside the door, pulling it the rest of the way open for her. He took one look at her bare feet, smiled a little, and shook his head.

"What is it with you and shoes, anyway?"

Her brows twitched together. He might be all that was standing between her and death, but that didn't mean she was happy with him.

"Probably it has something to do with the company I keep," she said tartly, and stood up. Her knees were wobbly, she discovered to her dismay, and as she rose she went unexpectedly light-headed. Grabbing the top of the door, she managed to steady herself before her legs gave out. Her toes curled against the smooth, warm blacktop for balance, and she took a steadying breath of the soft summer air.

"Don't even think about it." She glared at Nick when he gave every indication of being ready to sweep her up in his arms and carry her into the building. "You get to carry Muffy."

He looked slightly taken aback, then glanced into the backseat, where Muffy had so far been silent in her carrier.

"I forgot about the damned cat." His eyes swept her. "You sure you can make it?"

"Positive."

He looked skeptical but opened the back door and reached in for the carrier. Meanwhile, Katharine managed to stand on her own two feet and close her door, even if she did lean against it afterward, ostensibly to wait for him but really to gather her strength. She felt like she'd been run over by an eighteen-wheeler, but there was no need for him to know that. Her memories might have been messed with, but she retained enough of a feel for their relationship to suspect that the only way to deal with Nick without him taking charge completely was from a position of strength.

Carrier in hand, he closed the door and looked at her. "I can always come back for the cat, you know."

"Carry the cat."

The light-headedness had subsided, and even though her legs still felt weak, she lifted her chin and straightened her spine and relied on willpower to keep her upright as she walked into the building beside him. There were few streetlights anywhere around, about one per parking lot as far as she could tell, so the street and small yard and tiny, flat porch were dark. Cars were parked along the street and in the various lots. A man who looked like nothing more than a denser shadow among many walked along the sidewalk on the other side of the street, heading away from them. He was the only person in sight.

When they stepped inside, it was into a small central lobby that was dimly lit by only a single panel in the ceiling. One wall was taken up with a large rectangular metal grid of mailboxes, each with the apartment number and a slot for a piece of paper bearing the resident's name to be inserted in it. Many of those were empty. She counted four rows of four mailboxes each, which made for a total of sixteen apartments. Several smooth, brown-stained wooden doors opened off the lobby. One was marked *Emergency Exit*, another was marked *Laundry Room*, and the rest, presumably leading to apartments, were unmarked. There was an elevator beside the emergency-exit door. Nick punched the button to bring it to them while Katharine cast slightly nervous looks at the front door.

If someone had come through it before the elevator arrived, she probably would have had a heart attack.

They rode up to the third floor and got out. Besides the elevator and the emergency exit, there were two doors on each side of the hall, marked 3A, 3B, 3C, and 3D, respectively. Nick walked across to 3C, which was across the hall on the left, pulled his keys from his pocket, and unlocked the door.

Katharine moved past him into a small, dark living room, which was immediately illuminated by a white jar lamp in a corner by the couch as Nick entered behind her and flicked the light switch beside the door.

"Home sweet home," he said, closing and locking the door and setting the carrier down. Muffy immediately meowed.

"Poor cat, she's been in there forever."

Katharine moved to let her out even as she glanced around. The room was a long, narrow rectangle, with a round pine dining table and four chairs at one end, along with another doorless entryway that opened into the kitchen. The other side of the room held a brown-and-tan plaid couch pushed against the wall they had entered through. A brown recliner sat beside the couch, with a glass-topped metal table holding the lamp between them. A glass-topped coffee table sat in front of the couch, with a black remote control on it. Across from the couch, a small TV was tucked into a cheap oak shelving unit that also held various decorative knickknacks. Nondescript tan curtains that reached only halfway to the floor closed over one of the small windows that were a feature of the building.

"It rents by the week, and it came furnished," Nick said as Muffy cautiously emerged from the crate. "I stocked it with some food and other things I thought you might need, so you should be good for a while."

"What do you mean 'I should be good for a while'?" Katharine frowned at him while the cat looked from her to Nick and let out a piercing yowl. "You're not planning to just leave me here, are you?" Then, to the cat, she added on a softer note, "Hey, Muffy," and bent to stroke her. Muffy twitched her tail and started walking away with another piercing yowl even as Katharine's fingers grazed her back. Clearly theirs was not a touchy-feely relationship.

"I'm winding up an investigation here, remember?" He looked at the retreating cat. "You don't suppose it has to go to the bathroom, do you?"

"Muffy's a *she*, okay? And at a guess, I'd say it's either that or she's hungry." Katharine reached into the crate for Muffy's dishes. Unfortunately, like her shoes and purse, the cat food had been lost in transit. "And just so you know, there's no way in hell I'm staying here by myself."

Muffy had disappeared into the kitchen. Dishes in hand, Katharine followed, clicking on the bright overhead light as she went. Now that she no longer felt like she was in imminent danger, she was getting a kind of second wind. It was a galley kitchen, she saw at a glance: white linoleum, white tile, white appliances, dark wood cabinets. Nick, frowning, brought up the rear.

"The whole reason I got this place was so you could stay here and be safe." He sounded a little testy as he watched her fill Muffy's water dish from the sink and set it on the floor. The cat immediately crossed to it and lapped thirstily. She even let Katharine stroke her back while she drank. "There's tuna fish in the cabinet beside the refrigerator. I'm fresh out of cat food, but cats like tuna."

"She's going to need a litter box," Katharine pointed out, opening the cabinet in question. Sure enough, there were half a dozen cans of tuna, along with various varieties of canned soup, a jar of Jif peanut butter, a box of saltines, a box of Cheerios, a can of coffee, and a bag of sugar. And that was just the one cabinet. Five more just like it lined the wall. Clearly he didn't intend for her to starve.

"Shit," he said, and left the room, presumably to acquire a litter box.

In the meantime, Katharine opened a can of tuna and dumped it into Muffy's bowl. Muffy must have smelled it coming, because she looked up, suddenly alert. Her big blue eyes gleamed hopefully. She tracked the bowl's descent with radar-like precision, and as soon as Katharine put it on the floor she was all over it, eating in big, greedy gulps.

She was even, Katharine realized as she crouched to stroke her again, purring.

"You're . . ." *Welcome,* she was going to say, but her throat closed up before she could get the last word out. She was staring at her arm, the one that was extended in front of her as she stroked Muffy. Besides the two round burns on it—which she had already mentally dealt with and gotten over—there was a thick scattering of brownish dots of various sizes. At first glance, she had almost thought they were freckles—except that she didn't have freckles.

Katharine sucked in her breath and felt the room start to recede.

"What?" Nick asked, reappearing and dropping something to the floor. The sharp *slap* of its landing was enough to bring her head around in surprise and get her past the first acute stage of impending freak-out. "Jesus, you're white as a ghost."

"I have Hendricks's blood all over me." Her voice was very calm, and she managed to stand up without keeling over, which, under the circumstances, was a considerable accomplishment. What Nick had dropped on the floor, she saw at a glance, was a makeshift litter box, fashioned out of a cardboard box with strips of ripped-up newspaper piled high in it. She only hoped Muffy wasn't proud. "I have to go take a shower. Right now."

She was already moving toward the second exit from the kitchen, a doorless rectangle like the first, which opened onto a hall that led to the bedrooms. Presumably, she would find a bathroom back there.

If she didn't get Hendricks's blood off her soon, she would vomit.

"Okay." His eyes moved over her, and his lips tightened at what he saw. He followed her, a little at a loss, she thought, as to what to do. "You need help?"

There were two bedrooms. The master, which was easy to tell because it was much larger than the other one and had a queen-size bed while the other had twins, was bound to have a bathroom adjoining it. It did, she saw when she was about halfway across it.

"No," she said over her shoulder. "But don't you dare leave while I'm in the shower."

"No," he said. "I won't."

With his promise echoing in her ears, she stepped into the bathroom, turned on the light, and closed the door. Then she promptly walked to the toilet, opened the lid, and vomited.

It was probably twenty minutes later by the time she stepped out of the shower. The hot water had done its work: She was as clean as it was possible to be, and she felt limp and absolutely boneless. The strong scent of the Irish Spring soap—clearly he was partial to that brand—she had used lingered in the air even as she wrapped herself in a towel. A beach towel, big and orange, with a picture of a foaming can of Miller Lite on it. There were about a dozen identical ones stuffed haphazardly into the small linen closet, and she could only suppose that they had been running a special at Big Lots when Nick had gone shopping. In any case, there was enough terry cloth in that one towel to wrap it around herself twice over, and, with the ends tucked in, to cover her from her armpits to just above her knees. When she stopped in front of the sink to brush her teeth for the third time since she'd been in there—Nick had thoughtfully stocked the medicine cabinet with a handful of new toothbrushes and two tubes of toothpaste, and she wondered if he'd thought he was buying for an army—she was already nicely dry. She had put her hair up so it wouldn't get wet, and she was just pulling out the single bobby pin—clearly a leftover from a previous tenant—she had found in the linen closet when she noticed in the mirror over the sink that there were a couple of tiny spots staining the bandage on her nose.

She looked closer and felt her stomach drop. She couldn't be positive, of course, but the drops looked like blood.

Her heart speeded up as she contemplated removing the bandage. It was flesh-colored, not much larger than a Band-Aid, and it covered the bridge of her nose completely. It had been faithfully in place since her nose had been smashed. Thinking about what kind of damage might be under there, she shivered. For some reason, she felt a strong reluctance to take the bandage off. But she could breathe easily now, she realized, and her sense of smell was definitely back.

There was no mistaking the scent of that Irish Spring soap.

If her nose wasn't one hundred percent healed, it was healed enough, she told herself. And she absolutely could not live with the possibility that there might be drops of Hendricks's blood on that bandage.

Leaning in toward the mirror, working very cautiously, she pried up one corner of the bandage with a fingernail and started to peel it gently from her nose. Her face screwed up at the thought of what she might see. Her heart tripped anxiously. But when the bandage came off, what she saw was a slightly reddened but perfectly normal nose.

Her perfectly normal nose.

A little crooked, with a small bump on the bridge. Many times in her life, she'd thought about having it fixed, but she had always found an excuse—lack of money, lack of time, sheer cowardice—not to.

Jenna, honey, you don't want some little Barbie-doll nose.

The words echoed through her head. Somebody had said them to her once, a long time ago. A man. It was a man's chiding voice, filled with avuncular affection, that she was hearing in her mind.

Jenna.

Her eyes widened on her own reflection. Her heart began to pound. She could hear her blood rushing in her ears. The whole bathroom seemed like it was shifting around her, and a terrific pain shot through her head. She clung to the sink, gasping for air.

After a moment, the dizziness and pain receded enough to allow her to get her bearings a little.

Don't think about it.

If she did, she knew the pain would at least come back.

So she tried not to. She steadied herself, then, cautiously, let go of the sink and walked to the door. Opening it, she leaned against the jamb. Light from the bathroom streamed out around her. The bedroom was dark, but not so dark she couldn't see the bed with its simple white counterpane, the slightly shabby blue armchair in the corner with the floor lamp beside it, the stretch of cheap, tan wall-to-wall carpet.

"Nick," she called, her voice as weak as she felt. "*Nick.*"

But he must have been nearby, because he heard and walked into the bedroom. He had stripped down to a white T-shirt, which he wore with his black pants now, she saw as he looked at her inquiringly. Her eyes met his, clinging to them, even as his inquiring look turned to a frown and he lengthened his stride to reach her.

"What the hell?"

"Nick." If she hadn't been leaning against the doorjamb, she would have collapsed as the pain came back and the room started to spin around her. "Who's Jenna?"

24

"Damn it to hell." He caught her as her knees gave way, grabbing her by the upper arms, then, as she crumpled against him, gathered her up. "Okay, I've got you. Don't faint on me."

She dreaded saying it again, knowing that the pain would come with it, but she had to know. In fact, she felt that somewhere deep inside she did know, that the knowledge was right there beneath the surface of her consciousness waiting to emerge.

"Who's Jenna?" Her voice was the merest breath of sound. Her heart hammered. Her pulse raced. The expected pain attacked her, sharp and stabbing, and she moaned faintly as it shot through her head. Sliding an arm around his neck, she closed her eyes. He sank down into the armchair in the corner with her cradled in his lap.

"Everything's going to be okay." He was holding her close, his hand warm and gentle as it smoothed her hair back from her face. There was an undertone of harsh, driving fear in his voice, and she forced herself to open her eyes. Her head was pillowed on his wide shoulder, and he was looking down at her. His jaw was hard and set. His mouth was a tense line. His mild blue eyes weren't mild at all. They were the color of steel and fierce with concern for her. "You don't need to upset yourself about it. Just relax and let it go."

"I'm Jenna," she whispered, holding his gaze, feeling as if her heart was trying to pound its way out of her chest. "Aren't I? *I'm Jenna.*"

Not Katharine. Never Katharine.

She had known it all along.

As the knowledge burst through the barriers at last, defying every attempt of her subconscious to hold it back, the pain was so intense that she cried out. Her heart lurched. Her stomach dropped. But it was true, she knew it was true, she could feel it deep down inside herself—and he knew it, too. She could see it in his face. In that one split second, it was as if she could see the whole fabric of her life spilling out before her, the narrative of it undulating like waves of fine silk.

Then it was gone. All except for the certain knowledge that she was Jenna. Not Katharine. Never, ever had she been Katharine.

"Jesus Christ." His tone made it equal parts prayer and expletive. The distressed sound she made must have terrified him, because his voice turned harsh and his arms tightened around her. She could feel the heat of them, the hard, muscular strength of them, enfolding her in a protective cocoon, cradling her close. He was breathing too fast. She could feel the rapid rise and fall of his chest against her breasts. "They said they'd fixed it this time. They said you wouldn't be able to remember."

"They were wrong. I remember."

The pain was so bad that she was dizzy with it. It felt like it was tearing her head apart, ripping her brain in two. Her head spun. Her pulse drummed in her ears. She closed her eyes and clenched her teeth in an effort to fight it, curling up close against him, drawing her knees up against his side, pushing her face into the warm curve between his neck and shoulder, clinging like a barnacle to a rock. She lay against him like that, tense, unmoving, battling the pain while he murmured a mixture of curses and reassurances into her hair and held her close. Slowly, slowly, the pain receded. Gradually her body relaxed, and finally she took a deep breath, inhaling his comforting, familiar smell.

She knew his smell, recognized it instinctively, had probably subconsciously picked up on it from the moment she woke up in the hospital. It was a mixture of his own masculine scent with a spicy overlay of Irish Spring.

"Who's Katharine?" Her voice cracked a little on the name. Fortunately, no pain accompanied it. "*Is* there a Katharine?"

"There's a Katharine." His face was impossible to read. "She's Ed Barnes's girlfriend. And his personal assistant. She's been working for us as an informant, and when we had to pull her out, you took her place."

"*What?*" She couldn't get her mind around it. It hurt to even try. She felt like a newly hatched chick with its beak agape, only she was desperate for knowledge rather than food. "How?"

"The thing is, you look like her. Dead like her when you come right down to it, although because of the difference in your coloring, it isn't all that easy to see at first. Your height and general build are the same, although she was about fifteen pounds lighter. Once you got down to her weight, and you got your hair colored and styled like hers and we did a few other things, like fix the gap in your teeth and drill her mannerisms into you, it was hard telling the two of you apart. It's the facial structure—and the eyes. She's got the same beautiful green eyes."

The compliment went totally unappreciated. At the moment, she didn't care whether he thought her eyes were beautiful or not.

"The hypnosis—it made me think I was her."

"We thought it would be safer for you. Barnes isn't stupid, and he has spies and surveillance systems everywhere. You needed to stay in character twenty-four hours a day. There was no way you could give yourself away if you truly thought you *were* Katharine."

"You used me." The words came out of nowhere, sharp with accusation. The memory behind them shimmered just beneath the surface of her consciousness. On some deep level she knew what it was, what he had done, but she could not quite access the details.

"I made a deal with you." His tone was flat, uncmotional. "You agreed to it. Hell, you welcomed it."

The memory popped into her mind with the sudden sharp clarity of a snippet of video unspooling on a dark screen. On a Sunday some six months before, just as it was starting to get dark, she was standing at the sink in the kitchen of her own small house, looking out at a backyard dusted with snow. She was dressed in jeans and an oversized gray sweatshirt that concealed most of her curves. The unruly mop of her auburn hair was pulled back in a ponytail that still allowed long tendrils to escape and tickle her nose. Which was a problem, because she was wrist-deep in loam as she struggled to repot a Christmas amaryllis that had grown too large for its container. Gardening, it seemed, was one of her passions. She always had her hands in the dirt, and had the short, clipped nails to prove it.

Then someone knocked on the kitchen door—only friends and family ever used her kitchen door—and she rinsed her hands and went to answer the summons. When she opened the door, Nick was standing there—Special Agent Nick Houston, FBI—with his hair cut ruthlessly short and his face pale and tired, wearing a puffy green goose-down jacket and jeans with scuffed boots instead of his usual jacket and tie.

"Hey," he said by way of a greeting, and he must have read her intention in her eyes because he moved fast enough to prevent her from slamming the door in his face, which she fully intended to do. Instead, he strong-armed his way into her kitchen, then turned to look at her with the merest suggestion of a mocking smile.

"Good thing I'm not sensitive," he said. "Otherwise, you'd have me thinking you're not glad to see me."

At which point she screamed *"Get out,"* and when he didn't, she screamed it again and then took off one of the rubber clogs she was wearing and threw it at him.

He dodged, and the shoe smacked into a cabinet behind him. Then he grinned at her and held up a hand and said, "Stop! Wait! I'm here to make you a deal."

She hesitated, barefoot now, her other shoe in her hand, glaring at him. . . .

The pain attacked without warning and the memory vanished just like that, although she knew it was still there, still lurking in her mind just out of reach. Whimpering, she pressed a hand to her temple, doing her best to will the pain away. As she let her mind go blank, it finally did go away. She lay against Nick's chest, panting in its aftermath, wanting to know more but dreading another onslaught of pain.

"Okay, forget the whole hide-until-this-is-over thing." His voice was grim. "We need to get you to the doctor who did this, pronto."

She could feel his chest muscles tightening, feel the bunching in his arms and legs as he gathered himself to stand up with her.

"No."

The doctor—he was a psychiatrist. A government psychiatrist. An ordinary-looking man with a little paunch and intelligent eyes. She remembered him, not clearly but well enough to be sure. He had been one of the men in the woods that night with a flashlight. She had been terrified when she had realized they had come for her. She hadn't wanted to go with them, but she had to.

This time she felt the pain coming and tensed in dread. Then she deliberately let her mind go blank before it could grab hold.

Tightening her grip on Nick, she waited, shivering, until she was sure it had retreated.

"Look, you're scaring me here," he said. "I was supposed to take you to Dr. Freah and let him sort this out when the investigation was over anyway. I think maybe, under the circumstances, we should be heading his way a little early. Like now."

"No," she repeated, opening her eyes. "I'm not letting anybody do anything to my mind again. No way, nohow."

"Jenna . . ." He sounded like someone who was trying to reason with a stubborn child. But hearing him say her name felt incredibly right. It was as if she had been looking at the world through a distorting prism all this time, and now it had suddenly dropped away so that she could once again begin seeing clearly.

"I won't go," she said, adding, "I'll fight you every step of the way," just to make her position perfectly clear, and moved her head back on his shoulder a little so that she could see his face. There was a pinched whiteness at the corners of his mouth and a hardness to his eyes and jaw that told her his emotions were on edge, too. She didn't want to try summoning more memories, because she was afraid of the pain. But she wanted to know. She *needed* to know. "I remember throwing a shoe at you and then you telling me you wanted to make me a deal. What deal?"

She could feel him hesitating, feel his breathing deepening, feel the tension in his body. His face could have been carved from stone. His eyes slid over her face, and then he glanced away.

That was how she knew: Whatever the deal was, he didn't feel good about it.

"Nick," she said, and he looked back at her, finally meeting her eyes. "Please."

"You want to know about the deal? Fine, I'll tell you about the deal." His voice was flat. "Here's the bottom line: If you would agree to pose as Katharine Lawrence, I'd pull some strings to get your father out of prison."

The blow couldn't have hit her harder if he had shoved his fist into her chest. Her eyes went wide. She sucked in air.

Snippets of memory swirled through her mind like images in a kaleidoscope. Her father: the voice chiding her teenage self for thinking about getting a nose job. The parent who had raised her single-handedly after her mother had died in a car accident when she was four. The person she had always loved most in the world.

"My father's in—" *Prison*, she started to say, but before she could finish, a surge of memory hit her like a torrent of water spilling through a broken dam. A lightning-fast mental picture of her father grinning impishly at her made her heart lurch. She could see him plain as anything, stocky and not overly tall, wearing his trademark short-sleeved white shirt, red tie, and dark slacks, his thick, gray hair curly as lamb's wool, his jovial, blunt-featured face wreathed in smiles. He had met her on the threshold of his Baltimore financial services firm that day, hugged her, and then stood back to show her what was freshly painted in tall gilt script on the frosted glass in the top half of the front door: *Michael T. Hill and Daughter, LLC*. She'd been fresh out of the University of Maryland, armed with an accounting degree, and this was her first day on the job as his full-time—rather than summer or after-school—employee. She had meant to work for him for just a little while, to help him out and get some experience under her belt. But adding her organizational ability and work ethic to his talent for finding and charming clients proved a potent formula. The firm thrived and grew, and four years later she was still there, working flat out, a lot of twelve-hour days, a lot of weekends, a lot of holidays, whatever it took to get the job done. A couple of relationships fell by the wayside—she didn't really have the time to devote to them—but at its apex, Hill, LLC (she had talked her father into shortening the name) had sixteen employees and an annual billing of more than a million dollars. They were on their way.

Then one golden summer evening the wolf appeared at the door, in the form of Special Agent Nick Houston, FBI. Of course, she hadn't known that he was the wolf at the time. She hadn't known he was an FBI agent, either. She'd thought he was a client, because that was what her father told her. The first time she had set eyes on Nick was early on a Saturday evening some two years ago. She had been at the office for about an hour, totally alone in the empty building as she worked to finish up a corporate audit that had to be completed by that Monday morning before going to meet some clients at a nearby Morton's for dinner. Seated in her private office with the door closed, frowning over some figures that didn't want to add up, she heard noises in her father's adjoining private office, which, since he took weekends off as religiously as some people went to church, was unusual. When she went to investigate, she discovered her father, who usually spent his Saturdays playing golf, seated at his desk in front of his computer—which was equally unusual, because he barely knew how to work it—with a handsome stranger standing behind him, looking over his shoulder at the screen. Her father wore his golf clothes: a bright yellow polo shirt and madras slacks. The other guy—mid-thirties, close-cropped blond hair, tall, lean build—was dressed in gray dress pants and a navy blazer, white shirt, and gray striped tie. Practically the Fed uniform, but, of course, at the time she hadn't known enough about Alphabet Soup World to even begin to suspect.

They both looked up when she appeared in the doorway. Her father's expression made her think of a little boy with his hand caught in the cookie jar. He looked guilty, alarmed, and definitely not glad to see her, which was so unlike him that her antenna instantly went up. The other guy's expression was inscrutable.

"Jenna. I thought you weren't working this weekend." Wetting his lips, Mike Hill glanced over his shoulder at the other man, who had straightened and was looking at her with a spark of unmistakable masculine appreciation in the depths of his mild blue eyes. It was only then that she realized that she was dressed for her dinner date in a sleeveless little black dress that showed off her curves—and no shoes. She hated heels, and had kicked off her pumps under her desk. The knowledge that she was standing there in her bare feet made her feel self-conscious, which in turn made her frown at him. "This is . . . this is . . ."

"Nick Evans," the newcomer lied—although, of course, she'd had no clue then that it was a lie—stepping out from behind her father and holding out his hand. "You must be Mike's daughter."

"I'm Jenna," she confirmed, shaking his hand. "It's a pleasure to meet you, Mr. Evans."

"Nick," he said, smiling at her, and she had smiled back, both because he was a smokin'-hot guy and, she assumed, a client, although her father's demeanor still made her wonder what was up with that. But when she taxed him on it, once they were alone, he steadfastly insisted that Nick was simply a new, potentially very big, account, and told her that as a firm they should do everything they could to keep him happy.

Poor trusting thing that she was then, she believed him.

After that, Nick was around a lot, at the office and, later, as weeks turned into months, out of it. He never worked with her or any of the associates; instead, her father kept him as his exclusive client, which, again, was unusual. But her father brushed off her questions, and—as she saw later, with the useless wisdom of hindsight—she was too intrigued by the guy's good looks and easy charm to probe too hard.

The brutal truth was that during the course of bantering exchanges at the office and deeper conversations over cups of coffee and casual meals and the occasional poker game for three when she would, with increasing frequency, drop by her father's house to discover Nick there, she developed a real thing for him. A major crush. The kind of chemistry-based infatuation that would make her heart speed up when he walked into a room, that would make her go all warm and fuzzy inside when he smiled at her, that would make her daydream with embarrassing regularity about what it would be like to just walk up to him, wrap her arms around his neck, and kiss him senseless like she was dying to do.

But she held back, because he was a client and coming on to him did not seem like the professional thing to do.

The thing was, although she could tell that he was attracted to her, too, although she could see the heat in his eyes sometimes when he looked at her, although she could feel the electricity sizzling between them when he walked her out to her car after dinner at her father's house, say, or when he sat in her chair in her office with his feet propped on her desk while she tried to explain to him the intricacies behind different financial vehicles, he didn't so much as make a move in her direction. He didn't ask her out, he didn't try to kiss her, he didn't even make a suggestive remark. Not once.

He simply looked at her with eyes that she could swear burned for her and stayed strictly hands-off.

Until the day when she found out the truth.

It was a Thursday, a perfectly ordinary Thursday in late January, one of those cold, gray, slushy days when nobody wants to be outside. Wrapped up tight in her camel wool coat, with galoshes on her feet and her high heels in her hand, she was the last one out of the office, although not by much. Her father had stayed later than usual, leaving only some fifteen minutes before. It was full night at almost seven p.m., and she remembered thinking how tired she was and wondering whether, if she stopped by her father's house on the way home, she would find Nick there. He'd been in her father's office earlier, but he had left before she had a chance to do more than wave and smile at him through the open door.

It was embarrassing to admit even to herself, but she really, really wanted to spend some time with Nick, and that's what she was thinking about when she left the building via the side door, which opened onto the parking lot that they shared with a couple of other businesses. The wind was blowing a few sparkly crystals of snow around, and the macadam was shiny-wet and ringed with the previous day's snow. The smell of wood smoke hung in the air. There was no one, absolutely no one, in sight. She hurried through the dark parking lot with her shoulders hunched against the cold. She had almost reached her car—which she was careful to park under one of the two security lights, since it was almost always dark when she left work—when she happened to notice that her father's gray BMW was still in the lot. Surprised, frowning, she changed course and went over to check it out.

What she found was her father lying motionless on the asphalt beside his car.

"Dad! Oh my God!" She dropped to her knees beside him, grabbing his shoulders, the slush immediately soaking her black pants from the knees down, as icy cold as she suddenly felt all over. "Dad! Dad!"

To her everlasting relief, he groaned and moved and opened his eyes. Her first, immediate, reaction was a wave of thankfulness that he wasn't, as she had originally feared, dead.

"What happened? Did you fall?" Her voice faltered as she noticed that one eye was starting to swell up and his mouth was cut and bleeding. Her hands slid over the smooth surface of his navy overcoat, instinctively searching for other injuries. "Were you mugged?"

Glancing fearfully all around as the thought occurred—still no one in sight—she was already fumbling through her purse for her phone as she added, "Don't move. I'm calling for an ambulance."

"No! No, don't call anyone." His voice was surprisingly strong, and his grip was, too, as he grabbed her wrist to stop her from opening her phone. "Just get me into the car and let's get the hell out of here. They might come back."

He stirred like he was trying to sit up, but he couldn't do it, and panic clutched at her throat. Never in her life had she heard fear in her father's voice—until now.

"*Who* might come back?" Pulling her wrist free of his grip, she flipped open her phone even as she cast another scared look around. "Just stay still. I'm calling the police."

She was dialing 911 even as she spoke.

"No!" There was such panic in his voice that she paused with her finger poised above the last digit to frown at him. "Don't you understand? You do that and they'll kill me—they'll kill us both." Breathing hard, he managed to push himself into a sitting position, then flopped awkwardly sideways so that his shoulder was propped against the side of the BMW. "You gotta call somebody, call Nick."

"Nick?" Uncomprehending, she stared at him.

That's when her world as she knew it came crashing down around her ears.

"He's FBI," he said tiredly, closing his battered eyes and slumping against the car. Blood trickled from his cut mouth down over his chin, but she was too shocked to even think about trying to stop it. "Just call him, would you? His number's on my phone. In my pocket."

Still reeling, she fished out the phone, found the programmed number, and pressed the button. When Nick answered—a simple "hello" with no identifying information, which, in retrospect, said it all—her voice held no intonation whatsoever as she told him, "It's Jenna. My father's been hurt. He said to call you. We're in the parking lot outside the building."

"I'll be right there," he said, and he was. But with her father's fear that "they" might return as an impetus, she had already managed to get her father up and into the backseat of his car. He was lying across the seats, breathing hard, and she was tucking his legs inside when she heard a footstep behind her.

"Hey." It was Nick's voice, she recognized it instantly, but it came too late to prevent her from whirling and jumping with fright. He met her gaze fleetingly, but his attention immediately shifted to her father. He leaned into the car. "You hurt bad?"

"A couple cracked ribs, maybe. I've had worse." Mike's voice sounded labored.

"Was it Manucci?"

"Yeah. He didn't like the profit margin, so he sent two of his goons to let me know. Jumped me in the parking lot." His voice changed. "They said that if things don't improve, next time they'll hurt Jenna."

"Okay." He withdrew from the car, shut the door on Mike, and caught Jenna, who was hovering behind him, by the elbow. There in the uncertain light of the dark, newly scary parking lot, he looked hard, tough, and in no way like the charming man she had come to have a major jones for. "I need you to get in your car and drive to Mike's house. Stay right in front of me. I'll drive him, and then I'll come back for my car later."

He was propelling her toward her car as he spoke, pausing only to scoop her heels and purse from the pavement where she had dropped them.

"You're FBI?" she asked, still not quite believing it as she fished in her pocket for her keys. He nodded grimly.

"Yes."

"But what's going on?" Her head was whirling, and she knew she was in shock, but she still retained enough presence of mind to know that whatever was happening, they—she and her father and the firm—wanted no part of it. "Is it bad? Is it about us?"

"It's not about *you*." He took her keys from her and pressed the button to unlock her door, then opened it for her. "Get in."

"What do you mean it's not about me?" Panic tightened her throat and had her clutching at the sleeve of his navy jacket. "Is it about my father? Please, I have to know."

"You probably ought to ask Mike." Tossing her shoes and purse into the passenger seat, he disengaged her hands from his coat, bundled her inside the car, turned on the ignition for her, and pulled her seat belt around her. "Lock the doors. Drive. I'll be right behind you."

Then he closed the door on her, turned, and walked back toward her father's car. Her heart pounded like a jackhammer as she watched his tall, broad-shouldered figure stride away across the wet pavement.

It was her father who told her the truth, late that night, after they had returned to his house and Nick had called somebody—another shadowy government doctor—who had come, patched Mike up, and left again. Mike was lying in his bed, propped up on pillows because breathing was difficult with his injured ribs. Holding her hand, he wept as he confessed that he was using the firm to launder funds for the Mob, channeling "dirty money" offshore and from there investing it in legitimate businesses and financial vehicles so that the earnings would appear legal. Crime boss Phillip Manucci was one of Hill, LLC's biggest clients, although his dealings with the firm were known only to her father. Manucci was the target of Nick's investigation, and he had simply followed the money to Mike Hill. The investigation was almost over, and it looked like it was going to bring down the entire Baltimore-and-D.C.-based faction of the Mob along with a dozen or more basically unrelated businesses that were, nevertheless, part of the web Manucci had spun to mask his crimes.

Hill, LLC included.

"I'm so sorry, baby," her father said, clutching her hand as she sat on the edge of his bed, his usually cheerful face crumpled with worry and grief. "Money was real tight. I had you to raise, put through college. It started so small—I needed a loan to keep the business going, and Manucci was the only one willing to give me the money. Then he asked me for advice. What was I going to do, turn him down? Let me tell you, you don't turn down Phillip Manucci and live to tell the tale. Then it just mushroomed from there. Soon there was no way out. I was in too deep. By the time Nick showed up, I'd been laundering money for Manucci for years. Once the FBI found me, I knew I didn't have a choice. Like Nick said, if

I cooperate with him I'll spend a few years in prison. If I don't, when Manucci gets wind of the investigation—and he will get wind of it, sooner or later—he'll kill me without a second thought. And even if I was prepared to face that, now he's threatened you." His eyes closed, and he heaved a great shaking sigh as tears leaked out from under his closed lids. "I've made a hell of a mess of it, Jen."

Listening, her stomach cramped. Her throat closed up. Always, all her life, her father had been her rock, the solid, sturdy presence at the core of her life. No matter how guilty he was, to see him brought so low both terrified her and wrung her heart.

"It's okay, Dad," she said, tears falling from her eyes, too, as she hugged him. "We'll get through this together. Don't worry anymore, please."

She stayed with him until at last the pain pills the doctor had given him kicked in and he fell asleep. Then she headed for the living room. For her entire life, her father had done his best to care for and protect her. Now she was determined to do what she could to care for and protect him.

With that goal in mind, she went out to the living room to talk to Nick. He was sprawled on her father's big leather couch, minus his jacket and tie now, his long legs stretched out in front of him, his hands folded behind his head as he watched some kind of sports show on ESPN. A black shoulder holster was slung across the left side of his chest, unmistakable against his white shirt. There was no mistaking the gun that was strapped securely into it, either.

The sight of that gun made her stomach knot.

His head swiveled toward her. His arms dropped and he sat up a little straighter.

"How's Mike?"

"Worried. Scared." She walked toward the couch and sank down beside him. Because her pants had been soaked, she was wearing a pair of her father's silky pajamas with a matching robe that was cinched tightly around her waist. Her feet were bare. "Just like I am."

"I'm not going to let anything happen to you. You have nothing to worry about."

They were sitting so close that their arms brushed. Jenna turned a little sideways so that she faced him. Except for the flickering light from the TV, the small living room was dark.

"I'm not worried about me. I'm worried about my father." She picked up Nick's hand and held it in both of hers, her slim, cool fingers sliding with wordless entreaty against his big, warm ones. Her heart stuttered a little as their eyes met. Despite the circumstances, despite what she now knew about him, despite the threat that he posed to her father, she could still feel the heat sparking between them. "What's going to happen to him?"

"He's going to prison." His voice was flat. "I'll tell the court how much his cooperation meant to the investigation, and he'll probably get just a few years."

Jenna felt faint. "A few years." She lifted his hand to her face, pressing the palm against her soft cheek. His eyes narrowed. His mouth tightened. He didn't pull his hand away, though, and she took this as a good sign. "He's an old man. Prison could kill him."

"Prison won't kill him. Manucci will."

She took a deep breath. "There has to be some way, something you can do. . . ."

"There isn't."

"Nick, please . . ." She turned her head so that her lips grazed his palm. Deliberately, she parted her lips against his skin so that he could feel the moist heat of her mouth. She pressed a soft kiss to his palm and touched it with her tongue. His hand stiffened, he sucked in air through his teeth, and his eyes went dark and hot. Electricity arced through the air between them, and she could feel her body quickening with anticipation. Holding his gaze, she whispered, "I'll do anything, *anything*, if you'll keep my father from going to prison."

He moved then, leaning toward her, his hand tightening on her face as he tilted it up to him. For an instant his eyes slid over her face, seeming to linger on each feature. Then his mouth was on hers, hard and hot and fierce and absolutely mind-blowing. Her eyes closed, her lips parted, and her bones melted, all in a single sizzling instant.

Then he pulled his mouth from hers and stood up.

"Forget it, angel eyes" was what he said, in a low, rough tone, as she sat there gazing blankly up at him, her eyes dazed, her head spinning, her body aflame. "Even if I wanted to, there's nothing I can do. This thing's too big, and I'm not the only one involved here."

Then he scooped up his jacket and tie from the nearby armchair and walked out the front door.

Two days after that, late on a Saturday night when the rest of the building was deserted, she and her father were huddled in front of the computer in the basement offices where their back files were stored, at Jenna's insistence secretly going through every business dealing Mike had ever had with Manucci. If there was any way to make any of them look legit in the eyes of the law, that was what Jenna was determined to do, and to hell with whether she got in trouble for it or not.

Then two of Manucci's goons had appeared out of nowhere, shoving guns in their faces, pulling Jenna away from her father and tying her to a chair. It was, she realized immediately, the real-life basis for the dream she'd had in Nick's cabin. Manucci had gotten wind of a possible FBI investigation and meant to find out what, if anything, Mike Hill had told them. Once that was accomplished, he'd given orders for the pair of them to be killed.

At practically the last second, Nick and his team had shown up and blown the goons away.

Nick had untied her as Mike, who had collapsed and was lying in a pool of what turned out not to be his own blood, was surrounded by frantic agents. By the time Nick got her free and she was able to run to her father's side, it had been determined that Mike hadn't been hit: He had simply fainted. Then a medical team showed up and whisked him away, and she went with him. Mike was formally arrested later that night.

The last time she saw Nick prior to his showing up in her kitchen with his "deal" was at her father's sentencing. It was the previous June, and he'd sat in the witness chair, unemotionally telling the judge that Mike Hill had been instrumental in bringing down Manucci and his crime family.

She had been seated in the courtroom listening, and their eyes had met precisely once. By then she almost hated Nick—but still she felt the electric jolt of that contact clear down to her toes. And that made her hate him even more.

At the end of the day, the judge had sentenced Mike Hill to ten years, and she had collapsed in floods of tears. Not that it had done the least bit of good.

With her father in prison and the firm gone, its associates and clients dispersed, its assets confiscated, she had taken a job with a landscaping firm. The hours were flexible, there was no pressure or stress, and she had always loved working with plants. She hoped that tending living things would help her heal.

Then, on a wintry January day a little more than six months later, Nick had come knocking at her kitchen door.

Nick, whose lap she was presently curled up in, whose arms were warm and strong around her, who was right at that moment whispering soft words of reassurance in her ears. To be in his arms felt so good, so right, that once she would have wanted to stay right where she was forever. But now that she remembered exactly who he was and what he had done, she stiffened like somebody had goosed her. Her fists clenched. Her head lifted from his shoulder. Her spine straightened and she pushed herself upright in his lap. As he looked at her in surprise, pure fire shot at him from her eyes.

"You no-good, dirty, rotten son of a bitch," she said. "Get your hands off me."

Nick was still regarding her with transparent surprise as she whisked herself off his lap. Of course, as soon as she stood up her towel slipped—she'd forgotten that all she was wearing was a giant orange towel—and she had to grab at it to keep it from dropping like a stone to her feet. But she saved the towel, tucking the ends securely between her breasts and glaring at him at the same time, and never mind that her head was hurting and her legs were rubbery and she had just remembered the experience from hell. Actually, that was a plus, because it had provided her with a much-needed adrenaline boost. She felt totally herself for the first time in ages, and as a result she was so mad at him she could spit.

"For your information, I just remembered everything," she said through her teeth.

His expression turned cautious. He leaned back in the chair, his posture maddeningly relaxed as he looked up at her. "Did you now?"

"You said I'd be perfectly safe. You said you'd make sure of it. You said I would never even set eyes on Ed." She would have stomped her foot if she hadn't been afraid of dislodging the towel. Instead, she gripped it tighter and glared at him. "What you didn't say was that people were going to be messing with my mind. You lying *jackass*."

Infuriatingly, he smiled.

"Welcome back, angel eyes," he said softly.

As the endearment registered, Jenna felt as though steam should be pouring out of her ears.

"Angel eyes? Don't you dare call me that. Besides being brainwashed, I've been beaten and tortured and scared to death and almost killed about half a dozen times now, thanks to you. That's enough. I quit, do you hear? I *quit*." She was quivering with outrage. "I've kept my end of the deal. Now it's time for you to keep yours and get my father out of prison." She narrowed her eyes at him. "And you better not have been lying to me about that, too, because if you don't do what you promised, I'm going to run straight to a reporter I know at *The Washington Post* and tell him every tiny little thing I know about this top-secret investigation of yours."

"Are you threatening me?" He not only looked amused, he sounded amused. She felt her temper shoot through the roof.

"You're damned right I'm threatening you."

Without warning, he stood up, his height and broad shoulders making him loom suddenly very large in the uncertain light. *Intimidating? Oh, yeah*—or at least, he would have been if she'd been even the tiniest little bit afraid of him. The thing was, she wasn't. She now knew Nick Houston far too well for that. Glaring at him, gripping the towel just in case it should choose that inopportune moment to go south, she stepped back a pace. But only because he was crowding her and she refused to be that close to him voluntarily ever again. So what if her heart was beating faster now simply because, despite everything, she was discovering to her fury that she still wasn't quite over that thing she had for Nick.

"I don't blame you," he said.

She narrowed her eyes at him suspiciously, but he sounded sincere. The light spilling through the open bathroom door touched his golden hair; his blue eyes (and was their mildness deceptive, or what?); his long, mobile mouth; the strong, angular lines of his cheekbones and chin. The top of her head just about reached his chin, and the breadth of his shoulders was easily double that of hers. Scowling up at him, she had this thought: How unfair was it that her nemesis should be sexy enough to make her toes curl?

"You don't?"

"Nope. But you don't have to worry. It's over for you now, and the deal stands: Your father's early release is already in the works." He reached out and trailed his knuckles along her cheekbone. Ignoring the way the warmth of his fingers made her stomach contract, she frowned direly and jerked her face away and took another step back. But that still didn't put her very far away. She was not ready, she discovered, much to her own chagrin, to turn her back on him completely quite yet.

Some part of her—the stupid part—still wanted Nick.

"You better be telling the truth."

His smile was brief and wry. "You really don't trust me, do you?"

"No."

"Okay, I guess I can't blame you for that, either. Look, a lot of the stuff that's happened I didn't foresee. We were going to pull Katharine out while Barnes was out of town, and if things had gone down like they were supposed to, you wouldn't have had any contact with him at all. You were just supposed to kind of hold her place for a week or so while she testified before the secret grand jury that's been convened so we could get an indictment against Barnes to wrap this thing up. With an investigation of this magnitude, as high-level as Barnes is and as much dirt as he has on everybody in town, we had to make sure that he didn't get the slightest hint that we were working to bring him down. Obviously, something went wrong and he did get wind of it. But believe me, I never thought, when I brought you into this, that you would get hurt. It kills me that you got hurt." He took her hand, and she didn't resist, although part of her wanted to. His jaw tightened as he looked down at the small, round burns on her arm. When he met her gaze again, his expression was stark. "When I heard you scream tonight down in that damned bunker and I couldn't get to you, I almost lost my mind."

Lifting her hand, he placed it against his cheek. Her heart picked up the pace a little more and her breathing quickened as she felt the warm prickliness of his skin with its hint of stubble beneath her palm. Taking a deep breath, fighting to keep at the forefront of her mind the anger and hurt and sense of betrayal that were what she knew she should be feeling she still didn't pull her hand away. She realized that she wanted—no, needed—to hear the rest of what he had to say first.

"I was ready to take the place apart with my bare hands. If they hadn't brought you out when they did, I would have done whatever it took to get to you." He turned his mouth into her palm, pressing his lips to the sensitive skin. Her breath caught. Her heart pounded. Her mouth went dry. It was a deliberate repeat of the way she had kissed his hand on the couch in her father's house on that never-to-be-forgotten night when she had begged Nick to save her father from prison.

Which he hadn't done. He had, in fact, kissed her and turned her down flat, leaving her both heartbroken and humiliated.

The memory broke the shimmering aura of heat and electricity that was building between them like a bucket of water to the face.

She snatched her hand back, folded her arms over her chest, and glared at him.

"Is there a point to this? Because it doesn't seem to be going anywhere I care to go."

"There's a point." He gave her a small, rueful grimace. "And you're going to make me spell it out, aren't you? Fair enough. Here goes." He hesitated, and for a moment she thought he was going to reach for her again and tensed in automatic rejection. But he didn't, instead thrusting his hands into the front pockets of his pants and regarding her steadily. "From the first moment I saw you when you came walking barefoot into Mike's office, I was attracted to you. The more I was around you, the more I got to know the person you were inside the beautiful, sexy package"—here she narrowed her eyes at him warningly just to let him know that she was immune to his flattery—"the more I was attracted. But there wasn't anything I could do about it, because I was working a case that involved your father, and anything personal between you and me would be a huge conflict of interest. That night on Mike's couch when you begged me to fix things so he wouldn't have to go to prison, I almost lost it. You were tearing my heart out, and at the same time I wanted you so bad I—well, let's just say I wanted you bad. But I walked away because I had a job to do. And I stayed away, for the same reason, even though through all those months I couldn't get you out of my mind."

Her eyes were now clinging to his, no longer narrowed with suspicion but rounded with hope and vulnerability, and as soon as she realized it she immediately scowled in reaction. His mouth twisted in wry acknowledgment of her change of expression as he continued: "I knew Mike wasn't a bad guy, and I knew how close the two of you were. I kept looking for an angle to help you both, and when I came across Katharine Lawrence and saw how much she looked like you, I found it. She'd been acting as an informant for us for months, and we only needed about a week of testimony from her without Barnes suspecting anything was up to wrap things up, but that was a very dangerous week for our investigation. I thought the best thing to do was put somebody in her place while she testified, so that Barnes wouldn't even begin to suspect what was up. That somebody was you. I used your physical resemblance to her to give you what you wanted, which was your father out of prison, and I used it to get back in with you. And the reason why I did it is because I'm crazy about you."

As his words sank in, silence spun out between them, vibrating with an increasing tension that was almost palpable. Her heart, she realized, was beating really fast. There was a big knot in her stomach, and somewhere along the line she had completely forgotten to breathe. Exhaling slowly so that he wouldn't notice, she frowned a little as she searched his face. His jaw was hard, his mouth unsmiling. His eyes were narrowed, with a restless gleam to them as he watched her. He looked tall and dangerous and impossibly sexy standing there in front of her in the silent, shadowy bedroom, and her body responded to him the way her body always did.

It tingled and burned.

"You gonna say something here?" His voice was wry. "You know, that's how a conversation usually goes: I say something, you say something . . ."

"No," she said, and she didn't. Instead, she did what she had been dying to do. She took a step forward, went up on her toes, wrapped her arms around his neck, closed her eyes, and kissed him.

For a moment he didn't move, while her mouth plied his and her tongue slid between his lips and she pressed herself with abandon against every hard, muscular inch of him. His mouth was hot and tasted faintly of coffee, just like it had the last time she had kissed him, and as she registered that her heart slammed in her chest and her pulse pounded in her ears and her insides went haywire. Then he drew in a deep, shuddering breath and kissed her back. Wrapping his arms around her waist, he pulled her even tighter against him and slanted his mouth over hers and kissed her with a hunger that made her dizzy. His lips were firm and dry, and his tongue was hot and wet, and the kiss itself was so exciting that she trembled. His body was bigger than hers, far more muscular, thrillingly, unmistakably masculine. She clung to him, kissing him with the pent-up desire of thousands of daydreams, and when finally he lifted his head she made a husky little sound of protest.

"Jenna," he said, his voice deep and raw, and she opened her eyes. His face was flushed with desire and his eyes gleamed hotly down at her.

"Nick," she said back, holding his gaze, wonderfully conscious of the feel of him against her, of the hardness and heat of him, of the shivery desire rushing along her nerve endings that had its center somewhere deep inside her body. The electricity between them was so strong that it practically sizzled in the air. Breathless, quaking, she smiled up into his eyes and stroked his warm nape with her cool, slender fingers.

He caught his breath. His jaw tensed. His eyes were heavy-lidded and so hot that they practically scorched her as they moved over her face, touching on each individual feature, lingering on her eyes, on her mouth. His arms were hard and strong around her. His hips and thighs were tight against her own. She could feel the tension in him, feel the heat radiating from his body, feel—there was no mistaking it—the tangible evidence of his desire pressing against her.

"I want you so much," she said.

His eyes blazed at her. Then, unexpectedly, that quick grin of his appeared and was as quickly gone.

"I think that's my line," he said, and kissed her again, so thoroughly that she was bedazzled, absolutely lost in lust, clinging to him, kissing him back greedily. Her head spun, her heart pounded, and her legs trembled. She rocked against him, sliding her fingers into his newly long hair, kissing him as if she would die if she didn't, wanting to make him as hot as he was making her.

Nick, Nick, Nick . . . his name ran through her mind in a feverish refrain. She had wanted him for so long. Now she was melting for him, burning for him, on fire with passion for him.

His hand found her breast through the thick towel. The pleasure of it made her knees grow weak. Her nipple tightened and swelled under his caress. His mouth left hers to trail hot, wet kisses along the line of her jaw.

"Nick." His name was scarcely louder than a breath. She clung to his shoulders while her bones turned to water and her insides to fire.

"Hmm?"

"Make love to me."

He lifted his head and looked down at her. His jaw was set and his eyes were heavy-lidded and burning hot.

The smallest of smiles touched his lips, and the brief flash of humor in his eyes dazzled her. "Getting there."

Then he kissed her, his mouth hard and hot and compelling, and she kissed him back as devouringly as he was kissing her. He was still kissing her as he picked her up, swinging her clear off her feet with the easy strength that she'd come to know so well and that still managed to thrill her to her toes every time, even though she might not always admit it. He turned and took the two strides necessary to reach the bed, and then he lifted his mouth from hers so, she thought, that he could see what he was doing as he swept the covers out of the way with one quick yank. She busied herself in the meantime by pressing hungry kisses to the strong column of his throat.

"I've been thinking about this for so damned long." His suddenly hoarse voice bore no resemblance at all to his usual drawl as he lowered her to the mattress. It was only as her back touched the cool, smooth sheet that she realized that somewhere along the line she had lost her towel. The discovery caused her eyes to pop open. His arms were still around her, and he was still leaning over her, sliding his mouth sensuously along her collarbone. She shivered with reflexive pleasure even as her gaze sought and found the towel. It was lying in a crumpled heap where they had been standing, and as she saw the orange mound of it there on the beige carpet, she had a moment of absolute clarity in which she realized that she was totally naked and probably about a heartbeat away from getting it on with Nick. For a moment she backpedaled as she did a quick mental review of her many beefs with him and recollected how much she had hated him not more than ten minutes before.

But of course she hadn't ever really hated him at all.

Her eyes widened as she faced the fact that she was wildly, madly, deeply, in love with Nick, and probably had been for a long time.

Not that she meant to tell him so. She had to get accustomed to the idea herself first. In fact, the knowledge sent anxious little curls of panic tumbling through her system. She stiffened, just about to freak out, when he straightened away from her to pull his T-shirt over his head. She looked up at him as he dropped it to the floor and found herself totally distracted. His shoulders were broad and bronzed and heavily muscled. His arms were bronzed and muscular, too. His . . .

Here her thought processes faltered entirely as she realized that he was just standing there beside the bed, staring down at her naked body with eyes that burned her everywhere they touched. She was a nice toasty-golden color, she saw, glancing down at herself a little self-consciously, and thin, much thinner than she was used to being, but then that just gave her curves of a different scale, made her waist tinier and her hips narrower and her legs amazingly slender and long. Her breasts were smaller, too—she had an instant of regret for the usual lush fullness of her breasts—but they were still firm and perky, the nipples dark and erect as they swelled up toward him. From the diamond-hard glint in his eyes as they moved over her, he liked everything he saw, and the thought made her go all shivery inside.

Then, just about the time she remembered being in love with him and was once again freaking herself out with the thought, his gaze landed *there* and she remembered about the Brazilian wax and the heart tattoo instead and totally lost her train of thought once more as she blushed from the soles of her feet to the top of her head.

She must have made some small embarrassed sound, because his eyes suddenly met hers.

"Sexy." His eyes held a wicked glint over and above the heat in them, and his lips curved teasingly at her as he started unfastening his pants.

Her face was burning still, but she guessed that it was probably too dark for him to tell. Besides, the unfamiliarity of her own body was exciting, too.

"Hurry up." She arched her back a little and reached out to stroke his hard-muscled thigh through the smooth synthetic of his pants.

His jaw hardened. His hands stilled in the act of unzipping his fly. Passion blazed at her from his eyes.

"Darlin', two seconds and you're mine," he said, and finished stripping with swift, single-minded efficiency, ridding himself of pants and boxers and shoes and socks in scarcely more than the blink of an eye, clearly a man focused on a goal. Which meant she didn't have a lot of time to admire the view, but still she saw that his torso was the classic vee shape, wide through the chest and narrow through the waist and hips, with tight, toned abs and long, powerful-looking legs. He didn't have a lot of body hair, but what he did have was dark brown and formed a wedge in the middle of his chest before arrowing down to—well, she followed that trail with her eyes and caught her breath.

And she thought, *Wow.*

Then he came down on the bed beside her and kissed her again. His hands were everywhere, and suddenly her heart was pounding so hard and she was breathing so fast and her body was burning so hot that she couldn't think at all. Kissing him, she ran her hands along the width of his shoulders and down his back, loving the damp heat of his skin, loving the flexing strength of the muscles beneath it. Hot and wet, his mouth found her breasts, suckling them one at a time, and at the exquisite sensation, her body tightened and quaked. She cried out at the sheer pleasure of it, only to have the sound swallowed up by his mouth as his lips found hers again.

This is Nick, she thought, heart pounding, and wrapped her arms around his neck and kissed him back with hungry abandon. Nick, for whom she had yearned for so long . . .

His thigh slid between her legs, parting them, rocking up against that part of her that ached and burned and wept for him, and she gasped against his lips. Then his hand replaced his thigh, stroking her, caressing her, and finally delving inside the velvety cleft. In the process, she lost the ability to engage in any kind of conscious thought at all as she moaned and moved and dug her nails into his back.

His fingers moved within her, slid in and out, in the slow-handed, expert way of a man who knew his way around women, and she arched against his hand and gasped her pleasure into his mouth as her body pulsed with tremors.

"Easy," he murmured as lips left hers to trail hot, hungry kisses down her neck, over the dark-tipped globes of both breasts, and down the center of her rib cage. Breathing in fast little pants now, her pulse racing like she'd been running for miles, she slid her hands sensuously across his wide shoulders as his fingers continued to work their magic on her.

"Mmm" was her intelligent response.

"Great tattoo," he murmured a moment later, his voice thick but bearing a trace of humor, too, and it was the amusement that allowed her to catch her breath and focus enough to muster a reply.

"It better be temporary." She tried to interject a threatening note into that, but it was hard to sound threatening when she was weak and shivery with desire, she discovered, so she succeeded only in sounding breathless instead.

"It is. Think I could talk you into making it permanent?"

"No."

He pressed his lips to the small red heart, then trailed his tongue along the arrow that, she was only just realizing, suddenly seemed to have a purpose in life after all. It pointed directly to the place she most wanted his lips to go. Even as she had the thought, go he did. The feel of his hot, wet mouth moving over her sensitive skin sent streamers of delight rippling through her body. Heart pounding, pulse racing, she stiffened in anticipation. Because she knew what was coming next, and she was right.

His mouth inched its way down between her legs, crawling with exquisite slowness over the satiny mound with its tiny strip of fur, making her squirm, making her lift her hips off the mattress, making her quiver and pant and grab fistfuls of sheet. Finally he was there, his hands beneath her, cupping her bottom and holding her still for him, pressing lascivious kisses where she most wanted them, and she cried out again and again as wave after wave of scorching heat broke over her body.

"Nick, please," she gasped, tugging at his shoulders when finally she was so hot and hungry and absolutely wild with longing that she couldn't stand it any longer.

He lifted his head then and looked at her, his eyes heavy-lidded and burning.

"You taste like strawberries," he said in a low, hoarse voice. "I've been wondering forever."

He lifted himself up and over her, wrapping his arms tight around her, kissing her with a torrid eroticism that turned the air around them to pure steam. She could taste herself on his lips and thought, *Yes, he's right*, just as he thrust inside her, huge and hot and hard, with no more warning than that. It felt so unbelievably good, just what her body ached for—even the sudden fierceness of it was just what she craved. She cried out at the explosiveness of her response and clutched him and wrapped her legs around his waist and cried out again and again as she came in deep, shattering cataclysms.

"I love you, Nick; I love you, Nick; I love you, Nick," she moaned at the end, and he went very still for an instant as if absorbing that before thrusting into her with deep fast strokes that carried her away on another wave of ecstasy until, with a groan, he plunged inside her and held himself there and found his own release.

For several long moments, she lay there limp as a dishrag while the last sparkle of the late lamented fireworks faded from her mind. He was sprawled on top of her, his face buried in her neck, breathing hard, heavy as a collapsed building.

This, she realized, was afterglow.

Then her pulse quickened as she remembered the last comprehensible thing she had said to him.

I love you, Nick.

Her eyes popped open. She almost groaned. She really, really, really wasn't ready to let him in on a secret like that. Not yet. Not without some serious thought. Not . . .

He lifted his head and looked at her. Straight into her eyes. Just like that. No warning at all. *Boom,* and she was pinioned by a pair of not-so-mild blue eyes. Taken by surprise, she blinked at him, alarmed.

"We need to talk," he said, and rolled with her so that she was on top with their legs all tangled up. As the cool air hit her back, she saw that she was totally uncovered, slightly sweaty, and liable to get very cold very soon.

She also had her arms around his neck.

"I need . . ." she began, hoping to ward off the discussion she could see was coming by using the ever-handy excuse of running to the restroom. But before she could get another word out she was interrupted by something sharp that stabbed cruelly into her back.

She shrieked.

W hat the hell?" Nick grabbed her arms as she convulsed on top of him, alarm plain in his face.

Apparently startled by the commotion, the pale shadow that was Muffy bounced with all the grace of a rhino from the small of Jenna's back to the mattress, where she curled up, not a foot from Nick's elbow, wrapping her furry tail around herself and staring at the startled humans with big eyes that shone with obvious disfavor.

"Jesus Christ, that scared the life out of me." Nick sank back down with a sigh of relief, pulling a pillow that hovered precariously near the edge of the mattress under his head. Now that the attacker had been identified as the cat, all Nick's attention was on Jenna, who had rolled off him during those first frenetic seconds and was at that moment both rubbing her abused back and sliding off the bed with the intention of going for the towel.

"Scared *you?*" Supremely conscious of his gaze on her naked backside, she turned sideways and bent her knees in an effort to pick up the towel as gracefully as she could, doing her best not to give him any too-explicit views in the process. "She jumped on my back. With her claws out."

"Bad kitty," Nick said, not very severely. Then, "Wait a minute. Where are you going?"

Wrapping the towel around herself, Jenna felt marginally more in control. The sex had been great: earth-shattering, mind-blowing, pick your superlative. The realization that she was in love with him? Not so much. He'd said he was crazy about her, but what did that mean, exactly? Men said all kinds of things when they were trying to get a woman into bed. It did not necessarily mean the same thing as love. Anyway, letting him know that she was in love with him put all kinds of power in his hands, power that she wasn't sure she was ready to give him. Of course, she had stupidly blurted it out.

She was pretty sure that's what he wanted to talk about. And she didn't want to, not until she had time to get used to the idea herself. Until she got used to *being* herself again, with all the details firmly settled in her mind.

"To the bath—" *Room*, she started to say, turning to look at him. But the sight of him lying stretched out on the bed with one arm bent beneath his head, stark naked and totally at ease with it, while he stroked the cat was so arresting that she broke off. The man was hot, no doubt about it. And he was also clearly an animal lover. Muffy was looking as blissed-out as a furry Buddha, with her eyes listing at half-mast and a contented cat smile on her face. It was impossible to be sure over the hum of the air-conditioning, but Jenna was ready to swear that Muffy was purring. Ridiculous as it was, Jenna felt what was almost a pang of jealousy. Muffy had never looked at her like that. Then her brows contracted as reality hit. "Wait a minute. That's not my cat."

"No," Nick agreed, scratching Muffy's ears. If there was a kitty Nirvana, Muffy appeared to have reached it.

"That's *Katharine's* cat. The real Katharine."

"Yeah."

"No *wonder* . . ." Jenna said, then stopped as Nick frowned suddenly and shifted his gaze to Muffy. His fingers were buried in the thick ruff of hair under her chin. When they emerged, they were grasping the plastic ID tag Jenna had discovered previously.

"Jesus Christ." Nick stared at the plastic rectangle like he'd found gold. "I think it's a thumb drive. What the hell is a thumb drive doing around the neck of this cat?"

"No clue." Jenna stared at the thing in Nick's hand, too.

Muffy, tethered, was starting to look perturbed. Her tail twitched, her eyes widened, and she pulled her head back. As Nick slipped her collar over her head, she gave him an affronted look. Standing up, shaking her head, she stalked to the end of the bed and curled up again with her back to them. Clearly, Nick had fallen out of favor.

Nick sat up, swung his legs over the side, switched on the lamp beside the bed, and stared down at the gray plastic rectangle dangling from the pale blue leather collar. It had been secured to the metal ID loop with an O-ring. It was obvious that someone had put it there deliberately.

"She hid this thing on the cat," Nick said, picking it up to look at it more closely. "Katharine. I don't know what's on it, but that's a hell of a hiding place, I have to say. This is something she doesn't want anybody to find."

Jenna frowned. "Maybe that's what they were looking for. The men who broke into my house. They didn't find what they were after in the safe, remember. That other guy came back the next day."

Nick's eyes met hers for a pregnant instant. "Maybe it is."

There was a rising excitement in his face. He carefully put the collar down on the bedside table and stood up, reaching for his clothes. He, she was interested to note, made no effort to search for a flattering angle as he bent over. Not that he appeared to have an unflattering one. The guy was all sleek muscle and smooth flesh.

"There's one way to find out." He stepped into his boxers, pulled them up, and then did the same with his pants. "I have a laptop in my car. We'll just plug that baby in and see what's there."

"What do you think is on it?"

"No idea." He zipped his pants, pulled on his T-shirt, and stuck his feet in his shoes without bothering with socks. "But knowing Katharine,

I'll be real interested to find out." He headed for the door. "I'll be right back."

A jolt of anxiety struck her. She followed him with her eyes. "Promise?"

"Oh, yeah."

Then he was gone. She heard him walk down the hall and through the living room, heard the door open and close, heard the faint click of the lock. Then it occurred to her that this was a wonderful opportunity to get dressed. She thought of the pants and T-shirt she had discarded in the bathroom, realized that if the rest of her had been covered with blood they probably had been, too, and shuddered. Wait—Nick had said he had bought her some things—did he mean clothes? Opening the closet door, she found a Macy's bag on the floor. In the Macy's bag were two sets of silky underwear and bras, two pairs of khaki shorts, two T-shirts, and a pair of flip-flops. Choosing a flimsy white panty and bra, a pair of khaki shorts, and a navy T-shirt, she took them into the bathroom with her. She had just finished washing and putting on her new underwear and was in the process of pulling up the shorts when she heard Nick come back into the apartment.

She could tell from the sound of his footsteps that he was moving fast.

"Jenna," he called, not too loudly. There was an urgency in his voice, though, that had her hurrying to unlock the door even as she fastened her shorts.

"Here," she said unnecessarily as she opened it. He was already in the bedroom, striding toward the bathroom door, and clearly saw her. His eyes swiftly scanned her. Her eyes, however, didn't move. As soon as she saw him, they fixed on the big silver gun in his hand.

"We've got to go. Right now." He brushed past her into the bathroom, grabbed the navy T-shirt from the towel rack where it waited, and thrust it at her while she said, "What? What's wrong?"

"They've found us. They were around the Blazer, looking through it. If they don't know exactly which apartment we're in, it won't take them long to find out. Come on."

She had pulled the T-shirt over her head while he was speaking. Having her heart pound was actually starting to feel familiar, she thought as he caught her arm and started hustling her toward the door. Ditto with the dry mouth and the cramping stomach.

"Wait a minute." He stopped dead in the bedroom, turned to look directly at her feet, and frowned direly. "I thought so. Shoes."

She had forgotten that she was barefoot.

"Right." She ran for the bag, pulled out the flip-flops, and thrust her feet into them. Remembering, she spared a swift glance for the bedside table. Except for the lamp, it was empty. "You got the thumb drive, right?"

"Oh, yeah. Let's go."

This time he caught her hand, and together they rushed toward the door. Once there, he made her wait as he listened cautiously at the panel.

"Okay," he whispered, and quietly opened the door.

Muffy immediately darted past them into the hall, meowing loudly and waving her fluffy tail.

"Shit," Nick said, casting a narrow-eyed glance at the cat as he paused to close and lock the door behind them. "What are you doing?"

This was directed at Jenna, who had recovered from the mini heart attack the cat's unexpected rush past her ankles had given her and was doing her best to capture a recalcitrant Muffy.

"We can't just leave her out here."

"The hell we can't."

He grabbed her hand again, casting a hunted glance at the elevator while pulling her toward the door beneath the exit sign. Presumably, it opened onto stairs, which they needed to take because, she saw with horror as she followed Nick's glance, someone was coming up in the elevator. The little circular light above the elevator lit up over floor two as she looked at it.

Under the circumstances, in this sleepy little building in the middle of the night, she felt pretty confident that the occupants of that elevator were the bad guys. She and Nick had at best a few seconds to escape.

Her heart lurched. Her breath caught. If it hadn't been for Nick, for his solid presence and his strong hand holding hers and, not incidentally, his gun, she probably would have died of fright on the spot. At the thought of finding herself in Ed's hands again, she broke out in a cold sweat.

It didn't matter that she wasn't Katharine. He would kill her just the same.

They had just made it into the narrow, dimly lit stairwell and the door was closing behind them when Jenna heard the slight grinding sound that announced the arrival of the elevator.

Followed almost immediately by a loud *meow* that made Jenna jump and gasp, and that drowned out everything else.

Muffy streaked by them, racing down the steps.

"Damned cat," Nick said, and Jenna got the impression that this time he had jumped, too.

There were no sounds, no sounds at all, behind them as they fled in Muffy's wake down the hot, musty-smelling staircase. This struck her as ominous, although she couldn't have said precisely why.

"I don't hear anything," she whispered. "If that was them, shouldn't they be knocking on the door, or knocking down the door, or something?"

Nick snorted. "They don't have to knock down doors. If they want in, they're in. Which means they're probably searching the place by now. When they don't find us, you can bet your bottom dollar they'll be checking these stairs."

With that cheery bit of information, they reached the bottom of the steps. Muffy was there before them, standing in front of the door, waiting with waving tail to go out.

The landing was small, and the cat had nowhere to go. Jenna scooped her up.

"What are you *doing?*" Nick asked over his shoulder as he opened the door a cautious crack and peered out.

"If she follows us, and they spot her, they'll know which way we went." There was that, and also the fact that Jenna couldn't bear to turn Muffy out into this unknown neighborhood and leave her. No food, no water, dogs— she was pretty sure that Muffy wouldn't cope well with any of those. She wasn't a street kind of cat. Anyway, Muffy might not belong to her, but she felt responsible for her just the same.

"Fine. Here, give her to me." Nick either accepted her logic or didn't want to waste time arguing, because he scooped Muffy out of her arms, tucked the cat under his arm like a football, and opened the door wide. "Run as fast as you can to that building over there and go around the left side. Don't stop for anything, understand?"

Jenna looked at the building he indicated—it was another boxy apartment building very similar to the one they were in that faced the next street over, so that what she was looking at was its square brick back—nodded, and took off running toward it. It wasn't far, perhaps two hundred yards, but, with the security light above the door and the more distant glow of the lights from various parking lots, she felt hideously exposed as she darted through shadows and shifting patches of illumination. The uneven terrain made footing tricky. The small slap of her flip-flops hitting the ground sounded hideously loud in her ears. A sideways glance showed her the parking lot in which they had left Nick's car. She couldn't see the Blazer itself—the angle wasn't right for that—but, ominously, she could see three big, black Suburbans parked in a neat row right at the edge of the lot. They hadn't been there earlier, and just spotting them made her heart pound like a kettledrum.

There wasn't much doubt who they belonged to.

Dodging around a child's half-full wading pool, which she had nearly, and disastrously, missed seeing in her preoccupation with the Suburbans, she made it around the corner of the building and stopped, panting, to wait for Nick. He was right behind her, gun in one hand, Muffy, eyes narrowed and tail waving, under his arm.

Even as Jenna looked in his direction, she saw, beyond him, the small rectangle that was the door they had just exited through fill with light as it was pulled open from the inside. Four men in suits spilled out, looking around wildly.

She didn't doubt for a second who—or, rather, what—they were.

Sucking in air, unable to speak, she grabbed Nick's arm and drew him deeper into the shadows beside the building. Seeing her expression, he glanced back, too.

"Yeah," he said, and his voice was grim. "I didn't think it would take them long. Let's go."

Sticking to the shadows as much as possible, they ran across that street, through another backyard, along the back of a long row of buildings that might have been town houses, then across another street and through another set of backyards. Her heart pounded and her pulse raced, first from fear and then from fear mixed with exhaustion. Her legs started getting shaky. She had trouble catching her breath. Finally, she got a stitch in her side. If she hadn't known, as surely as she knew anything, that the search was on for them, she wouldn't have been able to keep going. At last, just when she thought she was going to have to stop, Nick stopped instead.

They were standing at the edge of a small, dark parking lot.

"What now?" she wheezed, bending double with her hands on her knees, gasping for breath and battling the stitch in her side.

"We get wheels."

"As in we call a taxi?"

"As in I steal us a car."

"You can do that?"

"Darlin', I got mad skills." He thrust Muffy at her. "Here, take this."

Muffy was heavy and hairy and didn't look at all happy with the situation, but she seemed to recognize the seedy, run-down nature of the neighborhood just as surely as Jenna did, and have enough sense to know that she didn't want any part of it. Neither did Jenna, actually, but there they both were anyway, with no choice in the matter at all. Casting nervous glances around—there were no security lights in this parking lot, and the only illumination came from the full moon overhead and the quick slash of headlights from a passing car—she saw nothing but a warren of brick buildings with only a few lighted windows, none nearby. They were in the midst of a large apartment complex. This was one of many parking lots.

If anyone besides Nick, who was peering through the windshield of a car not too far away, was around, she couldn't see them in the dark.

Not that that made her feel any better, particularly.

A moment later, a car pulled up beside her, making her jump. The passenger door swung open from the inside. No interior light came on. The car remained as dark as pitch.

"Hop in," Nick said.

Peering across the front seat—it was a bench seat, no fancy bucket seats for this ride—Jenna confirmed that it was indeed Nick behind the wheel, and got in. As she closed the door, Nick drove toward the entrance to the lot and Muffy vaulted for the backseat. Jenna let her tired arms sag for a moment in relief, then reached for her seat belt. There wasn't one. Or at least, if there was, she couldn't find it.

"It's probably lost under the seat," Nick said, having observed her fruitless hunt. "This is a 1972 Ford Fairlane. Seat belts weren't that popular back then. Hot-wiring cars only works on really old ones."

"Good to know." She was already looking at so many possible ways to die that driving around without a seat belt was the least of her worries. They were on the street now, heading west. A tall chain-link fence and a shadowy basketball court and another long row of apartments flashed past her window. They came to a cross street, and as he stopped at the stop sign, another car drove through the intersection in front of them. She gave it an anxious glance.

"We're safe now, right?" she asked, as he accelerated through the intersection in turn.

"Reasonably, I think. Whoever that was back there is searching for us big time, I guarantee it, but since they've got my car, they probably think we're still on foot. That buys us some time."

"What do you mean, 'whoever that was back there'? Weren't those Ed's men?"

"Probably. I just can't figure out how they found us." He turned down another street, a little better lit, and Jenna realized they were headed for the expressway.

"They're CIA. They can find anything," Jenna said. The thought made her shiver, and she cast another worried look around. They were nearing the on-ramp for the Beltway, and the overhead lights illuminated the inside of the car. As a result, she felt hideously exposed. There was more traffic, lots of vehicles, in fact, as they merged onto the expressway, but none of them seemed particularly threatening. Still, when an eighteen-wheeler zoomed past, rattling the old car right down to the frame, she jumped a little.

Face it, girlfriend, your nerves are fried.

"Where are we going?" she asked, hoping he had a plan. It had occurred to her that maybe they were running out of options.

"Someplace safe."

She looked at him for a moment. When no more was forthcoming, she said, "You going to tell me where?"

The quick grin that transformed his face was *almost* reassuring.

"I'd say something like, 'Don't you trust me?' but I think I already know the answer."

"You're right, you do."

"The thing is, though, just in case we don't make it to where we're going, it's better if you don't know where that is. Barnes isn't too particular about how he gets his information, as you undoubtedly remember."

"You think he'd try to torture it out of me?" Horror sharpened her voice. For just a moment, she had a flashback to those terrible moments when Hendricks burned her, and felt sick. Glancing out at the vehicles speeding around them again, she was conscious of cold chills racing over her skin.

Nick didn't answer, which she knew was an answer in and of itself.

Ten minutes later, they exited the Beltway way out past Bethesda, and he drove down a series of country roads that got narrower and narrower and darker and darker until Jenna was ready to bite off her manicured fingernails and actually jumped at the hoot of an owl.

Then he pulled off the road into some woods, bumping over what was scarcely more than a footpath. It was barely wide enough for the car, and several times Jenna thought they might not get through.

Finally, he slowed even more as a small, Cape Cod–style house came into view. There was a light on downstairs, and another upstairs in a dormer window. Just about the time Jenna saw that, registered that this must be their destination, and started to relax a little, a man stepped out of the night onto the path right in front of the car.

He was dressed in camouflage and carrying an enormous rifle, which he aimed straight through the windshield at Nick.

Nick cranked down his window. He had to do it by hand. Then he stuck his head out to speak to the guy.

"Yo, Baker, it's me."

The rifle—no, wait, Baker—moved a little closer, giving Nick a suspicious look. He then lowered the rifle, but only slightly. Jenna kept a wary eye on it.

"That's not your car. And you're not on the schedule."

"Yeah, well, I got a new one, and next time I'll be sure to make a reservation."

Baker seemed to hesitate, but then he stepped aside, waving the Ford through. Nick drove through more dense trees, following the track in a semicircle that led around to the back of the house. Except for the lights shining through several of the house's windows, the night was dark and shadowy.

"Who lives here?" Jenna asked, looking at the house with curiosity.

"Nobody, really." He pulled alongside a two-car garage—both doors were closed—and stopped the car. "It's owned by the Bureau, and we use it as a safe house. People come and go as needed." Turning off the ignition and lights, he scooted across the cracked vinyl seat toward her. "I love these old cars," he added in an appreciative aside, draping an arm around her shoulders. As she looked up at him with widening eyes, he slid his other hand along her cheek, stroking his thumb over her smooth skin.

"Nick . . ." she began.

He shook his head at her to silence her. "I've got something to say, and I want to get it out there while I've got the chance." His eyes swept her face. There was the slightest hint of a twinkle in them, but there was heat and tenderness there for her, too. "Just for the record, I love you, too, Jenna."

Even as she recognized the echo of the words she had said to him not very long before, he bent his head and kissed her. His body was firm and warm against hers. His lips were fierce and hot. Her stomach clenched and her heart pounded and she surged up against him, wrapping her arms around his neck and kissing him back.

Nick Nick Nick . . . I love you, Nick.

When he lifted his head she told him so, and so of course he kissed her again, quick and hard but amazingly thoroughly for all that. She was still reeling from it when he pulled his mouth from hers.

"Hold that thought," he murmured, nuzzling her ear, then reached around her and opened the door. "Right now we've got to go."

Yes, right. Bad guys trying to kill them. The stars falling like confetti through her mind cleared enough for her to remember. She looked up at him . . . *Nick* . . . and then she unwound her arms from around his neck and slid out of the car, once again back with the program.

With one vital difference: She was wrapped in a warm cocoon of happiness that had her smiling, even at Baker, who was watching them suspiciously from the thick line of oaks just beyond the garage.

Okay, get a grip.

Taking a deep breath, drawing in a lungful of the earthy scent of the surrounding woods and a slightly burning smell that, she thought, had to be the car, she waited as Nick got out, thrust his gun into the back waistband of his pants, and fished Muffy out of the backseat. She smiled at Nick—which was much more reasonable than smiling at Baker, after all—who smiled back at her, which made her heart beat faster and her stomach go all fluttery. Then she smiled at Muffy, who lashed her tail and looked grumpy. As they walked across the grass and climbed the steps to a small concrete porch that led to the back door of the house, the night seemed extra-beautiful. The moon was a softly glowing white globe in a midnight velvet sky. The stars were glittering diamonds adorning the velvet. The light spilling from the back windows of the house was a lovely golden yellow. Even the deep shadows ringing the trees seemed to dance with joy.

Then Nick punched a code into the keypad beside the back door, and they walked inside the house.

Into an exact replica of her kitchen in the town house.

Holy crap.

Jenna's jaw hit the floor. Her gaze swept the room—center island, bar stools, brick wall, microwave, everything seemed the same—before fastening on Nick, who was looking after Muffy, who had just jumped from his arms and was stalking away. Toward a doorway that opened into a replica of the town-house dining room.

"Nick," she said, in a completely different tone than she had used the last time she had uttered his name. An awful tone, in fact.

His gaze swung around to her.

"Jesus," he said, taking one look at her face. "I forgot. I should have warned you. We redid the inside of this house to match the town house. Don't you remember? So you'd be familiar with it. You lived here for almost a month."

Jenna's mind reeled. She was absolutely speechless. Then her eyes dropped to the floor. The terra-cotta floor with its twelve-inch tiles.

"My God." Crouching, she touched the tiles to make sure. Yes. There was no mistake. They were solid and real and indubitably the dirty tiles she had been nose to floor with on the night Lisa had been murdered.

Then the horrible truth broke over her like a tsunami.

"It was a fake. That night. That night Lisa was killed." Her voice was little more than a croak. Nick was standing over her now, looking worried—*good call*—and she slowly came back up to her full height to glare at him eyeball to eyeball. Well, except for the whole difference in height thing.

"Not a fake." His tone was placating. He reached for her, but she shrugged him off and took a couple of steps back, which ended when she came up against the counter. She stopped, folding her arms over her chest and scowling at him. The counter felt less than solid, she discovered as she leaned back against it, and with another sweeping glance around she realized that the entire kitchen, while visually virtually identical to the one in the town house, was actually a cheaply thrown-together replica. It might look the same, but the quality was vastly different. And whoever had done it had made a mistake on the size of the floor tiles.

"It was a re-creation," Nick continued. "Katharine and her friend really *were* attacked in her town house earlier on that same night. The friend—Lisa—was killed, but Katharine managed to escape just exactly the way you did. That's why the decision was made to put you in then, which was about a month earlier than we intended to do it. Everything had to be rushed at the last minute, because the attack threw our timetable off. If she'd been killed that night, our whole investigation would have gone down the tubes. We couldn't risk it."

"You *terrorized* me."

"I actually wasn't here for that. I was with Katharine, the real Katharine, who really was rushed to Washington Hospital after the attack. We substituted you for her later that night at the hospital. If I had been here when they were doing the re-creation, some things would have been done differently. You wouldn't have been hurt, for one thing."

"Well, I *was* hurt," Katharine said, glaring at him. "I suppose those were fake bullets they were shooting at me?"

"Yes."

"Somebody smashed my face into the floor." Indignation lent a shrill edge to her voice.

"That was Rimaldi. He was in charge here that night." Nick looked apologetic. "See, the one real difference that still remained between you and Katharine was your noses. Yours has that cute little bump on the bridge and hers doesn't. You nixed the whole idea of a nose job, and we were still brainstorming how to handle the difference when the people here had to make an immediate decision. The decision Rimaldi made was to smash your nose into the floor. That didn't actually happen to her."

"Lucky her," she said sardonically. Her head was hurting again, and she pressed her fingers to her temples. It was, as she had learned all too well, the sign of a repressed memory resurfacing.

I hate it when that happens.

The pain got worse, but she ignored it, concentrating. At first the memory was as amorphous as a cloud, but then, slowly, it took on shape and weight and color. She had been here in this house on that night, lying sleepless in the bedroom she'd been using, already heartily sick of learning to be Katharine but determined to see the thing through, both for her father's sake and to a lesser degree because—*yes, be honest here*—because Nick stopped by to check on her progress every day, and she was secretly pretty wild about Nick.

Not that, at the time, she had ever meant to tell him so.

Then there had been all kinds of commotion downstairs, and she had just been getting up to see what was going on when her bedroom door opened and about half a dozen people trooped into her room. Something had come up, they told her, and it was now showtime. Then the paunchy little doctor—Dr. Freah, that was his name—had cleared everybody else out and injected her with something, and then—her memory started going fuzzy again as she tried to recall, but she could remember how hard her heart had been beating and the panic that had welled up in her throat and how her hands had curled into fists in silent, futile protest—and then nothing at all except a warm, pleasant, floating sensation. A sense of safety and well-being.

From which she'd awakened as Katharine, with a man sneaking toward her through her darkened bedroom.

The feel of Nick's hands on her arms brought her back to the present.

Blinking, taking a deep, shaking breath, she looked up at him. He was frowning down at her, his eyes narrow with worry.

"You okay?"

"No." She flashed him a dark look. "I am definitely not okay." Then she had a thought. "What about the second attack? The one right after I left the hospital? Was that staged, too?"

Nick shook his head. "That one was real. And whoever did it really thought you were Katharine Lawrence."

Jenna had another thought. "The jewelry they were supposedly after, the inheritance I supposedly used to buy this ring"—she glared down at it—"none of that was real, either, was it? That weasly little doctor planted those thoughts in my mind."

Nick made a rueful face at her. "See, we didn't know what the first attack was about, but we were pretty sure it had something to do with the fact that Barnes was blackmailing just about everybody under the sun. At the time, I figured that he'd probably stashed some of the stuff he had on people in the town house's safe, which Katharine had no idea was there, and somebody had come for it. But now . . ." His voice trailed off, but then he seemed to give himself a mental shake and went on. "Anyway, since you were going to be playing the role of innocent Katharine, who wasn't an FBI informant, and since we couldn't simply cover up the break-in and murder at the town house because the local police were already on the scene, we had to program you with an explanation for the attack that didn't involve Barnes's blackmail gig but that would still be believable enough to you so that you could report it to Barnes, the police, whoever, with a straight face. We'd seen that *Post* photo of you—I mean Katharine—wearing all that jewelry, so we decided to use that. As for the supposed 'inheritance,' that was the money we paid Katharine to act as an informant. Just in case Barnes started checking her bank accounts, we gave you an explanation you could use."

"Oh my God," Jenna said. Before she could expand on that, she was interrupted by a woman's voice saying cheerily, "I knew I heard voices. Nick, is that you? What are you doing here so late?"

Nick looked over his shoulder and Jenna did, too. A woman walked into the kitchen. About an inch taller than Jenna and athletically built, she was wearing a navy skirt and a short-sleeved white shirt that buttoned up the front, with a shoulder holster complete with gun bisecting the shirt. But that wasn't what made Jenna's eyes widen. The woman's hair was short, feathery, and nut-brown. Her eyes were brown, too, a soft chocolate color that looked deeply familiar. And her face—the features—Jenna's breath caught as she had an epiphany.

She looked down. A delicate tattoo of a trio of interconnected butterflies adorned the woman's left ankle.

"Lisa," she gasped.

"Special Agent Mary Slater," the other woman corrected, meeting her gaze. "Hi, Jenna." Then, looking at Nick, who had turned to face her, she added in a chiding tone, "She's not supposed to be here."

"She played the part of Lisa when we restaged what happened to Katharine that night," Nick told her. "Complete with auburn wig, in case you somehow happened to see a picture of the real Lisa, who unfortunately was shot to death by whoever broke into Katharine's house." As Jenna was still absorbing this, he switched his attention to Mary Slater. "Until this is over, Jenna goes where I go. Too many people are trying to kill her out there."

"Kill me, you mean," a new voice said.

Jenna looked at the speaker, a blond woman clad in a pale green silky robe and slippers who had just walked up to stand behind Mary in the doorway, and her heart sped up as she experienced the weird sensation of looking at her own double. This, clearly, was Katharine Lawrence. The resemblance was uncanny—except, and it was almost unnoticeable, for the small difference in their noses. Unable to help herself, Jenna stared. After a quick, patently uninterested glance, Katharine did not stare back. The fact that she had a doppelgänger clearly wasn't news to her. Of course, she had probably been involved all along. Who else would have been able to provide such intimate, and accurate, information about Katharine Lawrence's life, down to the location of the front door key

under the mat and the picture of the Kappa Delts, which Jenna now remembered seeing?

"Hello, Katharine," Nick said, and there was a certain something in his
tone that told Jenna that her new twin wasn't his favorite person in the
world. "I'm glad you're up. There's something I want to show you."

"Of course I'm up. I'm a nervous wreck. Do you think I can sleep? I
watch TV instead, because there's nothing else in this hellhole to do." She
turned on her heel and walked away, throwing back over her shoulder,
"I'm watching *Letterman*. If you have something to show me, you can
show me in the living room."

"The diva rules," Mary whispered to Nick with a roll of her eyes, then
turned to follow Katharine.

Nick made a face, but he followed Katharine, too. Jenna followed Nick.

In the living room, which was a replica of the town-house living room,
gray walls, charcoal couch, glass-topped tables and all, Katharine sank
down on the couch, ignoring the trio that watched her from the doorway.
On TV, Letterman was interviewing Drew Barrymore. Nick gave
Katharine a grim look, then walked over to the coffee table, picked the
remote right up off the top of *Rose Gardens of the South*, and turned
the TV off.

"Damn it, I was watching that." Katharine slewed around on the couch
to glare at him.

"You can turn it back on—just as soon as you tell me what this is." Nick
pulled the cat collar complete with thumb drive from his pocket and dan-
gled it in front of her.

Katharine's eyes widened. For a moment she looked alarmed, then
sulky. She folded her arms across her chest.

"So you found that. So what?"

"I need you to tell me what it is."

Her lips pursed. She huffed out a breath and crossed her legs.

"A thumb drive."

"I know that. Now tell me something I don't know."

Nick was being very patient, in Jenna's opinion, but there was a tightness around his mouth and eyes that told her that his patience was stretching thin.

"It's insurance, okay?"

"What kind of insurance?" Nick waited, but Katharine didn't say anything else. "Look, you don't get the rest of the money or a free ride in the Witness Protection Program unless I'm satisfied that you've cooperated to the best of your ability." He paused, giving her the kind of look that reminded Jenna that he was an FBI agent first and foremost. "What kind of insurance?"

"You people are always threatening me," Katharine burst out. "I'm putting my life on the line here, and you're still always threatening me. Why do you suppose I downloaded that in the first place? To make sure the fucking FBI lived up to its end of the fucking bargain." She glared at Nick, then flounced into a different position on the couch, hunching an elegant shoulder at him and staring determinedly at the dark TV. "You can all go to hell."

"I'm going to go plug this into the computer in the office upstairs," Nick said to Katharine's averted face. "Is there anything you want to tell me before I watch it?"

"Go fuck yourself," Katharine said without looking at him.

Nick's lips tightened, and he and Mary exchanged silent glances. Then he turned without another word and headed for the stairs. Katharine picked up the remote from the table where Nick had left it and turned the TV back on. "I'd like my ring back, by the way," she said, stretching her hand, palm out, toward Jenna.

"Oh. Sure." Jenna glanced down at the big sapphire ring, pulled it from her finger, and crossed the room to drop it in Katharine's palm.

"And the earrings," Katharine said without looking at her. Jenna complied. Katharine glanced at the baubles in her hand, closed her fist around them, and thrust them into the pocket of her robe. Ignoring Jenna completely, she focused on the TV.

Jenna retreated toward the door.

"Want to watch *Letterman*?" Mary asked Jenna wryly.

Jenna shook her head. What she wanted to do was follow Nick. On her way out of the living room, she saw Muffy, who'd been keeping a very low profile since stalking away from them in the kitchen, emerge from behind the couch. She brushed against Katharine's ankles, and Katharine shoved her away with an impatient foot.

"Fucking cat," Katharine said.

Watching herself behave badly was not, Jenna discovered, a pleasant experience, so she headed up the stairs after Nick.

He was in the smaller, guest bedroom, which, she discovered, looked nothing like the guest bedroom in her—no, whoops, Katharine's—town house. This one had been outfitted as an office, with a state-of-the-art computer system. The door was open, so she walked on in.

Nick was standing in front of the monitor, leaning over a little, hands gripping the back of the chair that was pushed beneath the desk in front of him so hard that his knuckles showed white. She couldn't see what was playing on the monitor, but she could see his reaction. He was still as stone as he watched it. It didn't even look like he was breathing.

She was just about to say something to him when, from downstairs, a woman's shrill, obviously terrified scream sent every tiny hair on her body catapulting upright.

The scream was followed by an explosion of gunfire.

Nick and she whipped around as one, staring stupefied at the open bed-room door. Beyond it, they could see nothing but empty hallway. But still, menace hung in the air as tangibly as smoke.

"Run, Katharine," Mary bellowed.

More gunfire.

Another horrifying scream from downstairs sent Jenna's pulse rate sky-rocketing.

"No! Please, n—" a woman cried. Jenna was almost sure the voice was Katharine's.

The *pop* of a single shot interrupted.

Jenna's heart gave a great leap. Her stomach turned inside out. A cold chill snaked down her spine. It was impossible not to realize what had just happened: Katharine—possibly Katharine and Mary—had just been shot. The silence was ominous. If Mary was alive, wouldn't she be returning fire? Unless she was hiding, or being held at gunpoint . . .

In any case, the assailants were still in the house.

"Jesus." There was stark, cold fear in Nick's voice. He moved swiftly to the bedroom door, his gun in his hand, his feet almost noiseless on the hardwood floor. His face wore the harsh, hard-eyed expression of the government agent that he was.

He looked back at her, beckoning her urgently to join him. Heart pounding, Jenna did. He touched his finger to his lips, then put his mouth close to her ear and whispered, "I've got to go do what I can to help Mary, and I can't leave you behind. Whatever happens, stay as close to me as possible. Do what I tell you, when I tell you."

She nodded. He gripped her hand. Then he stepped silently out into the hall, leading with his gun, moving quickly toward the top of the stairs. Jenna followed him, her fingers entwined with his, trying to move as quickly and quietly as she could on legs that had gone all rubbery. She was breathing too fast, she realized, and her pulse raced. As they reached the top of the stairs, there was still no one in sight. The only sound from below was a faint explosion of laughter from the TV.

Straining her ears, she tried to listen for the telltale sounds of someone in the house. Between the TV and her own pulse thundering in her ears, she picked up on nothing. But she was absolutely sure that she hadn't heard the sound of anyone leaving the house, either.

Was it possible that the shooters knew she and Nick were there? Could they be lying in wait for them downstairs?

Jenna was horribly afraid the answer was yes.

With a single glance back at her, Nick started down the stairs, still leading with his gun, still holding her hand. Her heart was thumping so hard now that it felt like a living creature trying to beat its way out of her chest. Every tiny creak of the stairs, every small scuffling sound from their shoes on the wood risers, made her breath catch. Her scalp prickled with tension. Her knees shook. Nick kept his back to the wall, and she tried to follow suit. She could tell from the way his head was moving that he was carefully scanning the area they were descending into. About halfway down, their heads cleared the upstairs landing and they were able to see more than just the rectangle of hallway directly beneath them: a tiny slice of the living room, the dark wooden floor that stretched to the front door and, going the other way, to the kitchen.

As she crept down the next few steps in Nick's wake, her gaze swept everything she could see: floor, walls, furniture. Nothing seemed out of place. Still, the invisible tension she could sense in the air screamed *danger*. The sharp smell of recently fired weapons made her nostrils flare.

Near the bottom of the stairs, Nick hesitated for no more than a split second, sucking in air, his eyes fastened on the living-room doorway. From a few steps above him it was possible to see a little way into the living room—and what Jenna saw made her heart turn over.

Resting limply on the deep reds and blues of the Oriental rug was the lower third of a slim, tanned leg—and a slender foot in a pale green slipper. The hall wall concealed the rest of her, but Jenna knew without a doubt that it was Katharine.

Was she dead? The leg didn't move.

Jenna's breath left her body in an audible hiss.

"Shh," Nick whispered, throwing a quick glance back at her.

She nodded.

He stepped off the last riser into the downstairs hall, pulling her after him. As her feet touched the floor, Jenna got a better look into the living room. Katharine lay sprawled on her side in front of the couch, her eyes open and staring, a bullet hole neat and round as a dime in the middle of her forehead. The edges of it were black, with just the tiniest dark red center. The blood pooling beneath her cheek seemed to come from the back of her head.

Exit wounds are always worse. . . .

Jenna suddenly went dizzy. Her stomach turned inside out. She felt her knees start to buckle. Her grip tightened on Nick's hand, and he swung around to look at her . . .

Just as a gun exploded and a bullet smacked into the wall beside them in a trajectory that, if he hadn't moved precisely when he did, would have sent it rocketing through his head. Jenna shrieked and jumped, and both she and Nick reflexively ducked. Her heart thundered like a herd of wild horses. Her eyes were wide and wild as she looked all around. The taste of fear was sour in her mouth.

"Keep your head down," Nick screamed, putting himself between her and the living-room doorway and snapping off two quick shots—*bam! bam!*—at the shooter. Jenna got a quick glimpse of a man dressed all in black with a black watch cap on his head, leaping from one side of the living-room doorway to the other, moving so fast that he was scarcely more than a dark blur. There was a cry—had the man been hit?—and then in response to a gesture from Nick, she was racing straight toward the front door with Nick right behind her, running for her life, fueled by a tremendous burst of adrenaline that rushed through her veins like speed. A glance showed her that Nick was watching their backs, covering their exit, trying desperately to see everything at once. Out of the corner of her eye she got a glimpse of most of the living room, and there was Mary, too, sprawled on the floor several feet from Katharine. She was unmoving, but Jenna couldn't see her face and it was impossible to tell if she was dead.

Then her focus snapped forward again as she leaped for the front door.

Just as her hand closed around the cool brass knob and she turned it and yanked it toward her—*please, God, let there not be some kind of fancy dead bolt that keeps the door from opening*—another gun boomed and, behind her, Nick let out a cry.

Her blood seemed to freeze.

"Are you hit?" she cried, twisting frantically to look at him as she pulled the door wide. He was turned away from her, facing back the way they had come, firing at a black-clad man who ducked back into the living room as Jenna spotted him.

"Run for the car." It was just loud enough for her to hear, uttered as Nick pushed her out the door, and she obediently bolted across the small front porch, threw herself down the steps, and raced around the corner of the house toward where they had left the old Ford by the garage, thankful for the darkness that swallowed her and Nick so that they were no longer such obvious targets. She was breathing like a marathon runner, feet pounding over the grass and hard ruts of the drive, heart pounding faster than her

feet. The men inside could be anywhere now—they weren't just going to let them go—and she glanced fearfully all around as she reached the back bumper of the car.

Nick was farther away than he should be. That was what her glance around showed her. He was about thirty feet back, a black hunched shape in the darkness, lurching as he ran, and she realized with a sick twist of her stomach that she had been right, he was hit, he had to be if he was moving like that.

She was just turning back to go to him, to help him, when a hand grabbed her arm, snatching her off-balance, yanking her sideways.

Oh no . . .

She screamed like a siren even as she stumbled into a solid warm body and an arm fastened like a vice around her waist.

"Hiya, babe," a hideously familiar voice said in her ear, and she didn't even have to cast a quick, terrified glance over her shoulder to know that it was Ed. Her nails dug into his arm—it was useless, he was wearing a jacket—and she struggled desperately until she felt the hard jab of a gun being shoved into her side. She gasped and went still. "Keep fighting me, and I'll blow you in two."

He meant it, she knew. His arm tightened around her waist. The gun dug into her rib cage so hard that it was painful.

"Let her go, Barnes," Nick yelled.

"Drop it," Ed snapped over her head to Nick, who she saw had stopped dead and had his gun aimed at Ed's head, which was the only part of him she wasn't shielding. The gun ground viciously into her side, and she made a tiny pained sound and tried to lean away from it without success. "I guarantee you I can kill her before you can kill me."

Jenna's skin prickled as cold sweat broke out all over her body. Her heart was in her throat. She could scarcely breathe.

"You'd still be dead," Nick said.

Ed chuckled. Horrified, Jenna saw why. Dark shapes were creeping up behind Nick, at least half a dozen of them, bent low like some hideous nocturnal beasts bringing death closer with every silent step.

"Nick, behind you!" she screamed.

Even as he whirled, the night exploded around her.

She dropped like a stone, screaming, as the hold on her waist was suddenly released, sprawling on a combination of hardened earth and soft grass. Her ears rang. Stars burst in front of her eyes. A terrible smell—gunpowder and something else—assaulted her nostrils.

The good news was that she was pretty sure she was still alive.

"Jesus Christ." It was Nick's voice, tight with fear. She blinked, clearing away the stars, and saw that he was beside her, on his knees, one shoulder hunched in a way that she knew wasn't good, his gun nowhere in sight. His hand—only one hand—was on her side, feeling around her rib cage where the gun had been pressed, checking for injury.

Jenna sucked in air. A glance behind her revealed the shadowy outline of Ed's body sprawled on its back on the grass behind her. Some of the dark shapes—men, of course—were clustered around him. She averted her gaze, not wanting to see more.

"I'm all right," she said, sitting up. "He didn't shoot me. You were too fast."

"It wasn't me who shot Barnes." Nick sank back on his haunches, and she could see the long shudder that shook him. "I wouldn't have taken that chance for anything in this life."

"I shot him," a voice said out of the dark. Jenna looked up to see a tall, stocky man looming up out of the shadows behind Nick and felt her heart start to pound again. Was he friend or foe? "Vicious bastard deserved to die."

"Yo, Keith," Nick said, glancing back over his shoulder at the newcomer. "What the hell took you so long?"

Then he swayed. As Jenna reached for him, he collapsed in her arms.

When Nick woke up, he was in the back of an ambulance. The light was dim but it was still too bright for his eyes, so he opened them only a slit. The ambulance wasn't moving, and he guessed it was still parked outside the safe house, probably because they were waiting to load someone in beside him. He hoped it was Mary, hoped she had survived. He lay on a stretcher with his shirt off, still wearing his pants but with a sheet covering him to the armpits and a lot of white gauze wrapped around his shoulder. The wound wasn't fatal, but it hurt like hell.

Keith was sitting beside him. His square-jawed face was paler than usual, and there was a sorrowful look in his eyes.

"Where's Jenna?" Nick asked. He didn't like having her out of his sight. He'd aged a thousand years in those moments after he had realized that Barnes had his gun pressed to her side. He knew as well as Barnes did that he wouldn't have been able to kill the other man before Barnes could get a shot off. But putting down his weapon wouldn't have helped, either. If Keith and his posse hadn't shown up when they did, Jenna would have died. He would have died, too, but the thought didn't bother him nearly so much.

He'd realized over the course of this really harrowing night that in Jenna, he'd found the love of his life.

"She's inside. The paramedics are checking her out."

It took Nick to the end of that exchange to register that Keith was holding a black Beretta, its slender barrel elongated with a silencer.

This was not good news. His heart kicked up a notch.

"You planning to kill me, too?" he asked conversationally.

Keith stiffened, then smiled at him. It was a small, sad smile.

"You found out," he said. "I knew you would. I knew, from the minute you showed up at my house on the night Allie died, that we were going to end up like this. You're an obsessive bastard, Nick."

It was said in a chidingly affectionate manner that sent a chill racing down Nick's spine.

"Barnes had your house bugged," Nick said, and tried not to let the tensing of his muscles show. "Did you know that? That must have been how he knew he could target Allie. But it paid off for him in spades: He got you dragging her into your family room and hanging her from one of those overhead beams just like you were on *Candid Camera*."

"I know." Keith's jaw tensed. "That bitch Katharine Lawrence told me she'd found the video while she was snooping around for us, on one of Barnes's computers. She downloaded it onto a thumb drive and told me she had it, taunted me with it, said she owned me. Bad move on her part. I sent some guys to get it back, but they screwed up. It wasn't in her safe. I sent somebody back the next day to search for it again—of course, the dunderhead didn't realize Katharine had already been replaced and tried to scare its whereabouts out of your girlfriend—but we never did find it. Out of curiosity, where was it?"

Nick smiled grimly. "On her cat. Attached to its collar."

Keith looked stunned. "You're shitting me. I never would've found it."

"Probably not." While he had been talking, Nick had managed to surreptitiously unfasten the webbed straps that secured him to the stretcher.

"You told Barnes about that apartment I rented for her, didn't you? I knew it had to be you when those goons showed up, because you were the only one besides me who knew about it."

"I had to," Keith said. "Earlier today, Barnes got hold of a surveillance video of you with our little false Katharine, and after that he knew we were on to him. He came to see me about two hours ago, and threatened me with that damned video of what happened to Allie. I had to tell him about the apartment, and about this safe house." Keith smiled a little. "What he didn't know was that I outsmarted him: I was going to let him kill you, and Katharine, and then I was going to kill him. Problem solved." He grimaced, and his eyes seemed to harden on Nick's face. "Only he didn't kill you, so now I'm going to have to do it."

The gun moved a little, and Nick tensed.

"You don't have to do this, Keith," he said.

"Yeah, I do. You know I love you like a brother, man. I don't want to kill you, but I know you: You'd never be able to just let this go. It's come down to you or me, and since that's the case, I got to go with me." His jaw tightened. "Just so you know, Nick, I didn't plan to kill Allie. She told me that someone was threatening to blackmail her over those damned drugs, and I snapped. I just couldn't take it anymore. Always having to worry about where she was and what she was doing and whether or not anyone was going to find out. You have no idea what hell it was."

Keith stood up suddenly, bending a little in the close confines of the ambulance. Nick's heart gave a great leap. Adrenaline flooded his veins. This was it, he knew. The moment where he was going to either do or die.

"Look, I've got to go. I'm sorry, Nick." Keith leveled the gun. The flicker in his eyes gave Nick a microsecond of warning. He sensed rather than saw Keith's finger tighten on the trigger.

Summoning every last reserve of strength he had, he hurled himself off the stretcher and onto Keith just as the bullet smacked into the pillow his head had just vacated. Keith went down like a falling tree, tangled in the sheet, pinned by Nick's weight. The Beretta went sailing to the ambulance floor with a clatter.

Two fast, hard punches to the jaw, and Keith was knocked cold. Then Nick yelled for help.

While he waited for it to arrive, he looked down at Keith's unconscious face and said, "That's for Allie, you son of a bitch."

One week later, Nick was at home, in the small second bedroom he used as an office, sprinkling food into the fishbowl. He'd had to move it, because Bill and Ted had a pair of new housemates. They were fine with Jenna—actually, they seemed to like her almost as much as Nick himself did—but they didn't seem to think much of the cat. Muffy, who'd been adopted by Jenna in the aftermath of Katharine's death—Mary, fortunately, had survived—didn't seem to get the whole idea that since the fish had been there first, they should be treated with respect. Until Nick had wised up and moved them to his office, which had a door that he kept carefully closed, Muffy had passed her days sitting on the kitchen counter by the fishbowl, eyeing Bill and Ted with covetous eyes.

It just hadn't worked for the fish.

"Nick," Jenna called from the living room. "We need to hurry. We're going to be late."

To pick up her father. He was being released today. For the next couple of days, the old man would be rooming with the fish. Just until other arrangements could be made. Nick had to admit, he wasn't all that thrilled about having Mike Hill as a prospective father-in-law—oh, yeah, he'd popped the question, done the thing right, gotten down on one knee, the whole bit—but it was a small price to pay for getting Jenna for keeps.

"Nick," Jenna called.

"Coming."

He eased his jacket on—his shoulder was still in a sling—and as he did so the small framed photo that sat on his desk beside the fishbowl caught his eye. The shot was maybe thirty years old, and it showed him as a gap-toothed kid with his ponytailed big sister standing behind him, her arms wrapped around his thin shoulders, her chin resting on the top of his blond head. They were both smiling into the camera, happy that day. Nick looked at Allie, the big sister who had loved and mothered him until she couldn't anymore, and carefully tucked that image of her deep inside his heart. Then he turned and walked out of the office, carefully closing the door behind him. Next week he would be back at work, and life would start to get back to normal, or as normal as it was possible to get with the addition of three new family members. Call it the new normal. Anyway, he would be busy putting together a case against Keith and wrapping up the case against Barnes and filling out paperwork and working his ass off to catch bad guys and doing the hundred and one things that he typically did.

Including that old faithful: keeping the world safe for Bill and Ted.